Adventures of the Pirate
Prince of the Wampanoag

Carlomagno

John Christian Hopkins

BLUE HAND BOOKS

MASSACHUSETTS

Blue Hand Books Attn: Trace A. DeMeyer
442 Main Street, #1061
Greenfield, MA 01301
www.bluehandbooks.com

Publisher's Note: This is a work of fiction. Names, characters, places, and incidents are a product of the author's imagination. Locales and public names are sometimes used for atmospheric purposes. Any resemblance to actual people, living or dead, or to businesses, companies, events, institutions, or locales is completely coincidental.

Design and Cover: Trace DeMeyer (CANSTOCK photo with permission)

Ordering Information:
Quantity sales. Special discounts are available on quantity purchases by corporations, associations, and others. For details, contact the "Special Sales Department" at the address above.

Hopkins, John (1960 -)

Adventures of the Pirate Prince of the Wampanoag, Carlomagno/ John Christian Hopkins. -- 2nd Edition
ISBN: 978-1492363712

*"A man is not old until regrets
take the place of dreams."*

–JOHN BARRYMORE

ACKNOWLEDGMENTS

This work could not have been completed without the support, advice and assistance of Sararesa Begay Hopkins, Trace DeMeyer, Teresa Stevens and the inspiration I received from Douglas Fairbanks Sr. and Errol Flynn, two of the greatest swashbucklers to ever sail the seas.

Dedicated to
Sararesa Begay Hopkins, my friend, my confidante
and my wife; and to Louis L'Amour, a legend who
once took the time to encourage a young man ...

This book is the story of what could have happened to
the Pequot and Wampanoag Indians who were sold into slavery
in the West Indies.
The grandson of Massasoit, the chief of the Wampanoags,
and his mother were captured by the English colonists and
sold into slavery. He was only eight years old.
After escaping from the plantation owned by a cruel Spaniard,
Carlomango runs away for his freedom.
The writing is engaging, the dialogue is believable, and the
action scenes are framed in real-life settings. This is the kind of
book that as a teenager I devoured by the dozens. It harks back to
Natty Bumpo, Huck Finn, Tom Sawyer, and the early Faulkner.
It will make a good fit to a private holding or a school library.
John is to be commended for this book.

Dean Chavers, *Ph. D.*
Director, Catching the Dream (formerly Native American
Scholarship Fund)

Metacom meets Errol Flynn! John Christian Hopkins is one
of the most important indigenous writers from New England
today, and here he covers the region's painful, complex history
with insight and swashbuckling originality."

Siobahn Senier, *English Professor,*
University of New Hampshire

{ 1 }

Flight

The Arawak was coming!

One thought reverberated in the boy's mind. The Arawak was trailing him, even now. To be caught by him would mean a most unpleasant death. Pokanoket hurried fearfully through the darkness, certain he would be discovered at each step. The little light left in the day was swallowed under the jungle's dense canopy and the unfamiliar sounds of the beckoning night frightened the boy. Yet he had no choice but to go forward.

The Arawak—had he any other name?—was a native to this tropical land and prided himself on his abilities as a hunter and tracker. And as a fighter. None, it was said, had ever eluded him. No slave had ever escaped from the vast plantation of Don Pedro de la Marana and lived to boast about it. The Arawak had gleefully made sure of that.

Traditionally the Arawak people were docile, mainly hunters and farmers. But the one who chased the boy, it was said only his mother was Arawak, she was of the Taino. His father, they whispered, was one of the fierce Carib—the so-called eaters of men.

Pokanoket's small legs churned ever faster, racing to keep up with his pounding heart. But he knew, he knew for certain, the Arawak was behind him. And the Arawak would be relentless. Last night had been the most fearful he could recall, and though Pokanoket had seen only eight years, he had witnessed many horrible nights full of death and bloodshed. Pokanoket was young in years, but mature in hardship and suffering.

Only a short time ago he had been free, roaming at will the woodlands of his home. But that was far away, in a place the Englishmen called Plimouth. How far away, the boy did not know. Much had happened in the last year, too much for a small boy to comprehend. Plimouth was a world away, another lifetime for Pokanoket.

If he were home, he could draw in dirt and mark the place of his village; from there it would be no trick to mark where other villages, such as Agawam or Montauk, were located. But in this strange, new land drawing in the dirt was useless for he did not know exactly where he was nor what awaited him.

He had been free; he had gone to stay in a village where he was safe from the terrible war with the Englishmen. His mother was there, too. Though he worried about his father, he never for a moment believed anything would happen to him. His father had always seemed so strong, so sure of himself. His father was a great man. This Pokanoket knew by the way in which other men stepped aside for him.

The boy, too, was a native, though not like the Arawak. His people lived in the place now called Plimouth, in a village called Sowams. The men there were noted fighters and, the boy thought, *"So I will be one day. "*

Pokanoket was Wampanoag, the son of Metacomet, whom the Englishmen mockingly called King Philip and thought it outrageous that an Indian would carry himself as if he were the equal of a white man. His grandfather was Ousamequin, the Yellow Feather. He was the one the Englishmen who came to Plimouth knew as their friend, Massasoit.

4

What had happened to his mother, he wondered?

He had fled at her urging, though he had been reluctant to leave her. She had been different at the end. Always, even in the darkest times, his mother had been so confident, so reassuring. She encouraged those who had lost hope. Only something had changed her in the past few days, something had turned her heart bad.

Pokanoket—no, he must remember what his mother told him and hide his true identity; he must call himself by the name given him by his captors, first the English, then the Spanish.

Pokanoket's was a proud heritage, a legacy of greatness; he was the son of a warrior, the grandson of a great sachem. But that was all far from this place. Here, on the island of Hispaniola, the boy was just another runaway slave, and to be caught would mean death. For now, somewhere behind him, the Arawak was coming, and coming fast.

"They fear your father," his mother whispered. "If they suspect who you are, they may come to fear you, too. The white men kill what they fear, destroy what they do not understand."

The English who captured Pokanoket and his mother called him Charlemagne, after a long ago king. It was a joke between them, for Pokanoket's father was called King Philip, named for a king of ancient Macedonia. And Philip's brother was called Alexander—named for Philip of Macedonia's son, Alexander the Great.

"He's royalty, is he?" the Englishmen laughed as they mockingly knelt before him. "Who is he? Is he the Lion-Heart, perhaps?"

"That scrawny thing," another chortled. "He has no lion heart! He's a weakling, like old King James!"

"The hell, you say," the first man replied haughtily. "I say he's a bit of a fine fellow, a royal lord, he is. He's Charlemagne, I say. That's who the wee lad be! The bloke is Charlemagne!"

And so they all laughed and toasted him with cold mugs of ale; thus the son of King Philip was mockingly christened Charlemagne in honor of the French conqueror. When he was traded to a Spanish master, they interpreted his name as Carlomagno.

The boy did not doubt he would be free again. His mother had spoken of little else. But, she warned him, they must bide their time.

"We will have only one chance for it," she said. "We dare not fail."

But when the day finally came, it was without planning. Carlomagno had simply disappeared into the surrounding jungle, his only thought to put distance between himself and any pursuit. No doubt, Don Pedro would send someone after him, but the Don would not believe that a small boy might have actually escaped. Carlomagno had made a habit of letting Don Pedro think of him as less than intelligent.

Hopefully, Don Pedro might believe the boy had merely wandered too far. Soon the Don would have suspected differently and that is when he would have summoned the Arawak, the boy knew.

How much of a head start did he have? A few hours? Carlomagno had purposefully fled as dusk was coming on, to make it seem likely he had gotten lost. He drifted into the surrounding jungle and ran with the fluid, quick strides learned from his father. It was a pace an Indian warrior could keep for days on end. With luck, he might have gained as much as a day on the Arawak.

But he was only a boy and he had run as far as he could. He needed rest. He had to conserve his strength for that moment when he might come face to face with the Arawak. But what could he, a mere boy, do against a killer such as the Arawak? If only, the boy thought, he had something to use as a weapon. He had used a bow and arrow before; his father had taught him how to make his own bows and how to select the best arrows. But that took time, and time was something he did not have. There had been no time to grab anything when he fled; he had simply ducked into the woods and run.

Even in captivity, his mother, Wootonockuse, had carried herself well, keeping her head high. She did her work, telling her son that even the son of a sachem must share the hardship of his people. For

6

when their village had been surprised back in Plimouth, nearly 100 Wampanoag women and children had fallen into the hands of the English. It was decided to sell them into slavery, to make up for the expense the war was costing the colonists.

But Wootonockuse dreamt of her own freedom and that of her son. She harbored the secret hope that one day her husband—the proud Metacomet—would come for them. But a Spanish vessel had attacked the English transport, and the Spaniards had sold off their cargo, slaves included. Wootonockuse and her son were among those bought by Don Pedro de la Marana. And he had proved a merciless master.

Carlomagno did not understand why his mother had suddenly changed. But she, who had been his tower of strength, had become suddenly morose and withdrawn. Her laughing eyes now stared unblinking. Seldom did she speak to anyone, even her son. Was it because the two years of servitude had finally worn her spirit down?

At night, he thought he heard her crying. Then came the morning she told him it was time to run. Early, before they were sent off to the sugar cane field, she had turned to him with urgency.

"Tonight, you must not return here. When you see your chance, you must flee. Run to the mountains, it is your only chance, my son."

"And yours, Mother," Carlomagno told her, his voice pleading. "You will be with me?"

She shook her head slowly, reaching under her blankets on the floor and revealing a knife. "I have to do something today. Don Pedro has dishonored me, and today I must do what your father would, if he were here. I must kill Don Pedro."

"But, Mother, why can't we go together?"

"When I kill Don Pedro, the Spanish will be very angry with me. But I do not fear them I only want to know that you are free. If you come back, it will be hard for you. Remember how those Englishmen back in Plimouth wanted to kill you for the things they said your father did? If you come back here again, the Spanish will kill you for what I do today."

"It isn't fair," Carlomagno insisted.

His mother put a hand on his trembling shoulder. "It is life. No one has ever said it was fair. Now, you must do as I say. If I am able, I will find you."

All day, Carlomagno did his work in the fields. Once, as the afternoon grew long, Wootonockuse seemingly casually passed by her son. Bending near him, pretending to pick a stalk, she spoke without looking at him.

"If the gods will it, we will meet again, my son. From now on you must use the white man's name for you," she whispered. "But just once more, let my ears hear your true name. Be brave, my Pokanoket; remember, you are the son and grandson of great sachems."

When the daylight began to fade he had managed to work his way toward the edge of the field. When no one was looking, he had simply stepped off into the dense underbrush. He ran as fast as he could without rest, only slowing for a short time before running once more. But it was not only the Arawak making him wary. He had also heard the terrible stories of the man-eating monsters that roamed the wild jungles and mountains of Hispaniola. They were called Cimaroons, and were, it was whispered, a wild lot of savages. They were said to be half-man, half-beast. Most of the slaves on Don Pedro's plantation were afraid of the Cimaroons, and some refused to utter the word for fear it could be heard and they would be spirited away in the night.

Carlomagno's thought was to head toward the mountain regions where it was said the Cimaroons lived. There, the Spanish might hesitate to chase him. But what of the Arawak? Did he fear the Cimaroons, too? Or was he such a savage himself that he scoffed at the wild half-men of the mountains?

Carlomagno suddenly smiled. What a fool Don Pedro must feel now, he thought! *I deliberately led him to believe I was a half-wit*, Carlomagno nodded to himself with satisfaction. Rarely had he spoken in the Don's presence and when he had, he purposefully made mistakes most children would not. Often Carlomagno spoke his native language, knowing it would sound like gibberish to the cultured don.

Don Pedro had never guessed that Carlomagno was an unusually intelligent child. As the son of the Wampanoag sachem, he had been schooled in excellent fashion from an early age. First, from his father and the sachem's trusted advisor, Tuspaquin, he had learned the ways of war. His great-uncles, the brothers of Massasoit, were Unkompoin, a great shaman, and warrior-statesman Quadequina. From them, Carlomagno learned the secrets of the forest, about the plants, animals and medicines—and how to read men's hearts.

Much of his education was similar to that of other Wampanoag boys. But Metacomet recognized that the boy would one day be sachem and would need to lead the people wisely. Metacomet's friend—and later enemy—was called John Sassoman, and he had gone to the Englishman's great school in Boston, called Harvard. Before the friendship was severed, along with Sassoman's head, Metacomet had asked John Sassoman to tutor his son. Thus Carlomagno spoke English well. Always a quick study, in captivity he had managed to learn a good deal of Spanish as well.

Now, alone in the jungles of Hispaniola, the boy would need all of his knowledge to survive.

At that moment, Carlomagno thought back to his boyhood, and the tales the old people told. They spoke of Granny Squannit, a haggardly witch-woman. The people seldom spoke of her, for it was said she could hear all. Carlomagno shuddered as he thought of her, remembering his great-uncle, the medicine man, saying that Granny Squannit had eyes shaped like a cat's. Others claimed she had one square eye in the center of her forehead! But she was also described as being small, her hair a wiry mass of tangled white, falling long past her frail shoulders.

9

Mean as she could be, and she was said to sometimes abduct children, she could be equally benevolent. Granny Squannit, when the mood overtook her, was known to feed and care for shipwrecked people. She would at times send herbs to cure illness, or grant wishes if the cause was worthy.

"I could use some help, Granny Squannit," Carlomagno muttered. And then he hastily looked all about him, half expecting to see her.

Somewhere behind him, the Arawak was coming. He must reach the mountains.

The rugged Cordillera Mountains rose to dog the middle of Hispaniola. Cordillera was an old Spanish word for "cord" or "little rope." The Cordilleras were a mountain range of more or less even parallel peaks. Craggy and filled with deep gorges, they made it difficult for the Spanish soldiers to infiltrate. It had been tried a time or two, organizing well-armed troops to mount expeditions against the ragged, half-starved—but proud—Cimaroons. But there were few places where an army could march in force, leaving the soldiers strung out along the trail and easy targets for the sudden strikes from small bands of Cimaroons.

Most often, the Spaniards simply avoided the Cordilleras and ignored the Cimaroons. They were fortunate in a sense because the fierce Cimaroons had no organization; they fought as viciously among themselves as they did with outsiders. Scrapping out a meager existence in the rugged mountains, they were no threat to the Spanish Empire.

Hispaniola was located near the Windward Passage, through which ships from various nations had to pass on their way to the Caribbean or making the journey back to Spain, England, Holland or France. This Caribbean area, known as the Spanish Main, stretched from the so-called New World of North America to South America. But while Spain yet remained the dominant power, its once-iron grip was weakening as English cities sprung up in rapid succession. Not to be outdone, the fearless Dutch merchants had also begun to locate towns and make claims upon the myriad islands of the Spanish Main. So, too, had the French come.

The eastern end of Hispaniola was dominated by the Spanish, with most of the western side of the island claimed by the French. The northwestern edge of the island was another matter altogether, for there dwelt the dreaded buccaneers in makeshift camps as they prepared their vessels for raids on both trade ships and other pirates.

Pokanoket continued to run and as the miles fell away, the jungle closed more tightly around him. He stumbled once, over a stout branch. It seemed a good size for a club, so the boy hefted it in his right hand. Now, at least he had some way to defend himself. But the Arawak would be better armed, possibly with a musket, though he preferred his native tools of war, the bow and arrow and the blowgun. Few on Hispaniola used the blowgun. It was used more by the Carib, giving credence to the rumors of the Arawak's parentage.

Numb with fatigue, Carlomagno jumped with a start at the sudden croaking "*Coqui, Coqui*" of a tree frog. The boy had no good choices. To be caught by the Arawak meant death, or, at best, a return to Spanish slavery. The French also kept slaves. The Cimaroons might kill or even devour him! And the buccaneers might kill him just for sport! He had not a friend, unless Granny Squannit, somewhere in his beloved homeland far to the north, could hear the pitiful pleas of a lonely child all the way from the dark jungles of the West Indies.

Pushing onward, he climbed steadily, watching as the jungles gradually began to give way to the mountains. He paused to rest on a large rock and scanned his backtrail. Nothing, no sign of movement. Was he safe then? Had the Arawak turned back?

No, he wasn't the kind to turn back. But perhaps he has lost my trail, Carlomagno thought? He did, after all, know a bit about tracking, remnants of the woodland lessons taught by his father. He had been careful to leave as little sign as possible. But the Arawak was a sea-

11

soned tracker. While Carlomagno might delay his pursuer, he admitted there was little hope of eluding him completely.

Rising from his seat, the boy's eyes caught a flicker of something. Straining hard to see down the slope, he could make out nothing unusual. Turning his head, he looked sideways, knowing that often the side vision will pick up something not seen directly. But he saw nothing out of place.

Carlomagno continued on his way, clutching tightly the stout branch in his small, shaking hands. What had he seen, if anything? Was it a shadow, something wishing to remain unseen? Was it man, or beast? Or perhaps his mind playing tricks? A small boy's mind can often conjure monsters from the depths of innocent shadows. Several times he stopped to study his backtrail, but saw no sign of pursuit. Night had fallen like a blanket when he came across a stream. Drinking greedily, a delicious coolness easing his parched throat, Carlomagno decided to rest there for a few hours.

Where was this hillside? Was it truly the beginning of the Cordillera Central Mountains, or some lesser peaks? He had no precise way to know where he was, though his plan was to head inland, toward the mountain range. Carlomagno had no map, only the one etched in his mind by listening to snippets of conversation around him. Even Don Pedro had often spoken freely in front of the "half-witted" boy. Now he needed all that knowledge to save his life. To survive, he must lose himself in the Cordilleras.

Earlier, he had come across some plantains; now he took the time to eat them. He savored each bite. He found a place to sleep away from the stream. He did not know what creatures might come in the night, in need of water, but his father had taught him to respect all creatures, for the Creator breathed life into the animals as well as the people. He dozed off and on, tossing restlessly. He saw the face of his mother, Wootonockuse. Her life had been hard on the plantation, but until the very end she had continued to speak of gaining their freedom.

"Being a slave is no life for a Wampanoag prince," his mother had insisted. "Always remember who you are. Your father was the great sachem of his people, as was his father before him. That is who you are.

"For now you must hide from them, let them think of you only as Carlomagno, but in your heart you must remember who you are. You are a Wampanoag. You are the son of Metacomet, grandson of Ousamequin! Slavery is not meant for such as you, my son."

He did not escape for two years though several chances had come his way. Carlomagno stayed to be near her, to protect her as best he could. The boy knew that as a slave, he could never give his mother the kind of life a Wampanoag queen deserved. And always, deep inside, the boy yearned for the day his father would come to rescue both of them. For not one moment did the boy doubt that if he were able, Metacomet would have come.

His father believed in the old ways, believed in protecting his family and his honor. Once, Metacomet had chased a man for fifty miles because the man had spoken ill of his late father, Massasoit. It was an insult among the Wampanoag to speak poorly of the recently deceased. Metacomet tracked the man through fifty miles of woods and brush, and then killed the offender for his rashness. That was the father Carlomagno remembered. The man who would come for him, if he could. Carlomagno avoided all thought of what it might mean that his father had not come for them already.

But the days turned into blistering months and Metacomet did not come. Always Carlomagno listened for some word, any word on his father's fate. Was he dead then? Or maybe he had won his war? Maybe he had pushed the Englishmen from his lands? He had much success in the early days of the war and many new warriors flocked to him. Where, at first, the Wampanoags had stood alone in defiance, the Nipmucs, the Springfields and the Massachusets soon joined them.

Metacomet had traveled far to seek more allies for what the English called "King Philip's War." If the Indians could stand together they

13

could defeat the English, he insisted. He had been wooing the Narragansetts at the time his wife and son were captured. The Narragansetts were many and, if they should touch the hatchet beside the Wampanoags, the English colonies would run red. But the Narragansetts were divided. Some, like the brash, young Canonchet, spoke out for war; others, like the wily Ninigret, counseled peace.

It was while his father and many of his warriors were away in the land of the Narragansett that the Englishmen attacked the village where he and his mother were sheltered. Many were killed in a few bloody minutes. Carlomagno had slipped safely into the woods, but when his mother had been grabbed by an Englishman, he had turned back to help. Before the boy could free her, others came and both were subdued.

Exhausted, Carlomagno fell asleep in the midst of his thoughts, and in his dreams he saw a creature, dark and hideous, creeping slowly closer. Its hair was long and stringy as it peered through the brushes at him, yellowish slits for eyes. He turned his face away, afraid to look into those eyes. He knew instinctively it was Granny Squannit, and he was immobilized with fear. He had called to her and she had come! But would she grant his wish, or carry him away to the dark world?

Long, thin fingers reached out toward him, nails sharp as a hawk's talon. He shrank back in terror as she reached out for him again. The spiky points of her nails poked at him and he felt a sharp prick ... and opened his eyes.

{ 2 }

Pequot Refugee

A man stood there, a tall man with a spear. The point of the spear was inches from Carlomagno's throat.

It was not Granny Squannit, but a man not unlike himself. Carlomagno stared in disbelief. And the man, perhaps five-feet, eight-inches tall, stared hard back at him. But the spear did not waver. The man's skin was not as dark as the Cimaroons were said to be. Nor was he the color of the Spanish, or the native tribesmen. His hair was a salt and pepper mixture, and it was long, in the back, but shaved on the sides. He was not the Arawak.

"Who are you, boy?" the man demanded in a flat, harsh tone. "What are you?"

Carlomagno moved his lips, but only silence tumbled out. His eyes were wide in fear. For, if he had been frightened of the Arawak, or even the Cimaroons, he was doubly afraid now. His eyes took in the stranger's scalplock, and it rekindled thoughts of his boyhood home.

There was a people back home who wore their hair in a similar fashion. A fierce people, who were known as The Destroyers.

"Pequot?" Carlomagno managed in a hoarse whisper. "Are you Pequot?"

"Ah, you know the name?" the man sounded pleased, yet the spear remained where it was aimed. With one thrust the boy could be killed. "Yes, I am Pequot, I am Noank. It has been many years since I have heard that name from any lips other than my own. Tell me, boy, what do you know of the Pequot?"

"My father told me they were brave men. He said if they were on his side, he could win his war against the English."

"The English!" Noank spat in disgust. "It was the English who destroyed my people. It was the English who sent me here, to be a slave. But I escaped to the mountains. Noank is slave to no man!"

"I have escaped, too," Carlomagno said, daring to sit up.

Noank lowered the spear. "So you have. That is good, boy; maybe you have the makings of a warrior. Who are you? You have a look I remember from long ago."

"I am Wampanoag," the boy said proudly. "The Spanish call me Carlomagno. But my name is Pokanoket, son of Metacomet."

"Metacomet? I cannot recall that name."

"Are you not from the land of the Pequots? Are you not from Mashantucket, the place of big trees?"

Noank nodded. "Once, long ago, that was my home. But it has been many seasons since last I saw the much-wooded place. Know you of Mystic Hill, boy? Know you of the dark deed done there those many years past?"

"Yes, my father told me of how the English attacked your village and set it aflame, then killed your people as they tried to flee. It was said that 600 Pequots were killed in a single day."

"It was a bitter day, boy!" Noank stood silently, his head bowed for several minutes. "All you say is true. Families were slain, babies taken from their mothers' arms and dashed upon the ground, a sword run through them. Men, women and children murdered without quarter. It was my village, my people," Noank spoke, his eyes seemingly staring into the past. He was silent for a time, then, his voice softer, spoke again. "I was young then, about your age, I'd say."

"You survived Mystic Hill?"

"Had I been at Mystic I would have been dead, my pain over," Noank replied. "No, I had gone with my father to the nearby village of Sassacus, to visit relatives. We were only a few miles away, but too far to be of any assistance. That was how I was spared from the fate of so many of my family and friends. But the English were not content to destroy one village; they hunted us down with no end. I was among those who surrendered in the swamp. I was sold into slavery to pay war debts."

"What of your father?"

"He fled with Sassacus to the land of the Mohawk, to seek their aid. But the Mohawks killed them." Noank dropped, cross-legged, on the ground. "It has been more than forty years now, though it is hard to tell. The seasons seem much the same here, always the rain, always hot.

"I have lost track of how long I have been here. Some of my people were given to the Narragansetts or the Mohegans. But I was brought here. I always thought of going back someday, to die in my own homeland. But that is not to be, I suppose."

"I shall return one day," Carlomagno exclaimed.

Noank studied him for a moment. "Now, what name should I call you, boy? Are you Pokanoket or Carlomagno?"

The boy hastily explained how his mother warned him to conceal his true identity.

"As you wish then, boy. As you wish. You will be Carlomagno. But, who is your father? I do not recall this Metacomet."

"He was young at the time of Mystic. His father was Ousamequin, the one the English called Massasoit."

Noank's jaw dropped wide. "Your grandfather was Ousamequin! Him I have heard of. But you say you were sold into slavery, too? Was there more trouble then? More fighting after Mystic Hill?"

Carlomagno explained as much as he could of the war, of how there had been some successes, yet he had been captured before the outcome had been determined.

Noank seemed hopeful. "Maybe your father was successful, maybe the tribes were able to act together, to stand as one people," Noank sighed. "But could they forget old wounds? When Sassacus sought the aid of the Narragansetts, they could not forget their old an-

18

imosities. Though it would have been best for both tribes, Miantimomi refused to aid the Pequots."

"I have heard my father speak of Miantinomi. He was killed by the brother of Uncas long before I was born."

"Uncas! Ugh!" Noank spat on the ground. "He was always friend to the English. But Miantinomi? Dead? That must have taken some doing. Miantinomi was quite a man. But tell me more of this war your father led?"

"My father smoked the pipe with many tribes, and many villages listened to his words with open hearts. I think, grandfather, that maybe my father was successful."

"I would like to return home one day, to see if our people now live undisturbed in their wigwams," Noank said. Did they? Was it like it had been all those years ago, when he was but a carefree boy? Could the people roam the woods as they pleased? Did they still laugh as they ran along the beach during the time of catching fish? Did the women work the cornfields, their papooses in cradleboards on their backs?

Was anything the way he remembered it, Noank wondered?

"He follows you," Noank said, matter-of-factly. "Who is he?"

Carlomagno involuntarily flinched. "He works for the plantation of Don Pedro. That is where I escaped from. It is his job to recapture runaway slaves, and he is very good at it. He is an Arawak, part Carib they say."

"You slowed him down some, he lost time trying to work out your trail, I think," Noank said. "So you remember some of your boyhood training, anyway. The Arawak are said to be excellent trackers. I think now he doesn't need to look for your sign anymore. He has decided he knows where you are going."

"How could he know?"

"I think at first he did not think you were very smart; he followed your tracks expecting them to lead him to you. But as he followed your tracks, he came to realize you were much cleverer than he believed. You see, first he thought you aimless, just running with no thought in mind. Now, he understands that you had a plan in mind, a place to flee to," Noank explained. "He knows you planned to head to the mountains all along. Now he can save time and ignore your trail, he just comes to the mountain. He is sure he can pick up your sign here."

"He will, he is good. Very good."

Noank shook his head. "He will lose your trail and not find it again. I spotted you earlier and followed, taking care to wipe out both of our tracks. He will come and find nothing; soon he will begin to doubt himself, to wonder if his first inclination was right after all. He will, like most men, come to doubt himself. He will think you were running without purpose, no goal in mind. He will think you did not come this way after all. He will backtrack to the last point he spotted your trail and try to deduce where you went from there."

"You did this for me, grandfather?"

"For myself, boy. You were leading him right to me." Noank stood up, his movement fluid. "We had best move on."

"You live alone here, on this mountain?"

"It is better than slavery," Noank replied.

"But what of the Cimaroons?"

"I am Pequot. I do not fear the Cimaroons. Still, it is easier for me to avoid them, just as I keep away from the Spanish. Noank does not need anyone else, he can care for himself."

"I have heard the Cimaroons are eaters of men."

"It is not so, boy, not so at all. That is a tale the Spanish tell their slaves to keep them afraid to be out and about at night. To frighten them into submission, they tell tales of beasts they call Cimaroons."

"What are Cimaroons?"

"They are men, like you and I. According to their legends, the first Cimaroon was a runaway slave some two hundred years ago. He mingled with the natives who still lived free. In time more of the African slaves fled, marrying into the native tribes here. There are many now, in villages scattered throughout the Indies."

They talked as they moved along. The boy was good at hiding his sign, but Noank was better. With each mile Carlomagno became increasingly confident that the Arawak would never find him now. He was free, he sighed, no more chains, no whippings.

Yet the boy's heart was heavy, for he was free only so long as he was not discovered. The reach of the Spaniards was long and they could snatch him from his mountain hideaway at any time and return him to Don Pedro de la Marana.

Through the day they walked, resting only briefly. Late in the afternoon they climbed a ridge, looking back on the trail behind them.

"We stop here," Noank said. "We will watch our backtrail for a while, to see if the Arawak is still behind us."

21

"Do you think he can follow us?"

Noank did not reply for several minutes, and then he shrugged. "Who knows? Maybe he is a better tracker than I think. Maybe I have made a mistake and left some faint sign. It does not pay to underestimate an enemy, boy. Didn't your father ever teach you that?"

Carlomagno puffed up his chest. "My father was a great warrior."

"So you said," Noank replied without glancing at him. "But what of you? Your father is far away, if he even lives. What if this Arawak comes? Are you a great warrior, Carlomagno?"

"I will be."

"Bah, you are but a boy, alone in a world you do not even understand. You think it is so easy to become a warrior? How can you become a great warrior, boy?"

"I can learn from a great warrior."

"Is it so easy then? And where would you find a great warrior in these mountains?"

"He has found me," Carlomagno replied. "Now tell me, grandfather; why do we sit here?"

Noank let a brief smile skip across his lips. This boy had nerve, and the Pequot liked that. "We wait to see if the Arawak still comes. If he crosses that meadow below, that will mean he isn't turning back. If that should happen, I will have to kill him. It will be me or him then, Carlomagno. And I do not wish it to be me."

"Can you kill him?"

"It is never an easy thing to kill a man. The first thing you must understand is that he is equally determined to kill you. The one who forgets that, the one who makes the smallest mistake, is usually the one who dies."

They sat in silence, each captive in his own thoughts. For Noank, the sight of this boy sent his mind back to Mystic Hill, and his own days of endless summer dreams. How far away they were now. He could smell his mother's venison stew slowly boiling in her copper cookpot. Once again he saw his father, so tall and strong, as he worked with delicate fingers on chipping arrowheads or a new stone pipe.

Carlomagno, too, held his own thoughts. What fate had befallen his mother? Had she killed Don Pedro? Was she now dead? The thought left him feeling cold and empty. She had been his one connection to the life back home. When he looked at his mother, he had felt safe. He was certain they would return home one day. But if she was gone, so too was his hope. Was he ever to walk again along the shores he knew so well? Was Sowams stolen from him forever?

The boy was determined to stay awake. He would prove to his new friend that he was a warrior. How dare Noank think so little of him! *I am the son of Metacomet!* Back home, if he ever got there, he thought, he would be a king, a great sachem. Who would Noank be if he were back in Mystic Hill?

"Ugh! The Pequot thinks so little of me," Carlomagno told himself. *"But he will learn differently."*

After all, he nodded with satisfaction; he was destined to be a big man among the Wampanoags.

23

But somewhere along the way, weariness ambushed him and his eyelids clapped shut. He slept soundly, peacefully. For the first time in many days he slept without fear. The Pequot was with him, and the Pequot could protect him from the Arawak.

He awoke with the first rays of sunlight creeping across the sky. His rest had been peaceful, bothered only occasionally by the mosquitoes. Stretching, he sat up and blinked the sleep from his eyes. He looked around slowly and realized he was alone.

Alone!

The Pequot was not in sight. With rising panic

Carlomagno let his eyes search the area around him for some clue. Had the Pequot decided to leave him to his fate? Had the Arawak come and killed Noank? No, Carlomagno thought, he would have heard the struggle. His father, who was a brave man, even hesitated to fight the Pequots. They were, he insisted, as tough as their reputations. How good was the Arawak? Could he have snuck up and caught Noank sleeping? Carlomagno discounted that idea. He had heard too often about the Pequot warriors to believe that the Arawak could kill one so easily.

Could it have been the Cimaroons? No, of course not. They would have carried Carlomagno away, too.

It was more likely Noank did not want to be bothered caring for a small boy. The old man had himself to think about, and a boy would only be a nuisance, an extra mouth to feed.

But the Pequot had seemed to like him. And Carlomagno was not that small. He was very athletic, even strong for his age. He could prove useful around a camp as he knew how to cover his tracks and was a good hunter.

There was scarcely a sound, but something made Carlomagno turn his head and the Pequot was standing there, staring at him.

"I searched our backtrail," Noank said as he dropped the still bloody carcass of a wild pig on the ground. "As I suspected, he turned back. He does not know about me, and is certain you are not a good enough tracker to hide all signs. He goes back where he last saw your tracks and will follow another direction."

"What happens when he doesn't find me?"

Noank shrugged. "He may try another route, or assume you have been swallowed up by quicksand. Anyway, we will eat now. I will show you how to survive." Indicating the pig, Noank added, "Wild pig, boy! It is my favorite of the foods in this place. We will build a fire under that tree over there; its leaves will scatter our rising smoke, making it too small to see. You will need to learn these things, boy. Such knowledge is the price you pay for survival here."

And so Carlomagno's schooling began. Noank pointed out to him which plants were useful, and which to avoid. The Pequot taught him to read animal tracks and how to make his own tracks vanish. Always Noank would quiz his young ward, testing his knowledge about what he had seen or learned each day. It became like a game; survival was the prize to be won.

And Carlomagno, with time on his hands, made himself a bow and many arrows. The skin of a deer killed by Noank was used to make him a stronger quiver.

"These woods, the mountain, they provide me with all I need," Noank explained, waving an arm in an arc. "I have food when I am hungry, water is plentiful; I have no need of anything else. I need nothing from the Cimaroons and nothing from the Spanish or English. You will learn to survive here, too, Carlomagno. These woods will provide you with everything you want."

"I want to go home."

Noank lowered his head; he had felt the same when he first came here. But the waters were wide, and even if he built a canoe he would not have dared to sail away. Nor would he have known in which direction to go.

"You must forget about home, Carlomagno. It will only make your heart sad. Think only that you live, that you are free."

With bow and arrows in hand Carlomagno did feel a sense of freedom. He even thought should he meet the Arawak, he might have a chance against him. Of course, only if he saw the Arawak first.

He was able to kill small game with his arrows, and thereby make himself useful to Noank. They roamed constantly, never staying in one place too long. But Noank had his preferred spots, and often they returned to a favorite cave or secluded clearing close to water.

"Why do the Spanish tell such lies about the Cimaroons?"

"It serves their purpose, boy. The new slaves do not know any different, so they believe it. The Spanish know the slaves are superstitious, so they play upon the fact to control them. Remember, you can control people's minds if you use their own fears against them."

26

One day faded to the next and Carlomagno lost count of how many had passed. Every day he learned more, as Noank would suddenly ask him to describe the area they had just passed through, or point out a track or a plant and ask about it.

"You must always remain aware of your surroundings; keep your head about you, Carlomagno. If we should become separated, you must know enough to survive on your own. You cannot outrun death, only prolong life. Your mind will win you more battles than brawn ever could. So use your wits, boy. Avoid a battle if you cannot win it."

"What if it cannot be avoided?"

Noank's face seemed to soften as he broke into a grin. "Then sing your death song, boy, but plan to take as many of your enemies with you as you can!"

There came a time, during the rainy season, when Carlomagno became ill with fever and Noank stayed close to him, mopping his brow and forcing him to sip some concoction made by boiling particular plants. Tallow shrub—found in swampy or marshy areas—was a low-spreading tree, forming something of a dense thicket. The plant was smooth, with brownish-gray bark, and leaves narrow at the base. Noank had come to learn that the bark could be boiled and ingested to help ease the pain of typhoid, cholera and other fevers.

Noank kept a fire that night, and talked constantly to keep the boy's mind off of his suffering. Noank told the story of the fox and the bear.

"There was a time when Bear and Fox quarreled over who had the most beautiful tail. Fox said his tail was the most beautiful, but

27

Bear disagreed. Bear insisted that his tail was so full and fluffy, that it was the most beautiful tail the Creator had made. One winter's morning Bear awoke from his sleep and he was hungry. He wandered outside and, down by the river, he saw Fox eating a large trout." Noank paused to add wood to the fire. "Bear remarked how delicious that trout looked and wondered how Fox had caught such a large and tasty fish. 'It was easy,' Fox smiled pleasantly. 'See that hole in the ice? I sat over it and let my tail hang down. After a while I felt a sharp tug on my tail and when I pulled it up, I had caught this large trout.' So Bear sat over the hole in the ice and let his beautiful tail dangle in the water."

Noank tenderly mopped the sweat from Carlomagno's forehead, and helped him take a sip of the tallow shrub medicine.

"What happened next, grandfather?" Carlomagno rasped.

"Bear sat on the ice for a long, long time. He was about to give up when he felt a sharp tug on his tail. He tried to pull his tail from the hole, but it did not come. So he tugged harder and still harder. But the hole in the ice had frozen solid again and his tail was caught. Bear gave a mighty roar and tugged as hard as he could, and his tail snapped off! It had frozen solid from sitting all day in the icy water.

"That is why to this day Fox has a bushy, beautiful tail and Bear has only the short stub left over from the time he lost his tail in the ice."

The next day the fever broke and Carlomagno rapidly regained his strength.

"The fever is bad in this land," Noank said. "It is so hot here, not like our forests back home. But I have learned something of the plants here, and it has saved my life many times."

"Do you not miss having other people around?"

"Sometimes," Noank admitted. "But then I think of that day I returned to Mystic Hill. I can still close my eyes and see the smoldering wigwams, smell the charred flesh. I fear the thought of returning home from a hunt and finding all I know and love lying in ruins. It is easier for me to stay alone, to never have to face such a sight again."

"I don't think it is good to be always alone, grandfather. My father, he who led the war against the Englishmen, he would fight when he was forced to, but always found time to return to my mother," Carlomagno offered.

"That was your father's weakness, Carlomagno," Noank replied. "When a man has something he loves, something he clings to, he has something an enemy can use against him. My enemies can hurt me only by striking at me directly. I have no one else they can attack."

Only now Noank did have someone he cared for.

When he felt at full strength, Carlomagno slipped away from camp in the early morning hours. He wanted to go hunting, to surprise Noank with his skill. Always good with a bow, Carlomagno had grown better with practice. He also carried a spear, with which he was passable. Noank wouldn't worry about him, the Pequot knew by now that Carlomagno was a born woodsman.

Noank favored the taste of the wild pig and Carlomagno was determined to find one. Carlomagno plodded on for an hour, seeing nothing. By now the sun had crept over the horizon, its rays carrying the oppressive heat. Carlomagno was growing accustomed to the heat, finding it no longer as unbearable as when he had first come to Hispaniola.

That had been almost three years ago, a lifetime for a young boy. Standing in the shade, he glanced the way he had come. How far was he from their encampment? Three or four miles he thought, but he wasn't certain. For another hour he continued, and was about to turn back when he spotted the tracks. He could tell they were wild boars by the hoof marks, and he was sure the sign was not very old. He took a look around, following the tracks to the east. He moved slower now, not wanting to frighten away the pigs. He came to a narrow stream and followed it. The tracks were plain enough. At last, near a slight bend in the stream, he spotted a medium-sized boar as it rooted under a fallen log. The distance was not too great and he carefully notched his bow. He moved swiftly, drawing back the string and letting the arrow loose. It flew straight, coming to a sudden halt in the boar's throat. The wild creature gave a startled gasp, and stumbled. It rose again, took its final steps and fell.

Carlomagno darted forward, delighted with his good fortune. He knelt beside the fallen pig and touched its still-warm body. Silently, he said a prayer to the pig, asking forgiveness. It was a custom of his people to pay respect to all living things. He wished the pig to know he killed it out of necessity, not malice.

He had finished the prayer when his eyes chanced upon another track. The track of a man! It had been made not long ago. Carlomagno felt the hairs on the nape of his neck bristle.

He scooped up another handful of water and brought his hand to his lips as his eyes hurriedly scanned the area on the other side of the stream. His eyes discovered another sign: a smudged spot on the opposite bank.

His mind raced with a thousand questions. What should he do? What if the unseen stranger was watching him at this very moment? Or worse, maybe stalking him! Casually, Carlomagno stood up, clutching his bow in his left hand. He reached up and took an arrow from his quiver, half expecting an attack at any moment. But nothing happened. The track on this side of the stream was a footprint, but the other side was not. A smudge, like a knee? Whoever had made the track was stumbling. Was it from exhaustion, or was the person wounded? The footprint he had seen was a boot mark. Did the Cimaroons wear boots, he wondered? Or did they go about barefoot, as he did? Slave masters did not go around buying boots for their slaves, but Carlomagno's feet had long since hardened to the rough terrain of the Hispaniola sugar cane fields where he had spent most of his time.

Carlomagno followed the signs for a half-hour before he realized he had not been finding any new marks. He stopped, standing close to a protective tree, and looked all around him. The person had seemed to be stumbling without regard for tracks. Now they just seemed to fade out. Carlomagno was sure this person was in a hurry, for he had made no effort to hide his trail. That could indicate that he was wounded, maybe delirious, and not thinking clearly. Or he could simply not be a woodsman.

Suddenly Carlomagno had another thought. Who was this person fleeing from? He paused to consider. Of course, if this man he was trailing was fleeing in such a hurry, it was because he feared pursuit. Carlomagno silently cursed, he had been so intent on following his quarry that he had not made more than a passing attempt to hide his own tracks. By now, whoever was pursuing this stranger must know of Carlomagno's presence.

The boy turned back, moving with more care. As he went he used all the tricks Noank had taught him to hide his own tracks. At last he came to the spot where he had last seen the stranger's tracks. He knelt to examine them and by luck spotted the crucial clue. Hidden well behind overgrown bushes was a small opening. He knew at once that the person he was following must have gone into that opening. But now Carlomagno had other thoughts on his mind. He continued back toward the stream, wiping out all sign of his—and the stranger's—passing. At the stream, he managed to lift the dead boar. As he vanished back into the dense brush, he heard voices, speaking Spanish. The boy made for the cave. This time he was careful to leave as little sign as possible. He did not think the Spaniards were very good in the woods, as they had taken so long to reach the stream.

From what he had heard they were arguing over what to do. They had seen the boot print, but had not yet noticed the knee smudge. They did not guess the blood was from a pig, but thought it was left by the one they chased.

Carlomagno hesitated briefly near the cave. His bow would be useless in such tight quarters, but he had the spear. If he had to, he could jab with the sharpened point of his spear. Then he crawled under the bush and into the cave. It widened a little and took a slight turn.

Just around the bend he found the man, unconscious on the floor. He was not Spanish, looking more like the English. His clothes were filthy tatters, but his strong fingers were clenched around a pistol. Carlomagno knew about flintlocks, muskets and pistols from his father's training. He took the pistol, found the powder horn and carefully loaded it. Now, if this stranger caused trouble, Carlomagno had a chance.

The stranger hardly looked in any shape to cause trouble. He had been wounded, though the dirt now caked the nasty gash along his side. Using his waterskin, Carlomagno bathed the wound as best he could. There was little else he could do now. He crept back out to the cave's mouth and listened. Soon he heard Spanish voices. They had seen the mark on the stream's bank, but were unsure if it was left by the man they chased.

Now, having found no more sign, they were all for turning back. Except one man with a distinctive shrill voice. This one was certain they were near their prey. But the other two wanted none of it; they retreated the way they had come.

Still Carlomagno remained still. Noank had taught him not to be too trusting. His vigilance was rewarded. Ten minutes of waiting revealed that the Spaniards had not gone. He heard a voice: "I tire of this, Miguel. He is not in the area."

"I have a feeling," said Miguel, the shrill-voiced one. "Kerbour-chard was wounded! We saw the blood. He couldn't have gone far."

"He has a feeling," scoffed the first voice. "Well, I have one, too, Miguel. I say this man would not go inland. He would head for the coast, where he has the chance of meeting up with some of his pirate amigos!"

Pirate!

Carlomagno tightened his grip on the pistol. He had heard about pirates from his days on Don Pedro's plantation. The Spanish hated them, for they preyed upon Spanish vessels, stealing treasure, food and whatever else they desired at the moment. Carlomagno almost wanted to call out to the Spaniards. He could tell them the pirate had stolen him, to keep him from telling his whereabouts. Those Spaniards only wanted the pirate. They would probably return him unharmed to Don Pedro.

But Carlomagno kept quiet as the Spaniards moved off. This time he could hear them walking through the woods, making little attempt at stealth. Now, he turned back. He looked upon this man with new eyes, realizing that lying before him was one of the notorious pirates he had heard about. It was said they killed and maimed without reason, doing as they pleased. Well not this one, Carlomagno thought. If he gets one step out of line, he's going to regret it.

It was several hours until dark, so Carlomagno settled down to wait. He wanted to make sure the Spaniards had left. With nightfall he would make his way back to Noank to report all he had seen. Noank would know what to do. After a final careful look about, Carlomagno retreated deeper into the cave, where he could keep an eye on the wounded pirate. The stranger, he had been called Kerbourchard by the Spaniards, looked the worse for wear, his clothes more like the rags slaves wore back on Don Pedro's plantation. But the pistol was well kept. Carlomagno liked the feel of it in his hand. If his people had enough of the firesticks they would have easily beaten back the English colonials.

It had been a long day and Carlomagno, after all, was still a boy. He grew drowsy and his head dropped, chin resting on his chest. A moment passed, then two.

He opened his eyes with a start.

"How long did I sleep?" he wondered. What if the Span—

"*Buenos dias, amigo.*" The voice was soft, as if it were an effort to speak. The stranger had crawled to the wall and sat propped against it. The effort was draining him; the sweat rolled down his haggard cheeks. "Water, boy. *Por favor?* I need water."

Carlomagno raised the pistol. "I know how to shoot."

"I won't hurt you, boy. I need water. I see the waterskin beside you. May I have a drink?"

With one hand clutching the pistol, Carlomagno reached for the waterskin with the other. He came closer, warily handing the waterskin to the pirate.

"*Gracias,*" Kerbourchard croaked, before gulping a mouthful of water. He let it rest in his mouth before it trickled slowly down his throat. "I felt I was on fire, my friend. My name is Kerbourchard—Persifal Kerbourchard. You have a name, I suppose?"

35

"Carlomagno." the boy managed, hoping he sounded brave. Inwardly, he was shaking. "I know how to shoot."

"Ah, so you said. You're a heavy sleeper, too, I see."

"I dozed only for a moment."

"Yes, sometimes it seems that way, Carlomagno. There were times when I was sure I had only just closed my eyes, but had slept the night through and half the day!" Kerbourchard looked the boy over slowly. "You are not Taino or Carib. You might be him, the Red Indian they tell of. But from the stories they tell, he must be quite a bit older. You are his son perhaps?"

"My father is far away."

"Then you are a Red Indian? From the American Colonies?" Kerbourchard took another drink. "Ah, that's better. Now, let's see, you can't be the Red Indian they tell of. He was a slave from the colonies many years ago, but fled to the mountains. Sometimes he is spotted, but no one has ever caught him. If I recall, there is a bounty to be paid for his capture." Kerbourchard studied the boy. "Do you know such an Indian, boy? A Red Indian from the American Colonies?"

Carlomagno realized this man was talking about Noank, but he shook his head. "I am alone."

"I see. I have not heard of another Red Indian escaping to the mountains. But, of course, I have been preoccupied of late!" Kerbourchard groaned as he shifted his position slightly. "Boy, I need food. I have been shot. Can you get me food?"

Carlomagno nodded slowly. "I think so. I will have to move carefully, though, those men might still be out there."

36

"The Spaniards?"

"*Si, tres hombres.*"

"They followed me," Kerbourchard said with a grimace of pain. "I didn't think they were any good in the woods. Then again, I was in no shape to hide my tracks."

"I think they have gone," Carlomagno said. "I managed to hide some of your tracks and when they lost your trail they were turning back. All except one, the one with the high voice."

"Ah, Miguel! Miguel Souza. Yes, it's like him to want to keep on. He knew I was hurt, and knows what his life will be worth if Kerbourchard survives!"

"Miguel argued, but the others won and they all went back the way they came."

"Good, good. Then perhaps it is safe for you to go and bring me some medicine, boy. I see you have killed a wild pig? They are good eating, boy. Oh, and Carlomagno, maybe you should leave me the pistol— in case Miguel and his amigos return while you are gone?"

Carlomagno shook his head. "You might shoot me when I return."

"Why would I do that, my friend? You are helping me, and Kerbourchard does not forget kindness." The pirate closed his eyes for a moment. "There are two things you should never forget, boy—an enemy and a friend."

"You are a pirate." Carlomagno tightened his grip on the pistol. "I heard them say so."

"A pirate? You offend me, my friend. I am a rascal of some re-nown, a man who knows how to handle a sword—or a woman—with equal deftness. But, a common pirate? Bah! Never before have I, the Scourge of the Seven Seas, been so insulted! Why Kerbourchard is a proud name, Carlomagno. It was once a name that meant a lot in cer-tain places—and maybe it will mean something again someday."

"I do not know if I can trust you."

"I understand, my friend, and well it is for you to doubt me, for this old world is full of scalawags and cutthroats. Why to tell you the truth, my young friend, I was not sure if I could trust you, so while you were sleeping, I took the liberty of taking this." Kerbourchard held out his hand and a musket ball rolled around in his palm. Carlomagno stared from the outstretched hand to his pistol.

"You took the ball?"

"I had to know if you intended to shoot me, Carlomagno. Now, you see, we can trust each other. I could have taken the pistol from you, but I did not. I wanted to let you know I trust you," the pirate smiled. "But it is useless for you to go out there with an empty pistol. Besides, I may need it if those Spaniards return. Miguel Souza is a mean man, my young friend."

They boy hesitated; without knowing exactly why, he stepped forward and handed the pistol to Kerbourchard. An empty pistol did him no good any way.

"You are young, Carlomagno, but the world is rough, and you must learn if you are to survive. Never trust anything your adversary says, for he may lie to gain advantage over you. Take me, for example, I knew you dozed off only for a moment, but I also knew that you would not be sure how long you slept."

Carlomagno remembered Noank's words then, of how a man will tend to doubt himself at that last moment.

"Never doubt, when it is time to act, never hesitate," Noank told him. "To hesitate but a moment can mean the difference between life and death!"

It was the same lesson Kerbourchard had now shared. "I used your own thoughts against you, my friend. You see, Carlomagno, the pistol you just handed me is loaded. The musket ball I showed you was a spare," Kerbourchard it dropped back into his pocket. "If I were an enemy, I could kill you now. But, I am a friend, Carlomagno. At least I hope I am. I need one right now, myself. Are you my friend?"

Half angry at being tricked, the boy stood motionless before slowly nodding his head. "*Si*, I am your friend, *Señor* Kerbourchard."

"Good," Kerbourchard smiled. He had a nice smile, though he could do with a shave. "How about that food now, Carlo?"

Carlomagno gathered wood, made a fire, and began roasting slices of pork. Kerbourchard ate sparingly.

"Carlomagno, I need your help, son. If you don't come back to me, I won't leave this cave alive. I'm in a bad way, and I'm counting on you. Don't let me down."

"I won't." Carlomagno made his way back toward his own base camp with ease, moving slowly, but steadily. He made better time than he had in the morning, for then he had been meandering, following tracks while on the hunt. Now he knew right where he was heading. He moved at a good pace, always alert for jaguars or an alligator. The woods held many creepy crawlies and dangerous snakes that prowled the night.

And the mosquitoes! They were huge! To swat one only invited a half dozen others to land on you. But Carlomagno moved without distraction. He was eager to tell Noank all about this strange white man. He was not sure if it was a good thing he had done, to help this pirate, but Noank would know what to do.

At the edge of his camp he paused, letting his ears pierce the night as his eyes never could. Noank had taught him that, to be certain a place was safe before you entered. Too often, Noank told him, a person feels relieved when they reach home and they drop their guard at that precise moment. But Noank was not one to be taken off-guard, and through him Carlomagno was learning the ways of the warrior. In many ways, what Noank taught only rekindled the memories of lessons learned long ago in the forests of his homeland.

Cupping a hand to his mouth, Carlomagno imitated the croak of the tree frog—it was the signal he and Noank used for each other. There was no answering call. Carefully, Carlomagno inched forward. The camp was empty. Carlomagno was disappointed when he found no sign of Noank. He was not alarmed, however, as Noank had left him alone before when on the hunt. No doubt, Noank had merely followed a game trail that had taken him further afield than expected. After a careful look to make sure nothing was amiss, Carlomagno hurriedly threw a pack together. He found some food, wild yams and jerked meat, and some plants. He could not recall their names, but remem-

bered Noank saying that they could be used to make medicine to re-
duce fevers. Unsure of what to expect, Carlomagno wanted to be prepared if the strange white man suffered from fever. He recalled his own
bout—the sweating and shakiness—only too clearly.

At the mouth of the cave Carlomagno placed two rocks side by
the side, the smaller to indicate which direction he had gone in. It was
a simple signal, one he and Noank used to communicate to each other.
To an unknowing stranger, nothing would be evident. But when Noank returned, he would know in which direction to go if he wished to
look for Carlomagno.

The night was warm, with the "*coqui, coqui*" of the large tree
frogs surrounding him as he retraced his steps. Carlomagno was calm.
This surprised him, for he did not generally like being alone in the
jungle at night. But he felt a sense of confidence in himself. True, he
had been tricked by the stranger and handed over a loaded weapon un-
knowingly. Had Kerbourchard been unfriendly, he could have easily
been killed. But Carlomagno had lived to learn from another mistake,
and that is something many people cannot claim.

There was reason to be proud, too. He had successfully tracked
the wounded Kerbourchard to his hiding place, when three older men
had failed to locate him. But thinking of the three Spaniards made
Carlomagno uneasy. Would they return? What if they return with
more men to hunt for Kerbourchard? And what if one of those men
was a skilled tracker? The three he had seen were not, yet this Miguel
Souza, he seemed the type to come back.

Carlomagno knew the first chance he got he must move Kerbourchard. Unfortunately, he knew of only one place to move him to—and Noank wouldn't like that very much.

The pirate was asleep when Carlomagno returned to the cave. The boy rekindled the small fire and began to boil water. With some of the warm water, Carlomagno again bathed Kerbourchard's wound and affixed a poultice to it.

Kerbourchard opened his eyes, he forces a smile. "Ah, you have returned, *mon ami.* Kerbourchard is in your debt."

"We should move when you are up to it, in case those Spaniards come back." He dropped some of the vegetables he had brought with him into the boiling water and shaved some of the jerked meat Noank had stored.

"I doubt they will, but Miguel may come on his own. He'll be afraid for his life if I am still alive. He knows what happens to those who double-cross Kerbourchard! I thought him my friend, but he set me up to be captured. Greed got the better of him, Carlo. There is a reward for me."

"A reward?"

"Yes, a reward—just as there is one on your Red Indian friend. You deny it, but your eyes betray you, Carlomagno. I think you know of this Red Indian. He is nearby, perhaps?"

"Why do they look for him?"

"It is simply because he escaped—and has remained free. They want to make an example of him. But what of you, Carlomagno? Have you escaped from a plantation, too, then?"

42

"I ran away from Don Pedro de la Marana, and the Arawak follows me, I think."

"Ah, the Arawak. Yes, even we freebooters have heard of him. Don Pedro rents him out to wealthy men to capture their runaways. But no one has eluded him; how is it you, who are but a mere boy, manage it?"

Carlomagno shrugged. "Luck, maybe? I let on that I was slow-witted, so they would think I had simply gotten lost. I thought that would buy me a head start before the Arawak was sent after me. Also, I know how to hide my tracks—another thing they did not expect from me."

Kerbourchard smiled. "Wise, boy! Always use your enemy's own thinking against him. It's what the Spaniards do when they spread tales of the Cimaroons. Most of the slaves are afraid, and in their minds they imagine the Cimaroons to be worse than they are.

"Though they are bad, Carlo. I don't mean that in an evil sense, but they are bad to cross. They have been ill-treated by the Spaniards and trust no man. They have no love for the Spanish and do not hesitate to kill any Spaniard they encounter."

The stew was ready and they ate in silence, each enjoying the simple fare. As the days went by, Kerbourchard rested, slowly regaining some of his strength. Carlomagno hunted, scouted the area and spent time working on his footwear. Noank had killed a deer some time back and the hide was being used to make knee-high moccasins for Carlomagno. The boy had watched his father make a pair, so he thought he knew how to complete them.

43

"Why did you help me, Carlomagno?" asked Kerbourchard over dinner one evening.

"I don't know, a feeling, I guess."

"I have always found it important to heed one's feelings. Often your gut tells you something on the inside before there is any outward sign to go by. It's a good thing to have this intuition when you live a life on the run." Kerbourchard tossed the bone he had been gnawing on aside and wiped his hands on his pants. "Have you given any thoughts to what you will do?"

"I will live. This mountain gives me all I need."

"Is it enough just to survive? There is a big world out there, and a man can do more than just survive. You could come with me, take to the sea, Carlo. Adventure and life await us!"

"I don't know..." Carlomagno thought leaving would hurt Noank.

"If you stay here, on this mountain, you will always be on the run. One day you may find yourself in a trap, or sleep too soundly and be captured—or killed. No, there is no future for you here. The secret to dealing with your enemies is not to try to evade them, for sooner or later they will find you out. No, the best way to deal with an enemy is to become too powerful for him."

"I never thought of becoming a pirate," Carlomagno said. "I have heard many bad stories."

"There are some scoundrels, I'll not be denying that," Kerbourchard replied. "But follow your instincts and you'd be alright. On land, you couldn't hide; you'd always stand out as being different. But on a pirate ship less attention is paid to a person's skin color—all that matters is that you do your fair share—and share fairly."

Carlomagno settled down for a good night's sleep. He would think of what Kerbourchard had said some other time, now he wanted rest. And what, he kept wondering, had become of Noank?

{ 3 }

Pirate Kerbourchard

Carlomagno awoke with a start, sweat dripping from his brow. He had been dreaming of shapeless, shadowy monsters reaching out for him. He sat still for a moment until he recalled where he was: in a cave with a dangerous pirate!

And that pirate—or privateer, as he called himself—was sitting not ten feet away staring at him.

"You have a bad dream, my friend? You were tossin' about something fierce," said Persifal Kerbourchard.

"It was nothing, nothing at all."

"I have been out and about," Kerbourchard said. "Peaceful out there. No sign of any of those Spaniards."

"You can move around then? It is good; we should leave this place as soon as we can."

Kerbourchard leaned back against the wall and let his eyes close for a brief moment. "Where are you planning to go, Carlomagno?"

Carlomagno hesitated. He had a feeling he could trust this pirate, but how far? Dare he mention Noank, a runaway Pequot slave with a price on his head? Then again, Carlomagno smiled to himself, he was a runaway slave, too!

"I know about a place, a cave like this, but bigger. We can hide there," Carlomagno offered.

"No, I've had enough of caves, my friend. I'm for the coast, then to make my way back to Tortuga," Kerbourchard said. "You should come along with me. You've a good head on your shoulders, boy, and you could do well for yourself on the high seas."

The idea of going to sea was appealing to Carlomagno. If he could learn all he could about sailing, then maybe one day he could find his way back home. Yet he hesitated. Somewhere close by, maybe in dire trouble, was Noank. His friend must be in trouble; why else would he have failed to show up here?

"I have something to do first," Carlomagno said. "But maybe one day I will come to Tortuga to find you."

"Come then, and if I am not there, wait, for I shall return. Tortuga is a rough place, my boy, and no place for the weak of mind. If you come, be always on your guard for there are bad ones all about the place. Not the least of which is Levasseur himself, he who runs Tortuga with an iron fist.

"You've saved my life, Carlomagno, and I'll not be forgetting. In this life, boy, there are two things a man should never forget—his friends and his enemies. You and me now, boy, we're friends for life. One day I will come to your aid when you need it most!

"You wait and see, *mon ami.* Kerbourchard will not fail you!"

Carlomagno reached out and accepted the handshake offered by Kerbourchard. "I will be on my way then."

"I need my pistol, boy, but here's something that might come in handy," said Kerbourchard, reaching into his boot and withdrawing a plain sheath, with a jewel-handled dagger in it.

"It's beautiful," the boy exclaimed. "But I cannot accept such a fine gift. I have done nothing worthy of such a gift."

Kerbourchard mockingly clutched his chest. "Ah, my poor heart breaks! You have saved my life! Is the life of Persifal Kerbourchard then, so unworthy of such a gift? Has my existence been all for naught? Go ahead, my young friend, take this dagger—and use it well. He who last claimed rightful ownership will not be needing it any further. And I prefer a longer blade for my work. Take it and go; knowing the thanks of Kerbourchard go with you!"

Without a backward glance Carlomagno left the cave, and Kerbourchard, behind. It was daylight and travel was easy, but he took his time, stopping often to watch his backtrail. He didn't want to lead any enemies straight to his hideout.

But the birds of the jungle sang undisturbed. He slowed his pace as he neared the cave where he lived with Noank, his eyes darting back and forth for any signs of intruders, his ears alert for the slightest warning. He heard nothing, saw nothing, until the clearing opened before him. The cave had been ransacked, cooking pots strewn all about and Noank's bow snapped in half. A quiver of arrows had been dumped, the quiver tossed carelessly aside. The boy crept forward, his own bow ready to meet any challenge. But the camp was deserted.

He found a spot of blood on a rock. Was Noank injured? Or had he wounded an attacker! Carlomagno saw the footprints. He knew Noank's well. He also saw another, smaller pair. A child? But who? And how had a child found its way here? There was another set of prints, too. Carlomagno felt a chill creep up his spine.

The Arawak had been here!

Carlomagno cast about in a widening circle as he searched for clues. And he could soon read the story as easily as an Englishman might read the pages of a book. He found a spot where the Arawak had waited, watching the cave. He knew it because of the trampled grass and the small pile of discarded fruit peelings. The Arawak had spotted Noank and trailed him home, but had not seen the chance to capture him.

The Arawak had moved and stumbled across a child, for Carlomagno saw their footprints in the dust telling the story of a brief chase, a lopsided struggle and a drop of blood! So it was the child who was injured. Carlomagno found where the child had been taken and left. The cries of pain had alerted Noank and he came to investigate. That was when the Arawak had sprung his trap and captured the Pequot.

Though he could not know exactly what happened, Carlomagno could piece together enough to surmise that Noank had been captured as he came to the aid of the injured child. The tracks of all three then led off down the mountain. Was the Arawak taking them back to the plantation of Don Pedro de la Marana?

Panic gripped him. His friend was in the hands of the Arawak. At best Noank could expect to be returned to bondage. At worst—Carlomagno did not want to think about that. He had heard stories about the Arawak torturing his captives. A small voice inside his head told him to flee, to move higher up the mountain or deeper into the jungle. The Arawak had not yet located him; there was still time to flee. Ignoring the impulse, Carlomagno boldly followed the tracks.

What had Kerbourchard just told him? A man should never forget a friend, or an enemy. Noank was his friend, and Carlomagno could not abandon him. Nor could he forget his enemy, for the Arawak was relentless. No doubt when he was done with Noank, the Arawak would return here and resume his search.

Instinctively, Carlomagno knew the thing he must do was the unexpected. The element of surprise would be his only advantage against the Arawak. The Arawak, no doubt, still thought of him as a frightened, lonely child. He would never expect that child to have the nerve to follow him. Or would he? Was he using Noank as bait, just as he had used some helpless child to set a trap for the Pequot?

Whatever the risk, it was one that Carlomagno knew he had to take.

A sound caught on the wind and Carlomagno slowed. Now he moved like a panther. Ahead there was a small clearing. He crept closer until he could see into the clearing. Noank sat on the ground, his wrists tied behind his back and his ankles fastened together. The boy, no older than Carlomagno, was trussed in a similar fashion. The Arawak had left them to go off by himself, likely to hunt for some food, Carlomagno thought. Whenever the Arawak wished to rest or go off by himself he securely bound their legs so they could not run off. When he was taking them back toward Don Pedro's plantation he freed their legs only.

It was hot and Noank was facing the sun. He squinted and looked at the boy who sat a few feet from him. He was about the same height as Carlomagno, but stockier than the Indian youth. His skin was black, and seemed to glisten in the summer heat. The boy had dried blood on the side of his head from a nasty gash.

"Do not be afraid," Noank said.

The boy looked at him, unblinking. "I am Hausa. I do not know fear."

"Hausa? Is that your name?"

"My people are Hausa, from Hausaland, across the great ocean sea," the boy replied. "I am Koyamin, the son of Obasanjo."

"You are an escaped slave, then?"

The boy puffed out his chest. "I am no slave. I am Koyamin, I am free man!"

"Are you one of the Cimaroons?"

"My father is *jefe*, chief, of our village. He was brought here many years ago, when he was my age. He was stolen from his home in Hausaland. They tried to make him a slave but he escaped to the mountains. He proved himself valuable in our wars with other Cimaroon villages and married a daughter of the old chief. When the chief was killed, my father led the village."

Noank struggled with his bonds, but to no avail. The Arawak knew how to tie a knot! The Pequot looked about for something with an edge to it—a stick, or rock, something that he could work the ropes with. He didn't know where Carlomagno had gone off to, but was sure the boy had returned to their cave and could read the signs. He was certain Carlomagno would track them. He stopped in mid-thought. Was that what the Arawak was counting on?

"It is my fault you are a prisoner," Koyamin said. "I cried out, like a baby, and you came to help me. I am ashamed of myself."

"Don't be, Koyamin. The Arawak is a master at inflicting pain. When he gets around to it, I'm sure he could make most any man cry out."

"I have been watching you for a long time."

"What?" Noank was surprised.

"I spotted your cave a long time past. I come often to hide in the woods and watch you, to see what you do. My people know of you, the Red Indian—*el Indio Rojo*—they call you. I watch you and I learn much from you. I see how you move, how you never take the same path to and from your cave. I think you are too much alone, but my father says to leave you be. He says if you want to come to our village one day, you will come. If not, he says, it is best to leave you alone. But still I come to watch you. Then I come one day and I see you have a boy. A red Indian, like you, but a boy like me. I think to myself one day I will approach and talk to this boy. I would know how a red Indian boy comes to be on my mountain."

"He was sold as a slave, but escaped," Noank explained. "His name is Carlomagno. And, unless, I'm mistaken about him, I'd say he's on our trail right now."

"Maybe," Koyamin nodded. "Or maybe he is still caring for the sick man."

"What?"

"I found his tracks and followed. He was in another cave, not far from yours. I watched that cave and soon I saw a man emerge, a man with white skin. He looked like a poor man, and I could see that he was weak. Hurt, maybe, or sick. I realize this boy is helping the weak man.

I decide he—and you—are good to know as friends. I come to tell you where this boy is. That is when the Arawak catches me."

"I think he follows us, Koyamin. I think he will try to free us."

"My father says I am strong for my age, but I was no match for the Arawak. I do not know what your Carlomagno can do."

Noank did not answer. What could Carlomagno do? He was still only a boy and the Arawak was a dangerous man. He had overpowered Noank with ease—and the Pequot would not have believed any man could do that to him. Carlomagno was too small, only a boy who was afraid of the ghastly stories he had heard. Even if he started to follow the signs, how good a tracker was he? Could he find them?

The Arawak returned, carrying two rabbits. He started a fire, made a spit and began roasting one of the rabbits while he continued skinning the other. As he peeled the skin off the rabbit he glared at the Cimaroon boy.

"Soon, I will peel your skin," the Arawak threatened, an evil glint in his eyes. "I do not think you are worth the bother to take back to Don Pedro. He might give me a few pesos for you, but what of it? I need no peso. I take whatever I want. A handful of pesos cannot replace the pleasure I could have by listening to you scream."

"I am not afraid," Koyamin replied.

"Ah, the fly is not afraid of the spider, either—until one day he is caught in the web," laughed the Arawak. He turned his ugly eyes on Noank. "I think you know where the boy is? I do not think he could make it this far and you not be aware of him. But I will make you talk. It will be a pleasure."

"I don't know what you're talking about."

"Maybe you do, maybe you don't," the Arawak yawned. "In any case I shall enjoy making you talk. And you will tell me something, anything, as you beg for mercy. But I am Carib—and I do not know the meaning of mercy!"

The Arawak squatted by the fire, staring as his rabbit slowly roasted. The aroma wafted toward the captives, but they knew they would not taste the food. The Arawak would not bother to feed dead men. And though they weren't dead yet, it might as well be so. Soon, in his own good time, the merciless Arawak would begin the slow process of torturing his helpless victims.

Noank silently struggled against his bonds, but found no give in them. He knew all of his hopes for rescue lay in the hands of a scared young boy. A boy barely older than the one now bound beside him. But a boy who knew the art of fighting! Glancing sideways, Noank saw the boy, Koyamin, as he sat still, his eyes almost glassy as he stared into space. Was it the stare of a frightened child? Was that the kind of look Carlomagno would have when he laid his eyes upon the Arawak?

Koyamin was unaware of the Pequot beside him, or of the Arawak starting to eat his rabbit. Koyamin had The Gift; his father had pronounced it so after having a dream. Always Koyamin knew he had the protection of the powerful Otigbu spirits. It was the Otigbu who rewarded the just and punished the men who knew evil in their hearts. Now, his life in the balance, Koyamin was calling on the ancient spirits of his father and his father's father. He emptied his mind of all thought, seeking to make contact in the spirit world with his protector, with the *Oke Ololo*. The Old One would hear him, of that Koyamin had no doubt. Too often a man replaces belief with religion; he enjoys the trappings of his religious symbols, but does not cloak himself with the naked faith. Koyamin understood the balance; he knew *Oke Ololo* would come.

"Ha! Look at him," the Arawak sneered, gesturing toward Koyamin with the half-eaten rabbit in his hand. The second rabbit was now slowly roasting on the spit over the fire. "He was full of big talk about not being afraid, now he looks too frightened to even move."

"Let him go," Noank urged. "He means nothing to you. I'm the one you want. The Spanish will pay you a big reward for my capture."

"Bah, what do I care about rewards? I have food and drink when I want, women. What else do I need? The Spanish can offer me no reward beyond those things," the Arawak replied. "Everyone fears me; they know they cannot escape once I am on their trail. But now, this boy—a mere child—eludes me! Him, I want. And I shall have him, too. You will tell me where he is. Whether it goes easy for you, or hard, is up to you.

"I thought this boy was *stupido*, slow in the head. Everyone thought so. When he did not come in from the fields, Don Pedro sent a man out to look for him, thinking the boy had wandered away. But when they could find no sign of him, Don Pedro called for me.

"Never before has anyone escaped me. I am Arawak. I am the greatest tracker on Hispaniola. I, too, thought the boy was merely lost. I followed, sure I would catch up to him." The Arawak stood up and looked about before continuing. "I had not followed long when I began to think maybe this boy was not so *loco* as we thought. He was good at hiding his sign. I lost his trail a couple of times, but always found it again. Then I knew this boy was not foolish. He had a plan in mind, perhaps had been thinking of it for some time. I realized he was heading for the mountains and hurried here. But then his trail vanished. I see a footprint one day, then, *poof*, he is gone like smoke in the wind. Now I know the boy is smart, but not that smart. At first I thought I had mistaken his intentions. I backtracked, but could find no other trail. So I come back to the mountain.

"Only now, I think maybe the boy is not alone. I thought maybe Cimaroons had found him. But then I saw you. I have heard of you, the Spanish speak often of *El Indio Rojo*. I planned to capture you, sure that you could tell me where the boy is. Ah, but you are clever. Several times I had chances to capture you, but always the risk was too great. I do not intend to get myself hurt. So I must find a way to distract you, for the small moment I need. That is where the Cimaroon whelp came in. He is nothing to me, just a tool. Still, I have heard how tough the

Cimaroons are. I think I would like to see how much one can suffer before he cries out for mercy."

The Arawak started to lift the half-eaten rabbit in his hand when an arrow flew from the darkness and struck the rabbit, knocking it to the ground. Leaping back with a start, the Arawak stumbled and fell into the fire. He rolled quickly out of it, rolling to put the flames out. Then, his clothes still smoldering, he grabbed up his blowgun.

"So the boy has come, has he? It is well. It makes my job easier," the Arawak said. He had stepped away from the firelight and stood now in the shadows, letting his eyes scan the forest for any sign of Carlomagno. His eyes roamed, passing and returning to a spot where a shadow seemed darker than the others around it. Without warning, the Arawak suddenly raised the blowgun to his lips and fired a dart at the shadow. There was a crash, as Carlomagno leapt away, barely evading the poisoned missile.

"And so I have you!" Dropping his blowgun, the Arawak yanked the knife from his sheath. As he started forward, Noank swung his legs around in an effort to trip up the Arawak. Stumbling, the Arawak turned on Noank with fury and plunged the knife deep into the Pequot's side.

"I no longer need you, *Indio Rojo*! I have the boy!"

The Arawak turned toward the woods and there stood Carlomagno, bow in hand. Even as the Arawak saw him, the boy let fly another arrow, this one striking the Arawak in the leg. With a grunt of pain, the Arawak started toward Carlomagno, who stood dumbfounded, not even trying to take another arrow from his quiver.

"I have killed your friend, now you are next, boy," the Arawak growled.

Koyamin's eyes blinked and he flexed his wrists, giving a great tug as the Otigbu spirits came upon him and the ropes that bound him tore apart like wet paper. The Arawak was slowly advancing on Carlomagno, completely unaware as Koyamin hastily freed his legs and snatched up the spit holding the rabbit, which had fallen when the Arawak had stumbled over the fire.

With the spit held tightly in both hands, Koyamin jammed the sharpened end into the Arawak's back. The Arawak fell to his knees, howling in agony. He started to rise, but now Carlomagno was before him. With his knife, the gift from Kerbourchard, Carlomagno slashed the Arawak's throat. Blood gushed out as the dreaded Arawak toppled onto his side and made a last gurgling noise before lying still forever.

Once he was certain the Arawak was dead, Carlomagno rushed to Noank.

"I am sorry, grandfather! It is because of me you are killed," Carlomagno said, tears streaking his face. "Do you have to die? Please, don't die! I need you, grandfather."

"Death comes to all men, always out of season." Noank forced a smile. "You have given me a great gift, Carlomagno. You have allowed me to die like a warrior, to die fighting to protect something I love. Had I a son, I could have none better than you. Your father would be proud of you, Carlomagno, as I am. If I should meet Metacomet in the next life, I shall tell him of his son's bravery. Do not weep for me. I came to this land a slave, but tonight I die a Pequot warrior. I die proudly, grandson."

Carlomagno stared as Noank took his last breath and then remained still, a contented look on his handsome bronze face. Carlomagno looked up when he felt a hand on his shoulder.

"You have saved my life. I owe you a life now. I am in your debt. I am Koyamin, son of Obasanjo."

"I am Carlomagno, son of Metacomet."

{4}

Son of Metacomet

In a half-crouch Koyamin slowly circled to his right; with surprising quickness for such a big man he lunged toward his foe. Carlomagno stood still, seemingly unconcerned. Now he deftly ducked aside, swinging his left leg out and tripping up his Otigbu friend. Koy landed heavily in the dirt. He regained his feet in a moment and turned to face Carlomagno.

"I knew you were going to rush," Carlomagno laughed. "You give a quick blink of your eyes just before you lunge."

"But now that you have told me, I shall be aware of it," Koy replied gaily.

Many of the villagers had gathered to watch; wrestling was the sport of choice for boys on the verge of claiming manhood. Koyamin was taller than the other boys of the village and he was quickly filling out. His raw strength was unmatched by any of the other boys and promised to soon outmatch most of the village's men.

"You are too confident."

"Should I be less?" Koy asked. "I have never been beaten."

"After today, you will no longer be able to say that!"

Carlomagno closely watched Koyamin as he moved closer, his arms held wide. Koy blinked and Carlomagno moved aside—

Too late Carlomagno realized the blink had been a decoy to get him to reveal his next move. As he started to rise, Koyamin closed in, scooped him up and swiftly straightened, throwing Carlomagno over his back.

Though caught off guard, Carlomagno was quick to recover. He did not try to resist Koy's power move; instead, he let himself go into it. As he sailed over Koy, he twisted his body in mid-air to land on his feet. Certain that Carlomagno would land on his face in the dirt, Koyamin paused to acknowledge the giggling group of girls who watched and cheered shyly.

Carlomagno's feet barely touched the earth before he threw himself forward, striking Koyamin behind the knees. The African fell heavily, Carlomagno rolling him up. Finally, he was moments from pinning Koy...

"Enough!" Koyamin's father, Obasanjo, stepped into the circle and pulled Carlomagno away. "Our village needs food, and you waste your time in child's play!"

The two boys got to their feet, bowing their heads respectfully before their Chief, but grinning at each other. They moved off down the path and their audience slowly returned to their duties.

"I beat you."

"Did not," Koy defended. "I was about to make my move when my father stopped us."

"I know! We need food, so let us go hunting and see which of us can bring home the most game!"

"Fine! I will beat you twice in one day!"

Laughing, the two friends ran off to get their weapons.

"Why are you so angry, husband?"

Obasanjo sat in the shade in front of his thatched hut and watched his followers as they went about their routines. He was getting older, though the only outward signs of it were the gray hairs invading his head and beard.

"Koyamin lost. I did not want the others to see it."

"It's just a game," his wife insisted, "just boys playing around."

"It is not just a game, wife," he snapped. "I do not expect a woman to understand."

"Women understand more than men think. I tell you now that Carlomagno is no threat to Koy. They share a bond that goes deeper than blood."

"Maybe."

Age was an enemy no man could defeat. Obasanjo knew that one day he would be replaced by a younger, stronger *jefe*. It was his wish that when that day arrived it would be his oldest son, Koyamin, who would lead the village. There had been no doubt of the succession, even after the day when Koyamin had returned to the village with the strange red Indian boy, Carlomagno. Koyamin told the tale of tracking the legendary *indio rojo*, how together he and Carlomagno had defeated the Arawak. The boys had become instant heroes that day and rightly so. To kill the Arawak was a deed worthy of praise.

Obasanjo had welcomed Carlomagno to his village. What else could he have done? At first, he was amused by the boys' strong friendship. But the old chief was wise and watched with growing apprehension as Carlomagno quickly demonstrated his skills and made himself useful to the community. Carlomagno showed the other young boys how to set and bait traps as his own ancestors had done. While the Cimaroons generally preferred the spear, Carlomagno taught the other boys how to make bows and arrows and worked to improve their skill. It was done as a game, but one that would prepare the boys for when it was their turn to protect the village.

Obasanjo watched and grew more concerned about Carlomagno's growing prowess. Certainly the Indian youth was proving to be an asset to his adopted Cimaroon village. Obasanjo clumsily tried to explain his thoughts to his son. Koy was disinterested; talk of leadership was something to be considered at a much later time.

"You can only lead if people will follow you," Obasanjo told his son. "When the day comes, will the people follow you—or Carlomagno?"

His father's concern bothered Koyamin for a few days, but it was soon forgotten. He had never thought about becoming chief, and if he could appoint the next chief he could think of no one better than his friend, Carlomagno.

Obasanjo did not mention the subject again, but it was never far from his thoughts. Koy was still a child and did not yet think as a man would, his father reasoned. Power was the only thing that mattered to Obasanjo and as he aged he thought more and more about succession. He had worked too hard to groom his son for leadership to watch Carlomagno ruin his plans. This was a Cimaroon village and Carlomagno was not Cimaroon. He was nothing more than a ...

Obasanjo left his hut without a word to his wife. At the farthest end of the village lived Cuffie, who was a tight-lipped, dependable man. Obasanjo knew he could depend on Cuffie to do what must be done. After all, Cuffie had helped him before.

Carlomagno, the Wampanoag prince, and Koyamin, the Otigbu seer and son of a Cimaroon chief, grew ever closer. The other boys soon learned that to pick trouble with one meant fighting them both. They shared their knowledge, for Carlomagno knew the secrets from his

Wampanoag ancestors, while Koyamin carried in his heart and mind the mysteries from ancient Hausaland.

While Carlomagno told of his people's spirits, such as Granny Squannit and Manitoo, Koyamin told about the Otigbu and *Oke Ololo*.

"In Hausaland a boy can only become a man after he defeats a dangerous foe, be it man or beast," Koy said one day as they rested in the shade. "Is it the same with your people?"

"A Wampanoag boy must go alone into the forest to fast and pray, and to ask the great spirits to grant him a vision."

"A vision?"

"It's a special spiritual bond between you and the Manitoo," Carlomagno explained. "If you are worthy, you receive a vision and in it you find a path to follow."

After the discussion with Koy, thoughts of a vision quest held a prominent position in Carlomagno's mind. He knew he was at the age when a boy went to seek the wisdom of the gods. He had been young when he was stolen from his homeland, but he had been witness to the quests of others. With an uncle as shaman, the child's curiosity had been welcomed. But did he remember enough? Without a shaman to prepare him, could he undertake the quest on his own? Carlomagno began to plan for a vision quest. He could only try; it would be up to the Manitoo whether or not he would find what he sought.

"The Indians in your land were like the Cimaroons, many individuals with little unity?"

Carlomagno, squatting on his heels, had been idly tracing lines in the dirt with a stick. He thought for a long moment before replying to Koyamin. "Yes, much like them, I think. But there were some who talked of a different way, of maybe all the Indian people fighting together, acting as one."

"Did it happen?"

"I don't know for sure. I was captured when the war was still going on. The first time the tribes thought of standing together was long before I was born. My grandfather, Massasoit, once spoke of it. Massasoit was friendly with the English and had no trouble with them. But he could foresee difficulties in the future. I remember he told my father and my uncle, Wamsutta, that there would be trouble over land one day. The English always claimed more land for themselves, leaving none for the People. But no one seemed to take that threat seriously.

"My father spoke to me of the Pequot trouble, when their sachem, Sassacus, came to the Narragansetts carrying the wampum belt of peace. Sassacus urged the Narragansetts, who were many, to join the Pequots in fighting the English. Together, Sassacus predicted, they could drive the English away forever."

"What happened?" Koyamin asked.

"Sassacus told the Narragansett sachems, Canonicus and Mian-tonimo, that together they would be strong like a mighty oak, standing strong against the winds of change. But separate, they were like a weak limb and could be twisted and broken." Carlomagno snapped the stick he was holding. "Alone they could not stand against the English. But the Narragansetts and the Pequots had been old enemies since a time long before any could remember. What Sassacus asked was for an end to the bitter feelings. It was too much he asked, for the Narragansetts refused him. The English then marched against the Pequots, destroying them. My friend, Noank, he was of the Pequot village that was destroyed. He escaped when only a child because he had been visiting relatives in another village."

"The Indians of your land never joined as one?"

"My father, Metacomet, tried to do what Sassacus could not. He had some success, but not as much as he hoped. I do not know how it turned out in the end."

"I think your father was wise; by joining together people can better face great odds," Koy offered. "My father is from Hausaland, a great land in Africa. Strong cities have risen up from Africa, people who were mighty warriors. There was the Nok civilization, and others

John Christian Hopkins   *CARLOMAGNO*

came, strong cities like Tyre, Carthage and Kano. My grandfather was an Ofor priest and he was a much-learned man. He talked of these great cities often to my father and my father told me of these things. The Mongols were much like your people: many villages, but divided. Among them rose Temujin, a man driven to unite all the Mongols into one people."

"And what became of him?" Carlomagno wondered.

"He ruled an empire larger than any other ever known, or so my grandfather said. And my grandfather, Dan'landi, was knowing of such things. This Temujin became the Great Khan, who captured even fabled Cathay."

Carlomagno wracked his brain, but he could recall no mention of any such empire. Not one of his tribal elders, or his English tutor, had ever mentioned a Great Khan or a Mongol. And what was this Cathay? Was it a village, a people? Were they a strong, proud people, strong as the Pequots? Or maybe like the mighty Iroquois? Carlomagno started to ask Koyamin these questions, but caught himself. Did the Wampanoags know of such things? Did they not care because they happened so far away and so long ago? Was there a message in what Koyamin said?

That night Carlomagno lay awake recalling Koyamin's words, and wondering if he couldn't make his way back to the Wampanoag villages and bring the people together. Maybe he could become a Great Khan?

Life on the Cordilleras was spare, but mostly peaceful, each sultry day turning into a blistering month and the years bringing the two friends close to manhood. At seventeen, Koyamin was taller, well over six feet, and solid as an old Caribbean pine, with nary an ounce of fat. His people tended to be tall, though thinner. But Koyamin came by his muscle honestly and was twice as strong as he looked.

Carlomagno, too, grew taller than the average Wampanoag might have expected. He was four inches over six-feet with a broad chest and

63

powerful arms that boasted of strength. He was broad-shouldered, tapering in at the waist with strongly muscled legs. He combined power and fleetness as few men do. When the young men of the village held wrestling matches with each other, it was Carlomagno—and he alone—who could handle Koyamin. And even then, the Wampanoag often got as good as he gave in the rugged contests which often left both boys battered, bruised and, sometimes, bloodied.

The day began as most did on Hispaniola, with the coolness holding court under protection of the night, forced to flee as the sun began its blistering assault across the land.

Though the Cimaroon villages often worked small community gardens, there was never quite enough food available. There were wild pigs running loose, but the Cimaroons did not eat pork. Carlomagno, not wanting to offend his hosts, avoided hunting the pigs, as well. Once he had killed a pig and built a fire deep in the forest to cook his prize. The wild boars had been Noank's favorite food, he recalled. After he had gorged himself, the young Indian felt ashamed at having taken the pig's life only to see most of it left behind. It would be wasted because he could not eat it all, nor bring what was left back to Obasanjo's village.

As the pinkish sun peeked over the horizon, Carlomagno and Koy gathered up their weapons and left the village on one of their frequent hunting forays. Each carried the same arsenal, with Koyamin better with the spear and Carlomagno master of the bow. Carlomagno also carried a stone hatchet he had taken from Noank's cave. At first the hatchet had been too heavy for him to use effectively; he kept it because it reminded him of Noank. Years had passed since his days with Noank and Carlomagno found he could wield the weapon now.

"Let us go down to the flatlands," Carlomagno suggested.

"I don't know." Koyamin, like most Cimaroons, was hesitant to leave the safety of the mountains. In the rugged mountains they had no difficulty in escaping from the clumsy, armored Spanish soldiers that sometimes patrolled the valley to capture Cimaroons. On the flatlands the advantage swung dramatically in favor of the Spaniards, who could make use of their horses, lassos and nets.

"What if I knew a secret?"

"What could you know that I do not?" Koy demanded.

Knowing he had his friend's curiosity at full peak, Carlomagno grinned widely. "Oh, I know where Amina will be today."

Amina! She had once romped with the village boys, running further and faster than any other girl in the village. The boys of the village liked her for her sense of humor and adventure, and her willingness to attempt tasks usually reserved for the men, such as hunting. She was still well thought of by the boys of the village, only there was another reason now. Somehow, the skinny tomboy had turned into an attractive young girl with the power to make the boys' hearts flutter and give them new, strange feelings they did not understand.

Carlomagno and Koy were no exception.

"What do you know of Amina?"

"I overheard some of the girls talking. They are planning something special for your mother's birthday."

As wife of the village chieftain, Tilla was considered a queen by the Cimaroons. While her husband could be aloof, Tilla was always ready to help someone in need, or do what needed doing.

"You are my wife, the wife of a *jefe*," Obasanjo would insist. "It is unseemly of you to work the fields with the other women. I do not like it."

"It is good that the people see we do not think ourselves above them," Tilla wisely replied. "Should I sit around and grow fat on the labor of others? Is that not what we left behind on the plantation?"

Koyamin understood why many in the village admired his mother, and he knew Amina thought very highly of Tilla—a fact he was hoping might sweeten her feelings for him!

"What is it?"

"Some of the girls are going down to the flatlands today to pick flowers for her," Carlomagno said. "You could help carry someone's basket back up the mountain!"

"They won't go to the flatlands without guards," Koy said. "They know how dangerous it can be."

"You know Amina, she's not afraid of anything," Carlomagno said. "And she likes a dare. I bet if she was dared, she'd even kiss your ugly face!"

"She will kiss it often when we are married!"

"You? Married to someone as pretty as Amina? That would be like a beautiful parrot in love with a wart-covered toad!"

The friends always teased each other, so Koy was laughing when he commented. "If we were back in Hausaland, the people would not be able to tell your face from a baboon's backside!"

"You can have all the baboons' backsides; I'll be content looking at hers!"

"Bah!" Koy waved a hand dismissively as he stretched to his full height. "She does not even notice you with a real man, like me, around."

"Well, we could go and see Amina—if you weren't so afraid."

"Who is afraid? I am Koyamin, son of Obasanjo, I do not know fear." Koy slipped his quiver over his shoulder and took up his spear. "I am going to the flatlands. Come along if you want to see Amina make eyes at me!"

The Indian and the Otigbu seer ghosted through the forest, all thoughts of hunting lost to them now. Carlomagno wanted to see Amina just as badly as Koy did, and he knew that mention of her name would get Koyamin to go with him to the flatlands. They reached a ledge several hundred feet above the flatlands. Squatting on their heels, they used the protection of the forest to shield them as they studied the ground below.

"There!" Carlomagno pointed to what appeared to be small figures.

Koy frowned. "They are too far out in the open. If soldiers come, they could not make it back to the mountains."

Carlomagno happened to turn his head to scan the plains when he caught his breath. He thought he had seen a bright reflection in the distance.

"I don't see anything," Koy said after watching the plains for a few minutes. "If this is a joke, Carlo, it is not a funny one."

"It is not meant to be funny, my friend. I know I saw—look! There it is again!"

Koyamin saw the flash of sunlight striking something metal. "It could be soldiers," he admitted. "Though if it is, they are still far away."

The boys turned to each other with the same thought: Koyamin was right, the party of girls had wandered too far away from the safety offered by the mountains.

"We must warn them," Koy said.

They were on the face of the mountain and the drop before them was much too far for a man to survive. They would have to take a more roundabout route to reach the flatlands.

"Let's go," Carlomagno said, leading off back into the forest to find another way off the mountain. "We've got to hurry!"

Now there was no lighthearted banter, no delays as the two long-time friends rushed to reach the girls. They would be no match for even one Spanish soldier! They would be killed.

Amina and the other young women had slipped away from the village when it was still gray in the sky. They kept their plans secret because they intended to surprise Tilla, who was admired by all of the girls. There was another reason for secrecy, too. Obasanjo didn't like his followers going down to the flatlands unless absolutely necessary. There was no direct path down the mountain; they had to find their own way to the flatlands. Leaving the village meant making their way through the forest, which slowly thinned to a rocky, bald face on the mountain. Footing could be tricky here, and the girls moved slowly but with confidence as they crossed the bare space and entered another cluster of trees and shrubs. A boulder blocked the path at that point, but after skirting it the mountain fell away in a gentle slope, ending at the edge of the flatlands.

For a long while they remained hidden near the base of the mountains as they carefully scanned the plains. It was here where unwary Cimaroons were caught by slave hunters or soldiers. Though it was still a danger, no patrols had been seen for a couple of years. Rumor had it the Spanish were busy with a group of Cimaroon raiders further to the east.

"Come on, Amina. Let's go."

Amina smiled at her younger sister. "You must learn patience, Fiba. First we must be certain it is safe." Amina laughed softly to herself, thinking that she had been just as impatient as Fiba when she was a year or two younger. But Fiba was right; there was no sign of anyone else on the plains. "Stay close to me."

"I will," Fiba promised. At seven, she was excited to be making her first trip to the flatlands.

With Amina leading the way, the girls drifted away from the mountains. The plains were covered by a mat of grass and decorated with various flowers in colorful hues. A red and yellow butterfly floated past and Fiba, laughing, loped after it in a vain attempt to catch it.

"It's hard to think we were like that once."

Amina nodded at Darfa's comment. Amina had recently turned seventeen and her best friend was a year behind. "I don't think it was that long ago, Darfa."

"We're too grown up now."

"Yes," Amina glanced sideways at her friend. "Instead of butterflies, now you chase after the boys!"

"They are not very hard to catch," Darfa winked. "I think that, un-like butterflies, boys like to be caught!"

"Butterflies wander to every pretty flower, and remain with none," Amina observed. "I think boys are like that, too."

"Ha! A lot you know about boys, Amina. My mother says that a boy doesn't know what he wants until a girl puts the idea in his head."

Amina wrinkled her nose. "I do not want a man who does not think."

"Ma says they are easier to manage that way. Besides, all boys are like that—and men, too."

"I shall find a man who can use his mind."

"I hope you find him," Darfa laughed. "I only want a man that can use other parts of his body."

"Darfa! That's naughty!" Amina giggled.

"Oh, you have not thought of it? Not even with Carlomagno?"

Amina turned her head away, slightly embarrassed. Carlomagno was becoming quite a man; he was fine-looking and was already re-spected for his generosity. He would make a good husband.

So would Koyamin.

Suddenly Amina remembered her sister and hastily looked about for her. Where had she gone off to?

"Fiba! Fiba, where are you?" The rest of the girls were gathered around a batch of floral plants, chattering and giggling. They had not seen where Fiba had gone. "I told her not to wander away! Where could she be?"

"Maybe she went over there?" Darfa pointed to a cluster of trees further across the plains. "You know Fiba; she probably lost interest in the butterfly and started running after a rabbit."

"Come on, let's look for her."

They walked quickly toward the trees. The day was getting hotter and Amina had hoped to be back in the village by midday. She would have to find Fiba quickly and get the others headed back up the mountain. Glancing back, she frowned. Amina had not realized how far from the safety of the mountains they had come.

"Fiba!"

"I'm up here," Fiba chirped from her perch up in the trees.

"Get down here before you fall," Amina scolded her sister. "You had me worried."

Fiba swiftly descended the tree. "I am sorry, Amina."

"What were you doing up there anyway?"

"Watching the men." Amina exchanged a sharp glance with Darfa and then grabbed her sister's shoulders. "Ow! That hurts!" Fiba howled.

"What men?" Amina demanded harshly.

"The men," Fiba cried, "and their big dogs—"

"You mean horses?" Darfa demanded.

"She's only seven, Darfa," Amina said. "She's never seen a horse."

"What can we do?"

"Get her back, Darfa! Tell the others to run for the mountains. Now!" Amina ordered. "I will climb up the tree and see if they are soldiers."

Amina scaled the slim tree trunk with ease and sat on the same branch her sister had used. Her eyes widened when she saw the Spanish soldiers bearing down on them. In her panic, Amina lost her grip on the branch and toppled from the tree, landing heavily on the ground. Her head slammed against the grass and she fought a losing battle for consciousness.

The girls were happily filling their baskets with flowers when one glanced up and saw Darfa racing toward them.

"Why's Darfa in such a hurry?"

The soldiers crested a knoll that had kept them from sight of the Cimaroons; the men spotted the girls at the same moment and pushed their horses into full gallop. The girls ran screaming toward the mountains. A few panicked and ran the wrong direction as several horsemen cut away from the column and gave chase.

In her fear, Darfa released Fiba's hand and raced on ahead. Two laughing soldiers turned their mounts to head her off. While one blocked her path, the other quickly got off his horse and grabbed the frightened girl. Darfa struggled and screamed but her captor knocked her to the ground with a punch that broke her nose.

"What did you do that for?" his companion called as he dismounted.

"We do not need her nose for anything, *amigo*!"

The two men fell on top of the struggling girl.

Running down one of the fleeing girls with his horse, a soldier reined around and trampled her lifeless body. Another rammed a sword through a running girl's back. Two others were caught by the soldiers who tore at their clothes and laughed uproariously as the girls tried to cover themselves with the shreds they had left to wear. A rotund soldier stared down into Darfa's hollow eyes as her assailants continued to ravage her. She had ceased resisting and was struggling to breathe with blood from her broken nose smeared all over her face.

"No fair, I want a girl, too!" the portly horseman howled. "You two aren't leaving any for me."

"There is one, Esteban," one of the two men laughed as he pointed toward Fiba, who was churning her small legs as fast as she could to reach the mountains.

"You better hurry if you want to catch her!"

Esteban jerked his horse around and took off in pursuit. The distance between the soldier and Fiba rapidly melted away. Fiba would reach the foot of the mountain first, but it was steep; she would not be able to reach the ledge that offered a narrow path up the mountain and into the closest forest. Sobbing, Fiba clawed at the rocky slope as she tried to will herself up to the ledge. She glanced over her shoulder and saw the fat horseman thundering down on her. She grabbed for a handhold but the loose rock rolled and she tumbled back down the slope. She sat half-dazed as Esteban reached for her. "I have you now, girl!"

Suddenly Carlomagno hurled himself through the air, his bronzed body slamming into the Spaniard's, knocking Esteban from his horse. Carlomagno scrambled to his feet first.

"Run!" he hissed at Fiba, but the child had curled herself into a protective ball, trembling with shock. He turned to face Esteban.

The Spaniard was pulling out his pistol. Carlomagno lashed out with a savage kick, knocking the weapon free. He lifted his hatchet, ready to bring it down on the soldier's helmet.

The roar of a musket caused him to jump, but the bullet missed him, sending fragments of rock flying from the mountainside. As one man stopped to reload his musket, another ran toward Carlomagno. A hurried glance and Carlomagno saw the fat soldier was up on one knee. He could not win. Knowing he must flee, Carlomagno kicked the fat man to the ground, spun and whirled his stone hatchet toward the soldier closing in on him. The hatchet struck the man in the forehead; he was dead on his feet before he dropped to the dirt. Though the rocky face was steep, even for him, Carlomagno tossed Fiba over one shoulder and scrambled up. The soldier with the musket aimed carefully. A spear seemed to appear from nowhere as it shot through the air and lodged in the musketeer's throat.

"Good timing!" Carlomagno said, pausing to catch his breath.

"Where is Amina?" Koyamin asked Fiba. The terrified child could utter no intelligible words. Koy grabbed her forcefully. "You must tell me where your sister is."

"She's dead!" Fiba screamed. "Dead! I saw her fall from the tree!" Fiba continued to shriek as Koyamin held her in his arms. Within minutes, overcome by shock and trauma, the child slowly quieted and then simply dropped off to sleep.

The two young men crouched on the ledge watching helplessly as the Spanish soldiers finished raping the remaining girls and began to torture and kill them.

"She's not out there," Carlomagno whispered. "Maybe there's still hope."

Koy bowed his head, overcome with guilt and grief. "I should have come sooner. Now we must accept what the spirits have willed."

"Some of the girls made it back to the mountain," Carlomagno insisted, "they are probably lost in the forest right now. Take Fiba and go. Find the others and get them back to the village!"

"What about you?"

"I am going to find Amina. I have to know for sure."

The grass on the flatlands was nearly two feet tall, and with shrubs sprinkled about offering slight concealment, Carlomagno was sure he could make his way unseen to the stand of trees and locate Amina.

{ 5 }

Cimaroon Fears

"We must seek revenge!"

Obasanjo, looking much older, saw the angry faces of his followers. They had been enraged ever since word of the massacre had reached the village. Koyamin had brought the story, and the surviving girls confirmed it. At first Obasanjo had listened to the calls for retaliation. He had changed his stance after Carlomagno and Amina reached the village safely during the night. Amina had run immediately into Koy's arms, begging to see her little sister.

"We must protect those who survived. We are too few, and too poorly armed to fight the soldiers," Obasanjo lamented. "To attack would only invite further disaster." Later, Obasanjo was adamant when Carlomagno raised the subject again.

"Our weapons are useless against their muskets and cannon."

"What if we could get muskets?"

Obasanjo looked at Carlomagno and shook his head. "It would do us no good. We do not know how to use those muskets."

"I do," Carlomagno said. "My people have used muskets for years and I have been trained. I could teach you."

"No!" Obasanjo refused to listen. Instead he decided to move the village, to relocate in case the Spanish soldiers came in search of them.

"My father was once a slave to the Spanish and he has tasted their cruelty. He still remembers the feel of the lash," Koyamin explained later when he and Carlomagno were alone. "I think he fears to antagonize them. They will let us alone if we stay away, keep hidden."

"They did not leave the girls alone. They will keep coming, Koy. If an enemy thinks you're weak he will exploit it in his own good time. Your father can know peace only through strength. Only if the Spanish know many will die if they attack him, will they leave him alone."

"Your words are strong and stay in my heart. But how could we get muskets?"

"I know where there are muskets and swords, too. I have a plan, Koy. If my plan works we will have muskets—and more men to fight beside us!"

Carlomagno thought of the plantation of Don Pedro de la Marana. They could attack and take all the muskets there. And the slaves could be freed to join the Cimaroons in the mountains! With the added firepower of the muskets and the extra men, their village would become the most powerful of all the Cimaroon camps.

"Then we could unite the Cimaroons into one force, one that would make the Spanish afraid ever to come near the Cordilleras!" Koyamin exclaimed.

Carlomagno and Koyamin began making their secret plans. To reach the plantation of Don Pedro would mean leaving the safety of the mountains; if they were detected out on the plains, the Spanish would slaughter them.

"We must move at night, when the darkness will help conceal our advance," Carlomagno said. "We will have surprise on our side. This has never been attempted before, so the Spanish will never expect us to attack one of their plantations."

"Won't we be outnumbered?" Koyamin asked.

"Yes, as we cross the country we cannot afford a large group. We must move in small groups, with an agreed-upon destination where we can all meet before the attack. Once at the plantation, we will have the advantage of surprise. I will take some men and capture the storehouse, where the muskets and powder are kept. Some men will have to gather up the horses."

"Horses will be of no use in these mountains," Koyamin protested.

"We won't bring them all the way here, just use them to carry away what goods we can. We should have plenty of muskets, powder and shot, and even some grain and other food."

"What of me, then? Do I gather these horses?"

"Kamala can do that; didn't he say he used to be a groomer? He will know how to handle the horses. You, Koy, will go to the slaves' shanties and free them. They will join us. If they appear afraid, force them to come with us. I think they may be afraid of the Cimaroons because of the stories the Spanish tell. But I think once they see for themselves that there is nothing to fear, they will follow you willingly."

"It sounds good," Koyamin nodded.

"If all goes as planned, your father's village will suddenly have more food, more weapons and more fighting men than any other Cimaroon village. It will help you start building your own Cimaroon empire!"

With their plans in order, Carlomagno and Koy made another attempt to sway Obasanjo to their side. Obasanjo was a capable leader, able to feed his people and keep them in some semblance of security. But if he had one fault, it was that he was not a visionary. He saw no good in Carlomagno's plan. To raid a plantation would only provoke the Spanish and they would send their soldiers after the Cimaroons, Obasanjo argued.

"Let us leave well enough alone. Our men are few, and we cannot stand against the Spanish soldiers."

"Look about you, my Chief," Carlomagno countered with a wave of his arm. "This mountain is a natural fortress. Look at the thick woods, the huge rocks and deep gullies. The Spanish could never mount a force large enough to defeat us here. There are no roads, no way for them to drag their cannon up here. We could lead them to where they would have to march in a line and be picked off one by one!"

"It is too dangerous," the old man insisted.

"We would only be at risk while on the plains, that is where they could capture us. But if we plan it well, we could strike and be back in the mountains..."

"I said no!" Obasanjo growled, coming to his feet. "Who is *jefe* here? Is it Obasanjo, or Carlomagno? It is I who rule this village and it is I who will say yes or no. I say no to this. I forbid it!"

Later, when the two friends were alone, Carlomagno's frustration bubbled over.

"He is being stubborn! My plan would work!"

"It might work," Koyamin told him, "but it is a great risk. My father has said no and I will not go against him."

The village began preparing to relocate higher up the mountain. Carlomagno watched as crops were gathered, meat jerked and the Cimaroons seemed content to forget the massacre on the flatlands. Obasanjo asked his intentions and Carlomagno said it was past the time when he should have gone to seek a vision.

"I will go up the mountain and find a place where I can sing my prayers," Carlomagno said. "If I am granted a vision, it will reveal my destiny to me."

"Let it be so," Obasanjo nodded thoughtfully.

The *jefe* passed through the village until he reached the hut where Cuffie sat on a stump near the entrance. Their eyes met briefly and

Cuffie nodded. As was his custom, Obasanjo had vacillated over the decision, but had finally given his assent. Cuffie knew what to do.

{ 6 }

Vision Quest

Alone, Carlomagno held fast to his tenuous grip on a narrow ledge as his foot sought a toehold. He did not look down, knowing it might disorient him.

Anyway, what was beneath him was of no importance; he would climb higher up the mountainside, as high as he could go so that he would be as close to the Creator as he could be. When his toes found a solid place, he continued to scale the steep mountain. He was breathing heavily by the time he dragged himself over the lip onto a small, flat ledge. Here he would seek a vision from the Great Spirit. He had told no one of his plans, not even Koyamin, his closest friend. Working with swift, sure hands Carlomagno put together a small fire in the center of the table rock. Taking a small wooden bowl from his pack, he carefully arranged several leaves of dried sage within it. He had seen no sage in Hispaniola and was sure he would not be able to cleanse himself properly, but while bartering with a nearby Cimaroon village he had spotted some and made a trade for it. Sage could be used to flavor foods or even for medicinal purposes, but it held a deeper meaning for Carlomagno.

Setting a bit of flame to one dry leaf, he allowed it to smoke. The pungent scent took him back to ceremonies he had witnessed as a child, rituals that always began with the cleansing power of sage. Making a slow circle around the fire, he used an eagle feather he had hoarded to gently brush the fragrant tendrils of smoke around the edges of his camp. This was to prevent any bad spirits from entering the area.

There was a groove on the ledge floor, scarcely three inches deep, and he nearly lost his footing when he stepped in it. He would have to remember to move carefully in the dark; one misstep could send him off the cliff!

Carlomagno inhaled of the sage and then, using his hands, he pulled the drifting smoke toward himself, rubbing it all over his body. It was a smudging ceremony. The smoke of the sage would cleanse him of impure spirits. It was essential to his vision quest: to seek counsel with the spirits one must be free of bad thoughts and evil intentions. He spread his blanket and sat cross-legged. Silently, he began to pray to the Creator. He would remain without food or sleep until he was given some sign by the spirits.

He could look off into the distance knowing the village of Obasanjo was down in the Cibao Valley. Another, smaller village was located less than three miles away.

The Cimaroon villages were not unlike those of his homeland, the people sometimes forming brief alliances when the need arose, but more often than not going their own way. Each village was led by a chief and a priest. The greater the chief, the more followers would flock to him and the stronger he became. Obasanjo's village was small, a handful of families, so he avoided conflict whenever possible. Danger came not only from the Spanish or the buccaneers, but the stronger

Cimaroon villages—they often raided the smaller places. Food was scarce and every day was a fight for survival.

The sun dropped over the horizon and the last tinge of light in the sky surrendered to the hungry darkness; the timid stars dared not object. A cool wind blew across the mountain and Carlomagno sat unmoving as his long, black hair danced slightly with the breeze. The night grew colder and still Carlomagno sat, continually praying. It seemed as if the new day would never arrive, but at last a reddened sky released the sun. The day would be hot and sticky. But Carlomagno would not notice. He was deep in prayer.

Had his father undergone this same ritual when he was young? Certain he had, it gave Carlomagno a sense of closeness with his father, Metacomet. How many before him had sought the guidance of the spirits in this same manner? How many would follow? Having the world he knew ripped from him to be replaced with the bitter life of a slave on Hispaniola had taught him how fragile life could be. Many of the other Indians who had been sold into bondage with him and his mother had lost touch with their Wampanoag ways, finding that to convert to Catholicism might mean slightly better treatment from the slave masters. The Spaniards discouraged the Indians from practicing their traditional ways and saw their religious conversion as a sign that the "poor heathens" had seen the light of civilization.

Carlomagno vowed never to practice the white man's religion; the Creator had put his people on the earth to be the equal of any man, subservient to none. His father had taught him that.

"Never look down upon another man, or allow him to look down on you," Metacomet had said. "And always let your 'yes' mean yes, and your 'no' mean no."

Night visited again and Carlomagno's eyelids were heavy, his mind foggy for want of sleep. He could catch a quick nap, for just a few moments ...

He shook his head, as if the movement could throw the drowsiness off. He would not shame himself by falling asleep, nor would he insult the gods. At least it was cool, a delicious relief from the humid days.

How would it feel to float through the sky, gliding with the wings of an eagle?

The sky suddenly opened in a burst of colors, and he saw a large eagle soaring across a blue heaven. The eagle looked noble, its sharp eyes scanning downward as it searched for ... for what? The clouds that had been a puffy white suddenly darkened with anger, thunder rumbled and lightning flashed, the jagged streak aiming for the bird. Beating its powerful wings, the eagle veered to the side, then seemed to roll as it avoided another finger of electricity. Rain came in heavy, sullen drops that weighed the eagle down; it began to sink. Below, a mob of faceless people clamored and shoved, hands reaching menacingly. The rain stopped as suddenly as it had begun and just as the groping hands of the mob were about to seize it, the eagle gave a powerful thrust of its wings and began to climb toward the reddish-purple sun. The eagle grew smaller and smaller until it was but a speck on the horizon as it crossed the far, blue mountains and vanished on the other side.

Carlomagno found himself sitting in the dark, panting with powerful exertion. Slowly he turned his head and looked all about him. He was alone.

The vision! He had been granted a vision by the Creator, but what did it mean? In his lost homeland he would have visited a medicine man who would interpret the vision for him. To whom could he go here? He stood up, his head swimming slightly. The days without food or sleep had weakened him. He could not climb back down the sheer rock face; he would have to find another way off the mountain.

He tipped his waterskin to his parched lips, savoring the coolness as it dripped down his throat. Rekindling his fire, he wrapped himself in his blanket and nibbled on a piece of jerky. He wanted to taste the meat of a wild pig again. Before he returned to Obasanjo's village he would feast on pork to celebrate his successful vision quest. In the morning, Carlomagno thought, he would begin finding his way to Obasanjo's new village.

Fatigue overtook him and his eyes closed slowly, jerked open and then shut tight as sleep claimed him. Alarmed, he opened his eyes. How long had he slept? It was still dark and the fire was a small mass of red embers. Carlomagno sat still, alert to the slightest noise. What had awakened him? He wasn't certain he had heard any particular sound and yet he had an odd feeling, some instinct warning him.

His bow and quiver of arrows were beside him. With swift, sure hands he took up his bow and strung it while sitting silently in the shadows. He was probably being foolish, acting like a frightened child in the dark. After all, there was no reason to think there was any danger creeping up on him. Setting the bow down, Carlomagno stood up and peered all around. He saw nothing unusual, no shadow where a shadow should not be.

He was no scared boy, cringing in the dark, ready to jump at every slight noise. Still, he told himself, there is a chill in the air and it wouldn't hurt to put more wood on the fire. Stirring the coals, careful to keep the blanket hanging over his shoulders from catching fire, he fed two small sticks into the glowing embers and watched as the flames hungrily licked at the dry wood. A small circle of light surrounded the area by the blaze; Carlomagno could find no more wood. He would have to gather more if he wanted the fire to last through the night. But first, he moved to the edge of the cliff, just out of the firelight, to relieve himself.

He wondered if he even needed more wood; dawn couldn't be more than an hour away and his blanket kept him comfortable enough. His mind touched on the silence again. Strange, he thought, no birds singing or insect noises. It was almost as if ... as if something they feared was lurking nearby!

Turning from the ledge, Carlomagno saw a shadowy figure move to the edge of the firelight. Cuffie stood there across the fire, his spear held in two hands, ready to thrust.

"Why have you come here?" Carlomagno demanded.

"To bring you news," Cuffie replied smugly.

"News? What news do you bring, old man?"

"Amina is to wed Koyamin."

A gasp escaped Carlomagno's throat. "Wh... what?"

The firelight lent a malicious glint to Cuffie's dark eyes and he turned the spear slightly so the tip was facing Carlomagno. "I thought you would want to know that," he smiled malovently, "before you die."

The bushes rattled and Cuffie spun toward the noise with his spear poised to strike. A rooting wild boar emerged from the underbrush. Cuffie turned back toward his victim to find the rim of the ledge empty. His eyes scanned the area.

Nothing. It was not possible for Carlomagno to have gotten away. Then Cuffie spotted the crumpled blanket on the edge of the cliff. Perhaps, startled by the pig, Carlomagno had taken a reflexive step backwards and gone over the edge? Keeping his spear ready, Cuffie moved slowly forward on cat feet and peered over. Nothing. Of course it was dark so maybe...

In the instant the small sound reached his ear, Cuffie started to turn. Carlomagno—who had concealed himself in the slight groove in the rock—pushed him violently from behind, sending the assassin off into space, his scream echoing all the way down the craggy cliff face.

Dropping to his knees, his heart beating rapidly as the wings of a hummingbird, Carlomagno fought to calm himself, to resume breathing normally. He had killed a man from the village, someone he knew. Not just a man, he told himself, an enemy who had come to take his life!

He forced himself to gather more wood and build up his fire. The night had been cool, though not unpleasant, but now it felt different to

Carlomagno. It seemed somehow clammy, colder. He had been granted a vision and then killed an enemy. There was no doubt Manitoo was watching over him.

But what of Cuffie? Why was he there? To kill Carlomagno, by his own admission, but for what reason? Cuffie was a morose, unfriendly man, but Carlomagno recalled no particular incident between them. Cuffie never seemed to speak to anyone in the village. Carlomagno, try as he might, could only remember Cuffie speaking to one man—Obasanjo.

"No, it can't be," Carlomagno told himself. "That makes no sense. Obasanjo wouldn't send someone to kill me. What reason would he have?"

Even before the sun had risen, Carlomagno hurriedly packed up and made his way down the mountain to locate Obasanjo's new village. His plan to feast on a pig was forgotten; his thoughts were of Amina. He knew Koy was attracted to her, and often expressed a wish to wed her—so did nearly every other young man in the village. But somehow Carlomagno had never thought of Amina being with anyone but him.

Drums beat and people laughed and danced in celebrating the marriage of Koyamin and Amina. Carlomagno and his closest friend walked off into the forest to be alone.

"It all happened so fast. I mentioned something about Amina and the next thing I knew, my father was pushing for us to marry. He didn't want to wait," Koy explained, and then grinned. "I didn't want to wait."

"It all seems so sudden."

Koy nodded. "Yes, my father wanted it to happen right away, but I wanted you to be here, Carlo. My mother insisted you were like her son and it was not right to hurry into this without you there to share the joy." Koyamin looked down, a little uncomfortable. "You do share my joy, don't you, brother?"

"Of course, Koy. You need never doubt that. You are my friend, my brother. Give that to me and we shall make a pact." Carlomagno indicated the knife tucked behind Koy's belt.

Koy handed over the knife, not sure what was happening. "A pact?"

"This is what my people do, to make a brother friend pact," Carlomagno explained to Koyamin as he took the knife and made a small cut on his own palm. He did the same to Koyamin's palm and they clasped hands, letting their blood mingle. "We are family now," Carlomagno declared, "we are as one. We are brother-friends, pledged always to aid the other."

"It is good," Koyamin nodded.

"Your family took me in when I had no one. I shall not forget that. Your mother has treated me as a son."

"My father is glad you have come, too," Koy assured him. "I had an older brother who was lost in battle many years ago. Since then, my parents have not been blessed with any more children. I know my father always regretted not having another son."

Carlomagno had come to his own thoughts about Obasanjo, but did not reveal them to his friend. He could barely believe it himself; but who else would have sent Cuffie to kill him?

Carlomagno had been thinking a lot about his father's dream of saving his people from the encroachment of the English. He still dreamt of one day returning to his seaside home of Sowams. His friend, Noank, had spent decades alone in the wilds of Hispaniola, not even daring to dream of returning to his Pequot village. Carlomagno promised himself that he would not die an old man in this foreign place. One day he would return to his homeland. And when he did, he would go to the land of the Pequots, to Mashantucket, the much-wooded place, and tell them of how Noank refused to be a slave and had died as a warrior should.

It was the way Carlomagno hoped to die. He would never again be a slave to any man. Dreams of a life with Amina had been a pleasant distraction in his young, tragic life, but there comes a time when a man must accept his fate and move on.

"I am more grateful than you will ever know," Carlomagno began.

"But?"

Carlomagno smiled; he knew he couldn't fool Koyamin. "I wonder about my own mother. Is she still at Don Pedro's plantation? Did he sell her after I ran away? Or something worse? I think, too, of my father, Koy. Did he win his war? Maybe there is a great kingdom waiting for the son of Metacomet to claim his place."

"I understand, my friend. Were it my mother I would want to go back, too," Koyamin said. "But if you do this thing, my father will not allow you to return here."

Carlomagno sighed. "I have to go, Koy, don't you see? I have to know what happened to my mother. I must free her if she lives, or avenge her if she does not."

Koyamin did understand. He moved to uncover a sack cached under a pile of rocks and from it he withdrew a sword. The blade was tempered Toledo steel and as sharp as the day it was forged.

"This is what my father fears. Years ago, the day my brother was killed, my father went berserk and avenged him. He slew the Spanish soldier who carried this blade. My father took the blade as a trophy, but then became afraid the Spanish would send more soldiers after us. He was convinced if they found this sword, they would know what he had done," Koy explained. "He told me to take it away, to destroy it. But this sword is so beautiful, such fine workmanship, that I could not bear the thought of destroying it. So I hid it. Sometimes I would come alone into the woods just to hold it."

"It is a magnificent weapon."

"But it is not the weapon of a Cimaroon. I could never learn to use it as it should be used." Koy held the sword in two hands and offered it to Carlomagno. "Perhaps it is a weapon you can learn to master."

"Thank you, my friend," Carlomagno said softly. "I shall never dishonor this blade—nor the memory of he who gave it to me."

"I shall ask the *Oke Ololo* to hear your prayers, my friend." Koyamin extended his hand and Carlomagno clasped it strongly.

"And I will ask Manitoo to watch over you, brother." Carlomagno started to turn, and then faced his friend again. "Remember, Koyamin, we are brother-friends, no matter how many years separate us, or the number of miles between us, we are bonded still in spirit."

"Good luck, Carlomagno, son of Metacomet! May the gods to whom you pray open their ears to your requests."

Carlomagno turned away, thinking not of Koyamin or Obasanjo, but of the delicate features of Amina. He loved her, or so he told himself. He walked down the mountain, regretting that he had never held Amina, had never been with her as a husband with a wife. He was going into the world alone.

He had hoped to return to the plantation of Don Pedro to free his mother. He had told Koyamin he was going to try to find her, but he didn't know how he would do it. At a neighboring Cimaroon village a recent runaway from the area near Don Pedro's plantation remembered a native woman kept like a dog. He wasn't sure of her name, but after Carlomagno described his mother, the slave agreed it might have been the woman he had seen. Only he had not seen her for some time, at least six months, the slave recalled.

"She is no longer there," the runaway said. "Whether she died or was sold, I do not know. Don Pedro himself spends most of his time at his larger plantation, near Santo Domingo. He leaves his property on Hispaniola in the care of his son." The man made a sign and spat in the dirt. "The son is even worse than the father, if that's possible."

Carlomagno's first impulse was to return anyway and avenge his mother. But how? And what if she still lived, somewhere near Santa Domingo? He had to think, had to figure out how he was going to live without being picked off by a Spanish patrol. And eventually, get off the Island. So Carlomagno walked alone. Would it always be so? Was it his destiny, or his curse, to always be apart from those he cared for?

Carlomagno was confident when roaming the mountains; he knew he was the equal of any heavily armored soldier who might try to navigate the highlands. On the plains it was different; he had to be wary of being taken off-guard. Any man should be looked upon as an enemy. He moved cautiously across the plains, always watching for any signs of a patrol or slave hunters.

One day, exploring one of the most isolated areas of the mountains, he spied a small hut in a clearing near a narrow stream. A few palms offered some shade to the structure. A handful of chickens squawked and pranced in the dirt; a cow grazed undisturbed. Carlomagno was curious. Who would be living in the middle of nowhere, and why? It was far from any well-used trail. He spent half the day crouching in the woods, but saw no sign of movement from inside the hut. Was the hut empty? He doubted that, or if it was, it hadn't been left long ago.

He stood and cautiously stepped from the woods. He needed to refill his empty water skin, and, for that matter, his belly was complaining. Maybe he would find something to eat inside. If not, one of those clucking hens would make a fine meal. The stream was to the right of the hut, no more than two feet across and half as deep. It flowed from the forest and a stone basin had been built to catch the water. To the left he saw where the ground had been dug up and a garden planted. He recognized the cornstalks, though they were still only about three-feet tall. He saw a strange vine with red berries as large as apples growing on it, and some others he did not know.

Dropping his pack on the ground, Carlomagno held his sword in both hands and carefully made his way to the entrance of the hut. Its single room was spare and simple, but definitely appeared as if someone were living there. Grass mats covered much of the floor. Wooden bowls and cups sat on a small, round table. There was a sleeping area of palm fronds covered by grass mats and animal skins. Several books were lying on an overturned crate that seemed to be used as a chair. A wooden cross on a beaded necklace hung from a nail in the wall.

"Hello."

{ 7 }

The Wisdom of Ezra

Carlomagno spun around, startled to hear the voice behind him. Holding his sword up, Carlomagno studied the beefy, gray-haired man facing him, a stout wooden staff in one hand and the limp form of a rabbit in the other. The man had a kindly face, with florid cheeks and a hint of humor in his almond-shaped eyes.

His large hands and solid physique suggested the stranger had once been a brawny figure of a man. He wore sandals and a loose, brown robe held in place by a cloth belt. Carlomagno recognized the simple garb of a Dominican friar; such men had occasionally visited Don Pedro's plantation. .

"You won't need that weapon, my friend."

91

"Who are you? Why are you here?"

"I was going to ask you the same questions," the man smiled. "I am Ezra, once a student from Salamanca. Now but another wanderer in the world. I was checking my traps." He held up the rabbit. "Not much today, but it should be enough for us, don't you think?"

Carlomagno still held his sword ready as he moved away from the doorway and edged closer to where he had dropped his quiver and bow.

"I am unarmed," Ezra said. "Surely you are not frightened of an old hermit?"

"I am not afraid."

"Good, good! I do not often receive guests these days." Ezra tossed the rabbit to Carlomagno. "You skin that and I'll put a fire together. You have a name, I assume?"

"I am called Carlomagno."

Ezra raised an eyebrow. "Ah, a noble name! You do not appear to be Spanish. Taino, perhaps?"

"Not Taino. I am Wampanoag."

Ezra knelt beside a fire pit and began gathering tinder to start a fire. "Wampanoag? Just what is Wampanoag?"

Carlomagno put his sword down and drew the knife he had been given by Kerbourchard; keeping a wary eye on the friar, he began skinning the rabbit in a quick, expert fashion.

"You appear native, if I may say, though not a native of Hispaniola. Were you a slave, then?" When Carlomagno made no reply, the holy man continued. "You need not fear me, Carlomagno. I wish to avoid the Spanish, too."

"You were a slave?"

"No, not a slave, but something worse, perhaps," Ezra frowned. "I am a Jew, my young friend." At Carlomagno's confused shrug, Ezra couldn't help but laugh. "Of course you probably have never heard of the Jews, have you?"

"I'm not certain. There are tribes far to the west, past the Great Lakes I heard."

"Jews are from another land. The Catholics' Christ was born a Jew. We are God's chosen ones."

"What did he choose you for?"

Ezra chuckled heartily. "I don't think anyone has ever asked that of me before. Sometimes it feels He chose us for misery; many that now profess to be Christian feel it is their duty to kill Jews. We are not looked upon fondly by the Catholics who hold power in Spain these days. If I am caught I can expect a painful death at the hands of the soldiers. That is why I remain here, in the guise of a poor Dominican friar."

"Maybe they think Wampanoags are Jews, too?"

"Tell me about it."

As they shared a simple meal, Carlomagno explained his situation and how he came to be in this place. The Indian took an immediate liking to the older man, and the opposite was true as well.

"My people have been slaves," Ezra said as they rested in the shade after eating, "and warriors. I am neither. I want only to live in peace, to tend my garden and pray. As you know, it is unlikely one can evade the Spanish forever. Here, I am relatively safe. The Spanish rarely come this far west. It is French territory, but there is also danger of Cimaroon raiders and buccaneers."

"Yet you have managed to remain here."

He shrugged. "I am a poor man. The buccaneers— pirates—have been here, but I have nothing of value, so they let me be. I have studied medicine a bit, so I am able to be of service now and then. And, when necessary, I can defend myself."

"You?" Carlomagno was incredulous. "But you are old..."

"I was born neither old nor a hermit," Ezra replied. "I have studied in Salamanca, in the Castile region of Spain. It is not far from the city where your sword was no doubt forged. I recognize the workmanship, my young friend. Toledo was once the metalworking capital of the world! The swords made of Toledo steel are considered the best—and have been since Roman times. Do you use it well?"

"I have had no training."

Ezra clucked his teeth. "A shame, it is. To have such a finely crafted tool and not know how to use it properly."

"You can use a sword?" Carlomagno was clearly skeptical.

"As I said, I studied much while in Salamanca. It was once a place where the finest scholars congregated—Jews, Christians and Moors. Ideas were shared, examined and debated. I was a young man at the time, my friend; I made a study of fighting." He laughed gently and patted his soft belly. "Do not let my appearance fool you, young one. Being as strong as an ox does not make one a fighting man. Come, stand up. I want you to throw me to the ground."

"I do not wish to harm you."

"Are you afraid of being shown up by an old, fat man?"

Carlomagno leapt to his feet and charged, but Ezra nonchalantly avoided the Indian's grasp and caught his outstretched arm; with a rolling hip lock, he threw Carlomagno to the ground. Clearly surprised, the young brave was slow to get up.

"What say you now, my friend?"

Carlomagno grinned. "I say I have a lot to learn! If I can be of service to you, will you teach me in return?"

Ezra considered the younger man. "Perhaps. If you have what it takes? We will see. It is much too hot now; when the sun goes down we will discover whether you have the aptitude to learn the art of the sword."

As they rested, Ezra expanded on his tale of being a young man who wanted nothing more than to fight. He had been a soldier for a brief time, building his skill at hand-to-hand combat and learning to use various weapons.

When the heat of the day began to recede, Ezra put Carlomagno through a series of exercises with and without the Toledo sword. It took very little time for Carlomagno to prove himself.

"You have a good build," Ezra said with an appreciative nod. "And your reflexes are extraordinary. I can teach you what I have learned, but I suspect your natural ability will give you skills far beyond what I might offer. As for what you can do for me, perhaps what I need most is a student."

And so the days became wedded to months that gave birth to years of quiet coexistence and intense training. By day, Carlomagno helped out by working in the garden, or hunting for fresh meat. And, always, there was the training. Ezra taught Carlomagno the basics of sword play and schooled him in various types of hand-to-hand combat, including wrestling and boxing. Ezra had also learned some of the mystical fighting styles of the Orient.

As they rested in the evening coolness one night, Ezra listened intently as Carlomagno told him of the vision from Manitoo.

"Interesting," Ezra commented after Carlomagno had told of his vision. "Have you deciphered its meaning?"

"I believe that the eagle represents me, but I do not understand whatever Manitoo was sharing with me."

"Hmmm. Yes, I think the eagle was to represent you, Carlomagno," Ezra agreed. He rubbed his chin thoughtfully, "I think you are to soar high, like the eagle. The storms must show that you will face many challenges, coming from all about you. The way you describe the people on the ground, reaching for you, makes me think it means that your enemies will reach to destroy you, even as others reach out to you for assistance."

"And the blue mountains?"

"Have you ever seen these mountains before?" After Carlomagno shook his head, Ezra continued, "I think these mountains are the unknown; perhaps the future. After coming through the storms and evading those grasping at you, I think the mountains will be one last obstacle that you must overcome."

The Jewish friar had more to share, expanding his young charge's knowledge of the jungle plants and flowers, especially those which were edible or had medicinal uses. Carlomagno hunted and helped tend the garden, his eager mind soaking up all the knowledge he was offered. But he was often restless, wandering for long hours through the jungle. Ezra knew it was no life for a young man.

"I have taught you all that I can," the friar said one day after a strenuous wrestling bout in which Carlomagno pinned him in two out of three falls. "I think you are ready to resume your journey, my young friend."

"You have shared much with me, Ezra," the Indian said. "I have no gift of equal value to offer in return."

"You gave me the opportunity to share some of what I have learned over the years. Can a man ask for more?" Ezra wondered. "We all live and one day pass from this earth, and little remains to show that we once existed. I think the secret is to share what you have learned, to help someone else find their way in this world.

"I have no son, but if I had, I would have taught him the things I gave you. Use them well, my friend. And when the time comes, share your knowledge with others. We are all mortals, weak and tempted. No man is all good—or all evil. Each of us battles our own demons.

"If you make a bad decision one day, the next is an opportunity to start anew, to atone for your error. Do not let guilt steal your glory. In time, all men do something they wish they hadn't. You, too, will make mistakes. But never be petty, never cruel. You are a strong man, Carlomagno; strong, good men are needed to stand between the weak and those who would prey upon them.

"I am old and my time is near, I fear," Ezra said. "But you are young and your story is still to be written on the pages of time. If you want to repay me for what I have taught, then do this: when the final chapter is written in your Book of Life, let it say you helped more than you hurt."

As Carlomagno prepared to leave, Ezra hesitated before offering his final advice.

"You must choose your own course, my friend, but were I you, I would forget this search for your mother. From what you have told me, it seems doubtful that she lives. I have heard of the Don and he is a vengeful man."

"I must know."

"Do not let it consume your life, Carlomagno," Ezra said. "Live for the future, not in the past."

{ 8 }

A Bitter Lesson

His hands gripped the oar and Carlomagno, who had vowed never to be a slave again, was clamped in chains toiling below deck on a poor excuse for a ship. The bowels of the vessel were dank and musty, with rows of desolate, unwashed men seated on hard, wooden benches, the oppressive silence broken only by the occasional clinking chain or hacking cough. There was a good wind now, so the ship used her sails. The oarsmen sat, grateful for the respite. When the wind died, or was contrary to what the quartermaster wanted, the chained slaves powered the ship to the beat of a solitary drum and the cracking insistence of whips. It was in this world that Carlomagno now found himself.

There were two men per oar and Carlomagno shared his with a tired-looking skeleton of a man. He was one of those with a constant cough and hollowed eyes that spoke of little life left in his soul. Carlomagno thought the man's skin looked like wrinkled leather stretched over old bones.

"His name is Macomber, and a sorry bag of flesh, he is," croaked the red-bearded man across the aisle from Carlomagno. Red Beard was a giant of a man, his powerful muscles rippling beneath the tattered, stained shirt he wore. Dried blood on his back testified of the whips that had bitten into him in the not-too-distant past. "He's a pirate, you know. A dangerous rascal in his day, but by the looks of him his days are passing quick!"

Carlomagno's head was still a little groggy. He tried to recall what had happened to him. After he left Ezra of Salamanca, he had been intent on making his way back to the sugar cane plantation of Don Pedro de la Marana, determined to find out the fate of his mother. Preoccupied with his thoughts, he had made a fool's misstep—coming upon a hidden cove where a shabby-looking vessel was laying in supplies. Immediately spotted, he had decided to act boldly. To run was only to be caught, and possibly killed. So he walked openly into their camp.

"A fine sword, you have there," a man had remarked. He was a smallish, pock-mocked sort with narrow, shifting eyes. He introduced himself as Capitan Feroz. "Are you a pirate, then?"

"I have been upon the seas a little," Carlomagno had replied, thinking it better to let the captain think he was a fellow seaman.

"That is a fine blade; I have an eye for such things. It is Toledo steel?"

"It is."

Capitan Feroz held out his hand. "Here, let me have a look. It is a fine blade."

Carlomagno hesitated, putting a hand to the hilt of his sword. "I do not let other men touch my blade— except by the point."

"Well said," Feroz laughed. "You are a fellow pirate, I knew it! We are about to have dinner. Sit and eat. Perhaps you will consider joining my crew?"

Carlomagno knew little of pirating, but observed Feroz's crew to be a slovenly lot. True, he had known but one pirate, but even wounded and in shabby clothing Kerbourchard managed to convey a sense of style. Feroz was unkempt and his litter of bedraggled buccaneers added no glamour to his appearance. There was little to be done now. Car-lomagno accepted the capitan's invitation to dine.

It was an old trick, yet one new to a Wampanoag Indian on Hispan-iola. A drugged cup of wine was all it took. When Carlomagno awoke, his fine Toledo blade, his jeweled knife and his bows and arrows were gone. And he was in chains.

"We're all pirates in here, most of us anyway," said Red Beard. "You aren't scared of pirates are you?"

"I knew a pirate once, a corsair he called himself," Carlomagno re-plied, his voice carrying in the silence. "A good man, he seemed. His name was Kerbourchard."

The bony slave shackled next to Carlomagno let out a gasp.

"You know this Kerbourchard, Macomber?" asked Red Beard.

"I knew a Kerbourchard," Macomber managed, his voice a raspy whisper. "He fancied himself a corsair."

"Who was this corsair, stranger?" Red Beard asked. "What name does he use?"

"Persifal."

"Persifal Kerbourchard." Macomber blinked his eyes. "Tis him, right enough. A bold rascal. Few can cross blades with Kerbourchard. Where did you come by him, son?"

"On Hispaniola. He was wounded and I helped care for him."

"You have a friend then, stranger," Macomber said. "Kerbourchard is a good man and he never forgets a friend. On Hispaniola, you say. He must have been stranded, or escaping the Spanish."

"There were Spanish soldiers looking for him."

"God help the heathens if they corner Kerbourchard," Macomber said. "You got a good friend, boy."

"Lot of good it will do him, Macomber. Kerbourchard couldn't help this lad if he wanted to. A slave has only one way off this ship and it's not a good way," Red Beard grunted. "I've heard that Feroz is a devil himself. But what are you stranger? You don't look English, French or Dutch?"

"The Spanish call me Carlomagno, a name as good as any other. My land is far away, on the coast of what they call New England."

"Ha! 'New England' they call it," Red Beard snorted. "The English claim to discover everything! I'm Irish, lad, and my people have sailed the seas long before your Englishmen. I am Morgan Flynn and come from a long line of seamen, I do."

"Honest seamen?" Macomber wondered.

Flynn laughed. "A likely question from an English pirate! I'd say we've been as honest as most, and as brave as any!"

"So it was with my people," Macomber said. "Most of us Macombers were honest as the day was long. But honesty only gets a man so much, crumbs from the rich man's table. If you're not born into wealth, you have little enough chance of achieving it."

"There speaks an honest man, indeed! My ancestors had strong arms and willing blades," Flynn said. "We took off to fight in one war or another, hoping to come by a little."

"Mine, too, Flynn. 'Tis how I came to be here," Macomber said. "I was once a soldier; then, later, a trusted man to the king. But kings can change and to curry favor with one man in power might not sit so well with his successor."

What rations they received were little enough, and water was scarce, too, but Carlomagno shared his meager portions with Macomber. The older man seemed to slowly regain some strength. Spurred by Carlomagno's efforts, Morgan Flynn also began to share his food to help Macomber recover.

Myles Macomber had been a galley slave for nearly three years, as best as he could recall. Born into humble surroundings, he had joined the Royal Navy at a young age and quickly received recognition for his courage and cunning. He won promotions easily and soon earned the respect and attention of men who outranked him. He was pointed out as a dependable and loyal man and, in time, had come to the attention of King James II himself. The king was a man with many enemies about him, and some closer than he knew.

"James treated me well, like a son. He always wanted me present when he felt danger was close. And it was closer than he realized," Macomber explained, "or could bring himself to believe. And I failed him, for I saw it not myself."

"Aye, I have heard tell of King James' downfall," Flynn said. "His own daughter brought him down. By the saints, Macomber, it isn't fitting for a man's own get to turn against him!"

"Yes, his daughter—'Mary II' she crowned herself. With the help of her husband, William of Orange, they ousted old James in '88; and he fled 'ere they arrived at his castle," Macomber said, his voice thick with bitterness.

"What of James' wife, the Queen Mary?" Flynn asked. "I heard she was nearly captured by her daughter and killed?"

Macomber was silent for a long moment. "Mary of Modena, she was called. A good woman, she cared little for the pomp and circumstance of the royal court, but I believe she did care for James. You know how the royals are, marrying for politics. Anyway, Mary of Modena did fall in love with King James, and he with her."

"Yet he fled, leaving her behind," Flynn said.

"William's army was closing in fast. King James thought if he fled he might lead his enemies away, giving the queen a chance to escape," Macomber said.

"He should have stayed and fought to the death," Flynn said. "I would have."

"In war," Carlomagno interrupted quietly, "a man must do what he thinks best. My father had to be free to fight, to move quickly as the need arose. So he left my mother and me in a village deep in the woods, where he thought we would be safe from the war. But the English came deep into the land of the Wampanoag and attacked our village while most of the men were away. This was how my mother and I fell into the hands of the English. Looking back, I'm sure my father regretted leaving us where he did. But how was he to know?"

"Now you sit beside an Englishman," Flynn said. "It is a chance for revenge, to strike a blow for your people."

"In this ship, with these on," Carlomagno held up his manacled hands, "we are not English and Wampanoag, nor Irish and African. We are all one; we are slaves to the Spanish. It is only by working together that we might defeat a stronger foe."

"You are wise beyond your years, Carlomagno," Macomber said.

There was quiet for a time, soon broken by Flynn. "I wasn't meaning to stir up trouble for you, Macomber. Sometimes my big mouth gets to talking too much, is all."

"No hard feelings, Flynn," Macomber smiled. "My mouth has gotten me into enough scrapes of my own over the years. I think if we're going to get out of this mess, we need a leader—and I think we found one. Red Indian or no, I say Carlomagno is uncommon shrewd. I think if anyone can fathom a way off this vessel, it's him."

"When the time comes for action, Macomber, you count me in. It may be a lost cause, I'm thinking, but that never stopped a Flynn from fightin'!"

Three men came together in the bitter bowels of a Spanish galleon and forged an alliance for survival that would be tested over time and grow into an unbreakable friendship. Together they would bring an end to the Spanish stranglehold on the shipping channels of the West Indies, the Spanish Main.

"Macomber," Flynn said, "you never did tell us how Mary of Modena escaped."

"The king bade her fare thee well and left her in the care of a trusted man. This man suggested to the queen that she be at a certain spot on the riverbank at midnight. There, the trusted man told her a boat would be waiting to take her to safety. To be caught outside the castle by the forces of William of Orange and Mary II would have meant sure death for the queen."

"This trusted man could have earned himself a fortune by tipping off William," Flynn suggested slyly. "He might have won a high place with a rising power?"

Macomber nodded. "This, he might have done, were he not loyal to King James and Queen Mary of Modena."

"And so the queen escaped to safety," Flynn said.

"That she did, to rejoin her James in France."

"And what of this trusted man?" Carlomagno wondered.

"Naturally he fell from favor when William and Mary were crowned. He had spent his life in the British army, and now found many doors closed to him. Yet not all, for you see he had made some important friends along the way. One of these was George Monck; he would be second Duke of Albemarle. Through Monck, it was arranged for this trusted man to receive a commission in Jamaica. He was introduced to, and worked with, another acquaintance of Monck's—Sir Henry Morgan."

Henry Morgan was a name much on the lips of the people of the Caribbean. While Modyford was titled the Governor of Jamaica, it was loudly whispered that the real power lay in Henry Morgan. He had made a name for himself with a series of bold, reckless raids upon Spanish cities and their shipping a few years earlier. All this was done under the watchful, winking eye of the English crown. Morgan had fared well under King Charles, and then did the same with Oliver Cromwell. When the monarchy was restored, Morgan still sat well, retiring for the most part to Pencarne, his vast Jamaican estate.

"Morgan, you say!" Flynn was impressed. "He was the best. Why, his raid of Portobello is still talked about in every shantytown and pirate den!"

"Why doesn't this Henry Morgan try to ransom you, Macomber?" Carlomagno asked.

"Troubles of his own, I suspect. I have not seen him in nigh onto four years, I'd say. But I've been told the last few years have gone hard for him. He drinks too much, sleeps too little and his health is failing rapidly. Or so I hear."

Fair blew the winds for several days on end, leaving the galley slaves with naught to do but rest and enjoy their brief respite, if one could enjoy being chained in the belly of a ship where the stifling heat and the stench of dozens of unwashed men clogged the nostrils.

The crack of the whip brought the slaves in the galley to cringing attention. A man several rows ahead of Carlomagno jerked violently as the hungry lash bit across his shoulder blades; a pair of Spaniards, wielding whips, walked among the slaves, urging them on.

"Pick up your oars and row as if your lives depended on it, for they do!" barked one of the Spaniards as his lash snaked out and ripped an ugly gash across an oarsman's shoulder. "Move, you lazy dogs! Faster!"

There was muttering from row to row even as the slaves began working the oars furiously.

"What is it?" Carlomagno asked in a hushed tone.

"Either we're attacking, or being attacked," Macomber replied morosely.

"Being attacked, I'd say," grunted Morgan Flynn. "If we were attacking the drum would be sounding, to keep the pace even. They just want us to work these oars as fast as we can to put some distance between us and whatever is coming on."

"If we're running then it isn't another Spanish ship. It could be English," Macomber said. "If they overtook us, we might be freed."

"Ah, you're forgetting yourself, Macomber," Flynn replied. "There's a chance they'd hang you for a pirate. And if the ship is French or Dutch, we'd be no better off."

"Maybe we should slow down on purpose, take our chances," another man whispered.

"Anything has to be better than Capitan Feroz," another voice added.

Suddenly one of the Spaniards was looming over them. "What is all this talking? Row, I say. Faster, now, you dogs!" He emphasized his request with a vicious swipe of his whip at Flynn.

The ship lurched and the Spaniard lost his balance, falling across Carlomagno's knees. The Indian moved like a striking copperhead, twisting his chains about the Spaniard's throat. The struggle was brief and when Carlomagno relaxed his grip, his hand found the keys on the dead man's belt—and beside them was his knife! Hastily he unlocked his chains, reclaiming his weapon.

"Pull them through," he hissed to the men sitting in the row ahead of him.

The second Spaniard was only now becoming aware that something was amiss. His eyes searched the room for his companion. He started down the aisle, looking from side to side. When he saw his friend's boot heels hanging out into the aisle, he turned to flee, to summon help. Leaping to his feet, Carlomagno flung his knife through the air. It struck the fleeing man between the shoulder blades and he fell forward.

"I feel like a man again, with a blade in my hand," Flynn said, nabbing the fallen Spaniard's sword. He flashed a bloodthirsty smile. "Shall we go up and see what mischief we can cause?"

"Wait," Carlomagno said, putting a hand on Flynn's shoulder. "Feroz still has more muskets and swords. His men can cut us down in seconds."

The slaves had few weapons, only what the slave drivers had been carrying: a pair of swords, a pistol, the whips and a pair of knives. And Carlomagno had retrieved his own knife. Other slaves were planning to use the chains, or trying to break apart their wooden benches for makeshift clubs.

"So we do nothing?" Flynn asked.

"We wait for the right time to strike," Carlomagno replied. "When the Spaniards are busy concentrating on their attackers we will be able to take them from behind."

"I don't like skulking around and attacking someone when his back is turned. I'd rather face them man to man, blade to blade," Flynn said.

"Carlomagno is right, Flynn," Macomber offered. "We'll only get one crack at this, you know. When Feroz and his men are preoccupied, that's our chance to make a difference in the outcome of this fight."

They waited, listening as harried feet raced about the deck above them. They heard muffled shouts, unable to distinguish words. There was a loud boom and seconds later the ship seemed to shake.

"We've been hit," Macomber said. "They're closing in, then!"

Another boom roared in the night, louder then the first, and the Spanish ship was rocked again.

"Look!" one of the slaves exclaimed, his finger pointing toward the side of the ship at the water line. As they watched, a small fountain of seawater began to spurt.

"She's going down," Macomber said.

"And we're going up!" Carlomagno roared. "Come on, men! Freedom or death!"

He led the way up the stairs, emerging from the hatch just as a Spanish sailor turned to face him. Before the Spaniard could utter a warning, Carlomagno was upon him, his knife ripping upwards in the sailor's belly. He climbed to the deck and stooped to pick up the man's sword. Another slave grabbed the musket the dead sailor had been carrying; others piled out onto the deck. As Carlomagno expected, the Spanish were facing the oncoming ship, which flew the skull and crossbones. It could be seen in the light of the flickering flames from the Spanish ship, which was on fire in several locations.

"It's going down!" Macomber yelled over the din to Carlomagno. "We have little time!"

As Carlomagno planned, the Spaniards were surprised and soon overpowered, yet not all of the crew was captured. Feroz had escaped in one of the three smaller boats when defeat became imminent.

"Feroz got away," Flynn spat. "I wanted a crack at that slimy dog!"

"There will be another day," Carlomagno said. "He still has something of mine." Carlomagno thought of the Toledo blade, a gift to him from Koyamin.

The Spanish colors had been lowered as a signal of surrender and now the victors came aboard to view their spoils.

"Goddamn!" Macomber hissed into Carlomagno's ear. "You remember that chap down below saying it couldn't get any worse? Well, he was wrong. It's worse—much worse!"

"What is it?" Carlomagno asked. "What's wrong? They're fellow pirates, aren't they?"

"Aye, they be pirates, but the scurviest, meanest lot there is. Why they make Feroz look meek as a lamb."

"You're talking in riddles, Macomber, spit it out!" Flynn snapped. "Who could be worse than Feroz? Your Captain Morgan, perhaps?"

"Sir Henry would be a blessed sight now," Macomber groaned. "Look who's coming aboard there— it's Pierre Norville, the Chevalier de Fortenay!"

{ 9 }

Tortuga

The Chevalier de Fortenay swept aboard the sinking vessel, a sword held firmly in his left hand and a purple cape flowing about his shoulders. He moved as one acutely aware of the entrance he is making, barking out crisp orders to his men to hurry along their looting of the captured Spanish prize. His frown grew deeper as his men reported on their scant findings.

"Perhaps those who escaped carried off their plunder?" suggested a weasel of a man with a ragged kerchief tied about his head and more gaps than teeth.

"No such luck, Tulane."

Tulane, the man who had spoken, looked slowly around, as did de Fortenay. Tulane stared; his head bobbed in recognition.

"Macomber? Is it you?"

"Aye, you salty sea dog, 'tis Macomber in the flesh."

"You know this man, Tulane?"

"Aye, Captain. Macomber and I have sailed together before—on the Satisfaction, wasn't it, Macomber?"

Tulane had been lazy, often shirking his duty, but Macomber saw no reason to mention any of that now. De Fortenay let his eyes study Macomber.

"The Satisfaction was Henri Morgan's flagship, no?"

"It was," Tulane nodded. "And Macomber was a gunner. A good one, as I recall, Captain. Morgan swore there was none better."

"A gunner?" de Fortenay permitted his thin lips a brief smile. A good man on the guns was worth his weight in gold—and then some. "You are good with the guns?"

"Morgan found no fault with me."

De Fortenay flinched involuntarily at the tone. There was something in Macomber's voice, some trace of hostility. "Do I know you, *monsieur?*"

"No, we have never met," Macomber replied.

William of Orange and Queen Mary II had routed the queen's father from England, in part, over religious differences. William and Mary were staunch Protestants and sought to snuff out any other competing church in England. Their ambition had outgrown England and now the monarchs eyed France as tensions slowly boiled.

This was a fact not lost upon the Chevalier de Fortenay. "But, we are neither Protestant nor Catholic here, are we, Macomber? Nor do we dwell on French or English. We are buccaneers all! We can find common ground between us, if you are this good at the guns."

De Fortenay's men had finished plundering the food stores and what little coinage they could find.

"It's little we gained by this," Tulane muttered.

"Maybe this attack was not a total waste, Tulane. I have need of a gunner, Macomber. Come, join my crew."

"My friends, too?"

De Fortenay's eyes scanned the recently freed slaves. "The Africans, I have no use for; they are poor workers, and my hold is too small to carry them until I can sell them. The Spanish"—de Fortenay spat at the word—"I have no use for them, either. Frenchmen, I will take. And, for you, Macomber, I will allow any English or Dutch to join my crew."

Macomber indicated Carlomagno. "What of him? He is none of those things you mentioned."

"What is he?" de Fortenay asked, his lips pursed. "Not Spanish. Cimaroon, perhaps?"

"I am Wampanoag," Carlomagno said.

De Fortenay snorted. "I care not which heathen Carib fathered you."

"He's a native from the American colonies," Macomber said.

"Just another savage. Well, I do not like the looks of him. He stays behind."

"Then I stay as well," Macomber said.

"Suit yourself, *monsieur*. I will not offer again. This ship is sinking. You have, perhaps, an hour. You have no choice, Macomber—either come with me, or die here."

"I stay."

"Very well," de Fortenay shrugged. "Those who would live, come with me."

Some of the freed oarsmen of Anglo descent followed de Fortenay back to his ship. On the damaged Spanish ship remained an odd mixture of men, several Englishmen, a half dozen Africans, the Irishman Morgan Flynn and eleven of the Spanish sailors. And in their midst stood Carlomagno.

There were still several small boats like those in which Capitan Feroz and some of his crew had escaped, but there were not enough boats for those remaining. The Spanish sailors glared suspiciously at the men aligned behind Carlomagno.

"Who speaks English?" Carlomagno asked. Though he spoke Spanish, he felt his grasp of it was too sketchy to trust in translation for such a serious moment.

A straight-backed, dark-skinned Spaniard stepped forward. "I speak English, *Indio.*"

"Tell your men if we fight each other now, we waste time. We may all go down with the ship."

"What do you propose?"

"A truce. We are not of different races now, we are all just men trying to live. Maybe we can make it by working together," Carlomagno said.

The Spaniard was Diego El Negro, the son of a slave mother and Spanish father. He turned to his fellow crewmen and translated. His men nodded in agreement.

"It shall be so, *Indio.* We work together," Diego said. "But the ship is sinking and land is far away. What do you plan?"

"Carlomagno!"

There was a sudden sharpness in Flynn's booming voice and he pointed out to sea—where de Fortenay's ship was coming broadside.

"I thought the mangy dog gave in too easily," Macomber cried. "He means to give us a broadside!" The Chevalier's ship was coming wide around, slow in the light wind, but with obvious intent. "He never was a good loser."

"Let's get those boats lowered!" Carlomagno took command. "Hurry now, before he gets turned around."

"There are not enough for all of us," Diego commented, even as he ordered his men to help prepare the three remaining small boats.

"We'll take turns in them, the rest of the time we can hold onto the sides to help keep us afloat," Carlomagno said.

"It's too much to hope for," Macomber grumbled. "We're too far from Hispaniola."

"Feroz had changed course," Diego said. "He wanted to put in at Cape Tiburon. The Cape should be due north of us."

"Hurry with those boats!" Carlomagno threw a wprried glance toward de Fortenay's vessel; it was nearly in position. "How far do you suppose it is, Diego?"

"I think it is maybe five miles, give or take."

"That's a far piece on the open seas," Macomber interjected. "We'll be lucky if any of us make it."

"It's a longer way if we stay here and go straight to the bottom," Carlomagno replied. His final words had barely been uttered when the roar of the sixteen-pounders ripped through the night. De Fortenay had unleashed a devastating barrage and the Spanish ship was struck several times. One man screamed as the deck shattered near him, showering his face with a hundred splinters. The mast was torn down, a cannonball slammed at the water line.

"He's leaving us to our fate!" Carlomagno said.

"We're taking on water fast, *Indio*," Diego said.

"We can't get the boats in the water in time. The suction will pull us down!"

"Let the boats drop, we'll have to jump for it and swim to the boats. Grab anything that will float and let's take our chances!" Carlomagno said.

Men grabbed whatever they could find and began scrambling over the ship's railing, dropping into the water just behind the boats. Carlomagno stayed behind to help those weakened by their captivity; Macomber and Flynn stayed with him. Finally, they were the last three on board.

"Let's get off this deathtrap," Carlomagno shouted. He and Macomber went for the rail, but Flynn stood where he was. "Come on, Flynn! We have no time to waste!"

"No. No." All the color had drained from the giant's face.

Carlomagno urged him to the rail. "Here, look. The boat is right here."

Flynn moved cautiously and approached the rail slowly. "I don't see it."

"You didn't lean over far enough," Macomber said, catching on to Carlomagno's plan. "It's right there, against the ship."

Flynn leaned a bit further this time. Carlomagno and Macomber each grabbed a massive leg and heaved the giant over the side. They followed him, managing to get Flynn to one of the boats.

"You tricked me," Flynn protested as he gasped for breath.

"Hey, didn't you hear—I'm a savage," Carlomagno grinned as he held onto the side of the boat. "Don't you know you can't trust a savage?"

The roaring flames aboard the Spanish ship illuminated the dark night. The survivors watched it, even as they clung to the small boats, empty water barrels, pieces of the deck, or whatever debris might help a man stay afloat. The Chevalier's ship was like an ominous dark cloud as it sailed away, finally disappearing into the darkness.

Carlomagno was a strong swimmer; he kicked smoothly, one hand holding onto the gunwale, while Macomber clung to the other side. Diego El Negro paddled over to join them.

"Wait until I see de Fortenay again," Carlomagno told Flynn. "He'll pay for this."

"And what can you do, amigo?" asked Diego. "Even in Spain we have heard of the Chevalier de Fortenay. He is a legend to some, as bold as Henry Morgan or Rock Brasiliano."

"He's right, Carlomagno," Flynn replied. "De Fortenay is a big fish, and you are just a small catch."

"One with big teeth," Carlomagno replied.

"You will need more than big teeth, *amigo*," Diego said. "You will need sharp teeth like the barracuda!"

"'Then my teeth shall be sharp, like this barracuda!'"

Flynn laughed. "I'm privileged, I guess, to be sailing along with The Barracuda of the Spanish Main!"

One of the men swimming alongside the boat implored them to stop talking. "Especially about barracudas. They're all over these waters, you know, and they would rip us apart."

The barracuda was a ferocious fish with razor teeth and a taste for blood. The men fell silent then, as they thought of what might be lurking beneath them. Many were superstitious and in addition to barracudas and sharks, they envisioned the icy tentacles of giant squids stretching out for them or a plethora of sea monsters, serpents and demons ready to devour them.

The water was calm, for which they were thankful, as they headed slowly toward Cape Tiburon. Tiburon was a small island with no permanent settlements, located just off the western end of Hispaniola. Due to its wild forest and location it was a favorite stopping-off place for pirates looking to put on fresh water, stock up on wild foods or to scrape their ships free of barnacles. Of the latter, Tiburon was less likely to see, for the island was too easily accessible. A pirate ship being cleaned was vulnerable, so the buccaneers generally undertook that tedious, yet necessary, task in more isolated locations. The sun rose to beat down on the shipwrecked group, but onward they went. The salty water added to their thirst and fatigue as those who were able rotated out of the boats. It was their hope to make Tiburon and perhaps hook on with another pirate ship. It was, no doubt, what Feroz's plan had been when he had abandoned them.

Carlomagno thought much about this prospect on the way to the Cape, for whoever they encountered would no doubt be better armed than his ragtag party. He, Flynn and the other slaves were poorly equipped for fighting. The long days on the oars and poor nourishment had sapped much of their strength. What they had left would be depleted by this arduous swim. The work was hard and the thought to give up was in each of their heads, yet the will to survive remained strong within them. Carlomagno also thirsted for revenge. There would be a reckoning, he silently vowed.

One Spaniard gave a cry and released his hold on the boat. He dipped beneath the water popped up again and then vanished beneath the seemingly friendly sea. No one moved to try to save him; no one had the strength to spare. Onward they went, drawing closer to an unknown fate.

"Land ho," one of the weakened men inside the boat rasped, his throat swollen from lack of water.

"I see it!" Flynn agreed. "And a pretty sight it is, lads!" The sighting gave new energy to their limbs and they swam on all the harder. Land arose before them, and soon they crawled exhausted onto the beach. "You look terrible, Macomber."

"Ah, Irishman, but I'm glad to be alive."

Flynn put a hand on Macomber's bony shoulder. "You're in luck, too. If we stick with this Barracuda, we may see his sharp teeth take a bite out of the big fish."

"De Fortenay?"

"The very same, Macomber," Flynn replied. "But I think, maybe, that fish is too big for Carlomagno."

Under Carlomagno's direction they moved off the beach into the woods. A party of men was sent for food, another for water, as the remaining used palm fronds and branches to make crude shelters. There was no sign of Feroz.

"I'd like to give him something to think about," Diego said. "Coward! While we watch to defend his ship, he sneaks away."

"I thought you Spaniards stuck together?" Flynn asked. "Aren't you defending the Main against everyone else?"

Diego shrugged noncommittally. "I am half Spanish, Flynn. But half Mandinga, too. The Mandinga are a proud people, sir, and do not look kindly upon slavers."

"Slavery has been around a long time, since the world began," Macomber commented. "Even Africans had slaves—or helped to catch and sell them."

"It is true," Diego acknowledged. "I have read some of Tyre, Nok and other ancient civilizations. But not all Africans were involved in the slave trade. In Matamba, Queen Nzinga stood strong against slavery, which led to a long, bitter war between her and King Mwata Yamvo of the Benin. But the Portuguese aided Yamvo and together they pushed Nzinga back.

"And though Feroz was vicious and arrogant, you should not assume all Spaniards are the same, nor that they all support slavery. There was a Spanish nobleman named Las Casas many years back, nearly 200 years ago, who lost much of his wealth and power because he was outspoken in his views that slaves should be treated humanely."

"I doubt Feroz has heard of this Las Casas, nor would he care," Macomber growled. "But if we run into him, he'll have our number. Scoundrel, he may be, but he'll have us outgunned."

"I'm not so worried about Feroz, but if he is here, I'd like to get the edge on him," Carlomagno said. "We'll post sentries tonight. Tomorrow we'll send out small scouting parties. If he's about, we'll locate him. If we can surprise him, we can take him."

"What will we do with him?" Macomber wondered.

"I've some ideas," Flynn growled.

"Leave him stranded as he sought to leave us," Carlomagno said. "The thing I'd like is to take his weapons, so our men are better armed."

The days stretched into a pleasant week. The men scouted, finding no signs of Feroz, and ate and rested. They regained their lost strength. Using sticks, Flynn began working with Carlomagno to hone his fencing skill.

"You're a natural, Carlomagno—and your reflexes are unbelievably quick. It is good to know what I'm teaching you, but remember in combat it will likely be slash and cut," said Flynn, who was a respected swordsman himself. "Strategy is important, too. Lure your opponent into a false sense of security, get him to lower his guard or fall for a feint while you make your real move. Study your foe, Carlomagno, learn his tendencies. We all have moves that we prefer, things that come easier to us—or have worked in the past. The more you know about your enemy, the better chance you have of beating him."

They talked amongst themselves over the fire at night as they swatted away mosquitoes by the dozens. Diego told of his days in Seville. His Spanish father had treated him well and awarded him his freedom. He had studied some, though he had an itch to come to sea. He thought he was joining the Armada, but Feroz proved to be no more than a pirate. And a poor one, at that, Diego said.

"He rarely found treasure, avoiding taking any risks. You saw him with de Fortenay, at the first hint of danger his tendency is to run like the jackal he is."

"Good thing, Diego. De Fortenay would have been too much for Feroz," Flynn suggested. "And you, Macomber, I saw the way you looked at the Chevalier. Your hatred was obvious."

"He owes me a debt." Myles Macomber reluctantly told them of how his hatred for the Chevalier de Fortenay was born. He had lost out on any chance of court position when William of Orange came to the throne, so he had used his connections through a mutual friend to come to the Caribbean and make the acquaintance of Sir Henry Morgan. He had sailed with Morgan only a few times, before he was captured by a Spanish galleon; and soon found himself an oarsman for Feroz. Even then, Morgan was nearing the end; like all men, Henry Morgan had grown old. He had become somewhat of a court favorite in those last few years as he constantly told stories of his voyages. But he drank too much, and whored too often, and his power had waned. Some still feared his name alone, but the Henry Morgan who owned the Spanish Main was a memory that had long since sailed by.

"He was a tiger, that one, not a man to be trifled with. But the last time I saw him, maybe three or four years ago; he had grown fat. Too much rum, too many bumboos. Once he was maybe the best swordsman on the Main, now there are fifty to a hundred who are better. Levasseur, on Tortuga, is one. So is Gerard Labrosse, Rohan Levesque, Talon Chantry and Carlomagno's friend, Persifal Kerbourchard."

"Is one of them de Fortenay?" Flynn asked.

"He is. Everyone on the Main has heard of his skill with a sword, believe it. He is that good and better. And ambitious—Norville wants the notoriety that once was Morgan's."

When Henry Morgan's sailing days had come to an end, his crew drifted its own way, Macomber said. He had returned to Jamaica, where he had settled his family after leaving England. Their home was near a bay and together, Macomber and his wife would watch the sun drop away each night, to be replaced with a thousand sparkling stars. For a man who had spent his life in combat or upon the sea, it was the kind of restful retirement that had always seemed impossible.

"I was in Kingston, on a business trip. I fancied myself a trader. Morgan had done quite well as a farmer and planter; I thought I might do well for myself, by my own standards. I had gone to Kingston to talk business, to consider taking part in a trading expedition to the American colonies. When I returned I found my home burned, my family slaughtered and my life destroyed. One of my men, wounded fatally, had managed to crawl into the swamps to hide. I found him there, and before he died he told me the story of how de Fortenay and some of his men had come by. They had asked for a night's lodging, claiming they were traveling to Port Royal. De Fortenay made advances toward my wife, which were rebuffed. He grew angry—he cannot stand to be thwarted at anything—and he took her by force, as did some of his men after. Then they ransacked the place. They shot my worker, leaving him for dead. But he lived just long enough to tell me of this. And I swore that one day I would kill de Fortenay."

"You had your chance, *amigo*," Diego said quietly.

"It wasn't the time. He was better armed, had more men. But my time will come, Diego."

119

"We already have a barracuda," Flynn smiled playfully. "I guess you'll have to be the piranha."

One day soon after, one of the Spaniards, acting as lookout in a tall tree, spotted the topmast in the distance and gave the warning. A ship was coming in, but it was too far distant to see the colors. A Spanish ship might take the others back into chains, or vice versa if the vessel proved to be English or French.

"Are we agreed, Diego? We are of one crew now, no matter whose ship comes?"

"*Si*, Carlomagno. I like your style. My men speak of it, too. Maybe, they say, you are this barracuda who can swallow the bigger fish."

"We'll talk of bigger fish later," Carlomagno replied. "For now, we'd better concentrate on what we have on the line."

Staying out of sight, Carlomagno and his men watched as the ship sailed closer. Soon the Union Jack was clearly visible. Though this made the Englishmen breathe a sigh of relief, it did little to soothe Diego's men. The ship dropped anchor and soon smaller boats were lowered as the sailors rowed toward the shore.

"Well, I'll be damned! I know the captain," Macomber said. "It's Gerard Labrosse."

"Labrosse? Is he one of the swordsmen you mentioned?" Flynn asked.

"One and the same," Macomber replied. "He's a decent enough sort, salty if pushed, and probably no better than he has to be. My guess, Carlomagno, is that he's headed for Tortuga."

"Then let's see if we can hitch a ride. Macomber, Diego, come with us. The rest wait here. Flynn, you take charge if anything happens to us."

The seamen were frozen by surprise as Carlomagno and his aides stepped from the woods. Diego wore his Spanish uniform, a little worse for the wear, yet still striking. He had a sword belted on and had managed to save his musket. That he had no powder—none of them did—

was beside the point. Next came Macomber; he had put on a little weight since his days as a galley slave, yet was still thin. Labrosse's eyes touched on the Spaniard then fell on Macomber.

"Myles Macomber? What in blazes happened to you, man?"

"A long story, Gerard."

Labrosse's gaze centered now on Carlomagno. Black hair long past his shoulders, tall and strong, not gigantic in size but formidable none-theless. His father had not been so tall, though Metacomet had been a striking figure of a man himself. . The Wampanoag had a sword belted on and during their stay on Tiburon he had managed to make another bow and a handful of arrows. He had shafts for a dozen more, but had not had time to chip the arrowheads. Labrosse had never seen such a sight.

Macomber indicated the Indian. "This is our captain, Gerry. He is Carlomagno."

Labrosse nodded. "Captain Carlomagno, is it? An interesting name. But captain of what? I see no ship."

"Our ship was sunk by the Chevalier de Fortenay," Carlomagno re-plied. "We managed to make it here to await the next ship."

"The Chevalier is a bad man; I hope he's not still around."

"After he sunk us, he seemed to be heading west—maybe to Old Providence?" Macomber said. "We didn't have the chance to exchange travel plans with him."

"Of course not," Labrosse laughed. "From what I hear of de Forte-nay, you should count yourselves lucky to still be alive."

"That we do," Carlomagno said. "You wouldn't be on the way to Tortuga, would you?"

Gerard Labrosse smiled. It was well-known on the Spanish Main that after a successful raid many a pirate ship put into Tortuga—a safe haven for the buccaneers, and a place where every sin was available for the right price.

"I can take you there, but I'm making no promises after that. Macomber, you know how moody Levasseur can be. He might buy you a tankard of ale, or slit your throat for some fancied slight," Labrosse said. "I don't want any trouble. I'll take you there, and then you're on your own."

"You're a good man, Gerry," Macomber said.

"I'm a businessman," Labrosse said. "I can't afford trouble in Tortuga, it's one of the few ports where a, um, trader like me can dispose of his goods and get a few moments to relax without fear of a Spanish galleon bearing down on me."

"We understand, Captain," Carlomagno said. "We don't want to bring any trouble to you. Just bring us to Tortuga and we will make do from there."

"A word of caution, Macomber. You know Levasseur's reputation. For the right price he'll sell or buy anything—if he can't take it from you any other way."

Myles Macomber nodded grimly. Levasseur ruled Tortuga with an iron fist, like a feudal lord. He was the power on the island and all that came there paid his "tax" if they wished to survive.

"First Feroz, then de Fortenay,' Macomber grumbled. "Now Levasseur. It keeps going from bad to worse, Carlomagno. What the hell is next, the return of Sir Henry Morgan?"

{ 10 }

The Spanish Main

The night was calm, a warm breeze gently guiding the sails. Carlomagno stood on the deck, holding the rail, watching the stars as they winked in passing. But his thoughts were far away, deep in the woodlands that bordered Massachusetts and Rhode Island. Would he ever see his home village again? Did it even exist? He stood in the deck of a vessel that could take him home. But he knew that was a foolish dream, at least for now. He was the leader of a pirate crew and they wanted plunder. If he tried to sail northward, to his home, they'd mutiny and maybe even throw him overboard.

Piracy was a lonely, difficult life, a life that was generally short and ended with the merest warning. Maybe the last thought was of the cannon's boom, the swish of a cutlass whistling through the air or the sudden bark of a musket. The lucky few, like Morgan, were able to escape life on the seas, but it wasn't the case for most pirates. For most, the only escape was a prison cell, a noose or a lonely, watery grave deep beneath the greenest sea on earth.

Pirates were a hard lot, unaccustomed to taking orders, but certain matters of discipline had to be enforced. Though the buccaneer lived outside the general laws of the time, they did adhere to their own standards. One such of these, often included in the articles of agreement signed before each journey, involved the settling of disputes. Fighting aboard ship was prohibited among mates. If a dispute arose and could not be settled, the two antagonists would be brought to shore where they would face off at twenty paces. Upon order of the quartermaster they would turn and fire immediately. Failure to fire immediately would result in the pirate's pistol being knocked from his hand. If the guns did not settle the issue, they would then advance upon each other with their cutlasses.

"You have much on your mind, *amigo*?"

Carlomagno gave a start because he had not even heard Diego El Negro approach. "Just thinking of home."

"*Si*. I find myself doing that often. There is the home I knew in Yucatan, where my father was a man of some wealth with friends in high places," Diego said. "Then sometimes I think of the home I never knew, the place where my mother grew up. I am half Mandinga. What was it like for her? She told me stories, so I know a little of the Mandinga. These are always a part of me,"

"Have you heard of the *Oke Ololo*?"

Diego was surprised. "Ah, you have known someone from Africa, perhaps from Hausaland?"

"My brother-friend, Koyamin, is a Cimaroon."

Diego nodded. "The few I have known were ferocious fighters."

They spoke for a few minutes and then Diego retired. Carlomagno enjoyed the stillness of the night, disturbed only by the gentle lapping of the waves against the hull and the occasional splash as a fish sailed high into the air and fell back to its watery home. Carlomagno turned from the rail as Captain Labrosse was making his final rounds before turning in himself.

"Quiet night, Carlomagno. I like them like this, but don't be fooled. I've seen the wind blow up something fierce out of nowhere. Wait until you see a Caribbean hurricane. It's something you'll never forget. I've heard captains swear their ships were blown a hundred miles off course."

"Maybe that's something I don't want to see, Labrosse."

Labrosse laughed. "Trust me, you don't."

"What can you tell me of Tortuga, Captain?"

Lighting his pipe, Labrosse sucked on it for a few moments before replying. "Where to start? It might be the closest place to Hell on earth—unless that honor is owned by Port Royal."

Tortuga—the name meant "turtle"—was a natural rock fortress, an evil-laden humpbacked island just off the northwest coast of Hispaniola. Labrosse described it as the home of every type of dirty two-legged vermin, where every known buccaneer, corsair, freebooter or pirate showed up at one time or another. A place where, with enough money, a man could indulge in any sin ever invented by man—and maybe even invent a few new ones. Tortuga was a 25-mile island of rock rising up out of the water. The first recorded report of its occupation was by a buccaneer named Anthony Hilton, who led his men to the island and built a base camp that supplied passing pirates, Labrosse explained. The island soon became a buccaneer haven, as it possessed several natural defenses. One feature was a rugged climb to the top of the mountain, through a dense jungle of mangroves. It was virtually impossible to land a large force on the island, except at certain locations. The fierce Atlantic Ocean pounded the northern coast of Tortuga, while the south permitted only limited access because of shallow bays.

"On the mountaintop Hilton had a small area which was plowed into a garden," Labrosse said. "And a natural pool provided all the water anyone could ever want."

Hilton had been a visionary to see the potential of Tortuga, but he was not strong enough to hold it. Within a few years Tortuga had a new chief, a French Huguenot named Jean Levasseur.

"Levasseur was an engineer by trade before becoming a terror on the seas," Labrosse recounted. He re-lit his pipe, which had gone out. "Levasseur took the island and turned it into a pirate stronghold. He built a magnificent stone castle, known as the Rock Fort, on top of the mountain, looking down on the bay. The fort is manned by two dozen cannon. No ship can land without coming under his guns."

A cold, hard man, Levasseur was a feudal lord on Tortuga, his power was unquestioned. Tortuga was a safe place for pirates and privateers, though each paid a "tax" to Levasseur's "treasury."

"Bassa Terre, what they call the harbor at Tortuga, that's where we'll be going. If you show the skull and crossbones, Levasseur will let you in. But, if he doesn't like the looks of you, it's the end. No ship could withstand his cannon. They'd cut down an armada without as much as a dent in Tortuga," Labrosse said.

"Well, maybe we're risking a lot, but we have no choice," Carlomagno said.

"What is your plan?"

"That's the trouble, Gerard, I don't have one yet. I have to play it by ear, see what I can make happen."

"Like I said, if it comes to a fight, I can't take a hand. I won't be against you, but I won't risk Levasseur's wrath by helping you either," the captain said. "I'm sorry, but I'll have to deal with him later, and he's not one to forget a slight."

"I've heard that said about de Fortenay, too?"

"Another bad one. Two fleas on a mangy dog's arse, they are. Look, I like you, Carlomagno, and I've known Myles Macomber for years— and I owe him," Labrosse said. "Levasseur is hard to read, you never know how he's thinking. But if you're going to bargain with him you have to look the part. He can smell money and it's what he lives for.

You and your crew have had a rough go of it, and it shows. Levasseur won't be inclined to deal with you. He'll figure you're hard up and he can't make anything off of you. You need a suitable costume. We've some trunks below, taken in raids, but good material. Maybe you can find something suitable to impress Jean Levasseur?"

"Thanks, Labrosse. I'll do that, and maybe find something for Macomber, Flynn and Diego."

While most of the pirates were content with their rawhide breeches, coarse-linen tunic shirts and pigskin boots, Carlomagno immediately saw the advantage in playing up the image of a successful and daring corsair. After all, he told his comrades, the Barracuda of the Spanish Main was no common cutthroat. He donned a pair of crimson trousers, with a gold-embroidered serape. He set a plumed hat on his head, tilting it to a rakish angle.

"Well," Flynn chuckled, "if you ain't the most successful pirate on the Main, you're certainly the biggest dandy!"

Flynn, Macomber and Diego also found new clothes that fit them; nice enough, but far less flashy than Carlomagno's.

"You look the part, certainly," Labrosse nodded. He handed Carlomagno a small leather purse with a few coins in it. "You need the weapons to complete it. Come to my cabin, I have some captured arms that might be useful."

Carlomagno accepted a cutlass.

"A good weapon," Macomber said. "It takes a combination of skill and strength to use it effectively. It's somewhat like the Scottish claymores."

Carlomagno was also given a leather sling to wear about his chest, with which to carry the fine pair of brass-barreled .50 caliber flintlock pistols. Macomber accepted a double-edged sword and a prized French matchlock musket. The others, too, received swords and pistols.

"You've done a lot for us, Captain Labrosse," Carlomagno said.

"Thanks," Macomber added. "We owe you."

"It's all I can do. Good luck to you. We reach Bassa Terre today."

Tortuga was as Labrosse had described it: a wall of rock rising up. Though he couldn't make them out, Carlomagno imagined a dozen cannon staring gape-mouthed at the harbor. Once the landing was made, there was a narrow footpath leading through the mangroves and up to the town. It was a collection of wooden buildings and hastily thrown together tents and shacks. The streets were crowded with weaving, boisterous men. Every building seemed to offer strong drink or some native food.

"Be careful of what you eat, some will sell you anything. And if you complain about the service, 'tis best if you do so with a blade in your hand," Macomber said. "Keep one hand on your purses, men, and the other on the hilt of your swords. For as sure as the sunrise each morning, you're going to need one or the other while you're in Tortuga!"

"I have never been to Tortuga," Diego said, his eyes trying to take in everything at once. "What is your plan, Carlomagno?"

"We'll stop by the taverns and keep our ears open, maybe we'll hear something. But drink lightly, for we shall need our wits about us!"

Macomber and Flynn had been to Tortuga before, so Carlomagno sent Diego with Flynn and he began his search with Macomber. At the first establishment, he and Macomber edged their way to the bar and ordered drinks. They nursed their tankards as they casually listened to the talk around them. They continued this approach as they made their way down the street. Two hours of searching left them no closer to knowing how to approach Levasseur. But Flynn and Diego had had better luck.

"Feroz is here," Diego said. "It seems he reached Cape Tiburon as a small barque was taking on fresh water. Feroz killed the capitan of the barque and claimed it for his own."

"The barque's in the harbor now," Flynn added. "It's called the *Corazon*."

"The way I figure it, Feroz owes us," Carlomagno said. "I think we should take that barque as payment."

"Ah, *amigo*, that may be more difficult than you think," Diego warned. "You see, Capitan Feroz is sitting with Levasseur as we speak!"

"Where?"

Diego jerked his head. "Over there, in the Boar's Head Inn."

Carlomagno loosened his sword in its scabbard. "No use putting it off. Let's explain to Feroz why he will be needing a new ship."

Drawing on the dirt, Diego laid out the inside of the Boar's Head, including where Feroz was seated.

"Anyone else at the table with them?" Carlomagno asked.

"A pair of no-goods, but I do not know them," Flynn offered. "I'm sure there are some more of Levasseur's men about, too."

Macomber peeked in the door. "I know one of them, Carlomagno; a hard case named Smithers. He has a chip on his shoulder."

"We need to get our men into the room without drawing attention. Get them spread out so they can cover the room if anyone tries anything," Carlomagno said. "Have the men drift in, two or three at a time, and take seats at different locations around the room. But stay away from Levasseur's table. We don't want to arouse his suspicion just yet."

"What about us?" Macomber asked. "As I recall there's a back door to this place, it leads to the storeroom. Levasseur's back is at the storeroom door."

"Good, you and Flynn come in the back door. But don't step out until I've made my challenge."

"And me, *amigo*?"

"You will come in with me and take my back, Diego. If trouble starts, you take Feroz and I'll take care of Levasseur."

"That is a tall order," Flynn said. "But I have a hunch Levasseur will be peaceful once he knows Macomber and I have him from behind."

Carlomagno waited as the minutes ticked by. Finally, knowing his men were in place, he nodded to Macomber and Flynn. "Let's go, men. And may luck be with us."

"We'll need more luck than we've a right to ask for if Levasseur is in a foul mood," Macomber snorted.

"If we fight, amigo, don't think about being hurt yourself, just make sure you hurt someone else," cautioned Diego. "Even if Levasseur gets a cut at you, or gets his pistol into action, just concentrate on finishing him."

"He's right," Flynn agreed. "A lot of men are tough when no one stands up to them."

"Watch Smithers," Macomber added. "He is a man looking for a reputation. To impress Levasseur, he is likely to challenge you. If he does, you must be prepared to kill him without hesitation. You have to keep the edge once we get inside."

Crossing the street, Carlomagno pushed the door to the Boar's Head open with a fury and stood framed in the doorway. Eyes swung to him as he stepped boldly into the room. Diego, also looking splendid, was a step behind him. His eyes pinned on *Capitan* Feroz, Carlomagno crossed the room with quick, sure steps. Feroz sat with his back to the room and had not noticed him. Levasseur had seen him right away, and felt the crate beside him to make sure his pistol was still there. Carlomagno loomed over the table, letting his glance touch each man before turning his attention to Feroz.

"I believe you have something of mine, *Capitan*. Two things, in fact."

Feroz had been drinking and didn't like being talked down to in the presence of Levasseur, a man he was trying to impress.

'I'll take care of this," Smithers growled and as he rose from the table. Carlomagno drew one of his pistols and shot him in the head. Smithers fell back against the wall, and then slumped in a heap on the floor. Levasseur and the fourth man at the table did not move. Diego was staring at the fourth man; Levasseur was suddenly aware of someone behind him. But he didn't know whom. The room had fallen silent.

"And now, *Capitan*, we will conclude our business, if these gentlemen have no objections."

Levasseur stared hard at Carlomagno. "Do you know who I am?"

"You are Jean Levasseur, the king of Tortuga."

"And maybe you think you are the new king?"

"Not at all, Levasseur. I only came here to conduct business with Feroz," Carlomagno replied. "However, when I am finished with the Feroz I think we can reach an understanding to make both of us some money."

A cold smile played on Levasseur's thin lips. "Now, that, I like the sound of. And how would we make money?"

"I would make the raids and then come here, to pay my fair share of taxes to your treasury. You can observe my advantage for yourself."

Levasseur nodded. "You do seem to have the edge. May I ask your name?"

"Carlomagno."

"And you have a ship, Carlomagno?" Levasseur asked.

"I do, a barque called *Corazon*."

Feroz dropped his beer mug. "The *Corazon*! Why you double-dealing thief—that's the name of my barque!"

"It was your barque," Carlomagno said. "Now it is mine."

"*Monsieur* Levasseur, he is talking about taking my boat. We have an arrangement; I am to sail for you!" Feroz pleaded, his eyes on Levasseur.

Keeping his hands in plain sight, Levasseur nodded. "I did have a deal with the *Capitan*," he agreed. "It might not be in my interest to let you take his ship."

"But it is, Levasseur. How big a share can you expect from one who runs from a fight? He would never dare tackle the galleons, where the real treasures are. Your share from one of my voyages would be more than you'd see in ten years working with Feroz. Why, just a fortnight ago he fled his own ship—leaving most of his crew and all of his plunder behind."

"That's a lie!" Feroz blustered.

"It is true," Diego stepped closer to the table. "I was one of those he left to die."

Levasseur looked at Feroz. "What of this, *Capitan?*"

"We were under attack," Feroz exclaimed. "I had no choice, Levasseur."

Levasseur stared coldly at Feroz. "I think you are right, Carlomagno. I think we will make money together. The barque is yours. But you mentioned a second possession of yours to which Feroz has no rights?"

"Do you remember when we first met, Feroz? When you drugged me and had me chained as a galley slave?"

Feroz's eyes blazed with hatred. "You! I know you now. I should have killed you."

"But you did not. Another of your mistakes. Now I have come back for my sword of Toledo steel," Carlomagno put his hand to the hilt of his cutlass. "Unbuckle my sword, or die with it in your hand!"

For a moment it looked as if Feroz would fight, then his shoulders slumped and his fingers gingerly unbuckled the sword. His eyes downcast, he set it gingerly on the table.

"Is your business concluded, Carlomagno?" Levasseur asked casually.

"It is."

Levasseur reached down for his pistol and shot Feroz in the head. To conceal his shock, Carlomagno finished buckling on his Toledo sword. When he looked up, his steady eyes met Levasseur's.

"You are wondering why I did that, no?"

"He was not going to fight."

"Exactly! Men like you and I, we would openly challenge an enemy, with sword or pistol," Levasseur said. "We would fight and one of us would walk away, the matter settled. But a coward is more dangerous than a brave man, Carlomagno. He will appease you, hating you all the while. A coward stews in hatred and one day he will come after you when you are most vulnerable.

"I am protecting my investment, Carlomagno. I think you and I will make money together, but to leave a snake like that behind is to invite disaster. Feroz was a coward, but a vengeful one. He would have struck when you least expected it. I couldn't have him ruin one of your raids—and cost me money."

Carlomagno smiled. "I think we will do well together, Levasseur."

In his quarters, Carlomagno gathered Diego El Negro, Macomber and Flynn; with these three men would ride the success of his piratical career. His life was in their hands, for if they failed him all would be lost. But he knew men. Sitting beside his father, the mighty Wampanoag sachem, he had learned to sense a man's weakness.

"Look into a man's eyes if you want to peer at his soul," Metacomet had said. And his son had listened. He knew Macomber would rather die than betray a trust. Old Myles Macomber looked like he should have died ten years ago, but he was tough as the shell of a leatherneck turtle. Or tougher. He was said to be a master gunner, and a man who knew how to work the cannon was prized among a pirate crew. The difference between life and death often depended upon whose gunner hit the other ship first. It was no easy thing to gauge the distance on the sea, take into account the winds and use the proper powder and adjust the cannon accordingly. If Macomber could do all he claimed, they were in good shape, indeed.

Morgan Flynn was a tree trunk of a man, huge like some of the old oaks Carlomagno recalled from his childhood. He was a good man to have on your side, a first-class fighter who could equal any man with a cutlass. His strength was that of two men, maybe three. He helped

Carlomagno control the crew, which could become unruly on long voyages.

For quartermaster, Carlomagno had already decided on Diego El Negro. It was a shrewd choice, for though his mother had been a slave, his father had been a respected man of means. He had seen his unclaimed child educated as well as his legitimate children. Diego had been freed and treated as an equal by a wise and kind father. But a man in a powerful position made powerful enemies. Like carrion tearing at rotted flesh, his father's enemies wasted no time upon his death to attack his estate and seize all that was his. Diego was taken and forced back into slavery. After all, he had been born a slave, they reasoned. But Diego escaped and fled for the safety of the sea. On a pirate ship all that mattered was that each man did his duty as a man should. There was one vote per man on the ship and the majority held sway.

Diego El Negro—the name meant James the Black—knew that only as a pirate could an African live as a free man Diego was smart, seemingly two thoughts ahead of other men. The quartermaster was, perhaps, the most important man on the ship. He was in command, except during times of combat. He was responsible for stocking the ship with enough food, water, powder and provisions for any campaign. In most instances, a sailor was free to eat or drink as much as he pleased, but if supplies ran low it was the quartermaster who determined rations.

These men would become Carlomagno's trusted lieutenants.

Carlomagno pointed to a map unfurled on his desk. "We are about here, I'd say. Just off Hispaniola."

"*Si*, I think it is so," Diego agreed. "What is it you are thinking?"

"We need a quick strike. Levasseur needs to be convinced he made the right move. And by bringing him some loot in a timely manner, we will win ourselves a safe harbor."

Macomber nodded. "Sounds right to me, Carlomagno. What do you mean to do? We are moving dangerously close to Santo Domingo. You can't be thinking of taking that city—not with just a barque?"

"Santo Domingo is a trading center," Carlomagno said. "With any luck, we'll intercept a ship on the way in. We'll plunder her storehouse and turn back for Tortuga."

"It is a wise move, amigo," Diego smiled, his white teeth gleaming in the candlelight. "Such a strike would also give the men confidence in your ability."

"And that could come in handy when you have something bigger in mind," Macomber agreed.

The barque moved slowly against the wind, but all on board knew that same wind would help aid their escape back to Tortuga, for the Windward Passage was as dependable as a wind could be. What Carlomagno planned was a gamble, for many ships would be coming to Santo Domingo; the odds of encountering a mighty Spanish war galleon were increased ten-fold. Early on the morning of the third day after that meeting in the captain's quarters the crow's nest gave the alert. There was a sloop on the horizon.

"Prepare the deck for battle," Carlomagno ordered. "Macomber, ready the cannon. All men check and ready your arms. We will have little time to waste once we board her."

The barque hoisted its Spanish flag and turned its course slightly to intersect with the sloop. Most of the men kept out of sight, so as not to alert the sloop. A few sailors seemed to be going about their routine business. The sloop, also with a Spanish flag, sailed nearer. The distance grew shorter. Carlomagno watched a school of flying fish as they looked like silver streaks darting through the air. He thought how hot the day was, and it was just barely morning. The sky was the bluest he could recall, dotted with white, puffy clouds.

"Are you ready, Macomber?"

"They're in range. Anytime, Carlomagno."

"Diego, tell the helmsman to take us straight in as soon as we fire," Carlomagno took an arrow from the quiver slung about his neck. He fitted the arrow. "Fire at will, Macomber!"

The guns of the barque shouted a challenge that the sloop was unable to answer. As the barque closed in, Carlomagno raised his bow and drew back the string. He let his missile loose and it lodged in the chest of a sailor standing at the rail of the sloop. The unexpected firing of an arrow caused the sloop's men to hesitate for one moment too long. The barque came alongside and Carlomagno, sword in hand, led his men over the rail. The fighting was fierce, bloody and one-sided. The sloop was taken in a matter of minutes.

"Guard the prisoners, Flynn. Diego, take some men and gather the treasure. Take all we can carry."

"You make a mistake, *senor.*" The speaker was a distinguished-looking man with a rotund face. His uniform glistened with brass buttons and was festooned with ribbons. "This is the sloop of Don Pablo de Jesus."

"It is the don who made the mistake," Carlomagno replied pleasantly. "He should not have let his ship cross paths with the Barracuda of the Spanish Main."

"Barracuda, eh? I have not heard of you, *senor.* I am sure Don Pablo will want to know the name of the first man so bold as to attack a vessel belonging to the Duc de Castile."

Raising his sword in salute, the Indian gave a slight bow, "Give Don Pablo the compliments of Carlomagno."

"Carlomagno? Like the conqueror?"

"One and the same, *Capitan.*"

"And do you expect to conquer the entire Spanish Main?"

"Only that part which pleases me. Or rather displeases me. Now, if you will excuse me, I must be on my way. There are so many ships to plunder and so little time!"

"The time is shorter than you think, my bold rascal," the *Capitan* promised. "If I know the duke, he will have a fleet of his ships after you within a week of hearing of this atrocity."

Carlomagno leapt back onto his own deck, the barque already moving toward a course back toward Tortuga. "Tell the duke to load his fleet with treasure, *Capitan*! If I have to fight them, I at least want something for my troubles."

The wounded sloop limped slowly toward Santo Domingo, where its appearance caused a stir in the proud Spanish city. Few pirates ever dared strike so close to Santo Domingo, where there were always galleons about. The shaded brick streets were abuzz with noise, a hundred questions that no one could answer.

"Who dared such a feat?"

"Who is this 'Carlomagno,' where has he come from?"

Capitan Rodriquez admired the boldness of the buccaneer, a trait he once possessed in his own wild youth. But his looting days were long forgotten and now he was a Captain, serving an honored nobleman. Now he told the city's mayor all he knew about this man who called himself the Barracuda of the Spanish Main.

"The trouble with being a barracuda is that there are much bigger fish in the sea," said the *alcalde* of Santo Domingo.

"*Si*, bigger, perhaps, but few so dangerous," Rodriquez replied. Still, he knew the end that awaited even so bold a pirate as this Carlomagno, for Don Pablo had often boasted that no mere pirate would ever dare to attack one of his ships. The duke would catch Carlomagno, and the barracuda would find his teeth pulled. Still, Rodriquez raised his glass of rum and drank a silent toast to the only pirate who had ever managed to best him.

{ 11 }

The Anasarani

A dozen ships, of varying shapes and sizes, were anchored at Bassa Terre, the harbor beneath the rocky cliffs of Tortuga. With the skull and crossbones flying, the *Corazon* drifted easily into port. Their first haul and been successful, and its swiftness surprised the usually unflappable Jean Levasseur.

"I knew between you and Feroz, you were the better man," Levasseur said, as he piled high the dozens of pieces of eight that Carlomagno had poured from a burlap sack.

"We'll make more together, Levasseur. Much more," Carlomagno promised.

"Do you have something else in mind?"

"Not yet. The men want to enjoy their money."

"And you, is there something you desire, Carlomagno? Tortuga has it all. Women, if you want. There's food and drink. A card game, perhaps?"

"You've done well here," Carlomagno commented. "What happened to Hilton?"

Levasseur smiled as he set his mug down. "So you've heard that story, eh? Well, it's true. Hilton was smart to spot the potential of Tortuga, but he was too small-minded, he couldn't see the possibilities as I could."

"Did you deal with him as you did with Feroz?"

"Tortuga has become the place I dreamed it could be," Levasseur shrugged. "What else can I tell you? In such a place as this, there is room for only one chieftain. As you can see, I am he. Is that your desire, then? To become chief of Tortuga?"

Carlomagno laughed. "No, I have no such desire."

"Good, good. I'd hate to have to kill someone who brings me such wealth," replied Levasseur, clinking some of his coins together. "Your crew will be broke soon and they'll be wanting another prize. You'd best be thinking of that."

Carlomagno wanted little, so he had most of his share of the loot left. But, as Levasseur predicted, his crew was soon broke. It was time to sail again, and this time Carlomagno had a plan. It was risky and he needed more men than he now commanded. But where to find men—good, fighting men? Most of those he saw on Tortuga seemed little more than scurvy scoundrels. He had hoped to run into Rohan Levesque on Tortuga.

"Port Royal is the place, Carlomagno," Macomber suggested. "It's a better class of people. It's bigger than Tortuga with more vices available. But it's the place where Sir Henry Morgan spends much of his time. Modyford is the governor there and he's a fine sort if you know how the system works. Make him no trouble and he makes none for you. He has his hand out, like everyone else."

In the so-called civilized parts of the world, men felt protected by laws and society. There was a clear division between what was considered right and wrong, and the penalties for violating the norms were known. But even in places where proper gentlemen might find the natives uncivilized there were societal laws—perhaps not written in great

tomes or carved in stone, but laws and customs known through practice.

In his own world, the land of the American Indian, the Puritans saw
the natives as instruments of the devil, sent to tempt good Christians
from their righteous path. Yet the Puritan did not know the customs
and laws of the natives. Roger Williams, chased from the Massachusetts Bay Colony, had founded Rhode Island on land he purchased from
Narragansett sachems. Williams had occasion to spend much time
among the Narragansetts and found them a generous, kind people.
Should a guest visit their village, the Narragansett family would sleep
out of doors so the guest could have the privacy of their wigwam, Williams had noted in his letters. How many English families slept outside
on the ground so their visitors could have free run of their homes?
Roger Williams also noticed that thievery was a rarity among the Narragansetts. An Indian could leave his pipe and find it still in its place
when he returned. Though most of the Europeans saw their culture as
superior, they made the arrogant error of dismissing the mores of non-
European peoples. So, too, were there rules along the Spanish Main.

Law was inconsistent. A man could kill a man in one town and escape judgment simply by going to the next town. Law officials did not
work together to combat crime. In fact, crime was a way of life in this
rough part of the world. Spanish ships stopped English ships and took
their cargo or imprisoned their crews. And the English did the same to
other nations, as did the Dutch and French. They were the four European powers struggling for control of the Caribbean and the West Indies. Others were also starting trade expeditions, including the
Portuguese and the infant American colonies. For the year was 1692
and England's colonies had become profitable trading centers. England's monarchs had to press hard to force their belligerent colonists
to pay the proper taxes due. These were things Carlomagno learned
from talking with Macomber and Diego El Negro.

"So you know of the colonies? Are they at war?"

Diego shook his head. "They are at peace for now. Though in Spain they see the colonies wanting to expand, perhaps into Florida."

"They defeated my father?"

"I do not know your father."

"He is Metacomet." At Diego's blank stare, he added, "the English called him King Philip."

"Ah, yes, I have heard of that war, it bears your father's name," Diego said. He paused, adding softly, "but he lost it and the natives were defeated. From what I've heard, it was a costly war for all sides. Your father—I'm sorry—he was killed years ago, I think it was in '76."

Carlomagno stood frozen. His father had died not long after he and his mother had been captured. He had been dead for 16 years! All of his childish confidence, his dreams of being rescued by his victorious father, seemed to shrink to a cold, sharp lump in his gut. He was almost afraid to ask the next question.

"Are the natives all killed?"

"Not all. Many still live there, in smaller numbers, I understand. But the English roll relentlessly over the land, building great cities, such as Boston and Philadelphia."

Carlomagno felt his dream of returning to Massachusetts fading away. His life, for better or worse, was on the Main. And being a fast learner, he understood the law of the Main.

He was safe in certain harbors, as long as he played by the rules. On Tortuga, Levasseur charged his "tax," as he called it; he lived well and never had to leave his island. Every ship that sailed into Bassa Terre paid the tax. In return, the guns of the Rock Fort protected them.

There were other cities were a pirate could go unmolested. As long as he struck only Spanish targets, Carlomagno and the crew of the *Corazon* could sail safely to a number of places, such as Port Royal, Curacao, Nevis, Freetown, Old Providence and Guadeloupe. The rules were the same in each city, no matter which country claimed it. The governor of the city and the head constable, if one existed, had to be taken care of. At Port Royal, for example, a certain amount was given to Governor Thomas Modyford. From that Modyford forwarded a portion to his benefactor, the Duke of Albemarle. The duke, in turn, gave a gift or two or three to the king.

Piracy, of course, was illegal, condemned by every nation. Yet it was condemnation with a wink and a nod. The English Crown was deaf to complaints of piracy as long as the treasure was spread around—and English ships were left strictly alone. The other nations acted in the same manner.

Port Royal, on Jamaica, had started several years ago as a cow pasture. Located at the end of the Windward Passage, Port Royal had grown by leaps and bounds. When strong men like Modyford and Morgan arrived, they built Port Royal into one of the most bustling ports on the Main. Ships came and went on a daily basis. Pirates sold their ill-gotten goods and spent their money unwisely. Savvy traders brought their goods, including lumber and slaves, and carried sugar cane, rum and tobacco back to their own nations.

"This is the biggest place I've ever seen," Carlomagno gasped as they dropped anchor in the harbor.

"It can rough," Macomber warned. "Though not so bad as Tortuga or Old Providence."

"If you see any good men, bring them along. I'd like to find Levesque, if he's here." Levasseur had told Carlomagno that the last he had heard Rohan Levesque had gone to Port Royal. "And remember, men, we're new here so tread lightly. Everyone try to keep out of trouble."

Taking a few baubles and priceless gems, kept for just the purpose, Carlomagno walked down the gangplank and headed for the Governor's House. He would reach an understanding with Modyford, as he had with Levasseur. He was enticed by the sights and sounds of Port Royal. He saw men working on sewing sails, cobblers making shoes, others standing around in groups smoking pipes or sharing a bottle.

The aroma of roasted lamb teased him from some distant eatery and men of all shapes and sizes, some with an eye patch or a limb missing or dangling limply by their side, crowding the streets. The wharf area was busy with cargo being unloaded, bought or sold by sharp-eyed traders.

Carlomagno stopped to watch a man kindle a roasting pit; a dead hog was trussed up to go over the fire.

"I roasts my meats in the open, so all's can see's they be fresh, friend," the butcher said. "There's some 'round here, an' I not be namin' no names, who will sell you putrid meats an' claim they was made fresh that very day. You want fresh meat today, friend, you come back to see Calico Jack."

"Calico Jack? Is that your real name?"

Jack laughed heartily. "Why, youngster, you be the first to asks me that! Truth is, it's not me real name. My borned name was Rancid, friend. But I daresn't think that I'd sells much food if I names me place Rancid's Meat. Do you ken that, friend?"

Carlomagno laughed. "I'd say you have a valid point, Calico Jack."

"You be comin' back in a couple hours, youngster, and I'll be havin' some fresh pork today," Jack promised.

"I just might do that."

"See that you do, I is the bestest cook in Port Royal, even if I do says so my own self," Jack said, as he prepared his hog for roasting. "You have the looks of a new one to Port Royal?"

"I am that," Carlomagno agreed. "Fresh from Tortuga."

"Tortuga, is it? Aye, I could see the look upon you, friend. Well I needn't be tellin' you to watches your step 'round here. There are some mighty salty customers in Port Royal. Fact is things must be fixin' to blow up any time now."

"Why do you say that, Jack?"

Calico Jack snorted. "Things been too peaceable, youngster. Why Port Royal ain't had a killin' in two days! Gettin' to feels like a reg'lar church social, or somewhat likes it!"

Carlomagno waved. "I'll see you when that pig is done."

He strolled leisurely about the town, though it was larger than most towns on Jamaica. It held some 4,000 of the toughest men this side of Hell. Carlomagno noticed one such rowdy studying him.

"Alms for the poor, captain?" the man said. He had scrapes on his face and his bare chest showed marks, as well. Half an ear was gone and his left arm was mangled and useless.

"You have the look of a seaman about you."

"I was that once, I won't deny I was a freebooter. But I got mixed up with a petty lot and the gunner was drunken one day when he loaded our cannon. The four-pounder exploded and scarred me for life. I suppose I'm lucky to be alive, but my seafaring days are over. No one has much use for a one-armed sailor."

"This will hold you for a time, friend," said Carlomagno as he opened his purse and dropped a few coins in the man's waiting hand. "But it will soon be gone and you can go back to feeling sorry for yourself— or you can report to the *Corazon!* It's newly arrived in Port Royal and on the look-out for good men."

"Even one-armed men, captain?"

"It's not the arms I'm counting on, friend—it's the heart and the mind. Think it over."

"You are new here. What name do you go by?"

"I am Carlomagno. Go to the *Corazon* and ask for the quartermaster, Diego El Negro. Tell him I sent you."

"Thank you, captain—"

Voices were raised across the way and both Carlomagno and the one-armed man looked over. A well-dressed young man was facing three others, one smartly dressed, his two companions less so.

And then Carlomagno saw her.

She stood behind the well-dressed young man, a look of fear on her otherwise beautiful face, and a look of fiery anger in her green eyes. Her hair was long and loose, and of a bold red hue. A hint of freckles dusted her cheeks.

"They must be arguing over the woman," Carlomagno commented.

"Too bad for the gentleman," One-Arm said dryly. "He's about a minute from getting himself killed."

"You think it'll come to that?"

"I know it will, captain. That fellow he's arguing with is the Chevalier de Fortenay!" Carlomagno's eyes flashed with anger. He took a step forward and One-Arm grabbed at him. "Don't do it, captain. De Fortenay is the greatest swordsman on the Main!"

"He and I have met, my friend, and I lived to see another day. It is time to renew our acquaintance."

The argument grew louder as the well-dressed Englishman demanded de Fortenay apologize to the lady behind him.

"If I insulted her with my offer, I do apologize," de Fortenay said maliciously, as he gave a mock bow. "Perhaps if she is good enough I could pay another pence or two!"

"De Fortenay!" Carlomagno's exclamation caught the Chevalier by surprise as he was reaching for his sword. "I think you and I have some unfinished business."

De Fortenay, and his allies, turned to face this new threat. "I do not know you. Go, while you are able!"

"Once you decided I was not worthy to join your crew, de Fortenay. Remember, I was with Macomber? And though you left us on a sinking ship, you tried to hasten our finish with a final broadside."

"Ah, I do recall," de Fortenay sneered. "And how is dear, old Macomber?"

"He's around."

"A pity he didn't join me." The chevalier turned to face Carlomagno. "As for you, so we meet again, eh?"

"Maybe we meet once too often."

"You do not frighten easily. Ah, but you are a red Indian from the American colonies, is that not right? Perhaps you have never learned to count? There are three of us and but one of you."

A pistol barked in the sudden stillness and one of de Fortenay's men toppled into the dust.

"Now we are two and two," said a voice.

Carlomagno recognized that voice, though it had been several years since he heard it. "It is you and Tulane, now, Norville. And I stand beside the Barracuda of the Spanish Main!"

De Fortenay's eyes widened. "I have heard of this Barracuda. So it is you, is it? Maybe you are more dangerous than I thought." His hand remained poised on the hilt of his sword. "I should have killed you when I had the chance."

"You would be surprised at how often I hear that. But, you still have the chance, de Fortenay. You wear a sword, as do I," Carlomagno said. "Draw your blade, my friend, or drag your ass!"

It appeared that De Fortenay would draw his blade, and then he hesitated, slowly letting his muscles relax. "I do not like the odds now, Barracuda. But be assured that one day you will cross blades with the Chevalier de Fortenay."

"That will be the last day of your life," Carlomagno smiled. "I look forward to it."

The Chevalier, with Tulane in tow, turned and stalked away, leaving his comrade in the dust to feed the dogs and wild boars or whatever other creature might desire a meal. Carlomagno turned, a wide smile on his bronze face.

"Kerbourchard!"

"Ah, my old friend, I see you have grown into quite a man. Brave, or foolish, I am not certain which, for to challenge de Fortenay is madness in itself—but to do so when he has you outnumbered? Perhaps this barracuda talk goes to your head, no?"

"I couldn't see a good man killed by a rat like de Fortenay." Carlomagno turned to face the well-dressed Englishman, but the young man was angry.

"I will thank you to mind your own affairs!" the man snapped. "A gentleman does not presume to meddle in affairs that are none of his concern!" He turned, taking the woman by the elbow, and retreated.

Carlomagno watched the sway of her dress, and the way the light caught her hair as it flowed down her back.

"Was it the man you were worried about, Carlomagno—or the woman?"

"I have never seen anything so beautiful."

Kerbourchard laughed. "All women are beautiful in their own way. This I know, for I have loved a thousand times. Ah, but always a heart is broken. Sometimes mine, often it is the lady's. There are too many beautiful women for Kerbourchard to choose just one. It would not be fair to the others!"

But Carlomagno wasn't listening. He had just seen The One.

Macomber, Diego and Flynn joined them at Calico Jack's where they dined well on fresh pork, rice, salad and an assortment of fruit. There was never a lack of beverages at Calico Jack's either.

"You old buzzard, I can't believe you're still kicking," Kerbourchard teased Macomber. "What's it been—four years? Five?"

"Closer to five, I'd say. Last time I saw you, it was in Curacao," Macomber said, accepting another drink from a buxom waitress. "When Morgan sailed out, you were nowhere to be found, as I recollect."

The Frenchman flashed his easy smile. "Ah, I remember it like it was yesterday, Macomber! I was in the throes of passion with the sweetest angel I had ever known. At least the sweetest since the last port we had been in. Ah, but sweetness goes only so far and when I caught her hand in my purse! Well, she lost some of her luster."

"Only some?" Flynn chuckled.

"Well, a man still has certain needs, you must understand. When I finally made my way to the harbor, found that Morgan had sailed off without me. But there's always another ship ready to sail. Since then, I have taken on my own crew. I captain a sloop now, and she's a fast one. I'd have no other. And what of you, Myles?"

Macomber grimaced. "The years have gone fast, my friend, and none too kindly for me. After leaving Morgan I attempted to become a businessman, but returned home one day to find my family killed. I was filled with bitterness, with a desire only to destroy. fell in with a scurvy lot for a time, until the helmsman sailed us into a galleon."

"And now?"

"One last strike, a big one, is all I want and then maybe a little place of my own in some quiet corner."

"Quiet, you want? You are in the wrong company, Macomber! This barracuda you sail with is gaining quite a name. I have heard it said that Don Pablo de Jesus is outraged that one of his ships was molested. It is said that there is a reward out for you, Carlomagno. Quite a sizeable reward."

"I have only just begun. I have something bigger in mind. Are you interested, Kerbourchard? I have already located Rohan Levesque and Gerard Labrosse, and they are in."

"It must be big," Kerbourchard nodded. "If nothing else, it should be exciting. What is it you're planning?"

"The Spanish treasure fleet."

There was shocked silence. The treasure fleet was heavily escorted through the Windward Passage by a half dozen war galleons. It would be a fool's errand to attempt to take that ship. And Kerbourchard said so.

"I think Kerbourchard is right," Macomber added. "Not even Sir Henry would have dared that and I've seen the time he commanded 2,000 men."

"If you throw in with us," Carlomagno eyed Kerbourchard intently. "We will have about 450 men. A goodly number and enough treasure waiting to make us all wealthy. More gold and silver and pieces of eight than a man can count."

"But we'd face a fleet of galleons armed for combat. We'd be out-manned and outgunned," Macomber said. "It would be a foolhardy!"

Carlomagno turned to Diego. "Tell them."

"The galleons anchor off Nombre de Dios, where the treasure fleet sets sail. The treasure itself comes from the inland city of Panama. Pack mules carry Panama's treasure northward to the waiting ships at Nombre de Dios. Once the treasure reaches Nombre de Dios, we couldn't touch it, but, if we seized it somewhere between Panama and Nombre de Dios?"

"Can it be done?" Kerbourchard leaned his hairy forearms on the table. "My god, you'd need the devil's own luck..."

Using the plates and mugs on the table as markers, Carlomagno plotted it out. He showed Nombre de Dios, where the ships would wait, Kerbourchard's beer mug stood in as Panama.

"It takes about two weeks for the mule train to make its journey," Carlomagno said. "If we strike it about halfway, we'd have time to make it back to our ships and sail away before the galleons would even know what had happened."

"But how could we hide our own ships?" Flynn asked.

"We'll sail due south from here. That would bring us close to Car-tagena, but we'd veer off before we reached there. We would hide our ships in Darien Bay. Pine Island blocks the bay off by jutting out in front of it. The tall trees would help to hide our masts. From there, we'd march across the Isthmus and intercept the mule train."

"Maybe," Macomber muttered. "It just might work."

"What do you think, Kerbourchard?"

"I think I'll finish drinking Panama!" Kerbourchard took up his beer mug and leaned back in his chair. "I'm in," he grinned. "This is the damnedest plan I ever heard. And it's going to make us rich."

The talk drifted to other matters, and ribald stories of other days. Carlomagno sat quietly, liking the rough camaraderie of these men. Suddenly there was a fellow at his table, a well-dressed, nervous Englishman, who looked positively mortified to be seen in Calico Jack's.

"Excuse me," he addressed Carlomagno. "I believe you are the man they call the Barracuda?"

Carlomagno's eyes narrowed. "And if I am?"

"I am to deliver a letter to you, sir," the man replied, extending a fancy-looking envelope. "It is from Lady Annabeth Pickford."

"You must be mistaken, my good man, I don't know any such wench."

The man flushed. "I can assure you, sir, that Lady Pickford is no such woman as you may be used to trifling with!" The man turned abruptly on his heels and stormed from the room.

His friends stared at him until, almost embarrassed, he opened the envelope. The letter was in a smooth, feminine hand; there was the slightest scent of perfume on the paper. As he read, his smile grew.

"The woman on the street, the one involved in the argument with de Fortenay. She wishes to see me at the International House."

At the mention of de Fortenay's name Macomber's glass stopped halfway to his lips. "He's here? Norville is in Port Royal?"

"We neglected to tell you," Kerbourchard replied. "Our bold friend here nearly had himself a duel with the good Chevalier."

Carlomagno rose. "Gentlemen, a fond *adieu*."

"You can't go wandering off alone, not after having trouble with de Fortenay," Macomber protested. "He may have men lying in wait for you."

"She wants to see me, Macomber, and I would face a dozen de Fortenays for one more glimpse of that red hair and those emerald eyes!"

replied Carlomagno as he donned his plumed hat and started for the door. "What a vision, she was!"

"Ah, what the scent of a silky perfume can do to a man," Kerbourchard sighed. "It seems our young barracuda is as meek as a minnow."

"We better follow him. With his head in the clouds, this might be the chance de Fortenay is waiting for," Flynn said.

Oblivious to all about him, and his friends who shadowed him, Carlomagno hurried to the International House. At the door he paused, raised the perfumed letter to his nose and inhaled appreciatively. Then, stuffing the letter inside his shirt, he opened the door. He saw her at once, seated alone at a rear table. A pot of tea was being delivered. He approached quietly, sweeping off his plumed hat and offering a tentative bow.

"Won't you join me, captain?" At his nod, she deftly poured hot tea into a delicate cup. "Please be seated."

Suddenly self-conscious, Carlomagno dropped into the chair opposite her. "I received your letter, milady. I am not sure if I am fit company for a gentlewoman. I am, well ..."

"A privateer? A freebooter, perhaps?" Her eyes met his and there was a playful sparkle in them. "Or is the proper term pirate?"

"You are direct." Carlomagno smiled. He found himself drawn to this woman, and not just because of her beauty—which took his breath away—but by something about her personality, some inner steel concealed by her feminine charms. "Have you need of a pirate, milady?"

"No, but I'll keep the offer in mind," she laughed. "I wished to thank you for your kindness today. I believe my brother was about to be killed, had you not intervened."

"Your brother?" Carlomagno felt a tingling go through him, one he could not explain. "That young man was your brother?"

"Yes, Connor is four years my senior and, I'm afraid, he sees it as his duty to protect me from threats, imagined and real."

Carlomagno sipped his tea. It was hot. "This time the threat was re-al, milady. The Chevalier de Fortenay has slain a dozen men in fair combat—and who knows how many otherwise."

"Yet you risked your life, Captain? And for a stranger?"

"Your brother was brave, but foolish. He did not know the caliber of the man he was facing. He would have had no chance against de Forte-nay."

"And so you saved Connor's life?"

"You saved his life, milady."

Her eyes widened. "I? Whatever do you mean, Captain?"

Carlomagno sipped his tea, his eyes twinkling with mischief. "Why, had you not been so beautiful, my eyes would never have lingered long enough to see what was happening."

She flushed, but quickly regained her composure. "How very gallant of you, Captain. It is captain, isn't it?"

"I have no paper saying so; I suppose I am because the other men follow me. Where I come from, leaders hold their positions in just that way. You could call yourself a sachem—or chief, as you would know it— but a sachem with no followers has no clout. A sachem earns followers and power through his own actions, by demonstrating his ability to care for his people, to lead successfully in times of difficulty."

"Where is it you come from?" she asked as she poured them both another cup of tea.

Carlomagno hesitated, for his mother had warned him to protect his identity from the English. But when he looked into her eyes, he saw the sincerity of her soul. He told her, then, of Sowams, his home village, and of his people, the Wampanoag.

"How dreadful!" she exclaimed. "They sold you and your mother into slavery? And you were just a child, you had done nothing wrong!"

"I was lucky in that, I guess. There were some who wanted to kill me to make sure I didn't return one day to restart my father's war."

She looked him in the eye. "And will you do so?"

"That life seems far away and long ago, as if I had dreamed it." He glanced away for a moment, gathering his thoughts. "I want to do the best I can with the life I have now. I'd like to find a place for myself somewhere."

They chatted like old friends, though they had just met.

"Call me Anna, all my friends do. My father traveled quite a bit, he liked seeing new places. I was born in Hausaland, on the African continent."

"I know a little of the Hausa, and the Benue Valley." She seemed surprised. "I had a friend once. That, too, seems like another lifetime ago. But why Anna?"

"My given name is Annabeth, but Anna is short for *anasarani*, which means 'white girl' in their language. Every time my father called me Anna, we both knew he meant Anasarani."

"What of your father?"

"Father was a good man. He could be stern and somewhat aloof, but underneath he was kind to a fault. He was wise and had done well, trading all over the African continent. He did not inherit Father's keen business mind and he made bad investments. Also, he is too proud, he cannot admit his mistakes nor ask for help. That's why he was so angry with you today—you saved his life. Of course, he won't admit that, not even to himself." Lady Pickford hesitated. "That's why we're here, captain. I'm afraid my brother fell into debt with the wrong people. If he cannot pay them back, he could find himself in Newgate.

"The estates Father once owned have dwindled to next to nothing, our family's wealth all but vanished. My brother had to flee England or face arrest. So we came here. Connor is hoping to hatch some scheme to get enough money to pay off his debts and avoid being imprisoned."

"I don't have money yet, but ..."

She stopped him with a glance. "No, Captain. That is not why I asked you here. I wanted to thank you for saving Connor. I had no hidden agenda. It is getting late, however. I must be getting back up to my room."

Carlomagno stood, and offered his hand. "Will I see you again?"

"I should like a tour of Port Royal, but Connor says it is too dangerous for me to walk the streets alone."

"Your brother is right on this occasion, Anna. I offer you my services as your official escort—and protector."

"Thank you, Captain Carlomagno. Thank you very much."

He returned to his cabin on the Corazon, so lost in his thoughts he never realized his friends had trailed him. It was fortunate they had, for de Fortenay did indeed have thugs waiting to waylay Carlomagno. But the ruffians were merely tough men, not true fighting men, and Macomber, Flynn and Diego the Mandinga made short work of them. They left the roughnecks where they fell. It would arouse no suspicion when the bodies were discovered in the morning. Dead bodies were as common in Port Royal as was the hot afternoon sun.

Alone in his cabin, Carlomagno stripped off his shirt, his mind still in the International House and his thoughts revolving around Lady Pickford. Was it possible for a man to fall in love so quickly? It seemed unreasonable, preposterous, even! But how did one know? He thought of the simple beauty of a New England snowfall, when the forests were covered lovingly in a blanket of white. He recalled all he had heard about the King's Treasure House in Santo Domingo, the gleaming silver train of Portobello and the numerous wonders of the Caribbean, and yet he could imagine nothing as beautiful as the twinkle in the eyes of the Anasarani.

Her voice was so warm and melodious; every word she spoke danced along the paths of his sorrow-filled mind, bringing joy and laughter wherever they twirled. No parrot could sing so sweetly, no musician could play so enticingly as the merest sigh uttered by the Anasarani! She ... he noticed his reflection in the mirror and laughed at his longing thoughts of a woman he had just met!

"Am I going mad?" Carlomagno asked himself aloud. Yes, he thought, perhaps he was—madly in love!

Over the next week Carlomagno spent every free moment with Lady Pickford, showing her the wharf, dining at Calico Jack's and walking her throughout the city. Always two or three of his men followed behind, for the Chevalier de Fortenay was a vengeful man, and had been heard to make threats against the Barracuda of the Spanish Main.

Too soon, it was time to leave. To complete his journey, to reach the Isthmus of Panama in time to capture the elusive Spanish treasure fleet, Carlomagno and the Lady Pickford had to part. He left behind Myles Macomber, his trusted ally, to protect the Lady Pickford from the Chevalier de Fortenay. Macomber, crusty veteran of the seven seas, wanted to go with the winds, but was finally persuaded out of loyalty, and his admiration for his young friend.

"Our attack will be on land; if all goes well we shall not need a gunner, Macomber," Carlomagno explained. "If it goes wrong, a hundred gunners with unerring aim couldn't pull us out of the fix we'd be in. No, old friend, I need you here, to keep an eye on the Lady Pickford. I fear for her safety."

"It would be like de Fortenay to strike at you through her," Macomber agreed. "Alright, Carlomagno, I'll stay in Port Royal. You need have no fears; the lady will be safe until you return."

"I'll see you get your fair share, Macomber, enough to buy yourself that peaceful little home on the coast."

{ 12 }

Captain Morgan

"How does she look, Diego?"

The Mandinga straightened up. He had been studying a handful of papers spread over an upturned barrel he was using as a table. "I'd say we've got about everything. We may have to ration water before we get to Pine Island, but if we're careful we should be fine."

"I'd feel better with more guns," insisted Rohan Levesque, who was captain of one of the four ships in the makeshift fleet. Gerard Labrosse and Kerbourchard led the other two ships.

"Cannon are heavy, Rohan; the more of those we carry the fewer silver ingots we can bring back with us," Carlomagno said. "We don't want a battle against the Spanish fleet. This mission will be fought on land and won by planning. We have little room for error."

"We will be ready to leave within the hour," Diego said.

"Good, good! That gives me time to call upon Modyford."

"The governor? What's his role in this, Carlomagno?" Kerbourchard asked.

"I don't know, Percy, but he's sent me a message to come see him. You can tag along if you're of a mind to?"

"Not me," Kerbourchard winked. "I've got other plans. An hour, you say? That gives me time for a wench—after all we will be at sea a long time—and then a farewell drink or two."

"Sounds good," Levesque agreed. "Bur you can have your farewell drink, Kerbourchard, I may have a second wench!"

"If words got it done, Rohan, you'd be the father of your own country," laughed Kerbourchard.

"We sail in an hour, gentlemen," Carlomagno said. "If the gods are with us, we shall return wealthy men."

Carlomagno checked his weapons and started for the governor's mansion with Flynn, who had assigned himself as Carlomagno's personal bodyguard, at his side.

"Let's make this quick so I can say goodbye to the Anasarani," said Carlomagno as he rapped on a thick wooden door.

The door creaked open and a short, portly black man peered at them. "Can I help you?" His tone was cool, business-like.

"The governor has sent for me. I am Carlomagno." Carlomagno thought he saw a reaction in the servant's eyes before the man bowed his head obediently and led his master's guest into the building. It was as if the servant recognized him, but he was certain they had never met. "What is your name?"

"I am called Andrew, sir."

"Andrew, can you tell me why the governor has asked to see me?"

Andrew spoke quietly for Carlomagno's ears alone. "It's not that I'm listening, you understand, sir? Only sometimes a man can't help but hear a word or two. His Excellency is curious about your trip, I believe, and it may benefit his own plans."

Andrew knocked lightly on an inner door and opened it at a word. He stepped aside and bowed as Carlomagno and the others walked past him. The governor's office was modest, sturdy and practical, rather than stylish. Modyford was a competent man, but not overly imaginative. Seated behind his desk, Modyford rose swiftly as the buccaneers entered.

"It's not often one can extend a hand to a barracuda and not have it bitten," he smiled. "There's someone here who wants to meet you."

A thin, sallow man sat in a chair that seemed to make him appear even smaller. At one glance, Carlomagno could see the man had been powerfully built at one time. Now he was obviously ill; he coughed repeatedly into a dirty handkerchief. Another man stood at his side, introduced by Modyford as Dr. Hans Sloane "one of the best doctors in all of Europe," Modyford explained.

"He is the best," corrected the man in the chair. His skin looked draped over meatless bones. His complexion was sallow. Still there was a fire in his eyes, and his voice was commanding. "If you ever have need of a physician, Carlomagno, I highly recommend Dr. Sloane." He struggled to rise, finally doing so with assistance from Sloane.

"Carlomagno," the governor indicated the sickly man. "I have the pleasure of introducing Sir Henry Morgan."

Morgan held out a bony hand. "I have looked forward to this meeting. You have made quite a name for yourself, Carlomagno. You have taken chances, my friend. I have heard that Don Pablo de Jesus has sworn to capture you. It seems as if everyone is talking about the red Indian from America. You do things that attract attention—and powerful enemies. The Duc de Castile, for one. Be wary of him, he has many friends in many places."

"And the whole town has heard about your run-in with de Fortenay," Modyford added.

"What I have done pales in comparison to your legend, Sir Henry," Carlomagno said with genuine admiration. "Your raid of Portobello, Macomber has told me all about it."

"Macomber? Oh, so my old comrade is still active! Good old Macomber! He's a man to fight beside!"

The doctor helped Morgan back to his seat and Modyford called for Andrew.

"Andrew, bring drinks for the gentlemen. Rum?" They all nodded.

"My ship sails soon, governor, I cannot tarry."

Modyford sat back behind his desk. "I'll come to the point, Carlomagno. We've had a tentative peace with Spain, but it has crumbled. His Majesty wishes to inflict damage on Spain—unofficially, of course."

"It's the same as it was in my day, Carlomagno," Henry Morgan said. "A raid on a Spanish ship or town weakens Spain and if some of the plunder finds its way into English hands, so much the better! It is called privateering."

"We are hoping we can count on you, Carlomagno," Modyford said. "Officially, as I said, we can do little for you, just as it was for Sir Henry twenty years ago. But things can be done behind the scenes. I have the authority from someone very influential at the court in London to purchase 2,000 acres of land in your name, at a place of your choosing."

There was a map of the Caribbean on the wall and Carlomagno crossed to it. His finger touched a spot on Hispaniola, on the French-controlled third of the island—but bordering the Spanish holdings and the Cordillera Mountains. He had thought of a base there. He caught the surprise on Flynn's face when he suddenly said. "I want the land there, in the name of Lady Annabeth Pickford."

"It will be done," Modyford said. "We are in agreement, then?"

"We are, Governor," Carlomagno replied. "Now I must be off—to strike a blow for England."

The remark pleased Modyford, and he smiled as he called out to Andrew. "Show these gentlemen out, Andrew. And Captain Carlomagno is welcome here at any time."

"Yes, sir," said Andrew, bowing from the waist. The servant remained silent as he led them to the front entrance. Once there he peered about him before stepping closer to Carlomagno. "Sir, if I may?"

"What is it, Andrew?"

"You know how it is, sir, a man hears things sometimes, even if it's not on a'purpose?" Andrew looked around nervously. "I heard you were leaving on a ... on some personal business?"

"I am, Andrew, in but a few moments."

"It's none of my business, sir, and I pray you don't get angry with me for saying anything, but I do hope your business has nothing to do with Cumana."

"Cumana? Where there's been a huge gold strike reported?"

"What I heard, sir, is that there really isn't any gold strike in Cumana. Word is that the Duc de Castile started the story to entice you to go there."

Carlomagno put a hand on Andrew's shoulder. "Thank you, Andrew. I was not heading there. But why should you warn me? We've only just met."

"Peoples talk, sir, and things get heard here and there," Andrew replied. "It's been said you're a friend to the Cimaroons."

"Yes, I have friends among them," Carlomagno acknowledged. He thought of Koyamin, though he could not longer picture Amina. In fact, he could picture no other woman since first laying eyes on Lady Pickford. "Are you Cimaroon?"

Andrew smiled slyly. "I was born in the Cockpit Country, the home of the Cimaroons, where even the soldiers fear to go."

"If you went back there, wouldn't you be free, instead of a servant?"

"Yes," Andrew nodded. "But I wouldn't hear so many things—by accident, of course."

Carlomagno started away, then halted. "Andrew? Do you know Calico Jack's?"

"I do, sir."

"There's a man... "

"The Chevalier de Fortenay?"

"You do hear a lot!"

"I make a point of it, sir. What is it you want?"

"If you had a couple of friends who could go there tonight and make sure they sit at a table close to de Fortenay, these friends could possibly whisper a little too loudly about the gold at Cumana and how I plan to seize it."

Andrew nodded knowingly. "It will be done as you say, sir. And good luck to you."

"Thank you, Andrew."

"You ever run into troubles on Jamaica, you get to the Cockpit Country. You'll find friends there."

There was no time for other than a hasty goodbye with Lady Pickford before Carlomagno returned to the *Corazon*, which would be the flagship of this expedition. He met her on the porch of the International House.

"I wish you did not have to go," Anna said, surprised to realize how much she had come to care for Carlomagno. In one week! It was positively absurd.

It was much the same for Carlomagno. From the first day he had glimpsed her, he had felt something within his soul long to be near her. He would have laughed at the idea that one could fall in love at first sight—but now he wondered how he could have ever doubted it. As he stood on the porch beside her nothing had ever felt so right.

"It has to be done," Carlomagno said. There was a note of regret in his voice, almost as if he wanted to call the raid off. "I shall be back before you know it."

"Are you sure Mr. Macomber is necessary?" She had been deeply moved when he told her that Macomber would be watching out for her. She knew how much he counted on the man; leaving him behind was a clear declaration of his deep feelings for her. "I am sure I will be safe here. Connor assures me the governor will soon stem the lawlessness."

"The chevalier is a wily one, Anna. I will feel better knowing Macomber is here." Carlomagno glanced down the street where Flynn waited impatiently. It was time to be going. He told her of the land being set aside on Hispaniola.

"It is too much, Carlomagno," she protested. She searched his eyes. "Are you serious?"

He took her by the shoulders and drew her to him. "I know it all seems sudden. I can't even explain it to myself. I just want to be certain, should anything happen to me...at least you will have something to build on. You could sell it, repay your debts and return to London."

Annabeth smiled. Strange, she thought, since meeting this tall, handsome Indian she had not even missed London society.

Tilting her face upward, Carlomagno brushed her lips with his own. Emotions exploded within him and he wanted desperately to have this woman. He stepped back and smiled.

"You know," he said. "You have the cutest little nose."

"Get on with you," Anna laughed. "And if you don't hurry back, I'll come and drag you home."

Home! What a joyous sound that word made.

Though he'd been on Hispaniola more than half his life, he had always thought of home as some distant, fuzzy memory of a quiet place in the woods far away. As he joined Flynn at the corner, he turned and waved to the Anasarani, knowing there could never be a home for him without her in it.

"For a minute there, I thought you were going to stay," Flynn said, giving him a playful slap on the back.

"For a minute, I was."

Within the hour, de Fortenay would know Carlomagno had left; he had long since heard of the gold strike at Cumana and had been weighing making his own strike. Soon he would overhear a conversation and see his opportunity to snatch something right out from under the nose of the Barracuda of the Spanish Main! True, de Fortenay had few men with him, and no time to recruit more, but from all he had heard

Cumana was poorly protected. The soldiers stationed there were off in the hills, chasing after rebels. Maybe he could make a quick strike— and de Fortenay knew his ship's speed. It was one of the fastest on the Main! If he left soon, and skirted Margarita Island? Why he could slip into Cumana ahead of Carlomagno and clean out the gold before anyone knew what had happened!

"Tulane," de Fortenay put his hat on his head. "Get the men together; we're leaving as soon as we're provisioned."

On the deck of the *Corazon*, Carlomagno gazed longingly at the stars and thought how much they resembled the sparkling eyes of the Anasarani.

"So, tell me, Kerbourchard, what is the secret of life?" he asked suddenly.

The French corsair grinned, his teeth gleaming white in contrast to his golden-tanned skin. The sultry Caribbean night was a good one for thoughts of romance.

"Ah, the eternal question, Carlomagno. What answer can I, a mere mortal traveler, give you? I, like all men, walk upon this earth for such a short time, while the hills, the trees and the depths of the seas hold secrets they never yield to the living. Why, men have pondered this very question since they first walked in the Garden of Eden, I suspect. But you are in luck, Carlomagno! I have given it much thought, *mon ami*, indeed, I have!

"The secret of life is to live, and to live well. Eat of the finest foods, drink the sweetest wines, make passionate love to the comeliest women and fight the greatest battles. A man should do his duty, as he understands it to be. Never cheat a friend, nor let an enemy go unpunished. Ah, but most of all, Carlomagno, one must enjoy each day as it is given, for it might be one's last! Live with no regrets, *mon ami,* and that is how you die as well."

"Do you not long to leave something behind you?" Carlomagno asked. "To leave some mark upon the world?"

Kerbouchard looked out across the dark sea for a short time. "If you pick up a pebble and toss it in a pond, the ripples last for only a short time and then they are gone forever. Soon everyone forgets that the pebble even existed, but does that make the pebble any less real? A man's life is like that, like the ripples on a pond. We are visible for only a short time and soon, no matter how big our ripples once were, we are gone and soon forgotten."

"Still, I think it would be nice to be remembered."

"Why, *mon ami?* What does it matter? The whole world might love you when you are gone, but what good does it do you? You are the dead one, you are gone," Kerbouchard said. "A man is remembered for only so long, by his children and perhaps their children. But then what? If you are remembered beyond that, it is just as a name. They did not know you, the person you were, the struggles you faced. They know only a name; they do not appreciate the times, nor share your values. If you leave wealth behind, others spend it, living well, but say not one word of thanks to he who made their wastrel lives possible. The secret of life, Carlomagno, is to live for today—and let tomorrow be damned!"

Carlomagno walked the deck. Everything was orderly; Diego El Negro knew how to run a ship efficiently. Barnabas Greevey, a good, steady man, handled the helm.

"Evenin', cap'n. Nice night, it is."

"This is a nice place, Barnabas."

"It can get rough, cap'n. I'm thinkin' we might find that out before long."

"I hope it goes well, we've got it planned out to the smallest detail. Yet one unforeseen moment and it could be all for naught," Carlomagno said. "If the galleons spot us, we'll have no choice but make a run for it. Our barque and the sloops might have a chance against one galleon, but there may be close to a dozen at Nombre de Dios now."

"Word is, we're makin' for Pine Island?"

"That's right, Barnabas."

"The island juts out of Darien Bay and will help hide us, or it could help trap us if we're discovered there."

"I know, Barnabas. That's why we'll have to move quickly once we reach Panama."

"You ever been to Panama?" Carlomagno shook his head. "Best bet is to cut southwest to Venta de Cruces. From there, Panama City is about twenty-five miles away—but that's as the crow flies. I ain't got no wings, nor am I likely to be gettin' any. Unless you can fly, cap'n, we're going to have to hack our way through some heavy jungle."

"I didn't realize that," Carlomagno admitted.

"I did," said a voice from the darkness. The Mandinga emerged from the shadows to stand beside them. "I made sure to lay in a goodly supply of machetes. Greevey is right, we'll need them."

"I was getting ready to turn in, walk with me, Diego."

At his cabin, Carlomagno unrolled one of his charts. "I was thinking of Venta de Cruces. What do you think?"

'I'd agree to that, only we'd have to take out the whole village or skirt it so they don't raise an alarm."

"Is it a big place?"

"Very small, a few huts. A farming village."

"We'll herd them into one hut and post a few guards to keep them there. We'll free them on the way back," Carlomagno said. "By the time they could reach Nombre de Dios to raise an alarm, we'll be long gone."

"And the soldiers at Nombre de Dios might waste time by going inland to pick up our trail," Diego nodded. "If you're thinking about Venta de Cruces, you must be looking at El Cerro de los Bucaneros?"

"Exactly. Buccaneer Hill, as the English call it, overlooks Panama City—and you can even see the Pacific Ocean beyond!" Carlomagno said. "With a man there, keeping out of sight, we can watch for the treasure fleet. Once the mules cross the hill they will be out of sight of Panama City. We can take them anytime. Any survivors would retreat to Panama City and by the time the army reached the northern coast, we'd be gone."

"This should go off well, *amigo*," Diego said. "It has never been attempted before, to capture the treasure fleet while it is still in Panama. The guards should be minimal, probably grown fat and lazy from lack of action. I would like to see the look on those captains' faces when they realize their precious galleons have been of no use."

"Let us hope it goes so well, Diego."

"*Si*, I think maybe this will make you as famous as Sir Henry Morgan!"

The Caribbean winds picked up, filling out the sails, and the four ships slid gracefully across the green-blue sea. The day came, hot and heavy. Men went about their tasks, but there was time for leisure, too. For pirates were not fastidious about housekeeping or hygiene. Though they paid special attention to their arsenals and personal weapons, for their lives often depended on it.

Still, Diego had things in good order. What worried him was the lack of cannon. For four ships, their firepower was woefully weak. Together they might repel an attack, but any ship caught alone would likely be sunk. They made good time, coasting beyond range of Nombre de Dios in the early evening, making it unlikely their presence would be noted. Turning slightly eastward, they found Darien Bay empty and inviting. They sailed around Pine Island, lining up their ships in the bay.

"The island helps shield us from detection," Labrosse said. "But it also blocks our escape. It would be easy for a galleon to block us in and shoot us to pieces."

"It can't be helped now. We'll have to trust to luck," Carlomagno told him. "We'll leave a few men behind to guard the ships as best as can be done. Greevey is a good man; we'll leave him in charge here. He's got common sense and he'll know if it's best to fight it out or run."

"Greevey is the right man," Kerbourchard agreed. "If we lose these ships, *mon ami*, we'll be in for a devil of a long swim!"

"We'll probably end up rotting in Triana," Levesque said.

"Or swinging from a yardarm," Labrosse added.

"What if someone manages to slip away from Venta de Cruces?" Levesque commented. "If they raised an alarm, we'd be trapped. We can't risk having survivors left at Venta de Cruces."

The others looked at Levesque, but made no comment.

With a small band left behind to protect their ships, Carlomagno and the rest of the crew began the slow, methodical trek through the thick Panamanian jungle. Diego El Negro's machetes proved valuable as men took turns hacking at overgrown vines and protruding limbs. The tall trees provided shade, making it seem cooler than it actually was. Talking was kept to a minimum, for there was nothing to say. The captains had met with the crew to outline the plan before leaving the shoreline. Now, all that was left was the execution. The word sent shivers down Carlomagno's spine.

This one raid would make each man modestly wealthy. It was a day and an age when fifty English pounds was considered a small fortune. Each man could expect several times that at a minimum if they could seize the treasure fleet! No one knew exactly how rich the prize might be. Unconfirmed rumors abounded that only the Spanish king's Treasure House in Santo Domingo was a richer prize. At Venta de Cruces they met no resistance. The farmers were in their fields working when the pirates showed up. The men were herded into one hut, the women into another.

"You'll stay here, Levesque. Keep them separated. That way you can use one against the other; the men will behave for fear you'll hurt the women and the women will not want their men killed."

"There's scarcely two dozen people here, we could kill them all and be on our way," Levesque suggested.

"No, Rohan. There's no reason to kill them all, it serves us no purpose," Carlomagno said. "We'll leave a half-dozen men behind and move on."

After making their way through the jungle from the coast of Darien Bay to Venta de Cruces, the well-trod footpath toward Panama City was easy travelling. When they reached El Cerro de Bucaneros, Carlomagno sent Labrosse up the hill to keep watch for the treasure train. The rest of his men were to be concealed in the woods.

"What do you think would happen if I opened the attack from the jungle on this side of the road?" Carlomagno asked.

Kerbourchard's shrewd eyes needed only a hasty glance. "Why if they had any sense, Carlomagno, they'd run for those rocks over there where they could take up defensive positions."

"That's what I was thinking, too."

"You take the best shots so we can drop as many as we can in the opening salvo," Kerbourchard suggested. "Flynn and I will lead the hand-to-hand fighting when they reach the rocks."

Carlomagno scaled El Cerro de Bucaneros. The view was beautiful, the glimmering Pacific Ocean in the distance flanking the spectacular city of Panama.

"See, there it is," Labrosse said, his finger pointing south. "The mules are moving slow, but they should cross this hill by midday."

"How far from Panama City?"

"The air is clear and we're up high, so we can see pretty far," Labrosse said. "I'd say they're three days from the city—maybe more. It takes eight to ten days to reach Nombre de Dios."

"So we'll have about a week before the army will find out about us?"

Labrosse grunted in agreement, adding: "That is, if any survivors reach Panama City."

Right on time, the slow-walking mules appeared over the hill, teamsters struggling to keep the ornery creatures moving. The mules were loaded with sacks— sacks bursting with gold coins! An armed escort with the mule train consisted of ninety men on foot, led by. Capitan Perez, a proud, young man from a respected family. He had risen swiftly through the ranks; everyone who knew him agreed his future was bright. Until an arrow zipped through the humid air and slammed into his chest. Even as he clutched at the wooden shaft, a second arrow struck the man beside him. A volley of well-placed musket balls toppled another dozen men before a quick-thinking sergeant ordered the men to fall back to the nearby rocks. A few more musket shots hurried them along and Carlomagno got off three more arrows; one was a clean miss, but the other two struck retreating soldiers. The teamsters dropped the reins to the mules and made for the rocks, too. The Spaniards were nearly to the rocks when Kerbourchard burst forth at the head of the remaining pirates. The Spanish were flustered and paralyzed with indecision.

When Carlomagno led a charge against them, the few Spaniards who were untouched fled back down the hill.

"Let's get these mules moving," Carlomagno ordered.

Labrosse fell back with twenty men, in case any rearguard action was called for. The rest hurried back toward Venta de Cruces. Halfway to the small village they ran into Rohan Levesque and his men.

"You're supposed to be watching the villagers, Levesque!"

"Don't hurry any, them villagers won't be telling nothing to nobody."

Carlomagno scowled. "I told you not to hurt them," he roared, as his right hand dropped to his sword.

Kerbourchard stepped between them. "Not here, Carlomagno. We've got to make those ships."

"This isn't over, Levesque. You disobeyed my orders and there will be a reckoning."

"Any time," Levesque sneered. "Any time at all. I don't buy into all that barracuda stuff. You're just a man and you'll bleed the same as any."

The ships were waiting unmolested and soon they had the treasure loaded and were on their way. Eight of the mules had been loaded with gold and a like number carried silver. That was enough for most men, but add in the half-dozen mules loaded down with pieces of eight and it was a treasure fit for a king!

Only the Spanish king was never going to see it, not one single coin.

{ 13 }

A Trap in Cumana

Pierre Norville, the Chevalier de Fortenay, came from a family rich in heritage, modest in wealth and bankrupt of morals. Though he identified with the French side of his family—and had spent much of his childhood in a drafty, poorly-furnished manor located in the southern French area of Bayonne—there were also English roots in his family tree. An ancestor in the 11th century was said to have been in the army of William the Conqueror. Another member of his family allegedly fought in the Crusades with Richard the Lionhearted, and another family legend placed a Norville ancestor in the company of a certain Robin of Loxley, terrorizing hapless travelers passing through Sherwood Forest. On the French side, his family rallied behind Joan of Arc, though they were reputedly in it to grab what they could for themselves. Whether any of those stories were true or just ancient family rumor did not matter to de Fortenay. He was concerned only with acquiring wealth. Nothing was as beautiful in his eyes as a pile of gleaming coins on a silver tray, surrounded by solid gold ingots. A day did not pass when the chevalier did not dream of some scheme to further his ambition and enlarge his estate. His family once had money, and he made it his personal crusade to gain it back. For the cold, stone manor of his bitter childhood was evidence enough for him that his family had once enjoyed prestige and wealth in France.

The chevalier was of average height among men of the age, perhaps five-feet, six inches, with broad shoulders and a powerful build. He had the reflexes of a jungle cat—and the conscience of a beast to go with them. Anything that stood between him and what he believed was his due had to be destroyed, by any means necessary. His ancestors, French and English, had gone to the sea; they had sailed with Sir Francis Drake and plundered with L'Ollonais. For generations his family, or so it was whispered, were no better than they had to be. A problem had developed in France, however. The chevalier was from Huguenot stock, and France's King Louis XIV favored Catholicism. It was the very same situation that led Jean Baptiste du Casse, a de Fortenay family acquaintance who also grew up in the Bayonne region, to seek employment with a private trading venture that specialized in human cargo off the African coast. As was the case with de Fortenay, the Huguenot ties of the du Casse family barred Jean Baptiste from any preferment within Catholic France. When du Casse came home for a visit and seemed to be doing well financially, de Fortenay decided to accept a position with the same Compagnie de Senegal. Slavery was a fact of life and de Fortenay—like many men of his time—gave it no second thought as far as the right or wrong of it. It would be this same indifference which would make the switch from "honest" businessman in human cargo to a life of freebooting on the high seas a natural move for de Fortenay.

In 1680, du Casse had come to Saint-Dominique, as the French area of Hispaniola was called, with a load of slaves. De Fortenay was with him. They found the planters complaining about the quality of slaves being furnished them by the Compagnie de Senegal. In little time, due much to the ambition of du Casse, the pair was involved with a ship of their own and brought a load of healthier slaves to Saint-Dominique. They sold at a handsome profit. With the money, they provisioned a ship and went to privateering in earnest. By luck, they captured a large Dutch merchant ship. Here, du Casse and de Fortenay took their shares and parted ways.

But the take was so grand that when du Casse shared his treasure with the French Crown, King Louis XIV was suitably impressed. Deciding that a man of such skill was valuable—even if he was a Huguenot—the king named du Casse a lieutenant in the French Navy. From there du Casse's career would continue to rise, leading him to become one of the leading businessmen of Saint-Dominique.

De Fortenay's personal greed had caused him to miss out on winning the gratitude of the king, and he became nothing more than a common pirate. The wealth he had hoarded from the Dutch merchant ship was used to buy and furnish his own ship. A combination of solid planning and luck—seasoned with a liberal dash of ruthlessness—had made the Chevalier de Fortenay a man to be reckoned with on the Spanish Main. When hardy fighting men tossed off drinks and debated the toughest fighting men in the Caribbean, de Fortenay's achievements were toasted as often as Sir Henry Morgan's or Rock Brasiliano's.

With a sword, it was taken as faith, few men could equal de Fortenay—not L'Ollonais, or Levasseur or even Persifal Kerbourchard. With Levasseur refusing to leave Tortuga and the recent passing of Sir Henry Morgan, de Fortenay was the growing power on the Main. And then along had come that strange red Indian, that Carlomagno!

The Wampanoag cut a striking figure and had some quality that drew men to him. Norville did not recognize, nor appreciate, such a characteristic. To him, only success mattered. Still it rankled to go into every tavern and hear talk of The Barracuda of the Spanish Main! He killed a man once when he heard him say "barracuda," only to discover the man was talking about actually catching one of the feisty creatures. If any expected to see regret in de Fortenay for his rash action, they were disappointed. The Chevalier de Fortenay cared not one whit about taking the life of an innocent man.

"They should be talking of the Chevalier de Fortenay," he told his aide, Tulane. "I have done more than any man on the Main! I have never led a raid that ended in failure!"

He had had his chance to fight Carlomagno, and would have done so had not Kerbourchard been there. De Fortenay fancied himself a swordsman, but he had a grudging respect for Kerbourchard. He had seen Kerbourchard in action and secretly marveled at his quickness and skill. There was a part of him that wanted to test Kerbourchard, but another part of him recognized the great risk involved. That he could defeat Carlomagno, de Fortenay took for granted. From all he heard the red savages of the American colonies ran around half-naked and used bows and arrows. How primitive! Always he had planned his raids carefully, aware of every detail. But this time, overhearing a conversation in a tavern, he had acted rashly. In his envy over the rising glory of Carlomagno, the chevalier had decided to try and beat him to the gold strike in Cumana. He threw together a rag-tag crew, finding men willing to follow him based on his past successes. They had sailed unmolested into the harbor of Cumana when a sudden barrage tore the air. De Fortenay quickly saw it for what it was—a trap! The two ships with him were sunk, hundreds of men lost. His own ship was badly wounded and barely limped from Cumana. Taking on water and facing his own demise, de Fortenay's luck was nothing short of miraculous.

A ship passed by, a ship owned by Jean Baptiste du Casse! The chevalier was rescued with the few of his men who had survived the trick at Cumana. It had all seemed too easy and now de Fortenay understood why. There was no gold strike at Cumana; the rumor had been a deathtrap. But for whom? De Fortenay had his answer when the ship landed on Saint-Dominique and he was reunited with his old friend, du Casse.

"The word is that Cumana was a trap for Carlomagno," du Casse said over an excellent dinner, with the finest wine. Even as he enjoyed the man's hospitality, de Fortenay was vaguely resentful of du Casse. "I heard it was the work of Don Pablo de Jesus. The Duc de Castille has sworn to see Carlomagno hang."

"It all makes sense now," de Fortenay nodded. "I was meant to overhear a conversation. Carlomagno found out about the trap and tricked me into sailing right into it. And I, who had never tasted failure, have swallowed it whole."

"This Carlomagno does seem rather clever."

"He is nothing, the luck of a fool," de Fortenay insisted. "Give me a ship, du Casse, and I shall take his measure."

"I can't do that, Andre." Growing up together in Bayonne, du Casse knew de Fortenay's real name, and was the only one who still used it. Even the title was not one conferred officially. Andre liked the sound of it, so he adopted it, as he had adopted the name Pierre Norville. Though, again, family legend placed a Chevalier de Fortenay among his ancestors.

"I must have a ship, du Casse. You know it would profit you greatly. Give me a ship and some men."

"I have neither to spare," du Casse snorted. "It's those blasted Cimaroons. They've been coming off the mountains with more frequency and raiding outlying plantations. I need all my men to control them. I understand they're doing the same on the Spanish side of Hispaniola."

"How many men do you need to tackle that riffraff?"

Du Casse shrugged. "Something's changed with them. They have a new leader; he's like a king among the Cimaroons. He has organized them and they work in unison. Believe me, they are a fierce lot to deal with."

De Fortenay gestured with a mutton bone, "Come, du Casse, a man of your skills is surely more than a match for uneducated, godless heathens?"

"Well, we have had a stroke of luck, Andre. We have captured a woman said to be the Cimaroon queen. We are hoping, of course, that we can use her as bait to lure their so-called 'King' into a trap."

Du Casse proceeded to boast of his friends at the French court, but de Fortenay had ceased to listen. Suddenly he knew how he could get back at Carlomagno. Who was that woman in Port Royal, the one with whom he had spent so much time? Pickford. Yes, through Lady Pickford he could finally defeat Carlomagno. The lady had favored the savage, but was it a mere dalliance, or did Carlomagno care for her enough to come to her rescue? She might be just what he needed to gain his revenge!

Du Casse had a ship leaving for Port Royal the very next day and de Fortenay was on it with the remainder of his crew. Little did he know close he had been to his revenge. He had dined with Jean-Baptiste du Casse in the town of Miragoane. To the east, before reaching the town of Jacmel, there was a lonely land where the Cordilleras started the gentle slope that led high up to the stronghold of the Cimaroons. It was this land, 2,000 acres of it, which had recently been purchased in the name of Lady Annabeth Pickford! Had de Fortenay mentioned the lady's name, du Casse would have shared this information, for he had handled the arrangements as a special favor to Thomas Modyford, the governor of Port Royal.

England and France had on-again, off-again relations, but both courts were far removed from the Caribbean. This was a different world and it did no harm to do a small favor for someone who had powerful friends among the English aristocracy—for du Casse knew of Modyford's alliance with the Duke of Albermarle. There was no telling when Spain, which controlled two-thirds of Hispaniola, might decide to harass him and, if such a time came, it would be a comfort to know that Modyford might send aid—or, at the least, provide a safe haven if flight became necessary. Du Casse did not know why an English lady would want to live on such a wild, remote land, but he asked no questions. Sometimes on the Main, the wrong question could prove fatal.

The harbor of Port Royal, always bustling, was jammed with ships of every size.

"Many have come to pay last respects to Sir Henry," the captain explained to de Fortenay. "He was a great man."

De Fortenay snorted. "Now he is dead, and he is nothing."

"With Morgan goes the balance of power on the Main," du Casse's man continued. "The English are weakened. No one will challenge the Duc de Castile now, at least not after he gets his hands on Carlomagno."

"Carlomagno?" The name of his foe caught de Fortenay by surprise. "What do you know of Carlomagno?"

"Surely you have heard how Carlomagno plundered one of the duke's ships?" After de Fortenay nodded, the man continued. "The duke has vowed to capture him for his audacity. That whole story of the gold strike at Cumana, the word is that it was a ruse!"

"Oh?"

"Aye, the duke had arranged a trap at Cumana for Carlomagno, but some other bonehead stumbled into it!" The Captain did not notice as de Fortenay's jaws tightened. "Most of the raiders were killed, but they managed to get off a few direct hits—and in one blast, Don Juan Hidalgo was killed. The Duke set great store by his nephew."

"That is too bad," de Fortenay said, keeping his face blank. "How do they know it wasn't Carlomagno?"

"Because he was seen in Panama. The soldiers who survived described a wild, red Indian with long, flowing hair. It could be no other."

"Carlomagno, in Panama?"

"Ah, he's a bold rascal, he is! He slipped in and captured the entire Spanish silver train between Panama City and Nombre de Dios! And then he escaped without losing a man. My God, what a feat it was!"

De Fortenay's blood began to boil. *Damn the savage! He has toyed with me for the last time.*

"...but he may have signed his own death warrant," the Captain was saying.

"Oh?" de Fortenay's interest was suddenly piqued. "Why do you say that?"

"There was a small farming village; he massacred everyone—men, women and children alike. My god, but he's a cold son of a bitch! He's said to be on his way back to Port Royal loaded with treasure. This will make him the greatest hero since Sir Henry Morgan raided Portobello twenty years ago!"

The chevalier had his own ideas about who would fill the vacuum left by Morgan's passing, but he, too, realized that Carlomagno was an obstacle that had to be removed. On the wharf, shady characters were the norm and no eye was raised when de Fortenay stopped to chat with a seemingly aimless loafer. Now the Chevalier de Fortenay was thinking ahead, for, like du Casse, he knew the value of allies. He had a friend who had connections among the Spanish. He offered to deliver Lady Pickford to the duke, adding that by holding her Carlomagno would come to him. The friend, used to dealing in the shadows, nodded. "I am sure the duke will appreciate this. I will pass word along within the hour."

It took little time for de Fortenay to locate Lady Pickford, for she was still at the International House. She was well-liked and a frequent guest at dinners in the Governor's Mansion. But stealing her away would prove no easy task.

"It's Macomber," the foul-smelling Tulane explained. "He shadows her every move. We can't take her without dealing with him first."

"Macomber's no swordsman," de Fortenay mused. "I could challenge him to a duel."

"He's a cagey one, captain, and would take a lot of killing," Tulane said. "I don't think he'd fight you with a sword, it seems to me he'd just pull a pistol and shoot you. Besides, as the challenged party, he'd have the choice of weapons, no?"

Damn that Tulane, he was right, de Fortenay cursed. Of course, if he openly challenged Macomber the old war veteran would get the choice of weapons. Macomber was no fool; he could not be maneuvered into swordplay. It would be muskets or pistols. And de Fortenay knew Macomber had an even chance of besting him with gunplay. Still, there had to be a way.

"The woman's brother, what is he up to?"

"Pickford? He is hoping to arrange a marriage for her with some wealthy man and her dalliance with a mere pirate is interfering with his plans," Tulane said.

De Fortenay felt his fortunes beginning to shift. "A man like that, with some nudging, might be useful, Tulane...."

{ 14 }

An Enemy Revealed

The wharf and seaside corridors of Port Royal were full as the Corazon and her three sister ships cruised slowly toward the harbor. Carlomagno had climbed a few yards up the rigging and held there as he neared the place they would drop anchor. He smiled at the eruption of cheers, for he knew that word had arrived before him. It was amazing how quickly news could travel; in this case it seemed to fly on the wings of eagles. To the monstrous applause and catcalls, Carlomagno deftly tipped his plumed hat, his black hair flowing behind him in the wind. He had stripped to the chest, his quiver slung over his shoulder. He wore his twin brass pistols.

"Looks like the whole city has turned out," Flynn yelled up to Carlomagno.

"Not the whole city," he replied, his eyes scanning for any sign of the Anasarani. He saw no evidence of her, nor of Macomber. A smaller boat was lowered and Carlomagno, with his officers, sailed the remainder of the way to Port Royal. Governor Modyford met him, extending a hand with a huge grin stretched across his sagging jowls.

"Is it true, Carlomagno? Can it possibly be true?"

Accepting the hand, Carlomagno returned the smile. "All true, governor. We took the Spanish treasure fleet without losing a single man."

"It's incredible, Carlomagno," the governor exclaimed, rubbing his hands together. "As a feat, it ranks right there with Morgan's sacking of Portobello. It's quite a blow to the Spanish Empire."

"Aye," Carlomagno replied. "And a boon to William of Orange."

"He will hear of it soon. I shall forward an official dispatch to him on the next ship. Have you made an inventory?"

"Not yet, not a full one, governor. Send your men in the morning and we'll begin. I'd say there's plenty of treasure to go around."

"Do you feel up to attending a dinner at the mansion tonight?"

"I'm not sure, governor," replied Carlomagno, his eyes still scanning the streets. "I may have another engagement."

"I understand," Modyford said. He started to turn away, and then stopped abruptly. "Oh, I was sorry to hear about your friend."

"My friend?"

"The old man. McGyver?"

"Macomber? What do you mean?"

"He was shot," the governor said. "Some quarrel over a woman, as I understand it. There were witnesses. They said the man accused Macomber of making unwanted advances towards his sister."

"Is he...is Macomber dead?"

"He's alive. I knew he was a friend of yours and sent for Dr. Sloane. You remember Morgan's old physician? Well, Sloane says he'll pull through; that Macomber is tougher than rawhide."

"Where is he?"

Modyford motioned to his servant. "Andrew, take Captain Carlomagno to Macomber's room. And, Captain, the invitation stands—if your other engagement doesn't keep you too long."

As they set out, Andrew spoke out of the side of his mouth. "Sir, the governor doesn't know the true story. It was no fight over a woman, as he thinks. Oh, it was supposed to look that way. I spoke to Mr. Macomber, sir, and I know you asked him to keep an open eye on the Lady for you. Her brother pulled the trigger, that much is true, but Mr. Macomber courting the Lady? Nothing could be further from the truth, sir. It was that Tulane, sir, he went after Mr. Macomber. "

"Tulane was there? Then the Chevalier de Fortenay was involved, Andrew."

"Aye, sir, I agree! Tulane made a sudden move that caught Macomber's eye; when he reaches for his gun, his eyes are on Tulane. That's when the Lady's brother pulls his gun and shoots Macomber. Most folks thought they saw a fair fight. My people say it ain't so. They say it was a trick; that Tulane distracted Macomber so the Pickford boy could shoot him."

"Where is she now, Andrew?"

"I don't know, sir, but my people can open their eyes for her. Come to the governor's tonight and I'll have word for you, sir."

"Thanks, Andrew. I won't forget this."

"Mr. Macomber is in that boarding house, in room six. You'd best knock before you enter, sir. Mr. Macomber is a bit touchy these days!" Andrew said. He paused, looking Carlomagno in the eye. "I also know what they're saying is not true, about you killing women and children. I think I know men, and you are not the kind who would do such a thing."

"I didn't kill them, Andrew, but I am responsible. I left Rohan Levesque in charge and he massacred the whole village. I'll deal with him, I promise you."

"Sir, you ever get in trouble in Port Royal, make your way north-west, you hear? Get to the Cockpit Country and you'll find friends waiting. Good friends."

Carlomagno met with the captains, quartermasters and first mates on his flagship. Governor Modyford would send his people in the morning to supervise the division of plunder. It was a time when one hand didn't trust the other, so though they had an alliance, the gover-nor of Port Royal had to make sure the English king—and the gover-nor's coffers—received their proper portions. The remaining shares would be split up among the men, based on the articles of confedera-tion that had been agreed to at the beginning of the expedition.

The captains, as was custom, would receive the largest splits—sometimes up to five shares, though that was unusual. Other specialty officers—quartermasters, gunners, and helmsmen—could expect one-and-a-half to two shares each. The average crewman would get one equal share. With four ships stacked with treasure, even the lowliest pirate would receive a small fortune.

"Pick men you can trust to guard the storerooms tonight," Carlo-magno advised the captains. "We'll divide it up tomorrow and go our own ways."

"I'll be around town a few days," Gerard Labrosse offered. "If you have another expedition like this one in mind, look me up."

"Me, too," Kerbourchard winked. "You'll find me surrounded by wine, women and song—at least until my purse comes up wanting!"

"This was the easiest money I ever made," Rohan Levesque crowed. "You can count me in too, Carlomagno."

"No—you're out, Levesque. You disobeyed my orders. I should kill you right here and now," Carlomagno said roughly. "You'll get your share, but that's it. You'll never be invited to join me again."

"What? Because of a handful of peasants? They tried to make a fight of it, I had no choice!"

"You had orders, Levesque. Now get out of my sight."

"You're awful high-and-mighty, considering you and me are the same—we're goddamn pirates!"

"We're not the same, Levesque, and we never will be. When I kill a man he will have his chance, be it by blade or pistol. There is no honor in killing women and babies. Go now, Levesque, before I kill you anyway."

Levesque took a step backwards. "You believe all the barracuda stuff they're saying about you," he sneered . "But you bleed like any other man. You think you're better than me? We're both pirates and we steal."

"Carlomagno is right, Rohan," Macomber said. "We been friends a long time, but you had no call to kill those farmers. They were no threat to us."

Levesque looked at Labrosse. "I suppose you're against me, too, Gerard?"

"Killing a man in combat is one thing, but what you did, Rohan, was just plain murder."

"To blazes with all of you, then! You're weak, all of you. L'Ollonais would have understood what I did, or Brasiliano. There's no room in this world for sentimentality or conscience. Not if you're a pirate. That's going to be your downfall one day, mark my words. You're too soft, Carlomagno. You were never cut out to be a pirate!"

Carlomagno didn't see himself as a pirate, and maybe that was the problem. He hadn't asked for this life, he had been brought here against his will, in chains. But deep inside, Levesque's words stung. To make things right, he had done great evil. Would his good intentions matter in the end?

At the Governor's Mansion that night, Carlomagno drew every eye as he stalked boldly into the lavish meeting hall. His glance swept the room, seeking out Andrew. There was no sign of the servant.

"Glad you could make it, Captain," Governor Modyford smiled as he crossed the room to greet Carlomagno. "I'm afraid my guests would have been quite disappointed had they not had the opportunity to see our newest hero. All day, the talk in Port Royal has been of you, the daring Barracuda of the Spanish Main! With a few more exploits like Panama, it will be called the English Main!"

"May I speak with you a moment, sir, privately?"

"Certainly! We will slip away into the gardens as you slipped away from those Spanish galleons at Nombre de Dios!"

Once they were out of earshot of the other guests, Carlomagno spoke. "Governor, I don't think Macomber's shooting was an accident. I think the Chevalier de Fortenay was involved, at least in the planning."

Mdyford glanced about him and then lowered his voice, "The Chevalier is a powerful man, Carlomagno, and you are making a serious accusation. If you are wrong it could make a lot of trouble for both of us."

"I know, Governor, but, you see, Macomber was not making advances on Lady Pickford. I had asked him to protect her, so she could walk the streets of Port Royal unmolested."

Modyford whistled softly. "I see. So young Pickford misunderstood?"

"I think Macomber was shot to leave the lady unprotected. She has vanished. I have had my men search the city for her and she is gone, leaving no trace."

"First Andrew disappears, now, you tell me, an English gentlewoman? What is happening around here?" Modyford exclaimed. "I wonder if Andrew took her and fled to the Cockpit Country? As I said, I have always wondered if Andrew was mixed up with those Cimaroons. He is very intelligent, and dependable, but there is something about him, something I can't quite put my finger on. Strange that he would vanish now, just when there's been big trouble with the Cimaroons."

"Trouble with the Cimaroons? In Port Royal?"

"Oh, we have Cimaroons in Jamaica, captain, but few venture into Port Royal. When they do, they have little or nothing to do with our local Negroes. But to answer your question, Carlomagno, the trouble was on Hispaniola. In fact, it was in the area around the land you wanted. Near Jacmel, I think. There was a terrible clash with the soldiers and a few dozen were killed on both sides. But, in the end, I understand their leader was captured. A fellow named Koyamin, as I understand it. He's been causing quite a few headaches on Hispaniola. But they have him now."

Macomber, Anna, Koy—so many vows I have been unable to keep, Carlomagno told himself as he made his way back to his ship through an endless river of drunken men. One scruffy-looking rogue in need of a bath bumped him going by. The man muttered a curse, his breath reeking of alcohol. As he was undressing in his cabin Carlomagno found the slip of paper in his pocket. He read it by candlelight: *She is on Tortuga. Come if you dare.*

He crumpled the paper and threw it across the small room. So, it was just as he suspected! Norville had made his move; he had kidnapped Lady Pickford and was holding her prisoner on Tortuga. But what of Levasseur? He was no friend of de Fortenay, or had they made some unholy bargain? Jean Levasseur was, after all, a businessman. Had de Fortenay offered him something he could not refuse?

The next day they awoke to find a ship missing. Sometime during the night, Rohan Levesque and his crew had slipped away from Port Royal. The plunder from the other three ships was still considerable. Expecting something of the sort from Levesque, Carlomagno had instructed a few trusted men to lighten the ship of some of its most valuable treasure.

"Diego, didn't you keep your father's affairs in order?"

"I managed his affairs and kept his books," Diego said.

"I want you to do the same for me, Diego. There is something I need to do. You know the property on Hispaniola? I want a house there—a

186

grand house. But I want more. I want you to have full discretion over my money, to invest as you see fit."

"Land, *amigo*, land is the only possession whose value always increases. If you put your trust in me I shall not fail you. But how is it that you will be unavailable to care for your own estates?"

Carlomagno paused. "You mustn't speak of this, Diego, but I think de Fortenay is holding Lady Pickford on Tortuga."

"And you would go there? You must not, *amigo*, not alone."

"It is too dangerous, Diego, and I cannot ask anyone else to be a fool just because I am. Besides, I have a plan."

"I don't like it," the Mandinga protested. "Greevey is good with numbers, let him take care of the books and I will sail with you."

"No, it must be me, alone. You know the Rock Fort and the cannon overlooking Bassa Terra. We could never take the place by storm. But one man might slip in undetected. And don't forget, I can deal with Levasseur. With his help, I can get the best of de Fortenay."

Captain Stephen Anders was a reedy man, tall and thin, with quick eyes that missed nothing. But he was not the most ingenious pirate on the Main. His successes were few and seldom resulted in more than a week's worth of modest drinking. As a result he usually had trouble finding enough crewmen.

"Beggin' your pardon, cap' n?" Carlomagno was dressed in the dirtiest rags he could find and had his hair stuffed beneath a filthy stocking hat. "I was wonderin' if you might need another hand?"

"Go on, you beggar! I don't have time to learn you how to be a sailor," Anders barked.

"Cap'n, I was sent here by Governor Modyford."

Anders took a second look. "The governor, you say? You don't look like someone who would know the governor."

"I've had a rough go of it, but the governor told me you were outfitting for an expedition."

"Well, I'm on my way to Tortuga. From there... well, you'll find that out when the time comes. Alright, then, what's your name, man?"

"Philip King."

Anders jerked a thumb. "Climb aboard, Philip King, you made it just in time. We were preparing to raise anchor."

Anders had never amounted to much as a pirate, had never had a wealthy patron or protector. He was strictly small time in the scope of his raids and their successes, so it came as a sudden surprise to receive notice from Port Royal's governor. Not an overly bright man, Anders wasn't one to waste time trying to figure things out. He had no idea why or how he came to Governor Modyford's attention, but he was pleased. He felt certain all his years of struggling were finally paying off. Things were looking up for Stephen Anders!

Carlomagno kept to himself as much as possible for fear someone might recognize him. He did whatever duty was assigned him, swiftly and efficiently. Otherwise he tried not to catch anyone's eye. But he failed. Gil Blanchette was quartermaster and anyone who did his job properly aboard Captain Anders' ship was bound to catch his eye. Blanchette himself was an able seaman, but a sea battle had left him with a useless left arm. He thought his seafaring career was over, and for a man with few other skills that was a terrifying ordeal. Starving on the streets of Port Royal, he had resorted to begging for food or money. That was before a man the likes of which he had never seen had given him enough money to outfit himself, and more importantly, had restored his self-respect. He might only have one hand, but Gil Blanchette had a brain and years of experience. At first, Blanchette planned to join Carlomagno's crew, but he came upon a chance to be more than an ordinary sailor. Captain Anders, having difficulty finding crew members, took on the one-armed man and quickly found that even with a gimp arm, Blanchette was worth any three men onboard. The ship, never a model of efficiency, suddenly began running smoothly. Sailors did their jobs, if not well, at least often.

"I don't know why you're trying to disguise yourself, but I know you."

Carlomagno had been swabbing the deck. He stopped and looked around, ensuring no one was in earshot. "I have my reasons."

"After what you did on Panama, you could write your own ticket on the Main," Blanchette said, keeping his voice down. "Why here, hiding out on Anders' ship?"

Carlomagno knew once his ruse had been discovered, he had no choice but to put his trust in this one-armed man. He sensed the man was friendly toward him. "Anders is going to Tortuga. It's where I wish to go."

"Oh, of course, I should have guessed that, Carlo...uh, Philip. Of course, you're chasing after that girl, aren't you? Everyone's heard how your woman is held captive on Tortuga."

"I love her." Just speaking those words surprised Carlomagno, but he knew suddenly that they were true. He had never known another woman to live in his thoughts, her voice to linger in his ears, her kiss still whispering on his lips. Since the day he first saw her on the streets of Port Royal he had known there was something different about Lady Annabeth Pickford. "I love her, Blanchette, and I've got to get her away from de Fortenay."

"You'll be alone on Tortuga," Blanchette said. "Not a man will raise a hand to help, you know."

"I am hoping to sneak in unnoticed. If I can reach Levasseur, maybe I can talk to him, win his support."

Blanchette's jaw dropped. "You haven't heard? The news was all over the waterfront the last couple of days. Levasseur is dead. He was killed by the Chevalier de Fortenay."

"What?"

"Pierre Norville is top dog on Tortuga now. After the way he destroyed Levasseur, not a man will dare oppose him."

Carlomagno was shocked. His whole plan had been to slip into Tortuga and make a deal with Levasseur. Now he would be alone against the fearsome Chevalier de Fortenay—and every man on Tortuga!

"Here, now, what's all this talk?" It was Captain Anders. "Get this deck swabbed, King! We work on this ship."

Carlomagno moved off, mopping the deck. Actually it needed a lot more mopping than he could give it. Anders watched him for a few minutes before turning to Blanchette.

"Do you know him, Gil?"

"Just what you told me, cap'n. His name is Philip King, beyond that I know little. I was just asking him, he mentioned that he sailed with Kerbourchard before," Blanchette said. "Kerbourchard stands by his friends."

"What does that mean?" Anders demanded.

Blanchette shrugged. "Only that if he's a friend to Kerbourchard, maybe the Frenchman would remember us if we helped his friend out. Kerbourchard doesn't do anything without there being money in it, good money. He was part of that silver train raid, you know."

"There's money in it for me, Blanchette. You just do as you're told." Anders signaled to several men who suddenly pounced on Carlomagno and quickly subdued him. "You see, Blanchette, Philip King, as he calls himself, is Carlomagno!"

"What?"

"It's true, Blanchette. Modyford tipped me off that he was sending a man to me, a man that I would be paid handsomely for if I delivered him to the Chevalier de Fortenay! I had thought it was the other one below, until I saw Carlomagno. I recognized him right away."

His hands bound behind him, Carlomagno was led down a dark staircase and tossed into an even darker room. It was tiny, with small air vents in the door. The floor was littered with trash. Another bound figure leaned against the far wall.

"Sorry, sir, I thought I could help," said Andrew, his white teeth gleaming in the blackness. "I heard the governor talking with that de Fortenay just before that one left Port Royal."

Carlomagno suddenly remembered the bottle of French wine Modyford had opened in his presence. A gift from de Fortenay!

"The Frenchman paid the governor and promised more when you were dead, sir. He told the governor you cheated him, that you stopped on the way from Panama and buried some of the. When the other ship slipped off in the night, the governor believed this story."

"But how did you get here, Andrew?"

"I slipped away and joined the crew, hoping I could help you somehow once we got to Tortuga. Only this captain, somehow he knows; he threatened to sell me as a slave. I reminded him that I belong to the governor, but he said the governor will think I have run away."

"He thought you went to the Cockpit Country because of all that Cimaroon trouble on Hispaniola."

"Yes, I hear of it, sir. They finally captured Koyamin Otigbu."

"What will happen to him?"

"If they are wise, sir, they will kill him right away. But the Spaniards, they are proud. I think they will take him to Triana."

"Triana?"

"A prison, sir, a very bad place. No one wants to go there—no prisoner has ever come out alive."

As they sat in silence, Carlomagno couldn't afford to think of what trouble his friend, Koyamin, might be in. He was in enough of his own. He would soon be handed over to his worst enemy, the Chevalier de Fortenay! It wasn't the prospect of his own death that bothered him, but the idea that he had failed to rescue Anna. And the realization that he would never again kiss her tender, warm lips. They had spent much time together in Port Royal, but he had treated her with respect. They had held hands, he had brushed her lips with a soft butterfly kiss. But he had not loved her as he yearned to do. And now, when she needed him most, he had failed her. For him, it would mean a painful death. But what would it mean for her? A lifetime of indignity and shame? The thought enraged him and he struggled against his ropes, but there was no give. It was useless.

The Barracuda of the Spanish Main had been caught like a fly in a spider's web.

{ 15 }

Prisoner

Lady Annabeth Pickford sat very still, her eyes roaming over the dingy cabin. That she was a prisoner, she understood. Had there been any doubt, the fact that her cabin door was locked from the outside would have dispelled any misunderstanding. Her father had been a soft-spoken, yet wise man. He had often told her that to sit quietly and organize your thoughts was the first—and maybe most important—step to escape from a dangerous situation. Lord Pickford had carried himself proudly and with dignity; he had been a respected man in London and a frequent visitor to court. He had also known that his son, Connor, was not a man who took his responsibilities seriously. Connor had been too proud of his position, too vain and demanding. Father and son had not gotten along very well. For years, Lord Pickford had his business to occupy his time, but age and infirmities had robbed him of his independence in the latter years of his life.

Weak and unable to walk very far without taking time to rest, he had slowly withdrawn from his circle of friends.

Connor began to assume a larger role in his father's business, but not necessarily with his father's blessing. Too often, the father had no notion of what his son was doing until someone else told him of it. In those final, depressing years, his one consolation had been the attention of his daughter. A man who put stock on continuing his distinguished family name, Lord Pickford had tended to overlook his daughter. Under existing English law, his oldest son would inherit his estate anyway. Now, too late, he discovered that his daughter, named for his own mother, was far brighter than her brother and had a better head for business.

"Ah, pumpkin," he would sigh, "if only you had been the son. Then I could die knowing my affairs would be in good hands."

"Hush, papa," she gently scolded, "let's not speak of such things. You just need some rest and you'll soon be back on your feet."

But she was lying to him, for the doctors predicted that Lord Pickford would not see the New Year. They were right. But before he died, he imparted as much of his knowledge as he could to his daughter.

Now, a prisoner on a strange ship, Lady Pickford recalled his words. Think, Lord Pickford had insisted, for thinking can solve most problems. Annabeth Pickford was schooled in the Elizabethan world of womanhood; she was able to play the dainty lady at court, but also the shrewd businesswoman when the need arose. How many times had she gently gotten her way with Connor without him even realizing it? She had a way of making suggestions seem as if Connor had come up with the idea himself. She knew their family fortune had dropped dangerously low, though they would have no doubt been bankrupt had it not been for her. She loved her brother and wished him no harm. The idea of an arranged marriage had nearly caused an estrangement between them, until she realized how deeply he had gotten himself into trouble. Connor Pickford had not inherited his father's title, nor his acumen, and had lost large wagers to the wrong set; they could crush him on any day they chose. At best, Connor could hope for debtor's prison, but he might well be faced with the gallows if his enemies so chose.

In an effort to save her brother, Lady Pickford had agreed at last to accompany him to Port Royal and—if she found a man that interested her—she might consider marriage. But Connor was weak and the men he suggested to her were of no consequence; a handful of them were simply much too old for her, or too much like her brother. She was interested in none of them. Connor introduced her to mindless fops or spineless ne'er-do-wells. It wasn't that Annabeth Pickford was difficult to please, or too full of herself. She was, in fact, quite the opposite. Her beauty was classic, her eyes a penetrating green and her hair a magnificent red that attracted the attention of any man who saw her. Her figure was slightly plump, yet not unappealing. On occasion, the top of her bodice hinted at an ample bosom. She was a beauty, yet seemed unaware of it. Had she been told she was beautiful, she would have laughed it off, certain she was being toyed with.

She had a natural charm that attracted people to her. She was likeable. And she liked others. She was genuinely kindhearted, and not only to those who could do something for her. It was never second nature for Lady Pickford, or an afterthought. Her thoughtfulness toward other people was just a part of her, as was her winsome smile and robust sense of humor.

"I don't know what love looks like," Anna had confided to a childhood friend in her younger years, "but I shall know it when I see it."

She saw it that day on the streets of Port Royal, when the handsome, rakish buccaneer had gallantly defended her brother. The argument had begun innocently enough, as had many every day in Port Royal, the wickedest city on earth. The man, she had heard him called the Chevalier de Fortenay, had made a ribald remark at her expense.

"How ungallant of you, sir," she had replied, intending to continue on her way.

"Everyone in Port Royal knows you are for sale," de Fortenay sneered. "Your brother is offering you to the highest bidder. I only want a taste of what I might expect. After all, if a man buys a whore he has the right to expect quality for his money."

Connor, who had been standing dumbfounded, suddenly found his voice. He had never been involved in a personal duel before, but as an English gentleman he had taken fencing lessons. He demanded de Fortenay apologize to his sister at once. And Chevalier de Fortenay laughed in his face. Connor was taken aback. Always he had taken himself as a serious man, a man to be reckoned with. Now he realized he was far away from the streets of London, where his father's name might yet carry enough weight to extract him from the difficulty. He understood then that he was alone. He realized that other men had stopped to watch, expecting to see someone die. People were killed every day in Port Royal, where knifings and shootings were common, and the unusual news was when someone died of natural causes. Only now did Connor Pickford realize that they were all watching, expecting him to be the one to die. His knees grew weak with fear. He realized suddenly that he, Connor Pickford, was facing a challenge from the man considered among the greatest swordsmen of the Caribbean! In that instant, he knew he was going to die. Annabeth knew it, too, and her hand was already dipping into her purse for the dagger she always carried. If necessary, she was going to kill de Fortenay.

And then he stepped in. Her eye focused on her brother and the Chevalier, Lady Pickford—like everyone else on the street—was stunned when Carlomagno stepped in front of her brother and faced de Fortenay. He stood in contrast to Connor Pickford, who had so obviously lost his nerve and was a helpless pigeon waiting to be plucked. But this stranger, this strong, bold stranger confronted de Fortenay, giving as good as he got! He was bold, yet there was a certain self-assurance about him. Had someone mentioned his name at that moment, it would have meant nothing to her. English gentlewomen did not associate with bloodthirsty pirates! Only this man, looking so different—elegant, yet with a trace of savagery in his manner—had faced down de Fortenay and saved her brother's life!

Angry at being shown up for the coward he now knew he was, Connor had snapped at his benefactor and offered not one word of thanks. Lady Pickford had sent an invitation to this stranger. He had asked about him and found out he was new to the Main and already making a name for himself. He was Carlomagno; some called him the Barracuda of the Spanish Main.

"I will not offer any thanks to such a man," Connor insisted. "He's a killer, no better than de Fortenay. I will not meet him, and I forbid you to do so!"

"In case you do not realize it, Connor, you would be dead now, had it not been for Carlomagno."

"You are so quick to give him credit, and belittle my own chances. Perhaps, sister, I could have killed de Fortenay. Have you thought of that? No, I doubt it. Well, no matter, this man you speak of is a pirate. I have asked of him and he is a pirate, the same as de Fortenay. You will have nothing to do with him, Anna. With papa gone, I am the man of the family and I will decide who is fit company for you. And that man certainly is not. Carlomagno is a killer and a thief, and who knows what else!"

Annabeth Pickford already knew she would ignore her brother's edict and meet with Carlomagno. First, it was a matter of honor. He had saved her brother's life and had not been properly thanked. He deserved that, at least. But there was another reason, a personal reason. He aroused something deep within her. His powerful shoulders, soulful eyes and almost reckless disregard for danger spoke to the poetry of her soul and whispered lines without rhyme or reason across her heart. She had but glanced at him, their eyes sharing one brief introduction, and suddenly she remembered what she had told her childhood friend.

She had seen the face of love.

Annabeth Pickford was no blushing girl to be taken in by some dashing cad full of empty promises and sweet nothings, nor was she so foolish as to think she could take a handsome rogue and mold him into something he was not. She knew he was a pirate. That he robbed was a matter of fact; that he had killed was equally probable. Yet she was certain there was something more to him than that, some deeper ambition. Carlomagno was a violent man living in a violent world, and she accepted that. But she knew he was more than a mere savage. There was in him a gentleness of spirit, a lost boy quality. He was an American Indian caught in a world strange to him. And yet he was not one to whine of his misfortune— or to meekly accept it. He had confided in her how he had walked away from slavery, determined to be a free man.

But it would do her no good to think of him now, for he was miles away and completely unaware of her plight. She was a prisoner on a Spanish ship and on her way to Cuba. She knew that from the bits of dialogue she had overheard. She was the prisoner of Pablo de Jesus, the Duc de Castile. She had been kidnapped by the Chevalier de Fortenay and handed over to the Spanish duke as if she were common chattel. Now she sat alone in a small room aboard the schooner and looked for something, anything, which might aid in her escape. Carlomagno did not know where she was, nor did her brother, Connor. Ironically, he was responsible for her current predicament. De Fortenay had used her brother's greed and hatred of Carlomagno against him.

What was she thinking? The room, sparsely-furnished as it was, was full of weapons. The chair could be used to hit a man over the head. But could she lift it? She could always break one of the legs off now and have it handy as a club. But what then? Even if she knocked out the next person who came into the room, how could she escape the ship? If she ran up on deck she would just be recaptured. If she hid below, they would search for her, and there were only so many places she could hide. The schooner might very well have smaller boats aboard

198

for emergency use, but she would not know how to lower one. It was also unlikely she'd have enough time for that anyway. She could run up on deck and throw herself overboard. But that would only mean death.

Anna did not want to die. Like her Carlomagno—it made her blush to suddenly realize that she did, indeed, think of him as hers!—she wanted to live, she wanted to be free. And she wanted to defeat her enemies.

{ 16 }

Barracuda of The Spanish Main

The Europeans often failed to understand the American Indian. It was not just that the native people worshipped different gods, had different customs and thought of different things as important, it was their general outlook on life. The Indian was poor by European standards, for he had little that he did not make himself from animal hides, bones or sinew, or the very rocks of the earth and the shells of the sea. Some, like the Inca, may have made ornaments of gold, but most Indians put no value in such material things. An Indian was looked upon as wealthy if he possessed courage in times of danger, wisdom in times of doubt and generosity during the lean times. The Englishman who owned fifty horses was considered richer than his neighbor who had only thirty horses. But the Indian who was looked upon with the highest esteem was the one who gave his horses to his neighbors in need, who gave the choicest part of any game he killed to the widowed women who had lost their men and to the children who had no fathers.

Consequently, the European and the Indian experienced life in fundamentally different ways. The European would write with outrage in their journals of Indian guests who ate them out of house and home. Yet the Europeans did not mention that when the situation was reversed, the visitor to an Indian village could eat as much as he wanted. The reasoning was simple enough. Indians had to trap or stalk their food, so it was never a certainty that there would be a meal at the end of the day. So Indians would gorge themselves when food was present, and stoically go without when times were harsh.

The man known across the Spanish Main as Carlomagno was still an Indian. He had never forgotten who he was or where he came from. He was Pokanoket, the son of Metacomet. He was rightful sachem of the Wampanoag.

He was a prisoner now, but his time would come, he knew. When it did, his one goal was to take as many of his enemies with him to the next life as he could. It did not worry him, he accepted it. Besides, only fools fear the next life, for that is the world where loved ones wait, where game is plentiful and where laughter and happiness never ends. In the next life, the gods take care of their Indian children. Carlomagno was ready to see his father again, and his grandfather, Massasoit. For all he knew, his mother was in the next life waiting for him, and his sisters, too.

Because he could accept his fate calmly, it perplexed his European captors to find him sleeping soundly. With rough hands they yanked him to his feet.

"Look at him sleep," one chortled. "He's too stupid to even be afraid!"

"I knew it was just luck, the way he stumbled across that Spanish silver train," another added. "All that talk about him being so smart was just a bunch of malarkey."

The harbor of Bassa Terre looked the same; a handful of ships lay at rest, and the threatening cannon stared down from the top of the hundred-foot rock face. A path, littered with overgrown vines and unrelenting mangroves, rose steadily upwards toward the top of Tortuga.

His hands tied behind his back, Carlomagno struggled through the climb, but none sought to make it any easier for him. His captors were a motley crew of cowards and ne'er-do-wells. Men such as these reveled in the suffering of men greater than themselves.

Captain Stephen Anders was small-minded and petty. He liked living in the shadow of powerful men; he believed de Fortenay to be such a man. Partway up the steep path, the small party was met by Tulane, de Fortenay's aide, with a dozen armed men.

"We'll take him from here, Captain Anders," Tulane said. He smiled at Carlomagno with half-rotted teeth. "So, the famous Barracuda has lost his bite?"

"Loosen my hands, Tulane, and we shall see."

Tulane laughed as he gave Carlomagno a vicious shove. "I'll have my fun, if there's anything left when the Chevalier is finished with you."

"You'd better hope there is nothing left of me, Tulane, for I have you marked for death."

"Get moving, you're in no position to make any threats." Tulane's tone was harsh, but he kept his distance from Carlomagno. He assured himself there was nothing to fear: de Fortenay would see to that.

They trudged past the garden path, the deep well of cool, fresh water and the first few shanties that marked the beginning of Tortuga's "city." Carlomagno walked with his head up, his eyes looking at nothing— yet missing nothing. He saw no familiar faces, no men of whom he might expect any aid. Tortuga had always been a rough place, where violence ruled the day. It was even more so now, with the Chevalier de Fortenay firmly in charge.

He had friends, he knew, but none here now that he could identify. And, even if he had, they would be completely outnumbered. De Fortenay's reputation had attracted every bloodstained villain on the

Main. Carlomagno saw men he knew only by descriptions given when their savage exploits were recounted. As he walked forward, to where de Fortenay waited silently, he saw men who had brazenly committed every manner of heinous crime known to man.

"Welcome to Tortuga," de Fortenay smiled, giving a mock bow to Carlomagno. "Now, you see that you are no match for the Chevalier de Fortenay. From the moment you landed in Port Royal I had your fate in my hands."

"You bought Modyford?"

"Of course," de Fortenay grinned. "It was a wise investment; here on the Main, all things can be bought. Affairs in London have changed and the protection Modyford once enjoyed is waning. He needs new friends and was quite willing to make a deal with me. You thought he was your friend, maybe? Bah! You were just another pirate to him."

"Let me loose, de Fortenay, and let us settle this like warriors."

"It is I who will make the rules now, Carlomagno, for I am the headman on Tortuga. I will let you worry a bit before I kill you."

A wooden pole had been erected in the center of town and Carlomagno was pushed toward it, his arms twisted behind and lashed tightly, his back against the pole.

"Where is she, de Fortenay? Do you make war on women now?"

"You hurt me, Carlomagno," the chevalier said with mock sincerity. "The way I hear it, it is you who makes war on women. I have heard of Vente de Cruces."

"That was your friend, Levesque. I had nothing to do with that."

"But, of course you wouldn't do such a thing! You are a barracuda, no? You are too gallant, eh? So brave!" de Fortenay was enjoying his victory. "Maybe I shall use you for target practice? I think I can nick your ears at twenty-five paces. Anyone want to bet?"

"Do as you will with me, Norville, but let Lady Pickford go."

"Ah yes, Lady Pickford? Is she the reason you have come to my fine island? I am so sorry to disappoint you, *monsieur*, but you see Lady Pickford is not here."

"You lie!"

"I do many things, my friend, but lying is not one of them. No, Lady Pickford was never on Tortuga. I let you believe that to get you here," de Fortenay boasted. "Tulane, I want a guard posted at all times. No one is permitted near the prisoner without my permission."

"He is too dangerous, mon Chevalier, maybe we should kill him now?" Tulane suggested, in a pleading voice.

"You worry too much, Tulane. He cannot escape Tortuga and not a man here would dare to aid him. I shall enjoy this time, savor the taste of my victory. After I kill Carlomagno, not a man on the Spanish Main will stand against me! Henri Morgan is dead now and soon this mangy dog will join him. And then, the Chevalier de Fortenay will be king of the Caribbean!"

"Where is she, de Fortenay? If she's not in Tortuga, where is she?"

Deliberately, de Fortenay turned his back and walked away. The day grew hotter and Carlomagno remained bound in place with his defiant eyes scanning the town for any sign of help. In some of the faces he saw undisguised hatred, others tinged with malice for no particular reason. In a few he saw a glimpse of melancholy, but these looked quickly away, unable or unwilling to defy the Chevalier de Fortenay. Guards came to stand near him, to keep away any that might offer aid—even something as simple as a sip of water.

"He gets nothing, by order of de Fortenay!" one guard bellowed when a sailor would have offered a cool drink. "Now, move on!"

The ropes that held him were tight, and every now and then one of those guarding him would check to make certain nothing had changed. Carlomagno had long since ceased to struggle against his bonds, there was no point. Late in the afternoon a band of sailors made their way up the steep slope from the harbor, carrying a bundle among them. They dropped it at Carlomagno's feet. It was Andrew. He had been beaten senseless, his face battered and bruised, lacerations all about his head and face. But he had groaned when they dumped him on the ground, so he was still alive.

Barely.

"This is what you can expect," one of them said without warning he delivered a sharp punch to Carlomagno's stomach. The Indian gave a grunt of pain, but refused to cry out. "Think you're a tough guy, eh? De Fortenay will knock some of that out of you."

"Why don't you turn me loose and try to knock it out of me yourself?" Carlomagno challenged.

"Oh, you think I'm afraid?" The man pulled out his knife and pressed it to Carlomagno's throat. "Maybe I'll slit your gullet for you right now."

"I wouldn't." said Captain Rohan Levesque, flanked by a dozen of his seasoned crewmen. "The chevalier would kill you, Mac, if you took away his pleasure in watching Carlomagno beg for his life. And if he didn't, I would!"

Mac backed away, sheathing his blade. "I was just teasing, Levesque, I wouldn't have killed him."

Levesque stopped in front of Carlomagno. "My, how the mighty have fallen! Last time we met you were king of the world. Now, look at you. Ha! I knew you were nothing, I told them that."

"You have come to gloat, Levesque?"

"Oh, you bet. As soon as I heard how de Fortenay had set up this trap for you, I turned my ship around and headed here. I was in Tiburon when I heard the news," Levesque said. "I couldn't get here fast enough. If you are hoping for any help from your friends, don't bother. Kerbourchard has gone off to Villahermosa and I've heard that Macomber is still recovering from that gunshot wound. You're on your own, Carlomagno."

"You saw how easily I captured the silver train, Levesque. There's more where that came from. I have a plan to sack Panama itself. Help me, Levesque, and I'll let you in on it."

"Ah, so, first you threaten to kill me, now you want my help—and you'll make me rich, too?" Levesque shook his head. "I still have most of the treasure I took from the silver train, and even what little they had in Vente de Cruces."

"You will not have it long, Levesque. Believe me, even now de Fortenay is plotting a way to get it away from you."

"I know how to handle men like de Fortenay," Levesque smiled. "Never turn your back on him."

The day dragged by, the humidity nearly suffocating. Carlomagno sagged against the ropes, his throat parched. As night fell it became clear that de Fortenay was in no hurry to dispose of him. The chevalier was enjoying himself, occasionally taunting his prisoner by standing before him carelessly sipping ale and pouring half of his cup out on the ground at Carlomagno's feet.

"I wish we had enough to spare you a drink," he would chortle. "But there is no sense in giving a cool drink to a dead man, eh?"

The purple sky crept across the Caribbean and the pirates went about their carousing, paying scant attention to the helpless prisoner.

Myles Macomber was a man who had studied war and often he had shared his thoughts with Carlomagno. Now, bound without hope of escape, the Wampanoag kept his mind active by letting his thoughts recall things Macomber had taught him. He tried to remember everything Macomber had said of distant, ancient lands, such as Babylon, Macedonia and Cathay. The grizzled old gunner had also explained the tactics used by history's great generals, men like Alexander the Great, Richard the Lionhearted and Sir Francis Drake.

"Never give up, there's always a way to win," Macomber had insisted. To illustrate his point he told of how the Mongols, under the fearsome Kublai Khan, started out to invade Japan. "The Japanese were desperate; sure they could not beat back the Mongol horde. Then, when all looked lost, a great storm suddenly blew up and wrecked the Mongol ships, drowning thousands of men. Japan was saved, even when it had looked hopeless only minutes before!"

It looked hopeless for Carlomagno now, but at least the blazing heat was gone. The night air was humid, but a welcome contrast to the broiling sunlight. Carlomagno tried to keep his mind alert for the slightest chance to escape. Still bound, Andrew, badly beaten and barely conscious, lay at his feet. He groaned in pain.

"I'm sorry, my friend." There was no answer.

The guard who watched him now was particularly cruel, taunting Carlomagno by deliberating eating and drinking in front of him. He also went out of his way to give the Indian a sharp kick in the shins, or a sudden poke in the ribs. He came closer again, checking the ropes.

"Release me and I shall let you live."

The guard grunted, giving Carlomagno a jarring slap in the face. "You just don't get it, do you? You're a dead man. Maybe tomorrow, or the day after. Whenever de Fortenay decides he's had enough fun with you."

The guard went back to his fire; he sat staring into it. Carlomagno watched him with contempt. Even when he was still a boy among his own people, he knew better. A man staring into a fire ruins his eyes if he must look suddenly into the darkness. The moment it took for his eyes to readjust could make all the difference.

What a fool!

Andrew's eyes were open. He wiggled himself closer to Carlomagno, using his chin he seemed to be trying to communicate something. And then Carlomagno saw it. The tip of a knife barely sticking out from Andrew's pants leg!

Here it was, his one chance. Slowly, Carlomagno began to lower himself down the length of the pole. They had bound his hands to the pole, but had neglected to secure his feet. Attracting any attention would mean an end to this slim hope. But the guard, lost in his own thoughts, stared into the fire, the flickering flames taking him back to some pleasant memory. Andrew inched closer as Carlomagno came to a sitting position. Now his fingers stretched out as Andrew wiggled ever closer. His fingers found the knife. Working diligently, he sawed at the ropes, holding the knife blade in his fingers. He knew he was slicing into his own fingers every once in a while, but that was little enough price to pay. The ropes came apart and Carlomagno was on his feet in one fluid motion.

He moved soundlessly across the space between him and the guard. The guard looked up at the last minute. Carlomagno saw the frightened look on his face even as the blade was plunged into his throat. The man's lifeless body fell beside his fire. Carlomagno grabbed the guard's pistol and sword, hastily cut Andrew loose, and gave him his knife back.

"Can you make it?" Carlomagno whispered, helping the injured man to his feet.

"I can try," Andrew replied. "What shall we do?"

There was the slightest whisper of sound and Carlomagno whirled, raising the pistol. He stared at Gil Blanchette, the one-armed seaman who had spoken to him aboard Captain Anders' ship.

"Come this way, we must hurry," Blanchette hissed at them. "I've got some men for a crew, but they're antsy—afraid of de Fortenay."

Supporting Andrew between them, Carlomagno and Blanchette started for the path that led down to the harbor. They moved slowly, hindered both by the dark and Andrew's injuries.

"Leave me," Andrew gasped, as they stopped to rest. "You can make it without me."

"We go together," Carlomagno said. "Thanks, Blanchette. I don't know what will happen when we reach the harbor, but thanks for the chance."

"We have a ship --Levesque's." Carlomagno was surprised. "Some of his crew were angry about the way he slipped off from Port Royal. They wanted to stick with you, said your raid of the silver train was the easiest money they ever made. I talked it up with a man here and there and now we've got Levesque's ship. And the plunder he stole from you is still in the hold."

A drunken laugh pierced the air as three sailors wobbled up the path on their way to the town. Their laughter died abruptly as they saw the escaped prisoners.

Carlomagno yanked his pistol from his belt and shot the closest man in the chest. Then, with his sword, he darted in, ramming the blade into the second man's stomach. The third man was downed by Blanchette's pistol shot. There was a shout from the village as the three men made a desperate dash toward the harbor. They reached Bassa Terre and clambered aboard Levesque's ship.

"It's no good," Carlomagno said, pointing toward the top of the rock wall. "De Fortenay has already reached the cannon! He's going to blow us out of the water!"

"You're forgetting I know a little something about gunnery, Captain," Blanchette grinned. "I led some of the men up there and we spiked those guns."

Carlomagno watched as they slipped out of the harbor and the island of Tortuga faded behind them. He was free, but he still had no idea where Anna was. Could de Fortenay have been telling the truth about her not being on Tortuga?

"De Fortenay told the governor the lady accepted the invitation of a Spanish gentleman, that he himself saw her safely to 'the duke's' ship," Andrew said.

"The Duc de Castile! It has to be him. But where would he take her?"

"It could be anywhere, Captain," Blanchette said. "The duke is a powerful man and has contacts throughout the Main."

"I'll find him," Carlomagno replied. But first he would take Levesque's ship to Hispaniola, where the Mandinga was building up his plantation. There would be men there, supplies and weapons. From there, he would plan his next move. To Port Royal to deal with the

double-crossing Governor Modyford? Back to Tortuga to take the measure of the Chevalier de Fortenay?

"What did Levesque name his ship?" Carlomagno suddenly asked.

"He named it *El Tigre*—the tiger," a passing crewman replied. "He says the tiger is the real king of the jungle!"

"He may be right, but in the sea I would take the Barracuda over the tiger every time!" Carlomagno laughed. "Anyway, as of now she is to be the Anasarani."

But would he ever see his Anasarani, his Anna, again?

{ 17 }

Lady Pickford

The keys rattled in the door and the black woman stepped in carrying a wooden bowl of unappetizing mush. Her head was held high and there was a fierce fire in her coal-black eyes. She held a cloth-wrapped bundle under her arm that revealed a hunk of bread and a generous slice of cheese. This same woman always brought Anna her meals. There was always a sailor standing outside the door, but as Anna's eyes strayed past the woman, she saw the narrow hallway was empty. When she looked back, the cold black eyes were studying her, as if taking her measure.

"You might get past me, but what then, missy? We at sea, in the middle of no place," the dark woman said, setting the food on a small table. "You got no place to go, not no place at all."

"I need to escape, to get back to Port Royal. I can pay."

"On the Main, money can get you most anything. But not from me, missy. I don't need nothin' you got." The black woman made no move to leave. "'Sides, I gots my own problems."

Lady Pickford sat on the floor and picked up her spoon. In spite of how it looked, the food's had an appealing aroma. "What's in it?"

"Little of this, little of that, I'd imagine, missy." Usually the woman just set the food down and left; now she lingered.

"My name is Annabeth. I am Lady Annabeth Pickford."

"I am Amina. I do not know if I am a lady," she replied proudly, "but I am a woman!"

"Won't you join me, Amina?" Anna gestured as if she were inviting a guest to be seated in her drawing room. "There is enough food here for us both."

"You're just trying to make a friend," Amina replied, but she did sit down. "They don't feed me so much, but they figure the duke wants you kept well."

Annabeth broke the bread in half and offered a hunk to Amina. The black woman ate it gratefully.

"Where are we going, Amina?"

"I guess they'll be taking you to Cuba. The duke has a large planta-tion near Puerto Principe," she replied after a pause. She accepted some of the cheese. "But I think they're heading for Maracaibo first. They must be picking up supplies. He owns another large plantation there, and has storehouses full of pearls and silver. Or so it is said."

Annabeth leaned closer. "When we get to Cuba, I will need your help."

"I will not be going there with you," Amina replied. "I go only to Maracaibo."

"What then?"

"Then I escape and find some way to save my husband."

"Your husband is in Maracaibo?"

Amina stood up. "They take him to Triana. I will find a way to free him."

"Triana? That's the inescapable prison."

"I will find a way to free my husband."

"Maybe I can escape with you? I must get away before we reach Cuba! There, the duke will have allies and resources and my... the man I love would come there to rescue me and I fear for his life."

"You better forget your man, missy. Once you get to his lands in Santa Maria you will belong to the Duc de Castile. He is a man of great wealth and power in the Caribbean and your man would be no match for him. Not even Morgan dared lay hands on any of the Duke's possessions. Forget your man, missy, and make the best life you can with the duke. No man would be foolish enough to come to Cuba to rescue you."

"You say that to me? You, who would risk death in Maracaibo to save her man, you would tell me to forget mine?"

"You must be realistic," Amina replied after an awkward silence. She picked up the dishes from the table. "You believe in a fantasy if you think your man would dare to confront Don Pablo."

"If you knew Carlomagno ..."

Amina had been at the door, now she spun around. "What did you say? What name did you speak?"

"Carlomagno."

"Carlomagno? The red Indian?" Amina had to steady herself. "It has been many years since I heard that name spoken. Carlomagno, the red Indian from the American Colonies?"

"You have heard of him?"

"I know him," Amina said. Briefly she explained how she had grown up with him on the mountains of Hispaniola, along with her husband, Koyamin. "He and my husband have sworn a brother-friend oath. If he only knew Koyamin was in Triana, he'd come to rescue him."

"Amina, help me to escape when we reach Maracaibo. We'll find some way to get word to Carlomagno."

Amina said nothing. She slipped out the door, locking it behind her.

Anna had always been a good listener and quite capable of reading between the lines. She understood her situation quite well. Governor Modyford was in trouble in Port Royal. There were rumors that he was to be recalled. Sir Henry Morgan's death had begun the process, but Modyford's court protector, the old Duke of Albermarle, had passed away, leaving the governor with no powerful friend in a position to help him. Fearing recall by William of Orange, Modyford was looking to form alliances on the Main. It had been his hope to strike a bargain with the Chevalier de Fortenay. Modyford hoped to get some of de Fortenay's loot and forward it to London to save his own neck. That was why Modyford had agreed to let de Fortenay set his trap for Carlomagno. But Modyford had no way of knowing how ruthless de Fortenay could be.

The French corsair, too, knew of Modyford's shaky position and had no interest in allying himself with someone who could offer so little in return. The man to deal with, as de Fortenay saw it, was the Duc de Castile. He controlled the most men and ships in the Caribbean. Befriending the Spanish duke—and renewing his association with du Casse in SaintDominique—would put de Fortenay in an enviable position. He would have powerful friends strategically located throughout the Main. Taking control of Tortuga was only a first step in his plan. That he managed to do by backing Levasseur into a corner where he was forced into a fight to save face in front of his men. And Levasseur may have been a nasty sort of man, but with a blade he was no match for the skilled chevalier.

De Fortenay had toyed with Levasseur before disposing of him with ease. Now, he was finally in a position to claim his rightful place in the lore of the Spanish Main! He had given Lady Pickford to the duke and assured him that by holding her Carlomagno would walk right into his hands. He neglected to tell the duke that he, de Fortenay, planned to kill Carlomagno himself.

Only now Carlomagno was on the loose and more dangerous than ever.

"What are we going to do?" Rohan Levesque asked. He had been worried sick ever since the Indian had escaped. He had made his boast and now he might have to back it up! "What if he gathers up his men and returns?"

"Bah! He won't be that foolish, Rohan. He'll know the cannon will be repaired and ready by then," de Fortenay said. "We are vulnerable only as long as we sit and wait. That way, he can choose his own time and place. No, we must strike at him. It is him or us now, Rohan. He must be destroyed, or eventually he will track us down."

"What are you planning?"

"I cannot leave Tortuga now, so you must do this thing, Rohan. Go to Port Royal and find Macomber. Our barracuda will go to his friend and that will be his undoing!"

Rohan Levesque nodded. The plan made sense; he'd bring enough men with him to make sure the job was finished. They'd bring muskets and shoot Carlomagno down before he even knew what hit him.

Only Macomber wasn't in Port Royal.

Hobbling around on crude, wooden crutches, the crusty, old sailor tried to make himself useful as the main house was being built on the Hispaniola land owned by Lady Pickford. He had seen a lot during his forty years at sea, but nothing to equal the beautiful workmanship he was witnessing now. The craftsmen hired by Diego El Negro were understandably proud of their skills.

"It's coming along nicely."

Macomber turned slightly and saw Diego walking toward him. Macomber had always thought of himself as a fighting man, ready for anything. It rankled him how easily Tulane had distracted him before Connor Pickford shot him. He never thought the young man would have had the nerve. He also knew that Diego, also called the Mandinga, had learned of Modyford's double-cross of Carlomagno.

The Mandinga had wasted no time in gathering the crews together and departing from Port Royal. If Modyford had turned against Carlomagno, Diego reasoned, he might move against those loyal to the Indian. It would be the most logical thing for Modyford to do, and Diego was a practical man. Once decided, the Mandinga wasted no move. He left Greevey and Labrosse to ready their ships and warned the crew to go armed at all times—and to beware any strangers trying to board.

With Morgan Flynn and a half dozen others in tow, he went to retrieve Macomber, who was still recuperating at a downtown boardinghouse. Days before Diego learned of Modyford's treachery, Persifal Kerbourchard and his crew had accepted their split of the treasure and sailed off to the southwest, perhaps for Villahermosa or Old Providence.

Kerbourchard would find a place to hole up and spend his pieces of eight. He'd remain in port as long as his funds held out, that had always been his way.

"I can't believe how quickly they work, or how nice it looks," Macomber replied.

"I borrowed the design from my father's plantation. He liked the colonnades. I think Carlomagno is a man of similar tastes. We will build the house in a square, leaving an open area in the middle. I think he would like an atrium, an area where he can feel like he is back among nature," Diego said. "Carlomagno is unlike any man I have ever met. There is something about him that makes you want to do your best for him. I suppose, it's that he trusts me. I haven't felt that since my own father died. I don't want to let Carlomagno down."

"You won't, Diego. You seem to think of everything. Carlomagno's people live a very different life. Sometimes it seems amazing how quickly he has adjusted to life on the Main," Macomber said. "Now what is it he wants to call this place? I heard he picked a name out."

"*Sequanakeeswush*. He tells me it's a Wampanoag word for the celebration of their corn-planting time. He's planting a new life here."

"Thanks to you, Diego."

"The credit is his, Macomber. He told me to come here and to start building. He also knew those slaves possess wonderful skills not shown simply because they are slaves and kept at doing menial tasks. Among them, he said, would be builders, craftsmen and thinkers. It was Carlomagno who suggested buying slaves as I saw fit, then freeing them. It's his plan to create his own little world here on Hispaniola, something like what he left behind when he was sold here as a child."

"He's thinking ahead," Macomber nodded appreciatively. "By setting his slaves free, he gives 'em a stake in all that's being built."

"When the main house is completed, we will split the carpenters and shipwrights into groups. Carlomagno wants another ship. He wants to begin trading."

"From pirate to legitimate trader," Macomber mused. "Well, why not? It's been done before. That's what any of them were, if you look at it. Columbus, Cortes, Drake, they all came to someplace new and took what they wanted by force. Then returned home as traders or merchants."

"I hope Andrew is safe."

Macomber nodded. "He'll make out, Diego. He's a tough one, I'd say."

Andrew had returned to Port Royal, to reclaim his former position as a servant to Governor Modyford. Still sporting the bruises from his severe beating on Tortuga, he had rehearsed his story about how he had been grabbed and forced to serve on a pirate ship. It wouldn't have been the first time a pirate vessel gathered crewmembers in such a fashion. But Andrew, who knew of Modyford's dirty dealing, now returned as a spy for Carlomagno.

"Still, first chance I get I think I'll wander over to Jacmel and try and catch a ship for Port Royal," Macomber said. "I'll make sure Andrew is well, and I want to talk to that Pickford."

"Don't harm him, Macomber. Remember he is still the brother of the Anasarani," Diego said. "Carlomagno would not wish any harm to come to him."

Miles away, with the soft Caribbean winds caressing his cheeks, Carlomagno stood forward on the Anasarani as his ship rolled easily through the emerald waters. Beside him, smiling broadly, was the affable giant, Morgan Flynn. He had never been bested in a fight, never stepped aside for any man until he met Carlomagno. Flynn felt an obsessive devotion to the Indian; without him, Flynn was like an overgrown puppy. But with Carlomagno he became the deadly fighting machine that others feared. Not even Flynn could have explained why he felt as he did about Carlomagno, but he would do anything the Indian asked.

"Macomber was fit to be tied," said acting quartermaster Gil Blanchette. "He wanted to come along with us."

"He needed the time to heal, Gil. Besides, this could get rough before it's over. You sure you can handle it?"

"I'm game for anything," Blanchette said. "I might only have one arm, captain, but I have just as much heart as any man alive."

"I'm up for a fight anyhow," Flynn added. "Where are we heading?"

"Maracaibo."

Flynn and Blanchette exchanged shocked glances, but it was the quartermaster who spoke. "Did I hear that right, captain?"

"You did, Gil. Maracaibo, the pearling capital of the Spanish Main."

Carlomagno stood firm upon the deck of the rolling ship. His body was lithe, agile, and deceptively strong. His black hair had grown and he often wore it in two long braids on the sides and loose in the back. He had his sword of Toledo steel on his waist and the knife first given

him by Kerbourchard in that cave long ago. Tucked into his belt was a
hatchet, a fearsome weapon in close combat. He still wore the twin
brass pistols. The pistols, as were his sword and knife, had been left
behind with Diego when he attempted to join Captain Anders' crew.
He seldom wore the plumed hat now, preferring to wear a headband he
had acquired during a brief stop on Cape Tiburon. Usually he went
shirtless, even finding the time to make himself fringed knee-high
moccasins and a leather breechcloth. Ironically, he looked more like a
savage warrior than ever, and yet his bearing was regal, like his namesake, the great conqueror, Charlemagne.

His English captors had mocked the son of the Indian "King" him
by naming him after a medieval emperor. The original Charlemagne,
king of the Franks and conqueror of Saxony, founded the Holy Roman
Empire—though it took nearly twenty campaigns to accomplish. Charlemagne forced Christianity on the people he conquered, and put to
death any who refused or later repudiated the faith.

It was irony at its height that an American Indian—the Wampanoags believed in many gods—would carry the name of a staunch defender of monolithic theology. Yet it was not so unusual, for the
Puritans who came to New England had introduced their faith to what
they saw as a pagan people. And there were those among the Wampanoags who began to believe in Christianity. These religious conver-
sions had further divided Carlomagno's people. But Carlomagno did
not spend a lot of time worrying over philosophy or arguing religion,
he was primarily a man of action. He did not waste thought on whether
he was a good man or a bad man. How were such things measured anyway? He was a man. He did what he needed to do. He would beg for
mercy from no man, nor offer any.

He realized that half the battle could be won before a shot was fired
if he could get into his opponent's head. Carlomagno knew what Europeans thought of the American Indian and played up that ruthless savage image. Now, before an attack, he would wear a feather in his hair

and paint streaks of red, black and yellow across his face. At first sight of him many foes froze for that crucial second that allowed Carlomagno to strike first.

It was Macomber who had told him that in nine out of ten fights the winner is the one who strikes first.

"Never let an enemy get set for you," Myles Macomber was fond of saying. "Hit him first and keep on hitting until he gives way."

It was the white man's way to hoard wealth, but it was a way Carlomagno had to learn. It was money—and only that—which could buy him peace and freedom on Hispaniola. He had been double-crossed by Modyford, but money was at the root of that, too.

The Port Royal governor had simply made a business decision, believing he would make more in the long run by throwing in with the Chevalier de Fortenay. It was not personal, Carlomagno understood. He knew it was a reality of this world in which he found himself. He had a model to imitate.

Sir Henry Morgan had been as notorious a pirate as one could be, then became a privateer. The distinction was slight, but important. A pirate was the enemy of all nations, safe from none. A privateer acted with the unofficial blessing of some government, which in turn received a percentage of any plunder taken from enemy nations. Morgan had acted wisely and invested much of his loot. He owned land, lots of it. In the end, the pirate had become something of a national hero in London; even the king delighted in hearing his seafaring tales. By the time of his death, Sir Henry Morgan had been appointed a lieutenant governor of Jamaica and had lived out his final days without fear of the gallows or a deadly broadside at sea.

With enough wealth, Carlomagno could build his own place, safe from enemy eyes. *Sequanakeeswush* was a special word in his native tongue. It referred to a time when thanks are offered to the gods for the special bounties bestowed upon the people. But it was more than a simple corn-planting ceremony, for it gave thanks for life itself. After all, the Indian knew that all life came as a gift from the Creator. And that all things lived, from the birds of the air to the wildlife in the forest to the rocks, trees and even the stars that twinkled and winked all night long.

Carlomagno respected life, even as he took it. He was a pirate and had killed—and would not hesitate to do so again. But he saw himself now as being at war. He had been taken away from everything he knew, all he loved, when he was but a child. He was forced into this world and he was determined to rule it. He was the son of a great sachem. He would not cower in fear before his enemies. That was not the way he was made; his father would have expected no less from a son of his! If his enemies wanted him to be on the Spanish Main, they had better take notice. Carlomagno was here and he would not be subject to the white men's rules. He would make his own. He would create his own little world on Hispaniola. He realized that there were others like him, misfits who were brought to this place against their will, and together they could form their own community. But it would take wealth to create such a place. That longed-for place would be *Sequanakees-wush.*

The French to the west of his land could be bought off. Du Casse was an easy man to deal with and disliked conflict so close to home. The Spanish would be trouble, but they would find it difficult to come after him. The French would balk at having a large Spanish force marching so close to their border, for one thing. For another, part of the way was blocked by the Cordillera Central Mountains, making it difficult to move an army. And then again, the Cordilleras were home to the feared Cimaroons. The Spanish would have to fight them first, just to reach Carlomagno's land.

The Cimaroons were no threat to Carlomagno, for all of those proud warriors knew that the red Indian from America was a brother-friend to their own leader, Koyamin Otigbu. To Carlomagno, the brother-friend oath, to become a blood brother, was a sacred bond not to be taken lightly. It was his reason for going to Venezuela. He would sack Maracaibo, he was certain he could accomplish that, but that was just the pretext to get his crew to Venezuela. What he wanted was to free Koyamin who was being held in Maracaibo, awaiting a galleon that would take him to Triana—and a date with the hangman.

They dropped anchor near a small, unnamed island about a day's journey from the mouth of the canal leading into Lake Maracaibo. Lowering small boats, the leaders of the two ships went ashore to map out their strategy.

"I wish Kerbourchard had stayed," Gerard Labrosse sighed. "He was always a good man to have on a raid like this."

"Yea, that's for sure," Morgan Flynn said, his bushy beard flopping with each nod of his massive head. "You always knew your back was covered when he was around."

"I know Maracaibo is a rich port, Captain, but there are 4,000 people living there, some of them soldiers," Barnabas Greevey commented. He didn't say much, but generally what he said made sense. "Both ships together and we barely got four hundred men. We're outnumbered ten to one."

Carlomagno nodded. "Sometimes in war one must do something to achieve victory that he would rather not. It is this way for us. We must use their own fear against them in Maracaibo. Unfortunately, that means we must be brutal and bloody with de la Barra."

Looking at the men gathered on the small island, Carlomagno was confident that he had some good men with him. Yet there was a yearning inside of him, for he too would have liked the comfort of knowing Kerbourchard was beside him. Or Macomber for that matter.

"A lot will depend on luck," Carlomagno told his officers. "We will leave here and try to draw near the canal as darkness falls. Then we will lower the longboats and paddle past the fort in the dark; we will go by it and attack from the rear."

"The rear? Why, of course, that's so simple," agreed Gerard Labrosse. "The cannon of de la Barra are all pointed toward the canal or the open sea. The rear has the weakest defense."

"Exactly, Gerard. The Spanish knew that the fort controlled access to the lake and never gave any thought to a land attack from the rear," Carlomagno explained. That was something he had learned from Diego El Negro. But the plan he had devised was his own, and it was shockingly harsh. "Is everyone clear on the plan?"

They returned to their ships and weighed the anchors. The trip was uneventful, though once the crow's nest reported seeing—far in the distance—what might have been a topmast. It was full dark when they moved in closer to the shore. As silently as possible the longboats were lowered and the men—dressed and painted like Indians!—swiftly paddled forward. There were some lights on at the fort; they could make out a shadowy outline of the imposing structure as they swept past in their small boats. Carlomagno signaled and the boats swerved toward the riverbank. There was no need to talk now; the men readied their weapons.

With Carlomagno in the lead, and Morgan Flynn close behind, the pirates made their way back toward the fort, a half-mile distant. There they crept into position and waited.

A faint gray started to climb across the sky, the early dawn was quiet save for the usual croaking of frogs and chattering of birds. The animals had long since grown used to the men waiting patiently in the thinning jungle. They had spent the night creeping forward, reaching the positions from which they would launch their attack. To disguise them as Indians, Carlomagno had some of his men smear mud on their exposed torsos and tie bandanas around their heads. A few had feathers in their hair, others had managed to streak some paint on their faces. If the sight of one Indian caused fright in the hearts of the Spanish, seeing dozens of them at once would crush their resolve. Others wore their usual pirate garb.

It was lighter now, but not quite day. Carlomagno pulled back his bowstring and released his arrow. A guard patrolling a walkway along the riverside of the fort grunted in pain and toppled off the wooden walkway, crashing into the brush below. Hearing the noise, a second guard rushed to the scene to be met by a blood-curdling war cry—and a second arrow fired by Carlomagno.

The pirates leapt to their feet and rushed forward. The fort, built to protect the entrance to Lake Maracaibo, served that purpose well, but the rear walls had never been completed because no one ever dreamed that an enemy could get past the fort through the narrow channel leading to the lake. Now, behind Carlomagno, the pirates swarmed through the rear openings to do their bloody work. Their orders were to be vicious, to instill fear in the Spaniards so those who escaped—and some were to be allowed to "escape"—would spread tales of horror displayed by an army of savage Indians and pirates.

A guard caught flatfooted held his musket in idle hands as Carlomagno rushed upon him and crashed his hatchet through the Spaniard's head. He whirled and hurled the hatchet with accuracy as a second soldier began to lift his musket. The weapon struck the soldier and staggered him, but he regrouped and again raised his musket. Carlomagno had his sword out now and thrust the blade deep into the soldier's belly. The man's malevolent stare turned to blankness as he slipped to the ground. There was a stir to the right, in one of the soldiers' sleeping quarters. A man, rubbing the sleep from his eyes, staggered to the door. Carlomagno lifted one of his pistols and shot the man. He dropped the pistol into its holster and drew his second gun as he reached the doorway. Another soldier had just gotten out of bed and was reaching for his sword; Carlomagno shot him as well, finishing the wounded man off with his sword.

There was one more soldier in the room. He held a knife as he lay in bed.

"Get up, I'll let you get your sword," Carlomagno said.

"I wish I could, pirate. But I can't get up," the soldier snarled. "I broke my leg a few days ago. That should make it a little easier for you!"

"Yet you would fight me with a knife. You are brave."

"A man does the best he can with what he has at hand."

"So true." Carlomagno sheathed his sword and calmly began to load his pistols. "What is your name, soldier?"

"I am Enrique Rodriquez," the soldier said. "And you, I think I have heard of you. Can there be another like you? Are you not Carlomagno, the Barracuda of the Spanish Main?"

His guns loaded, Carlomagno put them away and dropped into a chair beside a shaky desk. "I am he. How old are you?"

"Nineteen," Rodriquez replied proudly. "This is my first assignment. I suppose it will be my last?"

Carlomagno shook his head. "You are too good a man to be killed in bed. Put the knife away, Enrique Rodriquez. Someday we may meet in combat; perhaps one of us will die. But not today, my friend. I can appreciate your bravery. I could use a man like you in my crew."

"No, captain, I am sorry. I am a soldier, loyal to the Crown."

"I expected as much," Carlomagno admitted. "There will be none left alive here to care for you. I will have a litter rigged and we will take you with us. We will leave you where you can get help."

"Where will that be?" asked Rodriquez putting his knife away.

"Maracaibo."

"My god! No one but you would even dare to think of sacking Maracaibo," Rodriquez exclaimed. "It would be an honor to fight beside a man such as you, Carlomagno, but my duty lies elsewhere."

Barnabas Greevey poked his head in the door, a musket ready. "You okay, captain?"

"Yes, Barney. Have a litter built; we're going to take this man with us. He's too good a man to die alone in the jungle." Carlomagno walked to the door. "Gil, light the signal flares so the ships know it's safe to come into the channel!"

Within the hour they were aboard ship and sailing straight for Maracaibo. The city was practically deserted when they arrived. As Carlomagno had planned, the survivors of the de la Barra battle fled to Maracaibo and warned them that thousands of savage Indians and bloodthirsty pirates were right behind them. People fled into the surrounding jungle, stricken with panic.

"Fill the ships with whatever we can carry," Carlomagno ordered Blanchette. "There are pearls for the taking here, pieces of eight, gold and silver. Load up some fresh water and food, too."

"We'll do it as quickly as possible, before those soldiers realize there are so few of us," Blanchette said.

Carlomagno spotted an old man sitting before his house. "Flynn, Greevey! Bring the litter over there. We'll leave Rodriquez with the old man." The old man stared at them as the pirates approached.

"Have you come to kill an old man?"

"Why did you not flee, grandfather?" Carlomagno asked.

"I am too old and lame, I cannot run very fast, or very far. I have no family to help me."

"This soldier, he is a good man, a brave man. You see that he is cared for, grandfather. His name is Enrique Rodriquez."

"You are a strange man," the old man said. "From the stories the soldiers told I thought you were ten feet tall and bit the head off of your enemies. My eyes cannot see so well anymore, young man, but I can still see with my soul. You are different, you are not a pirate. Not like one might think."

"What else do you see, grandfather?"

"Ah, I know it now!" the old man sat, rocking back and forth. "I had a dream a few nights ago, a very strange dream. It was the day they brought the Cimaroon here. You have come for him?"

226

"He is my friend."

The old man nodded. "I saw a painted indio in my dream, I saw him come and slay many enemies to free the Cimaroon. I told the captain of the guards but he thought I was a crazy old man. Ha! Look who's crazy now! The Cimaroon is here. There is a building at the end of the street, with bars on the windows and the door."

Carlomagno found the building. The door was ajar; he drew one of his pistols and entered. It was dim, though sunlight came through the barred windows.

Koyamin was standing inside his cell, near the door. Amina was trying to pick the lock and Anna Pickford was beside her.

"Carlomagno!" She rushed into his arms and their lips found each others' for a warm, exploding kiss.

"Hey, we have to hurry!" yelled Flynn, coming into the room. "Some of the soldiers are coming back. We've got the ships loaded, Carlomagno."

"I've got to free this man, but this lock won't give," Carlomagno said.

Morgan Flynn grasped the bars and began to push and pull with all his enormous strength; with a delighted cry Koyamin joined him. Soon, the bars began to bend and weakened mortar fell away until, at last, the bars were yanked from their sockets.

"Now, let's get out of here," Carlomagno said. "We've done all we can in Maracaibo!"

Indeed they had, for Carlomagno had sacked one of the wealthiest cities in the Caribbean, freed his Cimaroon friend—and been reunited with the love of his life!

{ 18 }

Red Indian

Sequanakeeswush was all Carlomagno could have imagined. Even the Lady Pickford, who had seen London, Paris and Vienna, was suitably impressed. The house was built of stone with expert workmanship. The colonnades were like Greek columns, with intricate designs etched in them. The house was comfortably furnished, tasteful, yet durable. Diego El Negro had learned much working with his father and had put his knowledge to use. There were other buildings, too: storehouses for grain and other products for sale, for the plantation raised sugarcane and tobacco, two important crops of the region. The sugarcane was also an important ingredient to the making of rum, a third major export of the Caribbean.

A ship, the Metacomet, had already been built and was off on a trade mission for its maiden voyage. Shipwrights and carpenters—all former slaves—were working at building a second ship and more housing for the freedmen. Though not as large as the main house, the freed slaves were each getting their own smaller homes.

"You have done well, Diego," said Carlomagno, between spoonfuls of green turtle soup. "I thought you were a man who would want the best," said Diego, pleased with the compliment, which meant more to him than the full share he had received from Maracaibo. "I see the ship is coming along faster than I would have thought."

"The men are good workers, and proud of their skill," Diego said. "It will quickly pay for itself once we start trading."

"Are you so certain?"

Diego nodded, "I am confident. And we have England to thank!"

"How so?"

"The king has issued an order barring the American colonies from trading directly with other nations, everything must pass through England's hands. As you might imagine, with no competition, the English can charge the colonists whatever they want. But, human nature being what it is, the colonists still want their few luxuries and necessities—and at the best price."

Carlomagno nodded thoughtfully. "And that provides us with a ready market for our goods."

Diego nodded. "Exactly, Carlomagno. We need only charge a little less than the king's merchants, and we shall have many eager buyers. I think we should immediately start on another ship after this one is finished. Believe me, we will need it!"

"None of this was possible without you," Carlomagno said. Finishing his soup, he pushed the bowl away, and added, "But these turtles might be the greatest of all your accomplishments!"

There were many varieties of turtles in the Caribbean, from the mammoth leatherneck, which could weigh in excess of a ton, to the hawksbill turtle, which was smaller by some two or three hundred pounds. But neither the leatherneck nor the hawksbill was edible. The green turtle, which was a true vegetarian, had a delicious flesh and was one of the main meat supplies in the area.

The green turtle was a favorite in part because it could be easily stored. There was no way to keep meat fresh in the tropical heat, save to salt it. And even salting had limitations. However, the large, clumsy green turtles could be kept alive for days on end simply by tipping them on their backs. When meat was wanted, one only had to butcher one of the green giants.

Another frequent dish was *salmagundi*, a mixture of a wide variety of uncooked herbs, including palm hearts, which were chopped up in a bowl. Mixed with oil, garlic, chopped meats and eggs and other flavorings, it was a favorite dish among the natives. Most Europeans passed up the vegetation and fruits the natives ate, preferring instead the meat of the cows and hogs they had imported.

Koyamin and Amina had stayed with them for a short time before returning to their Cordillera Mountain stronghold. Occasionally a Cimaroon would stop by for a meal or to trade. Often they provided news, for they saw much without being seen.

Carlomagno made sure to make healthy contributions to Jean Baptiste du Casse in Moagraine and to the governor of Jacmel. He seldom left his plantation, letting Diego or Gil Blanchette handle his business affairs. Once in a while, Barnabas Greevey even conducted small transactions. Carlomagno felt his reputation as a pirate might hinder him in conducting business, so he kept a low profile while his men acted for him. But always the final decisions were Carlomagno's.

The beachfront at *Sequanakeeswush* was quiet as the black waves rolled up into foaming caresses, a sharp white beneath the silvery moon. Carlomagno liked the cool of the breeze and the soft sand beneath his bare feet as he walked the beach beside Anna, their hands clasped tightly as they enjoyed the silence. The beach sand gave way to a steep hillside which overlooked the small harbor.

Atop the hill Carlomagno had set several twelve-pound cannon. Though not as numerous as the guns of Tortuga, the cannon could command any ships coming into the beach at Sequanakeeswush. It was his plan to add more cannon as time allowed. His plantation was situated between Moagraine and Jacmel, with Spanish territory to the eastern end, blocked by the Cordillera Mountains. Carlomagno felt certain the Cimaroons would alert him to any land invasions long before they neared his home.

It was the sea that worried him, for the harbor was small and could easily be bottled up. The island of Hispaniola jutted out slightly to provide barriers to his harbor, but also prevented escape if enemy ships suddenly appeared at the mouth. The cannon facing the sea would slow down one or two ships, but a fleet could not be stopped.

"It is lovely, Carlomagno," Anna said. They had been standing silently for a few minutes watching the stars. "It's a paradise here."

"Maybe it is possible to build a safe place here, Anna," he replied. "We could start a family."

"You know I want that, too. But I must be married first," she said. "It's the way of my people. Only a marriage performed by a priest of the church can be legal."

"It is different with my people. We do not have these church rules, though we have shamans to perform some rites of the spirit. Marriage is not of a church, Anna. To my people a marriage is a bond between two hearts. No church can make that, no man can order it to be so. It must be a feeling shared between two people, a willingness to give of yourself for the other's benefit, to do without so your partner might have.

"Maybe the white man sees love as something different, but I think love is not found on a piece of paper or written in some church records. Love is scrawled across the hearts, stamped on the souls and etched into the minds of two people."

She leaned close to him, her head on his shoulder. "You make it sound so simple, Pokanoket. Like it's just the two of us, alone."

"Who else does it need to be?"

"It's a big world out there, Pokanoket." When they were alone, Anna often referred to him by his given name. "We live in a world where there are laws, and we must live by them. What you do now, this privateering, it lasts only so long as England and Spain remain at war. Once they sign a peace accord both nations will turn against you."

"I have thought of that, Anna. I have spoken with Diego. He is very wise in such things. He has invested some of my money in other business ventures, all of which have returned modest profits. He is cautious, but it is better to start small and build bigger, he says. He believes in land, too. He has bought us land in Barbados and St. Kitts. If we ever have to leave here, we can go there."

She sighed. "I hope we never have to leave here."

"Yet, you leave soon?" he said. They turned and faced each other, his hand caressing her soft cheek. "Must you go, *Anasarani*?"

"You know I must, Pokanoket. I have to go to Port Royal and find my brother. I'm sure he regrets all that has happened. He was duped by de Fortenay; he would never have confronted Macomber otherwise."

"Yes, Macomber! You must inquire about him while you're in Port Royal," Carlomagno said. "We have heard nothing from him. Nor from Andrew. But you must not tarry in Port Royal; I shall miss you too much."

"I have to find my brother, he is all the family I have left," Anna said. "I will bring him back to *Sequanakeeswush*, if he will come. Then we will go to Moagraine and find a priest."

"I will try to make you happy," Carlomagno told her as they held each other in a tender embrace.

"You already do," she answered as their lips touched.

In the morning, she would leave on the *Metacomet* for Port Royal. The *Anasarani* was still anchored offshore, as Carlomagno liked to have at least one of his ships handy. A third ship, a three-masted schooner named the *Pickford*, was already on a trading expedition to the American Colonies. Captained by Barnabas Greevey, with Diego El Negro aboard, the *Pickford* was on its way to Carolina. Diego had it in mind to buy some land in the colonies, a place he thought might have a good future.

The next morning, as a touch of gold painted the eastern corner of the sky, Carlomagno stood on the sandy shore and watched the small boat move Anna across the water to the waiting ship. Once aboard the *Metacomet*, she stood at the rail and waved. Carlomagno returned her gesture and stood silently watching as the ship named for his father drifted away from Hispaniola.

He thought of this place he had built, this refuge against the world. But was it enough? Was he enough? What was he, after all? A common pirate. But he knew many a great man had started out much as he had. Alexander the Great was an emperor, yet his empire was founded on blood. All the great kings and conquerors of history took what they wanted by force of arms. It was ever the way with the world. Had not Macomber said as much? And the Mandinga?

Diego El Negro was wise in the ways of the world. He had read more than the average man of his time and could discuss history, philosophy and mathematics. He could talk of Thomas of Aquinas' Summa Theologica or speak intelligently of tiny "animalcules" discovered by a Dutch scientist named Van Leeuwenhoek. Diego El Negro would read anything he could find. He had even been in contact with several members of the Royal Society of England, the leading scientific body. Diego's father had been a learned man and encouraged his children in their pursuits. Like his hero, Leonardo da Vinci, Diego was a man who could paint well or sculpt marble, but most of all, he could think and reason.

Through men like Diego, Macomber and Kerbourchard, Carlomagno had slowly been exposed to a world he had never known. His people were comfortable in their eastern woodland world, knowing how to survive: what plants to grow, how to hunt whales in dugout canoes and how to make their clothes, utensils and other items from animal hide, bone and sinew. But the Wampanoags' world was small. They knew of white men, had heard of the Dutch in New Amsterdam and the

French trappers to the north, but they did not truly comprehend the size and scope of the world. Carlomagno knew that the wisest medicine men among his people would not have known about Carthage or Nok, would have been dumbfounded by names like Hannibal Barca, Cheops or Lao Tzu. Carlomagno knew so much, and it made him realize how little he really understood. He had wealth; by the standards of the day he was well-off. But his wealth had come from his piracy or because men like Diego or Gil Blanchette had invested wisely for him. They were honest men, in their fashion, and loyal to him. But if a day came when men less loyal held his purse strings? He would have to learn to read the white man's language better and to decipher their numbers. He knew some, instilled in him in his youth by a father who realized his son might confront different challenges than the world he had been born into offered.

His father, Metacomet, had done well to prepare him early for the life he would lead. Carlomagno would do no less for his children.

He thought of his mother. What had become of her? Had she died on the plantation of Don Pedro de la Marana? Or did she yet live? He must know the truth. Most of the sailors were with one ship or another, sailing under his banner. Carlomagno's flag consisted of a red background, to identify with his heritage—for he was known as the Red Indian—and a gold crown in honor of Lady Pickford; beneath it lay crossed gold hatchets. It was his personal version of the dreaded skull and crossbones.

Then he thought of Turang, a young Cimaroon who had stopped by to rest. The Cimaroons often came from the mountains and stayed at his plantation for a few days just for a change of scenery. Carlomagno had enough seamen on hand to sail the *Anasarani,* but not enough to attack Don Pedro's plantation. But he knew he could send Turang to the mountains and Koyamin would supply plenty of fighting men. A few years ago the Cimaroons used bows or spears, but they had successively raided surrounding locations and had acquired guns. Carlomagno had also captured firearms during his raids and had seen to it that Koyamin's village was well-armed.

It was time to pay Don Pedro back. The don had sent the Arawak after him when he was but a child. Carlomagno had defeated the Arawak, but not before the Carib had managed to kill his Pequot protector and friend, Noank. Carlomagno knew he likely would have died alone in the jungles of Hispaniola had it not been for Noank.

He owed Don Pedro, and Carlomagno would pay the debt.

A small carriage rattled over the uneven roadway and up the drive toward the main house. As it drew nearer, Carlomagno recognized the driver as one who worked for Louis Dearborn, one of the most respected merchants from Moagraine. Noted for his intellect, Dearborn had befriended Diego El Negro and the two held marathon discussions and debates on all manner of subjects.

"*Monsieur* Dearborn, it is always a pleasure," said Carlomagno as he opened the door to the carriage, "but Diego is not here."

Dearborn carried himself well, and those seeing him now in fashionable dress and with impeccable manners would not have believed that he had been a sailor, a soldier and an author at one time or another. If one looked closely the scars on his knuckles revealed his success in past skirmishes. But his rugged past was now well-concealed behind a pleasant smile and friendly eyes.

"Yes, I know, Carlomagno. He told me he was going on an extended business trip, one he encouraged me to invest in. I regret I did not have the capital at the time, as I believe Diego has an uncanny business sense."

They sat on the veranda, away from the sun. The horses were lathered so Carlomagno knew his guest had come in a great haste. Cool drinks were served, and a bowl of fresh fruit was set out.

"You have come far, and quickly, *monsieur.*"

Dearborn sipped his brandy. "You have excellent taste, Carlomagno. As you are no doubt aware, I am honored to enjoy a good friendship with Diego. He has told me on several occasions that if I were to hear news that might interest you, I should not hesitate to tell you. As you know, as a merchant I travel and sometimes find myself in a position to hear things."

"What have you heard, *monsieur*?"

"There has been much change in Port Royal, much has happened. Governor Modyford, I understand, was clamped into chains and shipped off to the Tower of London. It seems he lost some influence at Court following the death of his patron, the Duke of Albermarle."

Political patronage had probably been around since the world began. Knowing the right people could get things done; appointments granted could mean the difference between success and failure. Many a man failed only because he lacked family name or political clout, while others far less deserving succeeded because they were handed opportunities they did little to deserve.

Thomas Modyford was an able administrator and had done well. That he owed his appointment to George Monck, the Duke of Albermarle was just a fact of life. The duke had another friend, too—the uncle of Sir Henry Morgan. Using that connection, Henry Morgan had gained favor with Monck and then the king himself. But when the old duke died, it left no one to care for Modyford's career. Old enemies, jealous of the power he once held, now struck at him. False charges could take months—even years—to straighten out. In the meantime, Modyford would find less luxurious accommodations in the Tower of London.

"A temporary governor has been appointed, I understand, but he has not yet arrived," Dearborn said. "In the meantime, I fear Port Royal has become worse than ever. With Modyford gone, some of your old enemies are trying to move in. I have heard that the Chevalier de Fortenay has even left Tortuga."

{ 19 }

Old Providence

Old Providence was an island community deep in the Caribbean Sea, close to Yucatan, and yet it also offered easy access to the Dutch stronghold of Curacao, or Spanish ports like Coro or Santa Marta. It was a safe pirate haven, considered too small by the Spanish to be of any real threat. As a consequence it had developed into a buccaneer paradise. The island was one spread-out brothel of every ill thought up by mortal men. Mostly taverns and drinking establishments of all varieties dotted the island, some serving rum, brandy or a popular mixture known as *rumfustian*, which included eggs, broken and raw, mixed with beer, sherry and gin, flavored with cinnamon and nutmeg and sprinkled liberally with sugar. It was served hot. Beer was plentiful, too. There were different types of beer, as each tavern brewed its own. The cheapest was the "chowder beer" made from black spruce twigs, seeped in water and boiled with molasses. It tasted thick and nasty going down, but after a few glasses it either started tasting better or the drinker simply began caring less. Chowder beer was the cheapest and a man could get thoroughly drunk for only a little of his purse. Of course, after he had passed out there was always the chance that some wench might lighten his purse, if another brigand didn't seize the opportunity first. And of course much in demand on the Spanish Main was *bumboo*, a mix of rum and water with a hint of nutmeg and sugar.

The main export of Jamaica was sugar cane, with hundreds of tons a year being shipped to Europe. Rum, too, was plentiful. It was fast becoming a popular drink, though it was said most pirates guzzled brandy as the average man would drink water. A pirate, in general, was more skilled with a pistol or blade than many trained soldiers. Perhaps because the pirate found more opportunity to test his skills. That the pirate drank too much and played too hard could be excused, given his average life expectancy was not very long. If he survived the attack on a town or ship, he must still evade running into a larger fleet or some bounty hunter looking to make a living.

Life on the ships was no easy thing either, and there was often a lack of clean water and fresh meat. Men reeked of sweat, tobacco and alcohol. And women of any kind were all-mighty scarce.

When Kerbourchard was on his uppers, the booze flowed freely and the women flocked to him. Dangerous in a brawl, deadly whether drunk or sober, Persifal Kerbourchard was a man who admired the feminine charms of women and rewarded them liberally with jewels or a few coins here and there. Whatever port he was in—from Old Providence to Port Royal—the women of the waterfront dives knew Kerbourchard and came to see him whenever word reached them that he was in town. He was always a soft touch for the ladies; a well-turned ankle or a batted eyelash might earn a woman enough to live on for a month.

Old Providence was on a weeklong bender thanks to Kerbourchard and his salty crew as they ate, drank, whored and gambled their way through the modest fortunes they had won.

The life of a pirate was a hard one, often ending in sudden, violent death. They were a robust lot who lived their lives to the fullest, squandering no chance to take on a good drunk or share their bed with a willing wench. But, alas, as the money in their purses dwindled so, too, did the opportunity to satisfy their basest urges.

"The men are all broke."

Kerbourchard dunked his head in a bucket of cool water and used a hand to brush his hair down. His eyes were red from lack of sleep and he had a hangover. Yet he was dressed well and clean-shaven. He always believed in appearing at his best in public. Even when his pockets were empty—and they nearly were now— he looked the picture of wealth.

"Yes, Cedric, I supposed they might be getting restless."

"Do you have something lined up?" asked Cedric MacDonald, his quartermaster. "We need a quick score."

"I don't know," Kerbourchard yawned. "A quick score just means the money is gone that much faster and then we'll need to find another prize. Look at how long that loot lasted us from Panama! That's my idea of a strike. One raid and then we live like kings for six months."

"Yeah, we lived it up good, Percy, but we don't come across loot like that very often," MacDonald protested. "Too bad we can't find Carlomagno."

Kerbourchard stood quietly, looking up and down the street. "Maybe I have an idea, Cedric. What would you say to a raid of Portobello?"

Cedric MacDonald's jaw dropped. "Don't joke about that, Percy. Even Morgan had trouble pulling that off. I don't think Carlomagno would attempt that."

"Haven't you learned anything from Carlomagno?" Kerbourchard asked, playfully slapping MacDonald's broad back. "He always does what is unexpected. That's why he's successful. Now, admit it, no one on the Main would even think about raiding Portobello."

"Well, that might have something to do with the forts," MacDonald suggested. "They do make formidable obstacles to reaching Portobello—and then getting away again."

The first obstacle to reaching Portobello was the narrow, mile-long harbor. At the beginning of this treacherous harbor was San Felipe, known as the Iron Fort. A half-mile past that was another smaller fortress, called San Geronimo. To reach Portobello, both of these forts would have to be destroyed. But the harbor was so narrow, no more than one ship at a time could enter or exit. And the forts of San Felipe and San Geronimo combined to have over sixty cannon aimed at the mouth of the harbor. No ship could enter without coming under their blistering fire.

"It will take some studying," Kerbourchard admitted. "Let's get some breakfast and think it over some more."

"I'm done in, Percy. I got me a beef appetite, but a gruel budget."

"I've still got a bit, Cedric, and I want to talk with you." They had no trouble finding a place to eat, and after food was set before them they began eating in earnest. "You must have heard the stories they told of L'Ollonais?"

One of the worst of all the pirates was one named Francis L'Ollonais who hailed from Les Sables d' Ollone—the Sands of Ollone—in Britany. It was said he spent much of his youth as an indentured servant in the Caribbean, where he learned the arts of being cruel and rough. For, it was said, that was how a heartless master treated him. A bold and successful freebooter, as some called the buccaneers, L'Ollonais was known, even among the brotherhood of the lawless as a fierce, nasty man. Stories upon stories told of how he took a devilish glee in lopping the heads from his prisoners. Other times, it was whispered, he fed his captives only raw mule meat, watching as those who could not stomach such fare slowly starved to death.

"Are you trying to make me sick?" MacDonald wondered. "I've heard lots of tales about him. You'd be hard-pressed to find a worse scoundrel who ever sailed the Spanish Main!"

"L'Ollonais was a surly, friendless man. Yet he had a knack for finding plunder, and thus usually could find men to follow him," Kerbourchard said. "This often meant the difference between life and death."

"What are you getting at?"

"When you're successful, men want to join you. Since we've been in Old Providence I must have had fifty to a hundred men offer to join up." Kerbourchard leaned across the table. "Now I say we let some of them join us. We let them take care of the forts while we sail to Portobello."

"I'm listening."

Kerbourchard pointed out that a large party of men threatening Santa Marta might draw the soldiers from the Iron Fort. That would free his ships to enter the mouth of the Chagres River. Once past the Iron Fort, a second group of men would be set ashore to tackle San Geronimo, a smaller garrison with only about forty men stationed there. The majority of the crew would proceed to Portobello and sack the city.

"By the devil, Kerbourchard, I think you've got it figured out," MacDonald said, slapping he table top. "But what if the soldiers don't leave the Iron Fort?"

Kerbourchard smiled that familiar, reckless grin that inspired the men around him. "No one lives forever, Cedric! But don't worry, they will. They will because they would never suspect anyone of trying to sail down the Chagres. And men will follow us because of what Carlomagno did in Panama."

"And Maracaibo," MacDonald added. For word had reached Old Providence of the sacking of the Venezuelan pearling city.

"There is one other thing," Kerbourchard said. "There is a new commander at the Iron Fort; he is a man who lives for a fight. When he hears Santa Marta is under attack he will hurry there to involve himself in the action."

Kerbourchard's plan relied on luck, as had those raids of Carlomagno. But Kerbourchard did one thing Carlomagno did not—he put his fate in the hands of men he did not fully trust. But he needed more men to carry out his plan and he agreed to take on the extra hands.

"I don't like the looks of some of these scalawags," MacDonald said from the corner of his mouth.

"Nor do I," Kerbourchard admitted. "But we need the men."

A nervous-looking man, Captain Jacobson, was in command of one of the ships. He left Old Providence first, to give himself time to get into position. He was to appear in Santa Marta's harbor and fire off his cannon. Fearing a raid, Santa Marta would no doubt send a horseman to San Felipe, the Iron Fort, for help.

Giving Jacobson several days head start, Kerbourchard, with a second ship—a small barque— behind him, set out for the Chagres River.

"Even if the fort sends reinforcements to Santa Marta, it's unlikely they'll empty out the whole fort," MacDonald said.

"That's why I have Captain Husty's barque along. It's smaller and less imposing. We'll fill it with men and hoist a Spanish flag. It'll sail past the Iron Fort, and then put men ashore. Some will march to Felipe; the rest will attack San Geronimo."

A few more days passed and then, in the distance, Kerbourchard saw the solitary, distant peak of the Pilon de Miguel de la Borda, the 1,700-foot mountain that marked the beginning of the Chagres River.

"That is where we are going, men. We go to Portobello!" Kerbourchard ordered his anchor dropped and signaled Captain Husty to proceed. Anxiously, they watched as the small barque, crammed with hidden men, approached the mouth of the river. If the guns of the Iron Fort were going to fire, it would be soon, everyone knew. If that happened, they had no chance. Once in the Chagres there was little room to maneuver. The cannon remained silent as the barque slipped past.

"Weigh anchor," Kerbourchard roared. "Now we'll move in. With luck, the few men at the fort will be watching us while Husty attacks from the rear."

The defenders at the Iron Fort were too busy defending themselves to stop the ship that now entered the narrow river. The same was soon true of the tiny force at San Geronimo. Unmolested—and unexpected— Kerbourchard's schooner arrived in Portobello. The pirates struck viciously, causing a panic, as they slashed their way ashore and carried off whatever plunder they could locate. Back aboard ship they turned her about and started back down the river, the ship filled with treasure.

"I've got to hand it to you, Percy," MacDonald smiled. "Not even Carlomagno could have planned it better!"

Oh, how the lives and plans of men are like playthings to the fates! A life is like a thread dangling in the breeze. Some wave in a fierce storm, seemingly unbreakable, while others rip at the faintest whisper.

Captain Jacobson had arrived to threaten Santa Marta just as planned. His cannon shots had frightened the city's inhabitants, and an urgent messenger was dispatched to San Felipe. The commander of the Iron Fort lusted for action and immediately led the majority of his men eastward, toward Santa Marta. But that was when an unexpected disaster struck the pirate's scheming. Kerbourchard had not known that at nearby Rio Hacha, only a mile or so up the coast from Santa Marta, a Spanish war galleon had stopped for provisions. Resuming its leisurely course the galleon made an unexpected appearance at Santa Marta. Twenty-four guns rained cannonballs on Captain Jacobson's ship, blasting it to smithereens and sending the crew to Davy Jones' locker.

A second messenger was dispatched to San Felipe to cancel the request for reinforcements. Colonel Rubens was disappointed when he was met by the second horseman, but what else could he do? He retreated back toward the Iron Fort. As he drew near he heard gunshots.

Ordering his men forward at a gallop, Colonel Rubens arrived in the nick of time to spoil the pirates' plans to capture the Iron Fort. The small pirate force was wiped out to a man.

Captain Husty's barque was already turned around and San Geronimo was in flames as Kerbourchard sailed back up the river. Both ships made their way slowly up the Chagres, back toward the open sea. Then the cannon opened up from the walls of the Iron Fort and Captain Husty's barque was hit twice. It quickly began taking on water and turned sideways, blocking the narrow river. Kerbourchard ordered his own cannon to open fire, hoping for a lucky hit on the fort—maybe the powder room. Otherwise, he knew his schooner was a sitting duck in the middle of the river.

{ 20 }

Terror Unleashed

Port Royal had never been a bastion of morality but good women—and the roughest seamen could tell the difference—were generally not molested. But it seemed to Lady Annabeth Pickford that a new breed of pirate was now swaggering along the wide, muddy streets and leering smugly from every corner. She had thought her brother was being overly cautious the last time, when he forbade her to walk the streets alone. Now, she concurred with him. In fact Lady Pickford was glad her brother was not with her at the moment. Several rough-dressed scoundrels had hooted at her derisively and she knew her brother would have taken exception to it.

Connor Pickford was a nice enough fellow, but he was out of his element in Port Royal. He liked to think of himself as a tough man to

247

tangle with, but his sister had seen men of that stripe in action— men like Carlomagno and, yes, even the Chevalier de Fortenay—and she knew her brother did not the cast the long shadow he thought. Not that she would have told him so. Connor might believe he was protecting his sister, but Lady Pickford found that amusing. She was protecting him as often as not.

"Lookin' for somewhat, missy?" The speaker was a gaunt man in food-stained rags, with his stringy hair a tangled mat of dirt and sweat. He leered at her. "I got me two pence."

"You must be mistaken," Lady Pickford said, as she tried to step around the man. But he blocked her path, boldly looking her over. "I am not that type of girl."

"That's okay, missy," Stringy Hair sneered. "I like me all kinds of girls. Come wi' me, missy an' we'll have us a time."

"I think you heard the lady."

Stringy Hair swung his head around to match gazes with Macomber. "You takin' a hand in this, old man?"

"Careful, Billy," one of his partners hissed. "That's Myles Macomber."

"I don't care if it's Ol' Scratch hisself," Billy snarled. "I ain't afeared of no old coot, Peck."

"He ain't any old man, Billy. That there is Macomber; he's friends with Carlomagno, that red Indian."

Billy took a longer look. He saw the graying, thinning hair, the tanned wrinkled face and missed the cold, blue eyes. "Well, Carlomagno ain't here. I jus' see an old' broke down fool tryin' to horn in on our fun. There's four of us an' one o' him. An' I bet she's enough woman to go around, an' well worth fightin' over!"

"I ain't had no woman in nigh onto eight months," said a slovenly-looking man with blond hair.

Macomber had moved closer to Lady Pickford and he spoke to her without letting his eyes leave Billy and his partners. "You start walking now, ma'am. Two blocks up you'll see Calico Jack's place. Go in there and tell him who you are. He'll see you get treated right."

"She don't leave less'n we say so," Billy said.

"Boys, this is Carlomagno's woman," Macomber said softly. "You know if you touch her he'll hunt you down, each and every one."

"Way I hear it, he's running scared," said Latrell, the slovenly blond man. "He ain't been seen hardly since de Fortenay chased him out of Tortuga!"

As he talked, Macomber had seemed at ease, but he had moved his hand slightly toward the pistol in his belt. Now he drew it and aimed it at Billy. "Let her by." Something hit Macomber from behind and he stumbled slightly, but it was enough for Billy to knock the pistol from his hand.

The others moved in. Lady Pickford's hand dropped into her purse and withdrew a small dagger. She slashed into Billy Nedson's shoulder, tearing his rumpled shirt and leaving a reddening stain.

"You'll pay for that!" Nedson screamed as he turned toward Lady Pickford.

A short, muscular man stepped in front of Nedson. "You fighting women now, Nedson?"

Nedson was beyond caring and he had yanked his pistol from his belt. He leveled it at the newcomer. Latrell did, too.

"You in this, Ox?" Nedson snarled.

"No, Billy, not me," Ox replied as he slowly backed away, his hands half raised. He had delayed Nedson long enough for Lady Pickford to start running toward Calico Jack's. "I just wanted to watch the fight."

Nedson turned his head in the direction Ox indicated and saw Macomber and Tulane facing each other with drawn swords. Tulane, the lieutenant of the Chevalier de Fortenay, had shoved Macomber from behind as the old sailor was facing down Nedson and his comrades.

"I guess it is up to me to do what that Pickford whelp failed to do," Tulane grinned, showing his yellowed teeth in an impish grin.

"You sent him the first time because you were afraid of me, Tulane."

"I? Afraid? I am afraid of no one!" Tulane swung his blade in a wide arc, one easily deflected by Macomber. Their blades clashed noisily in the street as a crowd began to gather. Swordfights were nothing new in Port Royal, but this one involved two known combatants. Tulane believed himself the more skilled and his technique was flashier, but Macomber was steady, wasting no motion and awaiting his opportunity. He saw it and thrust his point home. Tulane grunted in pain and surprise. The aide to de Fortenay crumpled to the ground.

Macomber withdrew his sword and turned to meet Billy Nedson and the others. Macomber battled valiantly but in vain against four experienced swordsmen. One nicked his arm, another scratched his neck. Macomber's own blade flashed furiously, cutting deep into the fourth man who cried out as he fell. Macomber reclaimed his pistol, but a thrust from Peck drove into his side and the shot went wild. Macomber winced in pain and dropped his sword as Latrell's next swipe bit into his wrist. Now unarmed, they played with him, inflicting cuts at random. Macomber charged upon them with his bare hands, wrapping his fingers around Billy Nedson's throat. Peck's blade rammed into Macomber's back and the old sailor felt his strength drain away in his last moments of life. Their companions lying dead along with Macomber, Nedson and the others stood dumbly and stared.

"He was a tough old geezer," said Peck, throwing a glance at Tulane's body, only a few feet away. "He killed two men and nearly had you, Billy."

"I know," Nedson said, rubbing his sore neck.

"You know what I'm thinking? If that one old coot was that hard to tackle, I don't want me no part of Carlomagno," Latrell said.

Nedson turned his eyes on Latrell. "But you said Carlomagno was runnin' scared? You said so your own self, Latrell!"

"I might have been wrong," Latrell shrugged. "Maybe what I heard wasn't the way it happened at all. Could be that Carlomagno ain't had no cause to go back to Tortuga."

It took Calico Jack a few minutes to round up some of his men and get to the scene. He had a tough lot who did his bidding and they arrived with pikes, blades and muskets only to find the corpses. Billy Nedson and his friends had vanished, looking for a hole to hide in. Too many people had witnessed the altercation and one of them was bound to talk. Carlomagno would find out what had happened and they knew he would come for them.

"Green, Holton, gets some mens and takes Macomber for a burying. We'll do it decent. Carlomagno would wants that," Calico Jack said.

"What about them others, Jack?" Green asked.

"Let the hogs have 'em," some shouted.

"Poor hogs," Green said. "Chawin' on Tulane is likely to poison 'em."

"Alright, who seen it?" Jack glared into the slowly-gathering crowd. "I needs to knows, and soon!"

A short, stocky man stepped forward. Ox Czerkiewicz had intercepted Nedson and given Lady Pickford her chance to escape. A former shipmate of Jack's, he was bull-strong and as honest a man as one is likely to find along the waterfront of Port Royal.

"I saw it, Jack, and if I had me a sword I'd have taken a hand in it m'self. A scurvy lot they be, botherin' that girl. Macomber faced all four down until Tulane attacked him from the back." Wasting no words, Czerkiewicz described everything from when Billy Nedson first accosted Lady Pickford to the final stab in the back that finished Macomber.

"That's it for Nedson and them," someone in the crowd said. "When Carlomagno hears about this there won't be a safe place anywhere on the Main for them!"

"I say they are safe!" The crowd parted and de Fortenay stepped forward, flanked by a dozen of his crewmen. "This Nedson is under my protection. I will kill any man who touches him. Is that understood?"

"You tells that to Carlomagno," Calico Jack said.

"I am in charge of Port Royal now and Carlomagno will not dare come here, just as he is afraid to come to Tortuga. You are a good cook, Jack, so go back to the cooking before I slit your gullet. And that goes for all of you. The man who touches Nedson will deal with me!"

Lady Pickford was still shaking when she reached the International House, in spite of the stiff brandy and the stout escort Calico Jack had insisted upon. At the door they stopped and one of the men opened it for her.

"You be careful now, ma'am," he said, touching his cap. "There's a bad lot in town these days."

She thanked them and stepped inside. To one side was a dining area where her brother was seated at a table with another man, a rather good-looking man who appeared to be Spanish. He was dressed in the latest style with silver buckles on his boots and decorating his wide belt. She turned for the staircase, wanting only to lie down in her room, when her brother called for her.

"Annabeth, I'd like you to meet someone," Connor said, his smile broadening. "Lady Annabeth Pickford, I introduce Don Pablo de Jesus."

"A pleasure," she said, holding out her hand. De Jesus took her hand gently in his and kissed the back of it.

"You see, Don Pablo, isn't she as beautiful as I told you?"

"Connor!" Annabeth snapped at her brother. "What is this about?"

"I have seen you, senorita, and when I learned this man was your brother, I approached him to ask if I might escort you to dinner tonight?" De Jesus said, smiling pleasantly. He wore a mustache and small beard in the Spanish style and his eyes were dark and intelligent.

252

He was handsome, but there was something about him. Perhaps the nose, it was slightly hawkish, not marring his classic looks, but perhaps, offering a blemish?

"Thank you, Don Pablo, but I am tired."

"Later, perhaps? You must eat, senorita, and Port Royal has become a dangerous place of late. Too dangerous for one of your beauty to walk the streets without protection. I was suggesting to your brother that we could go to Calico Jack's later? His food is the best in Port Royal."

"I've just come from Jack's," she said. "I'd like to go to my room and lie down."

Connor noticed for the first time the tenseness in her body and her tightened features. "Are you all right, Annabeth? Has something happened?"

"Oh, it was awful!" she blurted, the tears starting to roll down her cheeks. "Those men stopped me; they were saying the crudest things!"

"What? Are they outside now?" Connor exclaimed. "Let me get my pistol!"

"No, they're gone now. Macomber rescued me."

De Jesus raised an eyebrow. "Macomber? I think I have heard of this man. A notorious pirate, I believe."

"He is a friend," Annabeth replied, glaring at her brother. "He saved me from those men. That Tulane struck him from behind." She was wise enough to leave out the damage she had done herself. "They fought. Macomber killed Tulane, I think. Someone in the crowd spoke out and Macomber told me to run. He was fighting with them when I ran to Calico Jack's."

"This is serious," De Jesus said. "If Tulane was there the Chevalier de Fortenay must surely have been involved. I fear for your safety, senorita."

Trying to regain her composure, she assured him she would be fine.

"I would like to offer my services. I have many men. I can make sure you have an escort wherever you wish to go in Port Royal," De Jesus offered. "If de Fortenay has any schemes in mind, my men will see that they are not carried out."

"I would appreciate that, Don Pablo," Connor said. "I cannot protect my sister at all times. I believe the Chevalier de Fortenay has attempted to harm her once already."

"Consider it done, sir," De Jesus bowed gallantly. "My men will be close by wherever you or your sister wish to go."

Lady Pickford did not feel safe until she was in her room with the door closed and locked. She sat on the edge of her bed and dropped her head into her hands. It had all been so horrible. Her little knife had been of little use. What of Macomber? Calico Jack would know and she would see him later tonight. She began to calm down. She thought of her brother. He always seemed to have some scheme in mind, but what could it be this time? Don Pablo de Jesus looked like a sincere gentleman and he had not hesitated to offer his men to protect her and Connor. The Don must be brave, she thought. Or maybe he did not know the caliber of man he faced in de Fortenay? But no, he did seem to know.

He recognized Tulane's name. And Macomber's.

This was not unusual in itself; each man had long been associated with two of the most famous pirates in the Caribbean. Still, for a gentleman to be aware of the names of such dangerous sorts...

She slowly unfastened her dress, letting it slip to the floor. She stretched out on her bed and was soon asleep. A light tap on her door awakened her. It was dark; she had slept longer than she had planned.

"Just a moment, Connor." She lit the candle on the stand beside her bed and a soft glow filled the room. She hastily picked out a new dress—a simple black one— and slipped it on. Back in London she had had to wear more undergarments, but it was too cumbersome—and much too hot—in Jamaica to burden herself with a dozen layers. The nights could get chilly, or maybe it was her blue English blood? She took up a red scarf and wrapped it about her shoulders. There was another rap on her door. Why was her brother in such a hurry anyway? "Alright, I'm coming."

She opened her door and two men grabbed her. One clamped a dirty, gnarled hand over her mouth. The other gagged her and roughly bound her arms behind her back, hefting her up onto his shoulder. It had taken only moments and they were gone, down the back stairs and out into the grey dusk. There was a carriage waiting and she was tossed inside. The vehicle immediately began rolling. She could smell the salt in the air and knew they were heading toward the waterfront. Determined to fight, she kicked out as she was dragged from the carriage and carried aboard a ship to be dumped unceremoniously in a heap in a darkened room.

"I don't understand it, senor," Connor Pickford said. "I knocked very loudly on her door, but she did not respond."

"I could see this afternoon that she seemed quite distraught. The rest is probably good for her, señor," smiled de Jesus. "Besides, there will always be another time."

"It is kind of you to be so understanding, Don Pablo. I assure you that my sister is not usually like this. She is very dependable, you'll see that as you get to know her," Connor said. "We are an old family in England and I have to think about our family name. I can't have it sullied by her consorting with pirates. I've had to look out for her since papa died. She is young and impressionable. I'm afraid she was too easily duped by this Carlomagno.

"But I'm sure it is just an infatuation. Once she gets to know a real gentleman like you, Don Pablo, she'll come to realize how foolish it is to pine for a common buccaneer."

De Jesus stood up. "I must be going. I sail in the morning."

"Oh, you're leaving so soon? I had hoped to give you get a chance to speak with my sister."

"I shall see her soon," De Jesus promised. "I have business which cannot wait, I'm afraid. I'm sure you understand, señor? Give my apologies to the Lady Pickford and I will see her upon my return."

Don Pablo de Jesus offered his hand to Connor and departed the tavern. Connor Pickford pulled his mug to him and started to lift it when a shadow fell across his table.

"Is your sister coming to eats tonight?" asked Calico Jack.

"No, she's sleeping. She was really shaken up by what happened this afternoon," Connor said. "Why she tolerates the company of such men, I do not know. I suppose Macomber saved her some grief. I owe him thanks."

"You saves your thanks, boy. Macomber deserved better than he gots today. You tells your sister that he's dead, boy. The man you tried to kills died saving your sister."

Connor gasped audibly. "I had no idea. I guess I was wrong about him," he said almost to himself. "He was truly protecting Anna."

"Aye, boy. He took Tulane with hims and another no-good, too," Jack said. "But five against one ain't likely odds, not evens for a tough mans like Myles Macomber!"

Connor Pickford was shocked. It wasn't that he had any love for Myles Macomber; he hardly knew the man, though he had once shot him. He had always regretted the incident because he knew he had been tricked into it. He was, he told himself, an English gentleman and not some common brawler. Now things just seemed to be spiraling out of control. He stood up from his table.

"I've got to tell my sister about this," he told Calico Jack, without making eye contact. "She would want to know."

"Aye, this is something she woulds wants to be knowin'," Jack agreed, wiping his beefy hands on his stained apron. "She mights wants to know somethings else."

Connor had started away, but something in Jack's tone stopped him. "What would that be?"

"She mights wonders why her brother be drinkin' with the Duc de Castile!"

Connor Pickford stared stupidly as Calico Jack's comment seeped into the morass of confusion in his mind. "The Duc de Castile? You mean... Don Pablo de Jesus is the duke!"

"Aye, boy, one and the sames."

Connor half-ran, half-stumbled to the door. He had to get to the International House; he had to talk to his sister! It was later than he realized and the streets were nearly deserted. He saw several rough-looking men passing down the other side of the street. They paid him no mind, but made him realize how vulnerable he was. His hand touched his belt reflexively, but he knew he didn't have his pistol with him. Counting on Don Pablo's offer of protection, he had not felt he needed his pistol. There had always seemed to be men around. Why had he not thought of that when the Don took his leave? Now he was alone on the street with no one to help. He thought of turning back and asking Calico Jack... But no, Jack would despise him if he did that. Besides, it was a short walk to the International House. And he was handy with the mitts when it came to that; he could handle himself quite well with the bare knuckles. He had been in a fracas or two back on London's tough end and had come out the better in each altercation. Ahead of him was the Black Horse Tavern, one of the rougher joints in the city, or so he had heard. A man stumbled from the door and then supported himself by leaning against the wall. His eyes were half closed and he reeked of stale sweat and strong drink. The man didn't seem aware of him. Connor looked cautiously to the right as he passed an open alley. No one was there. "I'm getting too jumpy," he thought. Again his hand went to his belt. Why had he been so foolish as to leave his pistol in his room?

"Excuse me, sir?" Even before he turned Connor's nose picked up the stale sweat and alcohol odor and he knew it was the drunkard from the Black Horse. "Sir, can you spare the price of a drink?"

Without thinking Connor reached for his purse. It would be wise of him to give the man a coin and then be on his way. Someone pushed him from behind and he fell forward. The drunken man caught him and started to drag him into the alley, where a third man suddenly appeared.

"Give it to him good, Nedson!" the drunk said as he gave Connor a sudden shove. Nedson, the man in the alley, slugged a sharp blow to Connor's chin and the Englishman sagged against a wall. Peck and Latrell, the "drunk," closed in and put the boots to Connor. They left him stomped and bloodied in the dirty alley. Peck spotted the purse Connor had dropped.

"A little bonus, Billy, in addition to what de Fortenay paid us."

Connor awoke to a cool, gray morning as a spattering of rain fell upon him. He sat up, his head pounded wildly. One hand was numb from being stomped on. It was bruised and sore, but not broken. His fingers moved, though stiffly. One eye was closed, his chin sore. His clothes were muddied and torn in several places. He remembered the men from the night before. It was no random act, he had been chosen for the attack. Robbery? Maybe. He felt of his purse, it was gone. He remembered he had taken it out of his pocket when the drunken man begged for a coin. He made his way back to the street and saw his purse lying open and empty on the street. He stooped and picked it up, not sure why he bothered when his head started to swim. He leaned against the wall. Connor Pickford bent over, his hands on his knees. He felt sick to his stomach.

"Sir, you will come with me."

He forced himself to look up, half-afraid of what he'd find. It was a boy, a skinny black boy. "Excuse me."

"Come, please. We must hurry. You are not safe here."

"I must see my sister."

"She is gone," the boy said. "She was taken away by the Duc de Castile. Andrew sent me to get you out of Port Royal. He is afraid that you will be used as bait to trap Carlomagno."

"Carlomagno? Yes, yes, I must see him," Connor said, he nodded his head but a wave of pain shot through him. "He must save Annabeth. Where is he?"

"He comes. But you must not stay here." The boy said his name was Cudjoe. Connor, in a state of disbelief, numbly followed the boy through side streets even as the rain grew heavier. "It will help our escape," Cudjoe called back over his shoulder. "There's a storm coming, a bad one my uncle says. I doubt many men will be out and about."

They came to the outskirts of the city where several tall, straight black men with sharp, piercing eyes waited beside the road with horses.

"You can ride bareback, sir?" Cudjoe asked as he deftly swung up onto the back of a strong-looking black horse with white stockings.

Connor nodded; once again the pain stalled him momentarily. But he got on the horse offered him and they rode off into the wild, unbroken country, the Cockpit Country. According to some, it was the closest place on earth to hell. The land was broken up with craters, the area scarred forever by the long ago eruption of a nearby volcano. Like the Cordilleras on Hispaniola, the Cockpit Country served as a natural fortress for the Cimaroons. The English currently claimed Jamaica, but some men of power in London thought it a waste to maintain a garrison there. Even as the English assigned fewer soldiers, the French were seeking to make inroads. The Cimaroons were determined to be free of both.

On Hispaniola, Obasanjo, the father of Koyamin, and other leaders had been afraid to rile the Spanish and took to hiding in the mountains and staying out of sight. Queen Nammy was not that sort. She was a proud woman and she instilled pride in the Cimaroons who followed her, and soon more followed her than any other leader in the Cockpit

Country. She couldn't read or write, and probably couldn't have identified the Bible, but she did believe wholeheartedly in an eye for an eye. Only she figured the English and French had more eyes than she did, so if they killed a Cimaroon she would order the death of three Europeans. Some saw her tactics as ruthless. But they were effective. Cimaroons were rarely bothered anywhere on Jamaica, particularly by the English.

The French, new to Jamaica, were still learning that terrible lesson from Queen Nammy. The English had sent men after her before, but they either became desperately lost in the wild Cockpit Country or, even worse, managed to catch up to the Cimaroons! Fierce fighters, the Cimaroons were adept at springing sudden ambuscades on the English with lightning hit and run strikes.

After several hours, the rain still poured down. Several of the men talked among themselves, then turned off the trail. Cudjoe dropped back behind Connor.

"It's getting too bad, we'll need to hole up!" he yelled, the words barely reaching Connor's ear as the wind howled wildly all about them. Connor was exhausted and in pain, and not in any shape to argue They made their way to a dry cave, a large one. The horses were led inside. One man went to a ring of burned rocks. Connor dimly realized that this hideout must be used often. The Cimaroon worked furiously and soon had a fire going. He fed it carefully and the cave gradually grew warm. The men broke out jerked meat and ate. Cudjoe brought some food and water to Connor and sat beside him.

"Thanks," Connor mumbled. "I never was good at saying thanks, but I guess you probably saved my life. I think Don Pablo tried to have me killed."

"I do not think so," Cudjoe said. "He left with your sister last night. Even while you were at Calico Jack's his men were taking her by force to his waiting ship. He goes back to his plantation in Cuba."

"You know a lot."

"My Uncle Andrew, he hears much. Information is important here," Cudjoe said. "I think the Chevalier de Fortenay set those men on you. They were the ones who killed Macomber."

"Why would your Uncle care about me?"

"He doesn't," Cudjoe said, standing up. "But he considers Carlomagno a friend and he was afraid de Fortenay might use you to bait a trap."

"Is Carlomagno in Port Royal?"

"No, but he is near," Cudjoe said. He returned to the fire, leaving Connor sitting alone. As the rain continued, they rested.

Connor slept badly, his thoughts on what a fool he had been all these years. He was a failure. His father had left him well off and he had squandered it away thinking his wealth knew no end. Only it did. He had found himself in trouble, and selfishly thought his only way out was to marry his sister into a wealthy family. Surely a wealthy man would pay off his brother-in-law's debts? Then he might leave this humid hellhole and return to London in good standing. But he'd been a fool. He'd gotten his sister kidnapped, or worse.

A hand on his shoulder brought him awake. "We ride." The storm had slackened and the Cimaroons led their horses outside the cave and mounted up again. They pushed on at a hurried pace.

In Port Royal, Calico Jack slowly stuffed his corncob pipe and lit it. He had an uneasy feeling something was wrong. Terribly wrong. Ever since the English soldiers had come and taken Modyford away, the city had had a different feel to it. Calico Jack wasn't a religious man, but he could only describe the feel of the city as evil. He said as much to Ox Czerkiewicz.

"You been working too hard, Jack," replied the Ox. He was a slow thinker, putting some thought behind each word. But, like his namesake, he was strong. He wasn't a tall man, but a rugged block of granite. Once, and witnesses had vouched for the truth of the story, Ox

Czerkiewicz had lifted a 600-pound anchor several inches off the ground by himself. "Things are just tense because of de Fortenay."

"Funny thing that." Jack's pipe went out and he paused to relight it. "De Fortenay left alls of a sudden earlier today. And Don Pablo de Jesus creeps off late last night. I thinks somethings is up."

"Their ships were docked next to each other," Ox commented.

"They spents some time visiting back and forth— or so I hears tell," Jack said. "But they never be seens together in public."

Ox accepted the frothy drink that Jack set on the counter before him. He took a healthy swallow. "Could be all of a chance, Jack."

Jack leaned closer. "I don't thinks so, Ox. I gots me this powerful bad feeling. I tells you there be evil afoot. I can't shakes it, this bad feeling I gots way down deeps inside me."

Czerkiewicz polished off his drink and pushed his mug forward for a refill. He'd known Calico Jack for years and damn if the man didn't have the sight. There was that time on the ship, years ago, when they had had the luckiest of breaks. They were young bucks then, pissin' vinegar. They had caught the eye of Sir Henry Morgan; he was planning a raid and they had been invited to join in. Young and impressionable, Jack and The Ox were sure their futures were made. Getting a chance to tie in with Henry Morgan was a once in a lifetime opportunity. His expeditions were among the richest ever and one raid could set a man up for life, that is, if he played his hand right. Czerkiewicz reflected as his refilled mug stood untouched on the bar before him. Calico Jack was a careful man and if he could get one good stake he would go someplace and set himself up in business. Ox hadn't been so sure what he'd do with his share of the money, he'd been more excited by the idea of fighting beside Morgan.

Then Jack had a premonition.

"I was thinking back, Jack, to that time with Morgan."

Calico Jack slapped a hand on the bar. "That's it, Ox! That's it exactacly! I gots me the same kinds of feeling now!"

Things had been going well that time with Morgan, anchored off Old Providence. Morgan and his chief lieutenants were planning the raid and the rest of the pirates were having a jolly time visiting back and forth between ships and drinking until they thought they would burst. And then Jack got his bad feeling, one he couldn't shake. He started telling everyone they should get off the ship, that he sensed something bad. Drunk and boisterous, the other pirates laughed at him.

But not the Ox. When Calico Jack walked down the gangplank Ox was behind him, though to this day he wasn't really sure why he did it. Some twenty minutes after Jack had left the ship a drunken sailor had let sparks from his pipe fall onto a powder keg. The ship exploded, dozens of men lost their lives and the raid had to be called off.

Ox pushed his mug away. "I think maybe I'd better have a bowl of that turtle soup, Jack. It's dark and wet out there. No time for a ride."

"I'll warms up some soups for us both, Ox," Jack said. "And packs some extry vittles, too. Might be a goods time to takes us a ride to Montego Bay."

Czerkiewicz buttoned his coat up and ducked out the door. The stable was next door, he'd get two horses ready for riding and one to carry packs. The wind was picking up.

Peck turned from the window of a second-story room in the run-down boarding house across the street from Calico Jack's. "Ox just came out. He's heading for the stable."

"Probably feeding the horses," yawned Billy Nedson, who lay in bed with his hands clasped behind his head. He started emptily at the ceiling. Of the three men in the room he was the only calm one.

Latrell sat at a small three-legged table, where he was cleaning his pistol. "I wish Carlomagno would show up. What's keeping him?"

"Yeah," Peck agreed. "De Fortenay said he'd be here by now. Do think he knows about us, Billy?"

"Nah. Maybe the winds are wrong, or he got a late start," Nedson suggested. "Don't fret, he'll come to Port Royal; he'll come to see Calico Jack to get the why and what of it all. And when he does, we'll be right here waiting for him."

"We should have taken out when de Fortenay did," Latrell said. Peck murmured an agreement, but Nedson ignored the comment. "I tell you, I don't like this. Why did de Fortenay take out so fast? He made all that talk about wanting Carlomagno dead, then he leaves Port Royal."

"Probably had to get back to Tortuga. Anyway, he paid us ten quid each to kill Carlomagno—and de Fortenay says there's more when the job's done."

"It's a tough job," Peck said. "Why, who expected that flea-bitten old man to be so difficult?"

Nedson waved a hand dismissively. "We made a mistake lettin' him get into action first. With Carlomagno it'll be different. We'll wait for him and when he walks out of Jack's door we'll just shoot him down!"

"I think there be a problem with that plan," said Peck, who was staring out the window again. "Ox just brought three horses out the stable. They're tied to Jack's hitch rail."

Nedson swung his feet to the floor and sat on the edge of the unkempt bed. "I'll take a walk over and listen up. You stay here. And, Peck, you keep an eye out for Carlomagno. You see him, you guys know the plan."

"But there will only be the two of us," Latrell whined.

"You shoot him as he comes out the door, Latrell. And where do you think I'll be? I'll be behind him, you fool—and I'll be shooting, too." Nedson buckled on his sword and picked up his pistol. "Hurry up and get that pistol loaded, Latrell. You know he's due anytime. Besides, you've already cleaned that pistol half a dozen times."

"Just want to be sure," Latrell said.

Nedson clambered down the rickety stairs and made his way past a couple of drunks stretched out in the hallway, snoring noisily. He wanted some of that fine rum of Calico Jack's, but Jack weren't likely to be too pleased to see ol' Billy. After he shot Carlomagno, he'd take Jack out too. Then he could drink all he wanted. As far as Billy Nedson was concerned, he was the equal of any man with a sword. It would be something to be known as the man who killed Carlomagno. Damn, Nedson thought, that would be a corker! Why, he wouldn't have to off Calico Jack, he could cadge drinks for the rest of his life...

Billy Nedson had taken several steps toward Calico Jack's tavern before he became aware of the man standing in the center of the street not ten feet away. The man's face was streaked with red and black and he was bare-chested save for the criss-crossed bandoliers and their twin brass pistols. There was a sword on his belt and a hatchet in his right hand. Nedson knew he had to move, yet his legs seemed frozen in place. The sight of this man frightened him. Him! Billy Nedson, who wasn't afraid of anything!

Peck, in position at the window, also spotted Carlomagno. "Come on, Latrell!" Peck raced down the creaky stairs, burst out the door and threw up his pistol, but rushed his shot and came nowhere close to Carlomagno. Whirling, the hatchet spun end over end as it hurtled toward Peck; the sharp edge slammed into soft belly and the would-be assassin fell backwards as blood spewed from the wound. Peck cried out in horror, blood spraying from his mouth, and fell. The movement galvanized Nedson's nerve and he drew his sword. He advanced timidly as Carlomagno drew his own Toledo-steel blade. Their swords clashed, the sound barely heard over the wind. Nedson swung his blade in a wide arc and almost carelessly Carlomagno thrust his point home. Surprised, Nedson took a step back. He dropped his sword, trying with both hands to stem the flow of blood from his chest. He dropped to his knees, reaching out a hand as if to beg for mercy as Carlomagno raised the Toledo blade. It came down swiftly, severing Nedson's right hand at the wrist.

"Now when we meet in the next life, you won't be able to raise your weapon to me," Carlomagno said.

Billy Nedson fell on his side and died with his eyes staring at his own severed hand, just inches from his face. The ground lurched and Carlomagno staggered before catching his balance. At that moment Calico Jack and the Ox rushed from the tavern. The ground rumbled, and the sounds of breaking glass and splintering timber could be heard from the waterfront. Carlomagno jumped on a horse and joined Jack and Ox as they raced out of town.

Port Royal, sometimes called The Sodom of the Caribbean, now paid the price as the evil Biblical cities had done in days long past. The ground shook violently. A few frightened horses managed to kick free from their stalls at the livery and bolt riderless down the quaking street. Buildings shook, men and furnishings inside sliding across the floors.

Latrell, his pistol finally loaded, came to the street, stepping over Peck's body. He saw Nedson lying dead and let his eyes follow in the direction the few men on the street seemed to be looking, naked horror on their faces. Latrell stood frozen in place as he saw the sea rise up from the harbor.

A gigantic wall of water came to life and rolled ashore, tossing thirty-ton ships about like mere playthings and crushing everything in its path. Latrell, like the other men, turned to flee. But no man could outrun the monster wave as it hungrily devoured a third of Port Royal. Man and beast alike were crushed by debris or drowned by the raging waters. The harbor disintegrated as buildings all along the waterfront and even toward the heart of the city were smashed to splinters. The earth surrendered underfoot and the merciless sea claimed the cluttered, filthy streets of Port Royal.

{ 21 }

Return of Pokanoket

Carlomagno pulled up and slid from the horse's back. His eyes scanned the circle of Cimaroons and fell on the frightened face of Connor Pickford.

"I...I had nothing to do with Mr. Macomber's death," Connor blurted.

"The men who killed Macomber are dead. The man who arranged it—the Chevalier de Fortenay—will meet his fate soon," Carlomagno replied brusquely.

"I've been a fool, Carlomagno. A bloody, big fool at that! I never saw what my sister wanted; I was too concerned with my own plans." Connor Pickford set his jaw firmly. "I don't expect you to forgive me. But I wanted you to know I've had a chance to think it over and I realize how wrong I was. If you have come to kill me, make it as swift and as painless as possible."

Carlomagno put a hand on Connor's shoulder and gave him a reassuring squeeze. "You have grown, Connor. It is never too late for a man to make amends."

Connor dropped his eyes. "It is too late for me. Thanks to me, my sister has been taken away by the Duc de Castile. Not even you can rescue her now," Connor explained. "She is at the don's Cuban stronghold—and it would take an army to defeat him there. He told me all about it. Members of the royal family use his plantation when they visit the Caribbean."

Carlomagno clenched his teeth in silent anger. His beloved was a prisoner of the Duc de Castile, and subject to every degrading outrage the Spaniard could devise. Carlomagno had reason to recall the Spanish knack for cruelty; he needed only to recall how his mother was abused by Don Pedro de la Marana.

"I will find Anna," Carlomagno promised, "and punish any who have wronged her!"

They had ridden at a blistering pace to escape the terrible devastation of Port Royal. The sea had invaded the city, taking a victor's portion back with it. The start Carlomagno and his friends had gained proved enough to avoid the dangers, though the ride did raise the hairs on their necks. It was as close as any had come to meeting his Maker. They had headed deeper into the Cockpit Country until they had come upon the collection of scattered huts. It was a village of Cimaroons. Andrew stood among them.

"I sent the boy for her brother," Andrew smiled, patting Cudjoe's head. "I knew you'd want him to be safe."

Carlomagno grasped Andrew's hand in a tight grip. "How did you know, my friend?"

"The spirits grant me visions sometimes. I see much damage," Andrew explained. "For the lady, I am too late, she was already gone. The spirits did not grant me the power to prevent it."

"It was the Duc de Castile. He has taken her to Cuba, but I shall go there, too."

"He waits for you to come."

"He might expect a raid, by a large force. And no doubt he could repel such an attack," Carlomagno said. "But has he thought of what one man can do alone? I will slip in and find Anna. I can get her away before the duke even realizes she's gone."

Connor shook his head. "But how will you get to Cuba?"

Carlomagno glanced at Andrew. "Has my ship arrived?"

"It has," Andrew said. "It was wise of you to have it drop you off near Port Royal and then come to our end of the island; the ship is undamaged."

"I thought de Fortenay was in charge of the city. Once I'd dealt with those who had killed Macomber, I'd planned to be in a hurry to get out of the city. You told me to come to the Cockpit Country if ever I was in need. I thought it wise to have a ship waiting here."

"You have men?" Andrew commented.

"Most of them are on my other ships," Carlomagno said. "But I have enough to sail the *Anasarani* to Cuba and drop me off."

Don Pablo's plantation was akin to a small fortress. It was located near Puerto Principe in the middle of Cuba in a town called Santa Maria. The don had boasted of his home to the impressionable Connor Pickford, who now gave as much information as he could to Carlomagno. The plan was for Carlomagno to debark the Anasarani on Cuba, while the ship continued on a trade mission to Grand Bahama. There was a small fishing village on the Cuban coast and on its return from Grand Bahama the Anasarani was to stop nearby.

"But what if you haven't made it back to this fishing village?" asked Connor.

"It will take the *Anasarani* three weeks to make its trip and return past the Cuban coast. If I have not reached the village by then, there is little hope for us," Carlomagno said. "In that case, the *Anasarani* will return here for you. It will take you back to Hispaniola, where Diego will know what to do next. You are welcome, too, Andrew. I'm sure Diego would appreciate your assistance."

The aging Cimaroon shook his head. "You honor me, Carlomagno. I knew the first day you came to the Governor's Mansion I had seen into the eyes of a great warrior. But my place is here. I must teach my nephew, Cudjoe, all that men must know. My people hide in the hills, afraid of capture by English, French and Spanish. I see the future, Carlomagno. It is for Cudjoe to lead the Cimaroons to freedom. But, first he had to learn from the warrior I'd seen in my dreams."

"I leave at first light," Carlomagno said, rising to his feet. "I thank you, Andrew, for all you have done for me."

"Remember, Carlomagno, you have friends among the Cimaroons, always," Andrew said. "If trouble arises, come to us."

Carlomagno did not want to think of trouble coming to Hispaniola, but if such a day should come he had already put his plans in place. He lay on his sleeping mat, staring up at the stars for what seemed hours. Even when his muscles slowly relaxed and he rested, he tossed and turned in his sleep.

A white mist surrounded him as he wandered along an unfamiliar path in a dense wood. His eyes could not pierce the fog around him. A shadow floated, a dark shape moving closer. To his shame, Carlomagno wanted to turn and run as fear gripped him. His leaden legs would not obey and he stood immobile as the darkness crept ever closer. Had Granny Squannit come for him? The mist thinned under a warm, gentle breeze. He saw a man before him. Shorter than Carlomagno but well-proportioned and muscular, his hair was shaved on the sides, two hawk feathers tucked firmly into his scalplock. The man's face was stern, as if taking measure of a possible enemy. Carlomagno knew him instantly.

"Father!"

The man's somber face lit up. Gentle eyes moved proudly over Carlomagno. "You have grown tall and strong, my son. No Wampanoag ever looked braver."

"Father, I wish I could have fought beside you, I wish—"

Metacomet held up a hand for silence. "My days have passed, my son. Each man must live in his own time. You go to a strange land, on a quest in which you dare not fail. I am proud of you, for you have learned to succeed in the world around you. To succeed in this quest, you must remember the ways of the warrior. They are waiting for a white man to come. You must not think as they do. Remember the things of your youth." Metacomet stood silent for a long moment as the mist slowly curled around him. "Remember the things you were taught by my brothers, Unkompoin, the shaman, and Quadrequina. Remember the ways of your father and your ancestors will walk beside you. Remember that you are Pokanoket, son of Metacomet."

Carlomagno reached out as his father faded away, his fingers clutching at the empty mist.

"Father! Wait, Father! Don't go!"

He woke in a sweat, his heart pounding like a hundred drums. He sat up and rubbed his eyes. The camp was silent. His father had been here! He knew it was more than a dream, knew that Metacomet was with him, and would guide him! Carlomagno lay back down and slept peacefully. He would need his rest for the coming ordeal.

Finding a sheltered inlet along the Cuban coast, the *Anasarani* dropped anchor. Carlomagno double-checked his weapons. Once ashore, he'd be completely on his own and any man he encountered must be considered an enemy.

"I still say I should be going with you," fumed Morgan Flynn. "If there's fighting to do, I've always guarded your back."

"I, too, should be a part of this," added Connor Pickford. "It is my fault that Anna is in such a predicament."

"I appreciate it, both of you. But the duke expects me to try and attack him with many men. He'll have the countryside on the lookout for groups of strangers. Alone, I can sneak in before he knows it."

Carlomagno slipped a leather quiver over his neck and checked the hatchet and knife at his belt. He wore fringed deerskin leggings and moccasins he had made himself. He started to take his pistols, then put them down, but strapped on his blade of Toledo steel. What he must do had best be done silently. He climbed down the rope ladder to the waiting rowboat.

"Three weeks from now, we stop in the fishing village up the coast," called first mate Rigger Bonham, a common hand whose bravery in Panama had earned him a promotion. "Luck be with you."

"If the Manitoo are with me, I will not need your luck," Carlomagno laughed. "If they are against me, all will come to naught."

The boat took Carlomagno closer to the shore and slowly made its return to the Anasarani. Carlomagno watched as the ship raised anchor and began to drift away. The fishing village was a few miles to the north.

He had to travel inland to reach Santa Maria near the center of the island. He turned and melted into the woods, which quickly grew dense. He moved swiftly, senses alert. Any man he met must be disposed of; he could not risk that an alarm might be raised.

A Wampanoag in his native forests could run forty to fifty miles in a day, but the going was slower for Carlomagno. The Cuban jungle was a mass of tangled vines and thick-waisted trees with drooping boughs. Carlomagno had to be wary of coming unexpectedly upon another traveler, as well as snakes, alligators or fierce jungle cats thinking him an easy dinner.

The *Anasarani* had dropped him off before dawn to minimize the chance that any local villager might spot the masts out on the sea. It also gave Carlomagno a full day to lose himself in the overgrowth. Arcing around the fishing village to avoid village dogs and using the sun as a guide, he picked his way inland.

Though it had been years since he'd seen another North American Indian, he had managed to maintain his native tongue by speaking aloud to himself or to the Manitoo. But the Wampanoag tongue was not practical on the Spanish Main, so Carlomagno had made the effort to learn English and Spanish. He even knew a little French. His Spanish was very good, though he was more proficient in English. He had learned a lot in his years on the Main, many things that never would have been necessary back at Sowams. He had learned how to survive in the Caribbean and even to thrive. He was among the most feared pirates in the region and one of the more successful. His success was enhanced by his disdain for the European concept of wealth. He was not intent on hoarding it, thus found it easier to spread around; buying favors and information often made a difference in his other ventures. Since his experience with Feroz, Carlomagno drank rarely and never to excess, avoiding a trap that ensnared many buccaneers. After a long, difficult journey, most pirates simply lived the high life, spending money as if there were no end to it. Only there was always an end.

Carlomagno made his life on the sea, as a pirate, because it was the only door open to him. He seized the opportunity it offered for a life of freedom—or death with honor, at the very least. He had expected nothing more than to punish those who had captured and enslaved him. At first, he wanted only to kill as many Englishmen and Spaniards as he could before he himself was killed. Slowly, he had changed. He began to think it might be possible to carve out his own place on the Main. For that, he needed the gold and silver white men prayed for. Carlomagno used the treasures he took for his own purposes. He bought slaves and granted them their freedom. They helped him to build his own plantation and lived as freedmen to come and go as they wanted. If a slave preferred not to remain after being freed, Carlomagno would give him a small stake so he could make a start. Many former slaves stayed and would prosper in time. With his friendship cemented among the Cimaroons, Carlomagno's plantation and livestock were never bothered. But his friendship with Koyamin, the Cimaroon leader of the Cordillera Mountains, had not gone unnoticed. Carlomagno's plantation separated the French towns of Moagraine and

Jacmel, and officials there had noted the potentially dangerous alliance.

What if Carlomagno and the Cimaroons decided to try and take over all of Hispaniola?

In Moagraine, Jean-Baptiste du Casse considered the possibility. Soon, he reasoned, the Cimaroons would start thinking about coming down off the mountains and inhabiting the flatlands. Backed by Carlomagno's fighting men and weaponry, the Cimaroons would be dangerous foes. Du Casse had made overtures to the Spanish governor in Santo Domingo. The French shared Hispaniola with Spain, but they had never had a formal alliance. Now, du Casse thought they might want to consider such a treaty. He was only half-thinking of the Cimaroon threat. If Spain were an ally, France could turn her attention to settling Jamaica. The French had already made inroads there and the earthquake that had wrecked Port Royal had further disillusioned the English. Du Casse saw the opportunity to rebuild Port Royal as a French seaport.

But there was the problem of Carlomagno.

Du Casse had to move carefully. If the Spanish spurned his offers, he could not hope to stand alone against the pirate king and his Cimaroon friends. But there were always other ways. He recalled the interest of the Chevalier de Fortenay in Carlomagno; if his information was correct, his old friend had a personal vendetta against the Indian. His arrangement with Governor Modyford of Port Royal had made alliances with the Spanish unnecessary. They had done some business together and each had profited handsomely. But things had changed. Sir Henry Morgan was dead, Modyford taken away from Port Royal in chains. Because of his dealings with Modyford and Morgan, du Casse had naturally sided with them during the struggles between Spain and England. Not that he had ever taken any overt action against Spain. No, that was not his style.

Perhaps he worried needlessly. His latest information was that Carlomagno was on his way to Port Royal, into a trap de Fortenay had planned for him. Carlomagno may even have been killed in the earthquake! Two thousand people were lost and a third of the city had simply fallen off into the sea. Carlomagno might be among the dead, du Casse thought. He slowly savored the bouquet of the wine in his crystal glass, holding the liquid briefly upon his tongue before swallowing.

Miles away, crouched in the dense underbrush, Carlomagno watched the riverbank where village women were washing their laundry. Several young children frolicked in the water. Even as he watched one of the three women took up her basket and called to several of the children; together they turned up a narrow path. Two women remained, with three children. Carlomagno edged closer, hoping to overhear something useful.

"Do you think he will come this way?" The speaker was a young woman whose tawny skin glistened in the sunlight.

"Shh! We should not speak of such things, Beatriz!" replied an older woman with flecks of gray in her hair. "If you speak of evil things, you invite them to happen."

"I don't think it is evil, Tia Elena," Beatriz sighed. "I think it would be romantic to have a man come so far for you!"

"You dream too much, they are foolish dreams," Tia Elena scoffed. "Take your head from the clouds and pay attention to your work."

Beatriz continued wringing out the shirt she had been washing, folding and placing it in a basket beside her.

"I think the duke is afraid of this man."

"You are young and speak foolishly, child. Why should Don Pablo fear a filthy pirate?"

"Then why does he have so many men patrolling the villages, looking for this pirate? Why does he offer so much *dinero* for information about this man?"

"I think it is just as the duke said, Beatriz. This Carlomagno is a bad man, a pirate; he robs and kills innocent people. Have you not heard of the village near Maracaibo? I think Don Pablo only looks out for us. Does he not treat us well, leave us alone to live in peace?" Tia Elena picked up her basket. "Come children!"

The older woman started up the path without a backward glance. The children, responding to the sternness in the older woman's voice, trooped after her.

Beatriz knelt by the river and started to wash another shirt.

"*Si*, Tia, the duke treats us well as long as we give him half of our crops," Beatriz muttered to herself. "He feasts on our hard work while many in the village have little to eat."

Carlomagno let the minutes tick by before he stepped from the woods. Beatriz was wringing out the white shirt in her hands when she saw the Indian. She took an involuntary step backwards, fighting down the urge to scream. She stared at him, her eyes wide.

"I will not harm you," the Indian spoke softly, his eyes darting along the trail. He knew her village was close. He had taken a great chance in showing himself, for she could now alert the countryside to his presence and the duke could target his search to a smaller area.

"You are the one," Beatriz whispered. "The pirate?"

"I am Carlomagno."

"You must love her very much to come to Cuba, where the Duc de Castile is at his most powerful."

"You know about the senorita?"

"*Si*, everyone knows. The duke, he says, she is under his protection. He warned us all that a dangerous pirate will come to steal her away. He said you would come with many men."

"Lady Pickford is to be my wife, Beatriz. It is the duke who has stolen her away. So I have come alone to take her home with me. Your aunt is wrong about me; I am not a bad man. I have done harsh things

276

because we live in a harsh world. But I did not massacre those villagers. I have killed men in battle, when it is them or me. Now I come only to get what was taken from me. I do not wish to harm anyone."

"It will not be so easy, senor. The duke has many men and he wants you dead. We are poor people and he has offered much for you," Beatriz said.

"If you scream now, you might make yourself a lot of money."

"To some people money is the most important," Beatriz offered. "For me, I believe it is love. I think a man who would come so far to rescue the woman he loves, such a man as this cannot be as bad as they have said."

"I have never been to Cuba before, Beatriz. If you could draw me a map in the dirt, give me some idea of where I am and where Lady Pickford might be?"

Beatriz smiled. "My aunt would be very angry with me. She believes Don Pablo is a great man. I think he is a parasite who lives off the work of others. I saw the woman when he brought her to Santa Maria and I did not see love in her eyes."

Using a stick, Beatriz drew a crude map in the mud beside the river.

"Thank you, Beatriz," said Carlomagno. He reached into a pouch at his side and offered her a gold piece.

Beatriz refused it. "What good would it do me? My uncle would only ask where it came from and when I could not tell him, he would beat me. My uncle and aunt believe everything Don Pablo says," Beatriz said. "There is no hope for me. I was born in a small village and I will die there. My parents died when I was a baby and my uncle and aunt raised me. They are very strict."

"You could marry and move out of their home."

"My uncle is a very quarrelsome man and will not allow any suitors to call on me," she said sadly. "No, Carlomagno, I have no brave man, like you, to rescue me."

"Would you leave if you had the chance?"

"*Si.* Nothing holds me here."

"In three weeks a ship will come to the fishing village on the coast. Be there in the early morning. If I am not back by then, you tell the captain that I sent you. He will take you away from Cuba if you wish."

"*Muchas gracias!*" She rose on her tiptoes and brushed his cheek with a kiss before he slipped away. "I hope you find the senorita."

Continuing with her laundry, Beatriz couldn't get the Indian out of her mind. How handsome he was, how strong he looked! She wondered what it would be like to have those strong arms wrapped around her. She flushed at the thought.

"It is taking you a long time to do the laundry."

Beatriz gave a start as she looked up to see her Tio Elian watching her. She never liked the way he looked at her. Sometimes she thought he chased other men away because...but no, it was wrong for her to think that way!

"I was daydreaming, uncle. It is such a nice day for dreaming."

"Get back to the village! There is much work to do," her uncle snapped. "Would you have your poor aunt do all the chores?"

"I will go now, uncle," she replied, lifting her basket. He watched her walk as she made her way up the trail; he liked the way her hips swayed. He told himself it was wrong, he was her uncle—but what harm did it do to look? He took a step to follow her when he saw the shirt she had dropped. Damn that foolish girl, he thought. Now the shirt will have to be washed again! Then he spotted the crude map drawn in the mud. He stared for a moment, not sure of the significance.

"Ah?" It dawned on him and he began to cast about for signs. He found a spot in the woods where the grass was pressed down, as if someone had waited there for a long time. Waited for what? For Elena to leave so he could be alone with Beatriz? Who would dare? What boy from the village would dare such a thing? Had he not made it clear that none of them were worthy of his wife's niece?

Later that night, Elian lay awake in bed thinking of the map in the mud. What did it mean? Were Beatriz and one of the village boys planning to run away? Why the map? She knew how to get to Santa Maria. Was the boy from another village? Was she to meet him there? What had the map shown? He thought it might be the area around the hacienda of Don Pablo de Jesus. But why there? He would speak to Elena in the morning. She was wise and she could help keep an eye on Beatriz in case she planned to elope with some useless peasant boy.

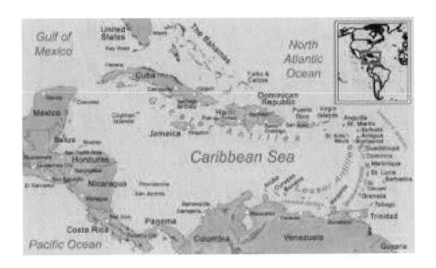

{ 22 }

Greed

Locked in a cage in the center of the parade ground of San Felipe, the Iron Fort, Persifal Kerbourchard was slumped, disheveled, in a corner. The sun beat down on him mercilessly and a bucket of water was just out of his reach. With half-closed eyes and swollen tongue, Kerbourchard stared at the wooden bucket. He had tried to reach out for it, to stretch as far as he could, but Colonel Rubens had deliberately placed it just beyond his reach. His men— those who survived the guns of the Iron Fort—were also imprisoned. Some were in the guardhouses, others had already been sent to work in the Spanish mines. When the cannon had opened up and sunk their ships in the middle of the Chagres River, the pirates had attempted to reach shore and escape through the jungle, but Colonel Rubens was not one to waste time. He had personally led a detachment from the fort and easily captured the demoralized outlaw crew.

Days in the stocks and near starvation had not loosened Kerbourchard's tongue, but Rubens was determined. The colonel loved the sounds of war, but that did not mean he did not enjoy the finer things in life. He was certain this bedraggled pirate knew where treasure was buried. Colonel Rubens was a patient man—to a point. Some of the other men were being forced to walk back and forth across the parade grounds under the same blistering sun. In spite of the Spanish soldiers standing watch, several of the men nudged the water bucket with a toe each time they passed. Kerbourchard watched wordlessly.

Later, when his men were led back to the guardhouse, Kerbourchard snaked an arm out from his cage and dragged the bucket closer. With a cupped hand he drew water to himself, splashing his face and letting a few drops trickle down his throat. The dashing Kerbourchard was now a dirty mass of mud and blood. But his spirit was no closer to surrender than the first day he had been caught. By now he knew what had happened to Captain Jacobson. It was the lot of the pirate, the unexpected thing that made the soundest plans useless. The war galleon had made short work of Jacobson, allowing Rubens to return to San Felipe just in time. Ten minutes more and the fort would have been in the hands of the pirates, and they could have used the fort's own cannon against Rubens.

"Ah, very clever!" A balding, heavyset man casually reached out a boot and tipped the water bucket over. "I do not know how you managed to reach the bucket, Kerbourchard, but it will do you no good. You will die here, you know."

Kerbourchard grabbed the bars and pulled himself to his feet. "I know you."

"I should say so," the balding man's laugh was even more annoying than his high-pitched voice. "Have I changed that much? I shot you a few years ago. Have you forgotten Hispaniola? I thought I had you. The others thought you were dead, but I knew better. I wanted to see your body, Kerbourchard. I wanted to know for sure."

"Souza? Is it you?"

"*Si*, old friend. I wanted the reward on you, but you escaped me. I did not think you were so good in the jungle. But you completely disappeared."

"I looked for you, Miguel. You hid yourself well."

"I hid in the one place I knew you couldn't reach me—Triana."

"Triana? But that is a prison."

"Not just a prison, but the one from which no man has ever escaped. And few who enter in chains ever leave alive, I'm afraid."

"You are stationed there?"

"I am *capitan* of the guards, Kerbourchard." Souza puffed his chest out, adding with flair, "I run Triana. If I do not like a man, he does not live long. Of course, in Triana, no one lives too long anyway. It can be boring there and I must think of amusements for the men. I wonder about Rubens, though, he seems to have a devious mind. Why does he not just kill you?"

"He wants me to tell him where my treasure is buried."

Souza raised an eyebrow. "Ah? And do you know of such a thing?"

"I might know a little more than I have told Rubens."

Stepping closer to the cage, Souza lowered his voice. "I can help you, you know. I have some influence these days. I am in favor with the Duc de Castile. I can get you sent to Triana."

"That's how you'd help me? Send me to an inescapable prison?"

"Maybe Triana would agree with you more than San Felipe? You would be away from Colonel Rubens," Souza said. "I could see that you were cared for, that no harm befell you."

"Like you did on Hispaniola?"

"Do not hold that against me, Kerbourchard, I was young and foolish," protested Souza. "I am in a position now to make all of that up to you. Rubens will kill you if you stay here, he has told me so. But in Triana, where I control things? Certain things might happen."

"Escape?"

Souza looked quickly about. "I could arrange such a thing, for a price."

"I don't know if I can trust you, Souza."

"I asked to be sent to Triana, Kerbourchard. You know why? Because I was afraid you would hunt for me, so I chose the one place you couldn't reach me. But I do not want to live all the rest of my days hidden in Triana. I want the cities, the taverns, the women! We can help each other, Kerbourchard. We will split the treasure, you and I. I will let you escape Triana— and you will forget all about seeking revenge for what happened on Hispaniola."

"My men, Souza—you must get them away from Rubens, too. I am afraid of what he will do to them if they remain here."

Souza nodded. "It is agreed. But, Kerbourchard, tell me, how much treasure is there?"

"More than most cites, Souza," Kerbourchard replied. Leaning closer to the bars, he added, "A king's fortune, I tell you! Mountains of gold and silver! More pieces of eight than you could count in a year."

"How can there be so much? Are you trying to trick me?" asked Souza. He was not a trusting man.

"No." Kerbourchard replied. He could see the greed sparkling in Souza's eyes. "I was with Carlomagno at Maracaibo, have you forgotten? We filled several ships with treasure, Souza. Treasure that has not been spent! I have been with him on other raids, too, and each was successful."

"Yes, I have heard of this Carlomagno. He even attacked a ship owned by the Duc de Castile."

"A ship filled with treasure, Souza. I have my share buried, but I also know where some of Carlomagno's is hidden. I can get that for you, too."

"*Si! Muy bien*! I will get you out of here," Souza said. "I can arrange this for you."

"And my men."

"Yes, your men, too. But if you try any tricks, Kerbourchard, I shall kill you and all of your men."

"No tricks, Souza. We understand each other," Kerbourchard replied. "You do your part and I will show you the greatest treasure there is."

Miguel Souza turned away from the cage and started for the headquarters of Colonel Rubens. The colonel was a greedy man and would hate to let Kerbourchard go—but what could he do, Souza thought? Not even Colonel Rubens would dare interfere with the plans of the Duc de Castile.

Rubens glanced up impatiently as Souza entered. A lifelong military man, Rubens had never liked the casual slovenliness displayed by Souza.

"That man in the cage—Kerbourchard? He is the one I seek. The duke wants him and his men sent to Triana at once."

Rubens' fist pounded the table and his teeth clenched as he tried to control his anger. "But this man is my prisoner! He is a common pirate!"

"He and his men attacked a ship owned by Don Pablo de Jesus and he wishes to have them interrogated at Triana."

"I captured them," Rubens insisted. "They are mine."

Nodding, Souza remarked, "I understand, Colonel. I shall inform the duke of your refusal to cooperate."

"No! No, Captain Souza," Rubens protested. "You misunderstand. Of course I will be happy to accommodate the duke."

Miguel Souza smiled with satisfaction. "That is better, Colonel Rubens. I shall tell the duke of your friendship and—" Souza paused before continuing. "I'm sure if there's any reward to be paid for these men that you should receive it."

"Reward?" Rubens sat down heavily in his chair. "Yes, reward. Of course, Capitan, I would be most grateful to the duke for any reward. The duke's ship, what became of its cargo?"

"Oh, it was recovered, every peso, Colonel," Souza laughed. "Is that what the pirate was telling you? That he had buried treasure? Bah, he has nothing. The duke only wants him to pay for daring to seize one of his ships."

Rubens nodded. "I see. You may take them all away with you. And do let the duke know of my cooperation. I am a great admirer."

{ 23 }

Cuba

Lady Annabeth Pickford opened the doors and stepped out onto the balcony. The sun was warm and a pleasant breeze playfully ruffled her hair. The view was magnificent, she had to admit. In the distance there were sugarcane fields; she could just make out the tiny figures of the workers. Closer to the main house a lovely garden of multi-colored flowers surrounded a marble fountain. At its top, an angel spouted water. Peering over the edge of the balcony, she spied the guards. There were two this time. Sometimes there was only one. But always she was watched. Don Pablo de Jesus had treated her kindly enough, but it was made clear that she was a prisoner. He had paraded her around Santa Maria and told a tale of their plans to wed. It was all concocted, for Lady Pickford had no intention of marrying the duke. Handsome, he might be, but her heart had already been given to another. She had not had time to prepare herself for this ordeal. She had been certain the knock on her door at the International Inn was her brother. She had been unable to utter a sound as two strangers grabbed and gagged her. Taken to a waiting carriage, kicking and struggling, loaded like so much dead weight onto a ship, she had assumed it must be the work of the Chevalier de Fortenay, until they were safely out to sea. Then she had been let loose and allowed on deck only to find her captor was Don Pablo, the man who had claimed to be protecting them. In fact, Pablo de Jesus was none other than the Duc de Castile, the man who had sworn to kill Carlomagno!

Annabeth knew she was only bait in this deadly game. If the duke was successful in killing Carlomagno, he might release her. But for what? What good to have life, but not to share it with the one man she loved? She might save Carlomagno, if only she could find some way to kill Don Pablo. The thought made her shudder. Had she become so callous that taking a human life meant nothing to her? No, she had been taken against her will and brought here by force—and then she realized that was exactly how Carlomagno had come to be in the Spanish Main!

She had no one to help her. The story in Santa Maria had been to scare the locals, make them think a jealous pirate was coming with his bloodthirsty followers to steal the duke's intended bride. The story would rile the locals into supporting the duke and reporting any unusual activity. Annabeth knew she could expect no help. She saw the people of Santa Maria and they either adored Don Pablo or feared him. She saw how some smiled openly at him, while others hid their frightened eyes.

But there was that one girl. She was young, her hair black as midnight, and her eyes as well. She had stared boldly at the duke, no hint of love or fear in her eyes. She was one who was not afraid of Don Pablo. Then Annabeth recalled the other two with her, both older. The man had been heavyset, with droopy eyelids and a menacing stare when he looked at the women. He was a man who might be dangerous, she thought. The older woman, Droopy Eyes' wife, perhaps, was one of those who fawned over the duke and lived for his every word. Neither of them would help. The young girl, their daughter, Annabeth guessed. What had they called her, Beatriz? But what could one girl do? And would she even help?

Lady Pickford went back into her room. It was nicely decorated and quite comfortable. Yet she knew it for what it was: a prison. Even if the girl were willing to help her, there was no way to get word to her; Lady Pickford did not even know where the girl lived. There were several small settlements near Santa Maria, most either along the river that split Cuba or on the coasts.

A servant was sent to bring her to dinner. They went down a wide staircase and the servant beckoned her out onto a screened-in veranda. A table had been amply set with food and the duke gave a bow as he held her chair for her.

"It is such a pleasant evening. I thought you might enjoy dining out here," he said as he seated himself. Immediately servants began to place food on the plates before them. "You might as well make your stay here as comfortable as possible, Lady Pickford."

"You do have a lovely home, Don Pablo," Lady Pickford said. She could see the compliment pleased him. "Why do you go to all this trouble?"

The smile left his face. "I must, senorita. You see, I have a reputation to uphold. No one has ever dared to seize one of my ships before. Not even Henry Morgan! But this Carlomagno dares. Oh, he's a bold fellow! But he must be made to pay for his insolence."

"I'm sure he had no idea the ship was yours. What if he made it up to you, paid you for the value of your lost items?"

"Oh, he will pay, senorita. I regret to refuse you, but I must make an example of Carlomagno. I will hunt him down and hang him. And then I'll display his head in the harbor of Port Royal as a warning to all the other scum along the waterfront."

"In Santa Maria you told the crowd of our plans to wed. I will marry you willingly and be your loyal wife—if you forget about avenging yourself against Carlomagno."

Don Pablo pursed his lips in thought. "An attractive proposition, senorita. Yes, most interesting indeed. But I cannot forgive this pirate his offenses. Now let us eat dinner. You will be treated well as my guest, and you will be free to leave once I have Carlomagno."

"You are mistaken if you think he will come to Cuba."

"Now you disappoint me, senorita. I know men. Carlomagno will come. He will sail his ships to the coast and come marching here with all of his men. But as you will see, it will not be so easy. I have my own private army, and they will not flee like the peons of Maracaibo." Don Pablo picked up his fork and speared a piece of meat from a plate piled high with roasted chicken. "Carlomagno will be in for quite a surprise when he comes to Cuba. And I will know of his movements long before he ever reaches here."

With his servants standing by, Don Pablo eagerly ate his dinner as he prattled on about his plans to expand his holdings. But Annabeth ate without really hearing him. She thought of refusing to eat at all, but decided she must keep her strength up in case an opportunity to escape presented itself. At every opportunity she managed to smuggle a bit of food to her room: an apple or plantain from one meal, a hunk of bread from another. Her mind was set on escape. She had the food hidden away in the rear of her closet. She needed a sack to carry it in, but so far had had no opportunity to get one.

Another servant appeared in the doorway; at Don Pablo's nod he entered and swiftly crossed the veranda.

"What is it, Pico?"

"I have news from Port Royal, Don Pablo." At the duke's nod, Pico continued. "There was a major earthquake and much of the city has been destroyed."

Lady Pickford dropped her silverware and a soft gasp emerged from her lips. Don Pablo glanced at her, then back to Pico.

"What of the pirate?"

"I'm not sure, Don Pablo. He was there, he had a fight."

"A fight?" The duke set his fork down. "Tell me about it."

"Apparently the Chevalier de Fortenay left some men behind to kill Carlomagno," Pico said. "There is no sign of any of them."

Don Pablo pounded the table. "Damn, that de Fortenay! I told him to leave Carlomagno to me. He ceases to be useful if he does not heed my commands! What of the pirate, Pico? Was he killed in the earth-quake?"

"I'm not certain, excellency. There was much destruction and many men were simply washed out to sea. No one is really sure what happened to Carlomagno."

"I knew he'd go to Port Royal when he heard about Macomber's death. That's why I told de Fortenay to leave the city, so Carlomagno would forget about him and come after the senorita." Don Pablo absently stroked his neatly-trimmed beard. "I must know if Carlomagno escaped Port Royal. Have any of the peasants reported anything unusual?"

"Nothing," Pico replied. "There was a man from a small fishing village on the northern coast. He said he thought he saw a ship sailing away early one morning. That was a week ago."

"What? Why did you not report this, Pico?"

"The man, he is old and drinks too much. He is known to exaggerate such things, he thinks to make himself look important so always he has a story to tell," Pico explained. "If you see an alligator, this mans sees one twice as big."

"I see," said the duke, nodding with satisfaction. "One ship, was it? No, that couldn't have been anything. A man like this Carlomagno will come here with all of his ships, looking for a total war. He knows my fortress is impregnable."

"The man said he saw one ship, my lord, and it was sailing away from Cuba. If there was a ship—and I doubt that—it must have been one sailing by on a trade mission to the Keys or the Bahamas."

"Yes, I think you are right, Pico. Thank you for the news of Port Royal," Don Pablo picked up his wine glass and took a sip. "But you must try to find out more about Carlomagno. I need to know if he survived the earthquake."

"*Si, senor,*" bowed Pico, backing toward the door.

Don Pablo de Jesus drifted off into his own thoughts. He was a man who lived by a simple code, one that insisted that those who violated him in any way must pay a harsh price. He had no hatred for Carlomagno, but an example must be made of the pirate. First, he must know if Carlomagno still lived. Leave that to Pico, he would find out the truth, the duke thought to himself. Pico was a dedicated servant and would never let him down.

Only Pico was dead.

The faithful servant had left the main house and remounted his horse, which had remained saddled and ready. He had suddenly thought of the small village to the northeast, closer than the one on the coast. There was a man there, his name was Elian, he might know something, Pico thought. This Elian was a selfish boor, one Pico suspected of being involved in smuggling and thievery himself. But he might have heard or seen something. Lost in his thoughts, Pico was unaware of the arrow that came whistling from the darkness and drove into his chest. He toppled from the saddle, hitting the ground hard without ever realizing what had killed him.

A shadow moved and Carlomagno stepped into the path. Speaking softly, he nabbed Pico's horse. It had taken only a few steps after its rider fell, and then stopped to look back inquisitively. Carlomagno stroked the horse; this bit of good fortune might provide him with the edge he needed to make a clean getaway with Anna. He mounted and went forward. He knew he was about a mile away from the main house of Don Pablo; getting in and rescuing Anna would be difficult indeed.

Carlomagno slowed as the jungle started to thin; he tethered the horse out of sight. There were fifty yards of open space before a guard tower loomed up. It was difficult to make out the guard in the tower in the darkness, but Carlomagno knew he was there by the reddish glow of the cigarette he smoked. Carlomagno snaked forward; the grass was tall enough to conceal him from the other towers. But if the guard on the platform before him was vigilant he could easily spot the creeping Indian.

The guard had been told to expect a large contingent of men and was certain he would hear the group long before they could reach his position. How many nights had he spent just like this one, relaxing and smoking his cigarettes? He had exchanged a word of greeting with Pico less than an hour ago. But Pico had been in a hurry. The guard raised his cigarette to his lips and took a healthy puff. He gave a short yelp as an arrow sank into him. He fell to his knees, disappearing behind the half-walls of his tower lookout.

Leaving his bow at the base of the tower, Carlomagno swiftly scaled the ladder. He needn't have, for the guard was dead. He was halfway down when he heard the sound of running feet.

"Ramon? Ramon, is that you?" Carlomagno continued to climb down. The ladder was in shadow and the man could not make out more than a dark figure on its way down. "Ramon, I must speak with the Duc! I found Pico. He has been killed!"

Carlomagno reached for his knife even as his feet touched the ground. The man, breathing heavily, came closer.

"It is the pirate, Ramon! I think he is here, I..." Too late Elian, the uncle of the girl who had helped Carlomagno, saw the long hair and felt the knife blade slide between his ribs. Carlomagno clapped a hand to his mouth and Elian died unable to scream a warning.

Using every bit of cover, Carlomagno slithered closer to the main house. He noticed a balcony on the second floor; beneath it two guards stood, conversing in hushed tones. In that room, he knew, the Lady Pickford must be kept. There was a vine-covered trellis leading to the balcony. He could make the climb to her balcony easily enough. But how to incapacitate the two guards? To use an arrow on one would give the other time to give warning. Carlomagno edged toward the side of the house, around the corner. He remembered the signal he had once shared with his Pequot friend, Noank. He made the sound of the tree frog: "Coqui! Coqui!"

He repeated it several times before he heard one of the guards approaching. The man turned the corner, peering cautiously around and mumbling about those frogs becoming a nuisance. Carlomagno took a long stride from the shadows and his hatchet split the guard's skull. Peering around the corner of the house, Carlomagno could see the back of the remaining guard standing idly below the balcony. It was an easy bowshot and the guard fell silently on his face. One pant leg was visible in a small circle of light from a window in the main house. But to try and move the guard into the deeper shadows would use too much valuable time.

Carlomagno shrugged off his quiver and dropped his bow at the foot of the trellis. Then, noiselessly, he climbed to the balcony. The door to the room was unlocked. Annabeth put a hand to her mouth to stifle a gasp as Carlomagno walked into her room. She rushed into his arms and they clung together for a long minute.

"It's a trap," she whispered. "You must flee; the duke only used me to bait his trap for you."

"I will not go without you."

"He wants to kill you, he knew you'd come," she pleaded.

"He expects a big army," Carlomagno replied. "He did not prepare for a lone warrior. Can you climb? There is a trellis against the wall.

Go down and turn to the left. At the edge of the woods, just beyond the guard tower, I have a horse waiting."

"Strip the covers off the bed. I have food, we can wrap it in a sheet," Annabeth said, moving toward the closet.

"You start climbing down, I'll wrap the food," Carlomagno said. He placed the food on the bed and grasped the corners of the sheet to form a makeshift sack. The door opened behind him.

"*Que pasa?*"

Carlomagno whirled around, swinging the food-filled bed sheet and striking the guard in the face. He stumbled back out into the hall and Carlomagno followed, kicking the man in the stomach. The man careened back and fell over the rail to the floor below. In a moment, a maid began shrieking. Carlomagno latched the door as he crossed to the balcony. Anna had already reached the bottom and was making her way toward the horse. As he began to swiftly descend, a musket blast clipped the wooden trellis a foot from his head. A man came out of the house holding a pistol but fired too hastily; the shot was not even close. The man began to reload. The yard came alive with shouting and the sound of running feet.

On the ground, Carlomagno gathered up a musket dropped by one of the guards he had killed, and snatched up his bow and quiver on the run. The door to the house flew open. With a hasty backward glance Carlomagno knew at once the man must be the Duc de Castile. He seemed to have an air of command about him. The man fired carefully, missing only by a fraction. As he hastily reloaded his pistol other gunshots erupted, kicking up the ground near Carlomagno's racing feet. A guard stepped before him with a musket in his hand. Carlomagno jammed the muzzle of his musket into the man's stomach, and then battered him over the head with it. There were too many coming! He heard the horse behind him and turned; it was Anna! He wheeled and ran, vaulting onto the horse. Anna managed the horse expertly as the duke raised his pistol for a second shot. They had barely reached the trees when the horse staggered; within a few steps it began to fall. The riders rolled clear as the horse kicked against death. It might have been the duke's shot, or some of the other fire directed toward them, but someone had shot the horse! Carlomagno had planned to go north, but the duke would expect him to follow the closest route to the sea. Instead, Carlomagno turned south. The river flowed swiftly from the heart of Cuba to empty some forty-five miles away into Twelve League Cays, a group of tiny islands at the tip of Cuba. They had gone but a little way when they came upon a small collection of thatched-roofed houses.

A watchdog's growl alerted someone; a door flew open and a man with a lantern stood there, irritably calling for his dog. After a few moments he started toward the water, a lantern held high in one hand and a pistol in his right. A small boat pulled ashore and the man glanced at it, his eyes widening as he saw Lady Annabeth standing beside it.

"Well, well, what do we have here?" the man said, clucking his teeth. "Is this my lucky day?"

"I don't think so," said Carlomagno as he prodded the man in the back with his musket.

"What is this? Are you stealing my boat? The boat of a poor working man?"

"Damn my blood for taking this vessel, for such I do not normally do! But I have urgent need of it, *amigo!*"

"You're the one Don Pablo warned about," the man suddenly realized. "*El Rojo Indio!* I must—"

"You must report me? Miserable dog! You would crawl on your belly and lick the boots of the rich man in hopes of a cast-off crumb from his table!"

The man shrank away. "No, no, I will not say anything, *senor.*"

296

"You are like all the sheep, doing the bidding of a wealthy man who robs you as surely as I do. The only difference, my friend, is that the wealthy rob the poor, who are defenseless. I rob the rich, making war upon them as surely as any prince on earth can declare war upon an enemy." Carlomagno said. "Prepare the boat, for I must take leave!"

The man glanced nervously over his shoulder. "Are you going to kill me?"

"Even as you ask that question, you are thinking of the reward offered by the duke."

"No, no, I wasn't," the man denied "I won't say anything to the duke! I swear to you."

"I must be certain of that." Carlomagno gripped the musket in two hands. Taking a swift step forward he brought the heavy stock crashing down against the man's skull. Working quickly, he bound and gagged the unconscious man. "By the time they find him, we will be long gone, Anna."

"I knew you were not going to kill him," she said smugly as he picked up the paddle and shoved off.

"You did, did you? I suppose you have me all figured out?"

"Not yet," she smiled to herself in the dark. "But almost."

"Try to rest; I'll keep moving until it gets close to daylight."

"Do you think he'll find us?" Anna sighed.

"In time," Carlomagno answered, "but it's our only chance. We've got to reach Twelve League Cays and hope to catch the attention of a passing ship—and hope it's not a Spanish one."

The odds were slim, indeed. After all, they were in Cuba.

{ 24 }

A Risky Retreat

To ride the river at night was dangerous, but they had no choice. Carlomagno dipped the paddle deep and kept a sharp eye out for crocodiles. Cold-blooded reptiles, crocs were unlikely to be in the water at night, but it was unwise to take things for granted. Carlomagno knew where he was heading only from the crude map drawn by Beatriz in the mud on the riverbank. She had explained that the Cays were a series of small islands, mostly deserted.

"We'll make it, Anna," he said softly. He could see the fatigue in her face and sense her apprehension.

"At least we're together to face whatever happens next." She smiled through her weariness. "There's no place I'd rather be."

They rode in silence. Just before dawn, when the gray shadows still protected them, they glided ghostlike past a slumbering village. It was getting light and Carlomagno knew that to remain on the water invited detection. A bit further downriver he spotted a place where tree branches drooped over the water, providing a hiding place. He eased the boat under the skirt of branches, nestling beneath the trees. Carlomagno helped Anna onto the tree-laden riverbank, dragging the small boat up after them. Without the branches, the rowboat would have been clearly visible; it was the best they could do for now. Carlomagno loaded his guns, grimacing as he noted his powder was almost gone. He would be hard-pressed to fight his way out of any scrapes. He had his bow, though the quiver held only three arrows. During the desperate fight at Don Pablo's hacienda he had been unable to retrieve any of the arrows he had used. He'd keep his eyes open for quartz or any similar rocks that could be quickly chipped to make arrowheads. Leaving his guns with Anna, he took the bow and scouted the area. He found no game, but did find a freshwater hole. Moving beneath the trees, they settled in a concealed spot to wait out the day. The coolness of the water was a tiny luxury as the day heated up rapidly.

"You think Don Pablo went north?"

"Yes, he seemed to be sure I'd land along that coast with many ships. It was the shortest way to his fortress. It was my plan to go that way," Carlomagno said. "The *Anasarani* will be cruising along the coast. I thought I'd have time to get back there."

"What do we do now?"

"Sleep, while we can. When the sun goes down we'll ride the river to the sea. From there, we'll need a bit of luck, I'm afraid."

Annabeth curled up on the ground, her head resting in Carlomagno's lap. The pirate sat with his back to a tree, his weapons close to hand. His fingers idly stoked her hair.

"I was so afraid when I heard about the earthquake at Port Royal. I was afraid for you, Pokanoket."

"I was lucky. Calico Jack and the Ox were planning to leave and had horses ready. We had a good start for the Cockpit Country before the city started to crumble. We crested a hill and looked back as the sea came roaring into town. I tell you, if I live to be a hundred, I never want to see anything like that again. Buildings knocked down like twigs, tiny specks—men, I imagine, just carried away."

"I'm afraid to ask, but what of Connor?"

"Your brother is safe—he's on the *Anasarani.* I can't explain it, Anna, but Andrew had a premonition and sent his nephew into Port Royal to get Connor out."

"Andrew is a good man," she said.

"Yes, and I think his nephew will grow up to be a good man, too," Carlomagno said. He let his eyes close, enjoying the moment of peace and quiet he now shared with the woman he loved. But how long would it last? How soon before the Duc de Castile realized they had taken the river south? How long before the man whose boat he had taken was able to summon help?

They were hungry, but neither spoke of food. The fruit and bread Annabeth had carefully hoarded was lost during the hasty flight forced upon them. The sky was still a dark purple when Carlomagno shoved off from the shore and began again to paddle southward.

"It is a lovely country," Annabeth said as darkness settled comfortably around them. Carlomagno's oar was practically silent against the water and the occasional calls of the jungle creatures reverberated in their ears.

"There's a rich history here," Carlomagno replied softly. Diego El Negro had spoken often of historical happenings and had shared much of the story behind the Spanish conquest of Cuba. Now, alone in a small boat coasting toward Twelve League Cays, Carlomagno told Annabeth all he could recall about Cuba.

Christopher Columbus came to Hispaniola in 1492. He actually made several voyages and during one of those he made contact with the Cuban natives. The natives were considered very peaceful. Columbus and his men went on their way, leaving the islanders undisturbed. But, by 1510 Spain decided to investigate the possibility of exploring for gold on Cuba. The governor-general of Hispaniola, Diego Columbus, Christopher's son, authorized Diego Velasquez, a wealthy planter, to lead the expedition. In 1511 Velasquez sailed from Hispaniola with four ships and 300 fighting men. The Spaniards had come to conquer and colonize. When he arrived in Cuba, Velasquez founded the island's first Spanish settlement at Baracoa.

Hatuey, a Taino chief, began hearing reports from the natives of Hispaniola about how the Spanish treated them. Hatuey organized a resistance against the Spanish in Cuba. His strategy was to attack and then disperse to the hills, where the Indians would regroup for the next attack. But the Spanish military might was too much for the natives. According to the legend, Hatuey was captured by the Spaniards and burned at the stake.

At the last moment, a priest offered him spiritual comfort, but Hatuey refused to have anything to do with a god that protected cruelty against Indians. With Hatuey gone and the resistance fatally weakened, Velasquez enslaved the remaining Indians to work the mines, cultivate the soil, tend the cattle, and perform other tasks as servants and porters for the Spaniards. Within four years of reaching the island, Velasquez had established seven settlements: Baracoa, the center of the colonial administration; Bayamo; Santiago de Cuba; Puerto Principe; Sancti Spiritus; Trinidad; and La Habana, later called Havana.

With the conquest of the natives well in hand, Velasquez began to conquer the land itself. Grants of land and labor were distributed among Velasquez' men according to their rank and valor during the conquest through a system of *encomiendas*, or trusts, and by allotments. The Spanish encomienda system established a series of rights and obligations between the *encomiendero*, the grantee, and the natives placed under his care. Much as serfs under their feudal lords, the Indians were required to provide tribute and free labor to the encomiendero, while the grantee promised to look to the Indians' welfare, assimilate them into Spanish culture and guide them to Christianity. Under the allotment provision, the Spanish Crown gave a permit to individuals enabling them to use Indian labor for specific tasks, such as working in the mines, on improvements to the community or on private farms. Later the encomiendero was replaced by the *repartimiento* system, only slightly different in that the local alcaldes—mayors— decided how the allotment of free labor was divided. Because the natives were effectively enslaved, both the encomienda and the repartimiento became sources of abuse. At the urging of Friar Bartolomi de las Casas, new laws were passed in 1543. Though he had come to the New World as a conqueror, Las Casas found religion and spent the final decades of his life fighting for humane treatment for the natives. As a young Spanish priest, Las Casas was sent to Cuba to assist Velasquez in the conquest, pacification, and settlement of the island. His firsthand observations of the destitution and misery of the natives prompted him to plead their cause to the Spanish Crown, where he openly challenged the racist overtones of the Spanish expansion. He became know as the "Protector of the Indians" and the "Apostle of the Indies."

"Some men live by a higher code, Carlomagno, like Las Casas. I'm sorry you have not met any of them. Men do many bad things to each other, don't they?" Anna said.

"All men are capable of it, I suppose." Carlomagno was silent for a moment. "I have learned much of your world, Anna, yet the more I learn the less I understand. White men speak from both sides of their mouths at once, saying two different things. I think it must be the same in their hearts. In your world the idea of what is right or wrong blows like the wind, in this direction today and that direction tomorrow.

"This question of slaves, for instance. It was not unknown among my people to take captives in war. But they were often traded back later for something of value. Sometimes they simply stayed and were adopted into the village. Turning a captive into a slave, to work him like an animal until he dies, this is not our way. It must be wrong, for I have never met a slave who is happy to be treated so, nor a master who insisted on trading places with his slave. Yet the Spanish priests come to the plantations and tell the slaves to be obedient, to work hard for their masters. They say their god loves the slaves and will reward them. What kind of a god would tell a man to put his brother in chains?"

Anna drew her knees up and wrapped her arms around them. "I have never met a man quite like you, Carlomagno Pokanoket. I have no answers."

"There are always answers, my darling," Carlomagno replied, as he turned to face her. "Only sometimes we don't know the questions. And always there will be men like Don Pablo de Jesus who use violence to seize the advantage."

"Have you not done the same?"

"Perhaps you are right," he sighed, "but I was given only disadvantages. The laws that were forced on me, and on my people, were never meant to help us succeed, but to keep us in the place the white man assigned to us, and when that did not succeed, to destroy us. It was against this injustice that my father fought.

"If an Indian ate an apple from a tree planted by a white man, he was whipped or ordered to pay many more wampum shells than an apple is worth. As if one could claim the fruits of the earth as possessions. But a white man could take the life of an Indian and the English courts looked the other way, or found some reason to decide the Indian was at fault."

"You are a revolutionary, Carlomagno."

"I do not know that word, Anna. I am just a man alone, trying to survive in a world which has marked him for death."

She touched his arm. "You are not a man alone. I am with you. And Death will just have to wait. I have found the man I have waited for and I will not give you up for fifty years, at least!"

Carlomagno laughed. "It is agreed, milady," he said with an exaggerated bow. "We will have fifty years together—and then if you change your mind, you can tell me goodbye."

When they reached the river delta, Carlomagno raised the boat's mast and her small sail. The river emptied into the Caribbean Sea and they sailed their boat to a tiny island and made their way ashore. There was a fresh water supply and fruits to eat. Carlomagno spitted a fat reddish-brown lizard over the fire for dinner. At first Annabeth wrinkled her nose at the roasting reptile, but hunger won out. After eating, she decided it was not as bad as she had feared. Fashioning a crude spear, Carlomagno was eventually able to catch fish.

Once a ship passed close to their tiny island; from their concealed position they could easily distinguish the Spanish flag. The days passed and they saw no one. When the *Anasarani* reached the Cuban fishing village and did not see him, Carlomagno hoped Morgan and Rigger would make a slow turn around the island before heading for Hispaniola. It was unlikely, but it was the only successful outcome he could foresee, and he wanted to keep Anna's spirits up.

Carlomagno sat beside Annabeth on a sandy, white beach as the emerald waves playfully tickled the shore. In the distance, like the glinting of a handful of silver coins tossed into the air, a school of flying fish shot from the sea only to disappear once more into the mysterious deep. The fading sun tip-toed westward, offering up a bright reddish purple wink as it left the sky to its celebration of winkling starlight and a large, silver moon.

Is love a matter of fate? Why does one man search a lifetime for it and come up wanting, while another stumbles over it unintentionally? Carlomagno and Annabeth came from different worlds, grew up believing different things; neither was living the life they had expected and been raised to live. But that day in Port Royal, when their eyes first locked, something had shifted in each of their hearts. There was a longing, even lust, but their connection went far deeper. There was an understanding between them; they knew they were meant for each other. Until they met, such a union was unthinkable for both of them. But on this sultry summer night, on a deserted Caribbean island, they tumbled into each other's arms under the watchful eye of the Creator. At that moment, loving each other without reservation, nothing else existed in the world. Their bodies welcomed each other, as their souls had done so many weeks before.

The comfortable days grew into anxious weeks as they saw no other vessels. Their food supply on the tiny island was shrinking along with their hopes of rescue. When at last they saw a ship on course to pass near them, they knew they had only one option. Building a smoky fire to catch the ship's attention, they sailed their little boat out to meet it.

"You'll be safe," he assured her softly. "Ask the captain to take you to Hispaniola."

They climbed aboard the ship and were met by Spanish soldiers. The captain was a portly, graying man with a stern but intelligent demeanor. He ordered one of his crew to take the guests to his cabin, where he soon joined them.

"I did not expect to find anyone on the Cays," the captain said, as he seated himself behind his desk. "It looks as if you had a rough time of it, senorita."

"I have managed as best I could." Knowing she had never looked less like the Lady Pickford, Annabeth lifted her chin proudly and smiled. "But, as you correctly guessed, *capitan*, it has been an ordeal!"

The captain turned his eyes to Carlomagno and measured him slowly. "Have we not met before?"

"I do not believe so, captain."

"Oh, but I am certain of it," the capitan said. "I have a memory for such things. As I recall, I was master of a sloop owned by Don Juan de Hidalgo, on my way to Santo Domingo. And you were in a barque, one called *Corazon*? Perhaps your memory improves now?"

Carlomagno smiled ruefully. "We have indeed met before, *capitan*."

"Yes, you told me you were the 'Barracuda of the Spanish Main.' And I have heard much since then of your exploits. I have been waiting to meet you again, Carlomagno."

"I surrender myself to you," the pirate said calmly, "but let the lady go home to Hispaniola."

"I won't go without my husband," Anna insisted.

The captain looked from her to Carlomagno. "Your husband, milady? I did not know. Do you have any children?"

"Not yet," Annabeth replied, looking the captain in the eye, "but we hope to someday."

"I have a son," the captain said. He went to a chest beside his bed. He removed a portrait and showed it to Lady Pickford. She offered a sincere compliment as to how handsome the young man looked in his uniform. "His mother and I did not want him to join the army. It is too dangerous and he is our only child. But he is headstrong; he did not listen to us. I was the same at his age, I suppose. In any case, a man must make his own path in this life, is that not so, Carlomagno?"

"Yes, *capitan*, I would agree with you."

"He has done well and his mother and I are quite proud of him." The captain put the portrait away and sat back down behind his desk. "Dinner should be arriving soon. I suppose you will both wish to freshen up before dining?"

"Am I to consider myself your prisoner?" Carlomagno asked.

"I have not asked for your weapons. You are my guests, Carlomagno. My son has been married a year now, and soon will welcome his first child. My wife is so excited; she is looking forward to spoiling her grandchild. As for me, seeing her smile makes me happy. My wife, she looks at me the way I saw the lady look at you."

"I don't understand *capitan*. You know who I am, and you must know the Duc de Castile is searching for me?"

"*Si*, the duke offers a large reward for your capture. That is why I had you brought down here so quickly, before any of my men might

306

recognize you. You see, Carlomagno, I owe you a larger debt. Were it not for you, I would have no son—and my wife would have no grand-child to look forward to," the *capitan* said. "My name is Rodriquez, Carlomagno. The name, I am sure, means nothing to you. But it should. Before your raid on Maracaibo you attacked a small garrison. Do you remember?"

"There was a lot of fighting that day. Many men died."

"But not my son, Carlomagno. Not my son," the Spaniard said. "He had broken his leg and you found him defenseless, lying in his bed. You spared my son's life—and I repay that debt to you now. I will take you to Hispaniola."

Carlomagno was stunned. "I did not think Spaniards knew the meaning of honor."

"Perhaps you have met the wrong kinds of Spaniards, Carlo-magno?" Captain Rodriquez suggested. "Honor is not inherent to any one race of people, or class of man."

At the captain's urging Carlomagno remained below deck during the journey from Cuba to Hispaniola. The less the crew saw of Carlo-magno, the better, the captain said.

"You take a chance in helping me," Carlomagno remarked over a simple dinner in Rodriquez' cabin. "The duke strikes me as vindictive."

"He can be. No man likes to be thwarted," replied Rodriquez. They dined on roasted yams and a rice dish mixed with beef and salt pork. It was simple, but seasoned for a mildly spicy taste. "I have been at sea a long time. This will be my last voyage. I plan to settle down and live out my life in peace. I have managed well over the years and my wife runs a boardinghouse in Cumana. I'll join her and we'll all live well.

"I will miss the *Arbol Grande*, though. This has been a fine craft to command. But there comes a time for every sailor when he must give up the sea. It is better to make the choice yourself, rather than to have it made for you, Carlomagno."

"You speak of piracy?"

"The times are slowly changing, my friend. Ten years ago or twenty there was little law. Each nation looked the other way as long as its own ships went unmolested," the captain said. "But that policy did little good. If anything, it encouraged freebooting. No, I think we will soon see an era of cooperation with the nations coming together to outlaw piracy. Then the pirates will have no safe port: every ship of every nation will be an enemy."

Carlomagno refilled his water glass. "There is always Tortuga."

"It seems indestructible, with the small harbor and rock wall, but it can be taken," Rodriquez said. "A blockade could be set up and the pirates starved out. It would take many ships, I grant you. But England and Spain have many ships; with the help of Holland and France, it can be done. And I have heard that even the American colonies grow weary of pirates along their costal waters."

"Have you been to the colonies?" Annabeth asked.

"No, I have not. I have sailed to Florida, to St. Augustine, but never to the English colonies. I hear they are becoming quite prosperous and civilized—um, well, I mean to say they are growing."

Carlomagno smiled and eased the captain's regret over his choice of words, wryly noting, "It is my greatest wish to remain uncivilized, *Capitan!*"

But it was not to be so.

Soon after their return to the *Sequanakeeswush*, Carlomagno and Anna were married in a civil ceremony that combined elements of his heritage with her Catholic beliefs. The smoking of the pipe to the four directions sent prayers to the Creator for a successful union, and the priest's Latin intonations drifted musically with the heavy incense. Father Sackett was from Jacmel, a friend of Louis Dearborn's. He offered some mild concerns at the irregular ceremony, but agreed to officiate.

"Your children? They will be raised Catholic, no?" the priest asked.

"Do Catholics believe in honesty and truth? Will they help the needy, defend the weak?"

"But of course, Carlomagno."

"Then they will be Catholic no matter how they are raised."

A lavish feast was followed by dancing. Food and stronger spirits flowed freely until the early morning hours. Everyone celebrated, from the newest arrivals, creeping onto the plantation under cover of night, to the former pirates who had proven their loyalty to each other time and time again. Even the priest partook of the fruit of the vine.

"Thank you for agreeing to marry us, Father Sackett," Anna said as the priest, tankard in hand passed the alcove where she and her new husband stood resting after a dance. "You were the only priest who would accommodate us."

"My pleasure, I assure you," the priest bowed, wobbling slightly. "If I have a weakness," he paused to take a healthy drink, "it is love! Love is a precious gift from God. I can't help but perform the act that binds two hearts together." His bleary eyes swept the crowded dance floor. "Imagine how grand the world would be if we knew only love, and never learned to hate?"

Nine months after their nuptials they were blessed with the birth of a healthy daughter, who was named Jennie Pickford Pokanoket, honoring Anna's mother. In the European tradition of taking surnames, the Wampanoag had signed his marriage certificate as Carlomagno Pokanoket.

Beatriz, the Cuban girl who had made it to his waiting ship, had acted as midwife. In spite of Carlomagno's look of horror, she had immediately placed the small wrapped bundle in his hands.

"What if I break it?" he protested.

"Don't tell me my brave warrior is afraid of a newborn?" Anna laughed.

"I assure you, *señor*, the *bebés* are much stronger than they look," Beatriz promised.

"Say hello to your daughter, husband," Anna urged.

Moving as if the blanket contained a deadly serpent, Carlomagno carefully cradled the bundle and used nimble fingers to peel back the cloth. A tiny face peered up at him as the baby seemed to wave her arms in greeting. Thus the fierce Pirate prince was conquered by a baby's smile.

Dinners at *Sequanakeeswush* were informal affairs with lots of food and even more generous laughter. Though they usually included Diego and Beatriz, Flynn, Labrosse and Blanchette, other members of the Hispaniola community were always welcome.

Guests were frequent and even some of the old guard came to relax in the sand and bask in the hospitality. The food was a major enticement. Calico Jack had come to Sequanakeeswush and soon set himself up as Carlomagno's cook; few could match his culinary skill.

As his plantation grew, Carlomagno gradually gave up his pirate ways, becoming prosperous and more worldly. Diego El Negro was a shrewd trader and had done well on each voyage. Diego's successes had also extended beyond Carlomagno's business interests. As the ship had reached the agreed-upon meeting place on the Cuban coast, a striking Cuban girl named Beatriz had insisted they allow her to leave with them as promised by the pirate, Carlomagno. The moment he saw her, Diego knew she would be his. They were to be wed very soon, with Father Sackett's blessing.

"If I am not careful, you will turn me into a gentleman, Diego," Carlomagno said over dinner one evening.

Feigning offense, Diego put a hand to his heart. "You insult me, *Señor* Barracuda! I would never stoop so low!"

As laughter died down, Anna raised her glass. "I believe you are both gentlemen; more importantly, my Carlomagno is a gentle man. I would not want him any other way! Besides, they do not call it the 'trappings' of civilization for naught!"

"Diego, tell us about your recent journey," Anna asked. "How are affairs in the colonies?"

Diego El Negro had returned from a trading mission to the American colonies. The reign of William and Mary was proving as onerous as that of James II and the New England colonists were growing increasingly discontented. At Carlomagno's urging, when his business was completed in Carolina, Diego had visited the city of Philadelphia for the first time. A few years back, Quakers in the area known as "Penn's Sylvania" had lodged an official protest against slavery in the colonies. It was one of the few places where colonists had refused to write into law the idea of lifelong slavery. Philadelphia was becoming a place where former slaves could live in freedom. They took it as a hopeful sign. Most of the colonies had moved to preserve their slave labor by doing away with laws that made it possible for some to earn their freedom.

Only the Rhode Island colonists had outlawed slavery in their jurisdiction.

"The colonists grow weary of the restrictions placed on them by the crown, but the atmosphere is vibrant," Diego explained. "Philadelphia is becoming a great city. It is still small as cities go, but I predict it will be the greatest city in the world one day. More people are arriving every day, not just from England, but all of Europe. They say the colonial population could reach 250,000 by the turn of the century. A push west seems inevitable."

"They say in the west, the native peoples still live much as they always have," Carlomagno noted wistfully. "It sounds like a place to see..."

""Your businesses aren't the only thing that's growing," Anna reminded him with a gentle pat to her belly. And don't you even think about going without me, Mr. Pokanoket!"

"I was only saying—"

Carlomagno, once a common pirate, was gradually becoming a man of substance. With his private fleet growing, there was always at least one ship in the little harbor, and sometimes two. He had holdings in Barbados, Jamaica, the Grenadines, the Bahamas and Carolina. His vessels would bring rum to the colonies and trade for timber or potash to be sold elsewhere. Many products passed in and out of his ships. But never human cargo.

"Soon you'll be one of the wealthiest men in the Caribbean," Diego said.

"We are all doing well," Carlomagno nodded as he closed their account book. Thanks to Diego, he had been learning how to add and multiply numbers. "But it is due to your diligence, Diego. Not just I, but all of us here at *Sequanakeeswush* owe you thanks. Most of us were former slaves without hope or future. Now we have our freedom and a chance to prosper."

"I have taught you much and you have been an apt student, Carlomagno. But I hope you understand the danger you face?"

"Danger?" interjected Morgan Flynn, who had been idly spinning a wooden globe. "Do you forget, Diego? He's a legend in the Caribbean—the Barracuda of the Spanish Main! No one would dare attack him now. Carlomagno is where Sir Henry Morgan was twenty years ago."

"What you say is true, Morg," Diego nodded. "But you do remember that Henry Morgan was taken back to England as a prisoner? It was only with the help of his friends in high places at court, those who had the king's ear, that he was pardoned. Carlomagno has no such friends, Irishman. If England turns against him, he has no one to state his case, no one on whom he can depend for support."

"What about Lady Annabeth's brother?" Flynn asked. "Now that his debts have been paid, he has returned to England and looks after our interests there."

"He comes from a good family, but has no title, no vast estate, nothing that matters to the English monarchy," Diego said. "He could not

312

hope to gain audience with the king or any of his top ministers. You see, Carlomagno, your success adds to your danger."

Carlomagno crossed the room and stared out at the green fields stretching away toward the sea. "I know, Diego."

He knew the governments of England, Spain, France and Holland would not take kindly to an upstart "state" growing in their midst. *Sequanakeeswush* was becoming more and more self-sustaining. With the European powers already squabbling over the fertile land, it would not be long before they looked to Hispaniola and the little empire of *Sequanakeeswush*.

Worse still, runaway slaves regularly found their way to his lands with hopes of gaining freedom. Only a week before, a representative from the Spanish-controlled region of Hispaniola had asked Carlomagno to return a runaway slave if he should turn up on his lands. Carlomagno had given no direct answer, nor had he openly defied the Spanish authorities.

"What will you do if this Shabaka shows up here?"

"I can't send him back to slavery, Diego. That is not a fit life for any man."

Diego El Negro smiled to himself, already knowing what Carlomagno would say. "It is a dangerous wind that fills your sails, my friend. You know it could lead to Spanish soldiers attacking us."

Morgan Flynn slammed his beefy fist on the table. "Let them come, Diego! We've men enough here to meet them. Good fighting men, too!"

Carlomagno watched the gentle sea as it rolled peacefully toward the shore. He had been trying so hard these past few years to avoid fighting, which cut into their profits. But remaining neutral was becoming increasingly difficult as tensions once again rose between Spain and England.

"There may be a way out for us, Carlomagno," said Diego. He crossed the room to stand beside his friend, "but it is not without danger."

Carlomagno sighed softly. "When have I not known danger, Diego? What do you suggest?"

"We could approach the new English governor at Port Royal. We can declare ourselves for England, perhaps obtain letters of marque? At least then we'll be operating under an English flag. That would give you some protection should the political tides change."

"And the danger?"

"If England should lose this war which is about to break out, all of Spain will be against us. We'll stand alone on the Main," Diego warned.

Dinners at Pickford Hall, as the main house at *Sequanakeeswush* became known, continued to be exciting affairs with the best of foods. Calico Jack followed recipes he recalled from his own childhood or simply invented as he went along. Green turtle soup was a staple, as Carlomagno had grown to enjoy it very much. The long wooden table in the main dining hall seated two dozen comfortably, and sometimes more would crowd around. Discussions were varied and moved between interesting news, humorous anecdotes and important happenings throughout the Caribbean. This night, Diego—easily the most learned of them—held their attention as he spoke of the legends surrounding the long-dead emperor known as Charlemagne. He was explaining about the hippogriff, the magical half-horse, half-griffin.

"The ancient poet, Virgil, had a saying: 'when horses mate with griffins.' Well, that was a good joke to all the Romans and it came to symbolize something that was impossible. Hundreds of years later, there lived another poet, an Italian named Ariosto. He was paid to entertain at the royal court, so he devised "Orlando Furiso," a tale involving Charlemagne and his knights. In this story Charlemagne's niece— he called her Bradamante—searches for her beloved Rogero, a knight held captive by a powerful wizard. This wizard rode a strange creature from 'beyond the ice-bound seas' who was half-horse and half-griffin. He called it a hippogriff."

314

"I understand the griff part," Labrosse said, "but where does the hippo come from?"

"Hippos is the Greek word for horse, so Ariosto just combined them," Diego explained. "He took Virgil's joke and used it to create a magical beast that few men could tame."

"That sounds like you, Diego—my sweet hippogriff!" Beatriz teased.

"But what of Bradamante? Does she rescue Rogero?" Anna wondered.

"Ah, she does, indeed, my lady," Diego laughed. "Charlemagne was a great warrior—and so were his daughters! Bradamante defeats the wizard in battle, frees Rogero from the enchanter's curse and tames the hippogriff!"

"Ah, ha! See, Carlo, women can be great warriors," Annabeth crowed. "Perhaps Jennie Poke will be a Wampanoag warrior yet!"

Carlomagno smiled faintly, but his mind had clearly been distracted from Diego's story. He delighted in bouncing his bubbly baby girl on his knee or playfully tossing her in the air and catching her as she giggled with delight. If Carlomagno was disappointed at not having a son, it never showed. He thought not of a son—though Anna's second pregnancy was beginning to show—but instead laughed and kissed the little auburn-curled girl who tugged on his ears and stood in his lap to peer into his eyes.

"How are the additions to your house coming along, Beatriz?"

"Very well, Annabeth." She looped arms with Diego. "We are both excited."

"She is anxious to be in your condition," Diego said.

"Diego! That is not proper talk at the dinner table," Beatriz chided him.

"Mama's going to have a baby!" Jennie Poke exclaimed. "A baby boy!"

"Or perhaps a girl, Jennie," Anna corrected.

"It's going to be a boy," Jennie insisted.

"How do you know, Jennie Poke?" Diego asked gently.

"I saw it in my head."

"What shall we name this baby boy?" Carlomagno wondered as he squeezed his daughter.

"Hippogriff!" the little girl announced, to the merriment of all at the table.

Watching him with Jennie Poke it was easy to forget the eager father they watched was also one of the most notorious pirates on the Spanish Main. Or so he had been.

{ 25 }

'Victory or Death!'

Sir Bertram Beerbohm Halifax was a round man, resembling a keg with legs. His face was florid and he smiled easily, even somewhat disarmingly. He would not dream of being seen in anything but the latest European fashions. Today he wore a powdered wig and high-heeled leather shoes that transformed his walk into a kind of sway as he took small, mincing steps. He was the new English governor of Port Royal.

"I have a thankless job, Captain Pokanoket! But do they care back in London? Of course not! They want results, sir. Results!" His jowls continued to waggle even during his dramatic pause. "England wants to rule the Caribbean and they expect me to see it done. They have faith in me, sir, quite a bit, I'd wager. That is, in me alone, since they gave me scant soldiers with which to subdue the Spanish army. That is why I appreciate your offer, sir, most genuinely." Sir Halifax struggled out of his chair with no small effort. He sashayed toward a map on the wall and jabbed at it with a stubby finger. "Old Providence!" he exclaimed, as if he had discovered something new. "The Spanish have captured Old Providence without a struggle. That was our only port in the area around Panama and Nicaragua."

Though considered an English town, Old Providence had been virtually run by the many pirates who congregated there.

"Yes, sir, Captain Pokanoket, we must do something, and I mean something dramatic, or those Spanish devils will think they have the run of the Caribbean." Jowls trembling sympathetically, Sir Halifax silently studied the map. "Have you heard anything about a Spanish fleet gathering near Hispaniola?"

"No, Governor," Carlomagno told him.

Halifax bobbed his head, reminding Carlomagno of a large, slack-faced dog he had seen during a visit to Old Providence.

"It's true, sir, I have it on the highest authority! Another Spanish Armada, it is, and it's being assembled at Santo Domingo! There will be fifty ships, galleons, barques, all loaded with cannon and soldiers!"

With the Governor's face in motion as he babbled, it was difficult for Carlomagno to maintain a polite expression. He had come to offer support, knowing it would be a delicate negotiation. Well, Carlomagno told himself, at least the man doesn't drool.

Later, at a dingy tavern that smelled slightly less foul than its neighbors, Carlomagno huddled with Gerard Labrosse, Morgan Flynn and Barnabas Greevey as they ordered up bumboos and discussed Governor Halifax's plan to attack Santo Domingo.

"Mad is what it is!" Flynn argued.

Labrosse nodded his assent. "Might as well fall on your own sword, it would end the same."

"Halifax is certain the Spanish mean to assemble a fleet and invade Jamaica," Carlomagno explained. Labrosse started to speak, but Carlomagno held up his hand. "Now, wait! Halifax is convinced that if we strike first, right at their heart, we will disrupt their plans and hopefully squash any invasion plans."

"While you were talking it up with Halifax, I was wandering around the waterfront keeping my ears open," Greevey said. "Way I hear, Halifax can't find any takers for this mission. I heard he even offered a commission to the Chevalier de Fortenay."

"De Fortenay, eh? And what was his response?" Carlomagno asked.

"Apparently, he laughed in Halifax's fat face."

"Hear that, Carlo? Even a fool like de Fortenay knows better than to accept this offer," Flynn said, thumping his near empty mug on the table. "I like a good fight as much as the next man, but a man would have to fall out of a coconut tree on his head to even think about attacking Santo Domingo."

By the governor's information, there were a dozen ships already gathered in the harbor at Santo Domingo. Carlomagno signaled the waitress for more drinks.

"I'm going to do it."

Shocked, they stared at him.

"But what of a crew?" Labrosse asked. "We'd never have enough men, not even if all the men who sail under your banner agreed to go."

"There are a large number of men who would jump at the chance if it meant their release from Little Newgate," Carlomagno replied. "I'll talk to Halifax tomorrow."

The filth of unwashed men and a sickening smell of festering disease and raw sewage clung to the air around Little Newgate, the English prison on Jamaica. The warden was a hawk-faced man with cruel eyes. Life in Little Newgate was harsh and death almost a certainty for those residing there.

"The prison holds a few harmless debtors and beggars, but most of the ruffians here are the vilest of men," Ricketts, the warden, commented. "Filth and trash, they are! Most would slit your throat for a dram of rum; the rest would do it after the dram!"

Prison guards had lined the men up in rows and Ricketts led Carlomagno and Diego through their inspection. As the warden stood
aside, the two men would stop to consider this man or that one, ex-
changing a few words, making queries. A few of the most bloodthirsty
were ruled out immediately; their complete lack of decency made them
undependable. At a signal from Ricketts, guards would take the dis-
missed prisoners back to their cells. About 250 prisoners remained in
place. It was this lot of criminals Carlomagno now addressed.

"Most, if not all of you no doubt belong in here." There was a mur-
mur of protest, which died quickly. "And most if not all of you are likely to die in here. You can wait for your trials, if you ever get them. If
you ever leave this prison, you will be old, broken men. If you stay in
Little Newgate most of you know what is waiting for you—the gibbet
or the block! Or you can join me-and earn a thousand pounds each!"

"A thousan' pounds?" a swarthy villain in the front of the crowd
challenged. "And pigs fly wit' tails for'ard."

"I niver in me life seen 'at much blunt," another muttered.

"What is it you be offerin'?" a voice from the rear called out.

"I offer you a chance to die like men—or, maybe, to live like kings!"
Carlomagno's voice carried boldly in the crowded space. "It's a dangerous mission. Few will return. Most of you are bound for the gallows.
But if you must die, as we all must someday, I say better to face that
moment with a blade in your hand, rather than dancing at the end of a
rope. Join me and the governor promises a full pardon for your past
crimes, a thousand pounds and a chance to start a new life."

There were excited rumblings throughout the crowd.

"Do not mistake me, men! All who take the oath to sail with me will
man their stations and fight," Carlomagno warned. "If you try to flee,
or shirk your duties, know that I will hunt you down and cut out your
heart."

"I'm with you, Captain!" someone shouted to an approving roar.

There were dozens of exhuberant shouts and a cry went up: "Huzzah for the Barracuda of the Spanish Main!"

With recruits made up of thieves and cutthroats, most of Carlomagno's old crewmates insisted on coming along. Their loyalty to Carlomagno was strong, but many also dreamed of heroism, or gaining the notice of the Crown. Many a great and noble family made its start through the strong sword arm of a man no better than these were. And then there was the satisfaction of humiliating the Spanish. Santo Domingo was considered untouchable, and with a strong fleet in its harbor, the city fathers had become arrogant. How grand it would be to raid such a prize, with an armada sitting in its pristine harbor!

In his cabin aboard the *Anasarani*, Carlomagno slowly unrolled a map and spread it out on the desk. He traced a finger around Hispaniola.

"There. That's the key, gentlemen."

Labrosse, who was to captain the *Pickford*, leaned over the table. "That spot is too far away to be in on the attack. There are better places to land much closer to Santo Domingo."

"The whole plan rests on you landing the *Pickford* right there," Carlomagno said.

"That cove is at least ten miles from Santo Domingo; we could never land there and get to the city in time to be of any help to you," Labrosse insisted.

"You shall not be part of the attack, Gerard. But the whole success of this mission depends on you," Carlomagno explained. "I will lead the *Anasarani* into the harbor, and Greevey will have the *Metacomet*. We're going to sail straight into the harbor, doing as much damage as we can to the Spanish flotilla on our way in."

"Two ships against a dozen, or even fifteen? You'll both be sunk, Carlomagno!"

"And so I expect to be, Gerard. That is why you must have the *Pickford* in this cove, and at the right time," Carlomagno told him.

"We will likely be coming fast and be looking to raise the sails in a hurry. You'll have canoes waiting for us on the shore, your ship stripped bare, to carry men and plunder only. Only a few guns will cover our escape if the Spaniards are close upon us."

"I see a couple of trouble spots with your plan," Flynn grumbled. "One would be to get close enough to Santo Domingo before our ships are cut down. Oh and then there would be the small matter of fighting our way through the streets of Santo Domingo to a little cove ten treacherous miles south of the city!"

"Well, I did promise them a battle, Morg," Carlomagno smiled. "Fighting is probably the only thing our new crewmen do well."

Santo Domingo was the oldest European city in the Americas, having been founded in 1496 by Bartholomew Columbus, brother to the famous explorer. It served for close to a century as the capital city of the Spanish Empire in the Caribbean. Enticed by the vast deposits of gold and silver on the South American mainland, Spain moved its capital to Cartagena, a heavily fortified city on the coast of Colombia. Still, Santo Domingo continued to flourish. The residents remained wealthy, fueled by massive exports of tobacco and sugar. They lived in grand mansions on wide, sun-drenched streets lined with palm trees. Considered a center of knowledge, Santo Domingo was home to the first university in what the Europeans liked to call the "New World." It was a prestigious accomplishment and the Santo Domingans were fiercely proud of it.

Three of Carlomagno's ships were to be involved, each with its own part to play. Labrosse would captain the *Pickford*, the largest of Carlomagno's ships. It would serve as the escape vessel.

Greevey, a fine gunner, would captain the *Metacomet*, one of the smaller ships, with Carlomagno on the *Anasarani*. The plan was to do as much damage to the Spanish vessels as possible, since it was expected that both of Carlomagno's ships would be lost. They were all fighting men and understood the chances of survival were slim. Luck had always been a part of his success, Carlomagno readily admitted; he knew he had had more good fortune that any mortal man had the right to expect. One day, that luck would desert him. Was that day to be in Santo Domingo?

With Spanish flags flying and only the friendliest-looking of crewmen visible, they sailed straight toward Santo Domingo's harbor, well within sight of the city. The galleon would be presumed to be one of their own, for the Spanish frequently used this type of heavy vessel, which could be outfitted equally well for commerce or for war. Carlomagno's luck held as they moved in easily, riding gentle currents. Spotting where he wanted to go, Carlomagno sent a message to the helmsman. There were a pair of galleons anchored about four hundred yards apart; the *Anasarani* veered slightly, heading for the narrow berth between them. The crewmen on the galleons shouted, as if they thought the new ship didn't realize they were there. On one of the decks, a sailor was waving his shirt, trying to catch someone's attention on the *Anasarani*. But Carlomagno held the course steady, gliding between the two galleons. He barked out an order and the cannon on both sides of the *Anasarani* roared their ferocious challenge. The peaceful summer morning was split with thunder as orange flames leapt from the barrels and Spanish timber cracked on the unsuspecting galleons.

They continued toward the wharf as the crew hastily reloaded the guns. Greevey swung the Metacomet off to the right and raked a smaller Spanish vessel with accurate fire, leaving it rapidly taking on water. There were shouts from the shore and men began to hustle about on the remaining ships, but the pirates still had the edge: they didn't need to sink the Spanish ships, just disable as many as possible.

Greevey fired his cannon again, striking a barque and a smaller pinnace. His own guns loaded, Carlomagno's ship bombarded another galleon.

"We caught the buggers napping!" Morgan Flynn yelled above the noise.

Carlomagno grinned. So far everything had gone perfectly. It was time to bring the Anasarani as close to the wharves as possible. The plan was to sidle up to the wharf, loaded guns facing inland. They would fire on Santo Domingo before rushing off the ship to sack the city. Even as they moved in, supported by a favorable wind, the remaining Spanish ships began to move, bringing their own cannon to bear. A barrage of cannonballs fell about the pirates, one slamming aft, and another striking right at the Anasarani's waterline. They slid closer to the shore, even as the ship began to list.

Greevey managed to damage another ship before his barque, too, came under heavy fire. The first hit was deadly. But the barque could run with sail or by oar, as planned. With the burliest of the prisoner-crew manning the oars, the Metacomet made its push for land. The plan was simple, but risky. Greevey would land his men and proceed to set the university ablaze; Carlomagno's would fight their way to the center of the town, to the King's Treasure House. The hope was that the residents, so proud of their university, would rush to beat out the flames, while the buccaneers plundered what loot they could carry away. Then, the Fates willing, they would make their escape to the hidden cove where Labrosse would be waiting. Those who survived would find the waiting canoes and paddle out to the *Pickford*, which would be ready to sail. The pirates would leave the enraged Spaniards standing on the shore, watching them sail off. If something went wrong, perhaps a Spanish patrol stumbling upon Labrosse, they would find themselves backed against the sea with thousands of Spanish soldiers and angry citizens snarling at their flanks.

Carlomagno heard the blast of the Spanish cannon, felt his ship shudder. Instinctively, he knew the *Anasarani* was going down. They were hit, and badly.

"Abandon ship," Carlomagno roared. "Swim to the shore, men! Gunners! Fire on the city and then we rush them!"

Men cheered wildly, bloodlust in their eyes as the cannon exploded, pounding the waterfront buildings and sending the Spanish residents of Santo Domingo fleeing in terror.

"Onward men!" called Carlomagno, brandishing his Toledo blade. "Victory or death!"

Men raced to leap into the sea and swim the final few yards to shore.

"Come on, Flynn! Jump!" Carlomagno called. But the giant shook his head, a terrified look on his bear-like face. "Jump, Morg, I will be beside you all the way!"

Flynn looked from his friend to the water sloshing across the deck. His eyes widened in fear. Another bombardment splintered the deck, sending sharpened fragments everywhere. With a deafening crack, the mast came toppling down. His eye on Morgan Flynn, Carlomagno looked up only moments before the mast slammed to the deck. Slipping on debris, he fell. He rolled desperately, managing to avoid being crushed and instantly killed, but the mast smashed down upon the barrels on deck, trapping one of Carlomagno's legs and pinning him to the battered deck. He struggled, but was stuck beneath the heavy timber. He would be going down with his ship.

Flynn stared hard at Carlomagno, frozen by the one thing he feared—water! The big man rushed to Carlomagno's side and tugged on the mast, moving it slightly. But not quite enough. The ship tilted; items not battened down began to slide about the deck.

"Go on, Morg! You can still make it!"

"Not without you!" Flynn strained even harder, the mast coming up a bit. His muscles at their mighty limit, Flynn planted himself and gave a growling cry as he battled for one more inch of clearance, then another...

Wriggling like a snake, Carlomagno squirmed out from under the deathtrap as Morgan's strength gave out. Another ship was coming into position for the finishing barrage.

"Jump, Flynn! I will be with you!"

"You are the best friend a man ever had," Flynn said. He effortlessly scooped up Carlomagno's two hundred-pound body the way a grown man swings a small child to his shoulders. Lifting his friend high over his head, Flynn tossed Carlomagno over what was left of the rail and into the teeming sea. Carlomagno spun in freefall, and then plunged beneath the surface; the sounds of battle were eerily quieted. He powered his way back to the surface.

"Morgan!" he cried, as a piece of the ship splashed into the water, sending a wave sloshing into his face. His last glimpse of Flynn showed the Irishman standing alone on the deck of the *Anasarani*, which was aglow in crackling flames. As Carlomagno watched in disbelief, the ship rolled, sliding beneath the sea. Carlomagno tore his gaze away and struck out with powerful strokes, determined to join his men, who were struggling to the shore. He climbed from the water and scrambled over a rock wall and onto a sandy stretch of beach as men rushed to join him. Wreckage and lifeless bodies began piling up in the breechway.

A man lying before him had managed to reach the shore only to succumb to his wounds: a sharpened piece of timber protruded from his back. The man's cutlass was still on his belt and Carlomagno snatched it up.

"Follow me, men!" With a strident war whoop, he charged toward the center of the town, crying out, "Beware, Santo Domingo, for the Barracuda of the Spanish Main has come to take his bite out of you! Come on, men, we shall all be rich!"

They rushed upon the city, meeting scattered but determined resistance. They battled for each step. Every yard a man fell, or cried out in pain. Still they fought forward. Flames roared to life in the distance,

on the outskirts of Santo Domingo. Greevey had made it to the university!

As Carlomagno had foreseen, the residents broke off the fighting
and rushed to save their precious institution. Left unencumbered, the
pirates made their way quickly to the King's Treasure House. They
battered down the door and, using every mule they could find, hurriedly packed their treasure train with every silver ingot, gold medallion
and piece of eight they could carry.

"Come men, come, we can't carry any more! Let's get out of here!"

Turning away from the Treasure House, they rushed down wide,
tree-lined streets heading away from Santo Domingo. Those greedy
few who hoped to pocket just one more bit of treasure were left behind.
Carlomagno knew the city would organize pursuit, but first they would
likely waste time arguing over what to do. Certainly they would send a
man to alert the nearby garrison. The garrison was to the north, lucki-
ly, in the opposite direction the pirates were taking. About five miles
out of town, Greevey and the rest of his men caught up to Carlomagno's band. Losses had been heavy at the university.

"For a bunch of shopkeepers and bookish types, they sure fought
hard!" Greevey panted.

"They will think we go inland," Carlomagno said. "Now we'll turn
for the cove, and trust that Labrosse is there."

They pushed on despite the terrible heat and stinging insects. One
man screamed as he was bitten by a snake, which slithered quickly
away. There was no time to stop, no chance to save him. The man's
messmate—for pirates generally traveled in pairs—was forced to end
his friend's misery with a quick knife slash. Men cursed as the mules
moved slowly despite shouts and cracking whips to urge them to pick
up the pace. The jungle vegetation began to thicken and the pirates
were soon forced to use their cutlasses like machetes as they hacked
their way toward freedom, step by agonizing step. The land dipped
away, the path leading through a ravine.

"This is a place a few men can easily defend," Carlomagno said. "Lead the men on, Barnabas, and I will stay here with a dozen men and ambush the Spaniards. That will slow them down. We'll catch up to you before you make the cove."

Greevey shook his head. "I'll stay behind, Carlomagno. The men are done in, exhausted. But the sight of you would inspire them to keep going. You take them on and I'll send those Spaniards to hell."

"Fire one volley and move on," Carlomagno warned, reluctant to let Greevey take his place. "We only want to make them stop and think. Be quick, for we cannot wait long."

They pushed toward the cove, using some effort to get the most stubborn of the mules moving again. It wasn't long before the jungle became less dense and their retreat picked up speed. Topping a rise, the cove came into view before them, the Pickford resting calmly in the sea. It took several trips, but the loot and men were safely loaded.

"Make ready to sail, Labrosse, for the others should be with us at any moment," Carlomagno ordered.

He had sent some of the men back in the canoes, ready to ferry Greevey and his men out to the waiting ship. The lookout yelled down that the canoes were coming back. A few men climbed aboard. Greevey and several others were not among them.

"Them Spaniards fought back," one sailor explained. "Greevey were right beside me. He took a musket ball to the heart. Killed, just that quick-like, Cap'n."

Carlomagno nodded gravely. "You're wounded, Gallagher. Go take care of it."

He turned away, staring at the shoreline as it grew smaller and smaller, his face streaked with sweat and grime. This victory held no satisfaction for him. The raid on Santo Domingo had been successful, but at what cost? More than half his men lay dead, littered throughout the streets of Santo Domingo, lost in the depths of the harbor or abandoned, lifeless, in the shadowy jungle. Dozens of men were gone, never to rise again. Never to laugh, or to dance with a pretty girl. Never to hoist another tankard of ale, or drink a bumboo. Gone, as if they had never existed. The loss of Greevey roused his anger. Greevey had been instrumental in so many of Carlomagno's victories, for his handling of the cannon had equaled Macomber's. Now, he was dead.

It was I who should have stayed, Carlomagno thought. *If only Greevey hadn't insisted on taking my place.*

Now Greevey had his own place back there, forever. And Morgan Flynn, too. It was so wrong, an underwater grave for a man who feared nothing save the water. Did the protection of the Wampanoag water spirit include these seas so far from his home? He made a silent request, just in case, that she hold Flynn gently in her arms. Carlomagno stood motionless on the deck of the *Pickford*, thinking of all that was changing about him. Greevey, Flynn, Macomber—they had trusted each other with their lives. Yet they were gone and he had survived. He struggled to control his emotions, aware of the men moving about the ship and in the rigging. At *Seequanakeeswush*, he would sing these men into the next life, and howl his grief from the mountaintop. The *Pickford* glided swiftly across the sea. As the sun went down, and the moon failed to rise, Carlomagno Pokanoket stood alone with his head bowed toward the west and feeling as if everything good and decent in his life was crumbling to ruin.

{ 26 }

A Traitor Plots

With gold earrings dangling from both lobes, Rohan Levesque smiled into the darkness. He was generally a careful man, one who saw wisdom in planning each move before it was taken. Some might consider him overcautious, but he was alive, and that was all the evidence he needed to prove to himself that his style was effective. Some mistook his caution for a lack of ambition. But those were the ones who did not know Levesque. He was driven by very definite goals, but wanted to make certain he lived long enough to enjoy reaching them. Why accomplish through brute force, and considerable risk, what could be done easily with stealth? Rohan Levesque was a plotter, a man who could be a dangerous foe when cornered and even more dangerous when underestimated.

Levesque had one desire he had secretly harbored for years. But he had had to wait patiently before the time was right to strike. That time was now, he knew. Levesque was pale, lack of sleep leaving him haggard, the constant strain of watchfulness drawn in fine detail on his face. He had not had a restful sleep since Carlomagno had escaped Tortuga. He feared the Indian would hunt him down for his betrayal and kill him. It was what he himself would have done.

Why had he been such a fool as to double-cross Carlomagno? The answer was simple: no kingdom could have two monarchs, and Levesque had been realistic enough to know that he did not yet rate in that discussion. Only one man could rule Tortuga, and, by extension, the Spanish Main. It would be the Chevalier de Fortenay or Carlomagno.

"Damn!" he cursed half under his breath. He had backed the wrong man! He had tried to tell the Frenchman to kill Carlomagno without delay, but de Fortenay would not listen; he had his moment of triumph and intended to savor its taste. Now the moment had slipped by.

All day Levesque had purposely allowed lazy crewmen to slack off on their duties as the Tigre fell further and further behind. With cover of night to cloak his movements, he had turned back for Tortuga. Now, with the Chevalier de Fortenay out of the way, it was time to make his move. When de Fortenay returned to Bassa Terre, if he returned, he would find the guns on the cliff overlooking the harbor turned against him. Most men would fear the prospect of double-crossing someone as ruthless as Pierre Norville. But, then again, most men did not plan as carefully as Rohan Levesque did.

Garrote was a good man and Levesque trusted him as much as he trusted any man. He had made sure Garrote was among the crew selected to be on board de Fortenay's sloop. If the chevalier survived the mission he envisioned, then Garrote would know what to do. Garrote was a man who knew how to use a knife or pick the lock on a cabin door. Like the cabin of a sleeping, unsuspecting captain. Years ago, when he saw how Jean Levasseur controlled Tortuga, Levesque knew it was his destiny to become king of the island stronghold. But he had waited, as de Fortenay killed Levasseur and claimed the right to rule Tortuga. With his fearsome reputation as a swordsman, none had dared to challenge him. A naturally suspicious man, de Fortenay had taken few men into his confidence, limiting the number of those who might get close to him. But he had a close bond with Tulane and when his henchman was killed the chevalier needed someone to count on. That was the moment for which Levesque had waited. He had taken up residence on Tortuga and begun assisting de Fortenay. He quickly found the chevalier's iron-handed style of leadership bred both fear and enmity. Levesque was careful to cultivate friendships where they might prove the most useful. Whoever controlled the guns on the cliff controlled the harbor—and Tortuga! Levesque had carefully cultivated a friendship with the chief gunner.

And Garrote had been helpful. A pirate's life was a rough one, so no one raised an eyebrow as some of de Fortenay's most loyal compatriots were suddenly killed in drunken brawls or raids that went awry. Now, Rohan Levesque sailed contentedly back toward Tortuga.

{ 27 }

Clash of Steel

His narrow face seemed more pinched than usual as the Chevalier de Fortenay grimaced on the forecastle deck. A heavy fog had rolled across the Caribbean during the night and it was to play a pivotal role in the savage plans of Pierre Norville, the Chevalier de Fortenay.

"I think it's clearing up, cap'n," said his quartermaster, the aptly named Jim Orr. "It was thicker when I first came on deck."

De Fortenay grunted as he stood in his usual finery, including a blue cloak trimmed in gold, and a large hat of matching hue with a white plume attached. His customary sword was belted on and he wore a pistol tucked behind a wide black belt.

"It must ease up soon, Orr," de Fortenay insisted. "We should be close to him."

"If he came this way."

De Fortenay glared at Orr, a raised eyebrow serving as reproach. "It is the way I would come, Orr. It is the only way to make such a quick escape. And the escape must be quick, no? Or the plan works not at all!"

Jim Orr had started to reply, but bit his words off short. De Fortenay could be touchy and it didn't pay to anger him. He was especially aggressive when he was irritated and the quartermaster knew the captain was in a foul mood. The fog was only part of it. Sailing was a tricky proposition even in clear weather. The best methods of determining location and speed were not much more than estimates. Dead reckoning—determining the speed and location of a ship based on a previously known location—relied on the accuracy of a captain's charts and his ability to calculate measurements taken by sextant.

With little formal education, de Fortenay had relied upon Tulane or another experienced sailor to do the mathematics. Every common sailor learned how to judge speed. A rope knotted at equal intervals was dragged alongside the ship. The pilot kept time on the sandglass, while a sailor counted the knots as they slipped through his fingers.

De Fortenay was gambling that after the successful raid on Santo Domingo, Carlomagno would flee southward along the bottom of Hispaniola. He envisioned the *Pickford's* cargo hold loaded with treasure and trade goods, with many of the men lying wounded or exhausted from their assault on the proud Spanish city. The ship, de Fortenay believed, would be lacking cannon, as every effort would have been made to make room for the men and plunder during the hasty escape. It was what de Fortenay would do, and he had finally accepted that Carlomagno was his equal. Well, almost so. That was why the Chevalier de Fortenay was in the vicinity of Hispaniola on this overcast morning.

De Fortenay had learned from a trusted source, who swore he got it from Lord Halifax himself, that Carlomagno had undertaken the challenge to sack Santo Domingo. After double-checking to avoid a repeat of the Cumana debacle, he had gone into action. First, and most likely, Carlomagno might fail in the attempt, de Fortenay knew. But the savage had the Devil's own luck in pulling off supposedly impossible raids. If successful, he would have a ship laden with mouth-watering trophies. De Fortenay sat down and studied a map of Hispaniola. How could it be done? He could not at first conceive of a way to get past the war galleons in port at Santo Domingo. It was Rohan Levesque who solved that problem.

"Where in hell is Levesque?" thundered de Fortenay to no one in particular. All yesterday Levesque's ship had lagged behind. It was old and needed a good careening, but still de Fortenay felt it was up to the task. As evening had fallen, the *Tigre* was not to be found.

"I thought he'd catch up during the night," Orr offered. Getting no reply, he excused himself to go below deck and rouse the lagging crewmen.

Levesque had looked at the map and recalled the cove located close to Santo Domingo. If Carlomagno could get into the city limits he'd never have time to load his plunder and get away, not with a dozen well-armed Spanish galleons lurking close by. But, Levesque supposed, what if Carlomagno was willing to lose his ships? In that case, he might blast his way into the city and make his escape in an unexpected direction. De Fortenay listened to Levesque's theory and knew at once it was precisely what the infuriating upstart would do. The small inlet was just big enough to hide a single ship and close enough to Santo Domingo that a forced march could reach it in a few hours. But could Carlomagno's men fight off the Spanish pursuit?

The pirate captain glanced around; sailors were coming from below deck, beginning their duties. He recognized none of them, but Levesque had assured him these men were the best available. How he missed Tulane! De Fortenay had relied heavily on his longtime friend. Levesque had proven useful after Tulane was killed, but where was he now?

"*Bonjour, mon Capitaine.*"

De Fortenay could not recall seeing the man before this voyage, but Garrote did his work and seemed very dependable.

"The fog is lifting," de Fortenay replied. "When it does, we will be in good position to intercept Carlomagno."

"Just the way it has been planned," Garrote said. "Your meal is being served below, mon Chevalier."

De Fortenay permitted himself a smile. Levesque had been his insurance, but even without him the plan would work. De Fortenay's ship carried twenty guns of different sizes and he was certain he could disable Carlomagno's craft and leave him floundering in the water. "Keep a sharp eye," De Fortenay snapped.

"Of course, *mon Capitaine*," Garrote replied. *I'll be keeping watch*, he thought. When the opportunity came he'd earn the bonus promised by Rohan Levesque.

Everything seemed to be going smoothly for de Fortenay. When Tulane was lost, he had suddenly realized how much his aide had done for him. So many small details were involved in planning a voyage and preparing a crew, things de Fortenay had never been bothered with when Tulane was at hand. Then de Fortenay had another thought. If the loss of Tulane disrupted his usual planning, might not the loss of Macomber hinder Carlomagno in the same fashion? Of course Carlomagno was a savage, a red Indian from North America, and probably did not grieve over his loss as a civilized man would, de Fortenay reasoned. But that loss would still impinge on his ability to execute. That word sent a shiver up de Fortenay's spine.

Execute.

It sounded so calculating, so callous—and so final. The Indian would sorely miss Macomber's skills. And what of the clever Kerbourchard? A satisfying rumor had circulated that Kerbourchard had finally met his end. And soon, de Fortenay smirked, Carlomagno will join him.

Restless and unable to sleep, Carlomagno had ordered the Pickford further out to sea. The fog had been extremely heavy in the early morning hours; he didn't want to run aground. Now, as the fog lifted, the *Pickford* was once again moving closer to the shoreline.

Labrosse opened his spyglass and examined the still expanse of sea. Bemis, a good man with keen senses, had been up the mainmast earlier in the morning. He reported to Labrosse that he thought he had seen another vessel in the fog. Labrosse could see nothing, but the fog was beginning to dissipate. He hesitated to wake Carlomagno, who had been withdrawn and sleepless since the raid. But if there was another ship out there it likely meant trouble.

"Any sign of her?"

Labrosse gave a start; he had not noticed Carlomagno standing beside him. The Indian seemed to materialize out of the fog. "This glass is no good. I can't see anything, Captain. But I trust Bemis, sir."

"We're in no shape for a fight."

Labrosse nodded. "We've got two twelve-pounders, two eight-pounders and the swivel gun, but some of those galleons carry a hundredweight of tonnage and forty cannon. If we run into one of those, we'll have less chance than a free beer on a hot day!"

Starting to turn away, Carlomagno caught himself in midstep. There was something. As he glanced out to sea the fading fog seemed alive, almost a living, breathing thing! For a moment he thought he saw an eagle soaring through the mist, a large eagle, like the one he had seen in his vision!

"I have a feeling," Carlomagno said. "Have the guns loaded, Gerard."

Labrosse turned on his heels. He'd been around Carlomagno long enough to know the Indian had an uncanny sense for doing the right thing at the right moment. He hurried to find the gunners and rouse them into action.

With the ship travelling southward, ready to make its run after the Santo Domingo attack, all the guns had been placed on the starboard side to help drive off any land pursuit.. It left the *Pickford* vulnerable to a portside attack, but the vessel didn't have enough guns to fight off an attack in any case.

Carlomagno returned to his cabin and belted on his sword. He had once again lost his blade of Toledo steel back in Santo Domingo and now carried a spare sword he had picked up. He carefully cleaned and loaded his twin brass pistols, securing them in their bandolier; at the last moment, he snatched up his hatchet and tucked it into his belt at the small of his back. Returning above deck in only a few minutes, he saw the fog had thinned considerably. There was a dark outline in the mist no more than an arrow's flight away!

"What are her colors?"

"Can't tell, captain," Bemis said, peering hard at the shape. "But I got me a feeling she's bad company."

There was a stirring in the distance, as the other ship had spotted the *Pickford*. Frantic shouts carried on the air, as both ships were desperate to be ready if the other proved a foe.

"Are the guns ready?"

Gerard Labrosse replied affirmatively. "And I think they're set for right about this range, Carlomagno."

"Give the order to fire and then have the pilot turn us starboard. We've got to get close and board her," Carlomagno said. "It's de Fortenay!"

"Are you sure, Captain? I mean at this distance—"

"Do it!"

Between Bemis' keen senses and Carlomagno's hunch, Labrosse had already begun to hurry the crew to prepare for battle. That decision had now given the edge to the *Pickford* as the fog burned away before the bright, morning sun. Through the final wisps of white fog the black muzzles of the Pickford's few cannon belched orange flame toward the perfectly situated enemy vessel. The cannonballs smashed into the chevalier's ship, ripping canvas sails and splintering the hull and port side of the vessel.

"Reload!" the master gunner yelled, though his trained crew had already begun the process.

Labrosse raised his spyglass again, seeing more clearly now. "It's a scurvy lot, Carlomagno! Pirates, to be sure. Why, it's the chevalier!"

"Let's take her in!" Carlomagno called. "Ready the grappling hooks! We're going to board her, men!"

A scattered cheer went up as the *Pickford*, aided by its leeward course, swiftly cut the distance between them and the enemy ship. Cannon barked and the ball tore a sail as it soared over the Pickford and splashed in the sea. A second cannonball fell wide of the target with a harmless plash. The ships were soon trading direct hits, but the gap was closing fast. Carlomagno stood on the rail, holding tight to the rigging.

"Get ready, men! It's all or nothing now!" Carlomagno shouted. Musketeers from his own crew traded shots with the enemy vessel, with the *Pickford* scoring the most damage. Staring grimly toward the oncoming ship, Norville barked commands. Now he was sure it was Carlomagno he was facing; the tricky fog had spoiled his hand and stolen the cards he had planned to be holding. Despite the heavy cannon, he had lost another advantage by allowing Carlomagno's ship to get too close. The *Pickford* had gotten off the first and most telling shots, and now the fighting would be brutal, hand-to-hand.

Grappling hooks locked onto the rails of both ships and hearty sailors pulled the vessels closer. With his hatchet in his right hand and a knife clasped between his teeth, Carlomagno was among the first to leap onto the enemy ship. He chopped down with his hatchet, severing fingers as the sharp stone head slammed into a man trying to fend him off with his musket. The knife jabbed forward and up, ripping into the unfortunate sailor.

There was a clash of steel, the occasional roar of a pistol or musket and the grunts, screams and howls of desperate men struggling for their lives. Carlomagno was everywhere, slicing and hacking with both hands. A man came at him with a pike; he knocked the point away with his hatchet and thrust his knife home. The falling man jerked the knife from Carlomagno's grasp and as he bent to retrieve it, someone bowled into him. He tumbled to the deck, rolling over a mass of broken, bloody bodies. Dazed, yet struggling to regain his feet, he saw a pirate with a gold front tooth charging him with a ready sword. Carlomagno flung his hatchet and it whirled end over end, crashing into the pirate's skull. Labrosse, who was battling as hard as his friend, downed another man with a sword thrust, finishing him off as Carlomagno regained his feet. Trading a wink with Labrosse, the Indian pulled his twin pistols. His first shot struck down an enemy about to attack Bemis from behind. A big man, using his empty musket as a cudgel, swung wildly at Carlomagno. Hit by a glancing blow, Carlomagno stumbled back. He brought his second gun up and squeezed it off just inches from his attacker's face.

An unnatural lull in the fighting seemed to take hold as Carlomagno drew his sword, looking for a nearby challenger. At that moment, one of the *Pickford*'s sailors fell over dead and the Chevalier de Fortenay, bloody sword in hand, was left standing face to face with Carlomagno.

"And so we meet, Indien!" smiled de Fortenay. "Always you have avoided meeting me with a blade, and wisely. I am the greatest swordsman on the Main! Today you die, *Monsieur* Barracuda!"

Circling warily, Carlomagno replied, "I have been taught by a better man than you, de Fortenay."

"Better than I? Bah, no such man exists!"

"Macomber was better."

"Macomber? Better than I? Preposterous." De Fortenay gave a thrust, easily parried by the Indian. "But I am a gentleman, so I will see that on your gravestone it is written 'He was trained by Macomber'!"

"Is it so hard to believe? You were so afraid of him you tried to have Connor Pickford kill him. And when that didn't work, you sent Tulane and four others to do what you couldn't do yourself!"

"You shall pay for the insult, Barracuda," Norville sneered. "We shall see how well he taught you."

De Fortenay lunged forward suddenly, but Carlomagno easily deflected the attempt. They circled each other, each man taking an opportunity to probe the other with searching, basic maneuvers.

"So, Macomber did teach you a thing or two, eh?"

There were different styles of fighting, even when using the same weapon. Macomber had been a student of war and had worked with Carlomagno to teach him different styles. A Frenchman, for example, might favor certain moves over others, while an Englishman might prefer completely different maneuvers. Under Macomber's tutelage—and from his sessions with Noank, Ezra, Flynn and Kerbourchard—Carlomagno had practiced classic sword fighting, as well as methods favored by the Moors, Middle Eastern techniques and other tactics, too. Most of all, he had learned that battles were won by thought as much as by might. Carlomagno realized now that he could hold his own with the Chevalier de Fortenay, and he knew his advantage was in his opponent's brash overconfidence.

De Fortenay was arrogant enough to believe he was the greatest swordsman to ever cross blades on the Main; he thought Carlomagno undeservedly lucky in avoiding a fight. For his part, Carlomagno took pains to make himself look clumsy, to lure de Fortenay into a false sense of security. Once, Carlomagno miscalculated and the chevalier's point ripped a gash across his bare left shoulder. A few inches more to the right and de Fortenay's blade would be lodged in his throat, he realized. The blooding only added to de Fortenay's self-assurance.

The two battled on, unaware that the fighting around them had died down as men stopped to watch what they knew would be remembered as one of the greatest sword duels ever to take place on the Spanish Main.

De Fortenay lunged, but Carlomagno parried, his enemy's blade sliding harmlessly away from him. He stepped in close as they pushed blades against each other.

"How does it feel to know you are so close to death, eh?" de Fortenay hissed.

Carlomagno swung a closed left hand and clobbered de Fortenay on the side of the face. The French corsair staggered back as his face darkened with anger.

"How does that feel?" the Indian asked.

De Fortenay inhaled sharply. "I forgot that you are a savage, no? You do not observe the ways of a gentleman." He rushed in, his sword flailing wildly as anger overcame his common sense. It was a deadly few moments as Carlomagno fought to fend off the assault. A sharp blow from de Fortenay landed just right and Carlomagno's blade snapped off short. There was a collective gasp from the onlookers. Carlomagno hurled his broken cutlass at de Fortenay and, as the Frenchman ducked aside, he ran in, bowling his foe over. De Fortenay lost his grip on his sword as they rolled across the deck, clawing and slugging at each other. De Fortenay wrestled his way to his feet and reached for the knife on his belt. Carlomagno, only half-upright, threw himself at de Fortenay's knees. They both fought themselves to their feet. De Fortenay drew his knife as a taunting smile played across his too-thin lips.

"You have fought well, but it is *finis*," Norville said as he started to circle.

Wordlessly, Carlomagno watched his enemy and then, as de Fortenay made his move, Carlomagno used his left hand to slap the knife aside and with his right he gripped de Fortenay's shirtfront and tugged him off balance. He slugged a solid punch to his rival's windpipe and as de Fortenay wheezed, the Wampanoag followed it up with several crunching blows. Reeling, De Fortenay lashed out with his knife and, leaping back, Carlomagno tripped over a body. Seizing the opening, the Chevalier de Fortenay launched himself forward.

As he fell over the dead man Carlomagno's hand found a dropped pike and he clutched at it, tipping the point upwards as de Fortenay rushed in. The Frenchman grunted in shock as he impaled himself. The knife dropped from the chevalier's hand and he gripped the pike sticking through him. He tried to tug at it with weakening fingers.

"*Non, ce n'est pas possible! Je suis...le Chevalier...*" His eyes glazed over and he crumpled in a pool of blood and gore. Carlomagno shoved the man's body aside and stood over him.

"*Adieu,*" Carlomagno addressed the corpse as he picked up de Fortenay's fallen sword. With a slash, he severed the fingers on the Frenchman's right hand. "So I won't have to be bothered fighting you in the next life."

"Who is quartermaster here?" Carlomagno called out as he surveyed de Fortenay's beaten crew.

Jim Orr limped forward, his right arm dangling uselessly at his side. "I am he. The ship is yours, Captain Carlomagno. Men, drop your weapons!" Swords and pistols clattered to the deck.

"What does this ship carry?"

"Very little, captain," Orr said. "The chevalier was in a hurry to find you. He was certain your vessel was laden with treasure."

"Why would he think that?"

"Santo Domingo, *monsieur.* The word is that your men were off to sack the city. The chevalier plotted to intercept you," Orr explained. "There was a second ship, but Captain Levesque seems to have fallen behind."

Both ships were heavily damaged, though the *Pickford* was in better condition. "Put this trash overboard," Carlomagno said, gesturing toward his fallen foe. He recalled stories Diego had told him of people called Vikings who sent fallen heroes to Valhalla on floating funeral pyres. He thought the chevalier would have liked that. But he did not deserve such honor. "He was a scoundrel. Let him be remembered as such."

Carlomagno abandoned de Fortenay's crew, leaving them to their own fate as he ordered his vessel on. Though its sails had suffered some damage, the *Pickford* soon outdistanced the other pirate craft.

"We'd better make our way back overland," Carlomagno said.

Labrosse frowned. "Overland, Carlomagno? But it's Spanish territory we'd have to cross, and carrying the loot from the King's Treasure House!"

Putting the *Pickford* in to shore was dangerous, but perhaps less so than remaining at sea in a damaged vessel that could not hope to outrun any pursuer and without guns enough to fight off an attack. On land, they had a chance, however small it might be.

They hugged the shore, hoping to find another cove, but were disappointed. At last, Carlomagno ordered his prize ship to a halt and, using the longboats on board, transported men, supplies and plunder to dry land. Then he sent Gerard Labrosse with a skeleton crew to try to bring the *Pickford* back home.

"If you are in trouble, Gerard, take to the longboats and come ashore. It's the best chance you'll have."

"'I'd hate to leave her," Labrosse said. "She's a fine craft."

"That she is, but she's not worth your life. Leave her if you have to, Gerard. I'd not lose a good man for the sake of a ship." Carlomagno stared off across the waters as he thought of all the good men he had already lost. "Move the guns to the port side and keep her as close to land as you dare."

Carlomagno didn't wait for the ship to sail before he got the remainder of his men moving. To linger on the coast invited danger. He knew their best option was to move inland to ensure no passing Spanish warship spotted them. Carlomagno sent scouts ahead to bring him information. He didn't want to stumble across any army patrols. It was slow going as the men had to carry everything themselves, but since they were bearing a fortune, none seemed to mind! Despite the walking, the men were in good spirits, no doubt buoyed by the knowledge that they would all be rich if they could escape Spanish territory. They were halted for a midday rest when one of the scouts returned.

"There's a plantation up ahead, looks to be good-sized," said Rochambeau.

"Horses?"

"Lots, cap'n. Wagons, too. I saw some slaves working the fields," Rochambeau said. "I didn't see many Spaniards around. I think we could slip in and take the place over."

Rochambeau was a studious man, not one given to exaggeration. He did his work without argument or mumbling, and he did it well. Carlomagno had selected him to be one of the scouts precisely because he felt Rochambeau's observations would be the most accurate.

"We'll go on ahead, with as many men as we can spare," Carlomagno said. "Dinwoodie, you'll take charge here. Bring the men up. If the packs are too heavy, discard some of the food. I'm sure we can replenish food supplies up ahead. All right, Rochambeau, lead the way. If we can get horses and wagons, we can get out of Spanish territory before they even know we're here."

The plantation was three miles away, according to Rochambeau. Carlomagno started out at a rapid clip, slowing as they neared the place. He stopped about a half-mile away and had each man check his weapons.

"It'll be easier if we wait until dark," Rochambeau suggested.

Carlomagno shook his head. "That's still several hours away and the longer we delay, the greater the chance we'll be discovered. The fields are our best way in. There are only a few guards there, you say?"

"I saw three, perhaps four."

"Take some men to the fields and take the guards out. The slaves might even help us fight," Carlomagno said. "If nothing else, they can tell you the layout of the place and how many Spaniards there are. I'll take a dozen men and make my way to the main house. We'll try to locate the weapons and secure them."

They filtered silently through the dense foliage, the only sound an occasional grunt as one of the pirates slapped another mosquito. As the jungle thinned out Carlomagno led the way to edge of the tree line. He studied his men; they were mostly untested.

"It gets tricky from here, men. Keep your heads down and follow my lead." With his men trailing, Carlomagno crawled forward on his belly, his head barely off the ground as his sharp eyes scanned his surroundings. In shock, he realized where he was. This was the plantation of Don Pablo de la Marana! He froze and struggled to contain his anger, fighting down a powerful urge to rush in and attack. A man had to remain cool in a fight if he wanted to have a chance to win. The main house was silent, but that didn't mean there weren't people around.

A sharp crack split the air, followed by an audible grunt of pain. Carlomagno recognized the sound at once: someone was being whipped nearby. Voices echoed from behind a building a short distance away. There was a snort of laughter, another crack of the whip. He crept closer to the main house, rising to peer over the low wall of the veranda. He swung a leg up and soon disappeared from view. After a moment he gave the prearranged signal, the soft croak of a tree frog, and the others glided silently toward him. Crouching on the veranda, they spoke in hushed tones as Carlomagno sent half the men into the house with orders to secure any weapons and hold any prisoners. If any of the

Spanish men made a fight of it, they would be dispatched as swiftly and quietly as possible.

"You, take the rest and secure the blacksmith shop. There should be someone there; if he starts to raise a fuss, kill him. When you see Rochambeau coming from the fields, you gather up horses or mules, and hitch up any wagons if you find them," Carlomagno said. "Then get back down the trail to Dinwoodie and get the treasure loaded up."

When the others had gone, Carlomagno rose to his feet and stepped off the porch. Judging by the voices, he could picture where the men stood on the other side of the building and he simply walked around to come up behind them. There were four Spaniards. A young man with shiny, black hair held the whip. He lashed out again and chuckled as the dark-skinned slave grunted in pain.

"Come now, Shabaka, you can cry out louder than that!" the young Spaniard taunted. "Beg me, Shabaka, and I might let up a bit."

Shabaka! Here was the runaway slave whose return had been requested by the Spanish. Carlomagno had not found him, nor would he have returned him under any circumstances.

"Ah, come on, Luis, you hog all the fun!" croaked a fat man, his half-unbuttoned shirt stiff with sweat. "Let me have at him. I can get him to beg."

"You, Esteban? Hah! You are fortunate I do not put you in his place. You let him escape! Besides, you know nothing of how to punish a man. It is an art, Esteban. You must make him beg, plead for mercy. You can't just kill a man without taking your time to work up to it."

The pistol shot gave them a start and Luis, the young man holding the whip, rose to his toes and pitched headlong into the dirt.

347

{ 28 }

Carlomagno Returns

Esteban, the fat man, stepped back hurriedly and tripped. He fell to a sitting position with a heavy thud. The other two Spaniards stood staring at the strange sight before them. Carlomagno was bare-chested, wearing buckskin leggings with high moccasins, a bandolier and a belt into which was tucked a battle-tested hatchet. He stood calmly, a pistol in each hand. The gun in his right hand was still smoking.

"Your friend was wrong," Carlomagno spoke conversationally. "See how easy it is to kill a man?"

"You have made a grave mistake, senor." The speaker was the oldest of the group, a dignified-looking man of middle age. "You have killed the don's youngest son."

Carlomagno put away his right-hand gun, shifting the still-loaded second pistol. "You, fat man! Get up slowly and release the prisoner."

"Stay where you are, Esteban!" The middle-aged man spoke with the voice of one used to command. "You are but one man and we are three, my friend. I suggest you drop that pistol. Now!"

Carlomagno smiled. He was amused and impressed by the man's nerve. "I think I like you, my friend, and I have no wish to kill you. But, as I'm sure you realize, your fat friend is in no position to be of any help. Before he can get his backside off the ground I will have killed you."

"You cannot hope to escape," the man countered coolly. "There are a dozen men on this plantation and a dozen more due by nightfall."

"I do not doubt your counting, senor, but by now I suspect there are somewhat fewer men on this plantation." He waggled the end of his pistol. "Move, fat man, or I shall split you like a hog."

Esteban rolled to his hands and knees and began to push himself erect.

"I gave you an order, Esteban. Stay down—"

Carlomagno's pistol shot cut off the man's sentence. He gripped his stomach as he fell to his knees. The dirt around him was spotted with blood, his blood. His pistol empty, Carlomagno dropped it in its holster and drew his sword. "Last time, fat man. Move!"

Esteban scrambled to his feet and hastily loosened the ropes holding the African. Carlomagno turned his attention to the last man, the one who had made no sound. But he was not to be any trouble; he had been so frightened he had wet himself where he stood, immobilized by fear.

"Are there more men due back here tonight?"

The man moved his lips, but was unable to speak; he shook his head. More gunshots rang out and there was the sound of excited voices from the distant fields.

Rubbing his chafed wrists, his back bloody and ripped by the lash, Shabaka looked down upon the dead body of Luis. He spat on the man's head.

"He was nothing. He was the don's son; he did not earn anything in life."

"He earned one thing," Carlomagno corrected. "And he got it today."

Esteban was beginning to find his courage. "You cannot hope to get away with this. Do you know who owns this plantation? Why, with but a snap of his fingers Don Pablo can summon a hundred men!"

"Then let him snap his fingers, for I shall kill those hundred men. You tell the don when he arrives that Carlomagno did this to his son."

Esteban gasped, for he had heard horrendous tales of this pirate king. As for the other man, he fainted dead away.

"Are we far from French territory?" Carlomagno asked.

"Not so far," Shabaka replied. "I have been there."

"How did they catch you?"

"I returned."

"You came back on your own?" As he spoke, Carlomagno casually reloaded his pistols. "Why?"

"I made a promise to someone who was kind to me. I told her I would return for her. She wanted nothing more than to taste the sweet air of freedom once more before she died. I came back to take her to the mountains."

"She is alive?"

"She lives yet, for what good it does her. The story told is that when she was brought here, the don sought to force himself on her and she fought back, tried to kill him, they say. So he blinded her, making her crawl around like a filthy animal and beg for scraps." Shabaka was working up to a rage. "But she was kind to me. The first time I tried to escape the don had me chained outside and forbade anyone to bring me

350

food or water. But this old woman gathered up her scraps and shared what little she had with me."

"She sounds like a brave woman."

"She is that. Blind though she is, she never lost her dream of freedom. Nor her desire to kill the don."

"She never tried again? To kill him, I mean?"

"Don Pedro seldom comes here these days. He is old, and they say even fatter than Esteban. But he will come when he hears of his son's death."

"Where is this old woman?"

"Luis had her locked in that shed over there, so she could not bring me food this time." The tall, thin African went to the shed and raised the bar. The door creaked open and he stepped inside. Carlomagno heard him speaking softly. A moment later he emerged, guiding the slow steps of an old woman, walking with the hunched-over posture of one who has seen much hard work. Carlomagno could only stare.

"Wootonockuse?" he queried.

The woman stopped in her tracks, swinging her head toward the voice. Even with the changes of age and mistreatment, there was no mistaking her. Carlomagno's blood went cold.

"Is it you?" she whispered. "Has my son returned?"

Carlomagno rushed forward and swept her gently into his arms. For a moment, the most fearsome pirate on the Spanish Main was a lost little boy. "Mother, I dreamt of you often. I prayed for the Creator to protect you."

"The Creator has protected me, my Pokanoket. He allowed me to live long enough to see my son again," Wootonockuse said. "I knew one day you would return."

Tenderly, Carlomagno clung to his frail mother. When he stepped back and studied her, his anger grew. She was malnourished and clad in filthy rags. He turned to Esteban and madness flashed in his brown eyes.

351

"You." Carlomagno jabbed a finger in the fat man's direction. "Do you wish to live?"

Esteban gulped, his Adam's apple bobbing as if he had swallowed a rubber ball. "Yes, yes, please, I beg you."

"You will take care of this woman, very good care of her. Do you understand?" Esteban nodded. "Take her in the house and have a maid bathe her and clean her hair, and dress her in the finest garments. You will attend to her and if she utters one single complaint, your life is forfeit."

"It will be done," Esteban said, his large head bobbing furiously. "She will be treated as a queen."

"As well she should."

Carlomagno turned his attention to Rochambeau, who led a contingent of laughing, blood-splattered slaves up from the cane fields. Their laughter faded as they approached Carlomagno. The women whispered anxiously to one another.

"Do not be afraid," he told them. "You have worked here with no reward. Now it is your time. Take what you want from this place. Rochambeau, when these people have everything they need, put this plantation to the torch."

Esteban found his voice, though it was barely audible. "But this plantation belongs to Don Pedro de la Marana!"

"As fine a reason as any to burn it. And if he were here, he'd burn with it!"

{ 29 }

"It is Time"

Though age was getting the best of Louis Dearborn, the Frenchman still sat a saddle well. His rolled-up shirtsleeves revealed thick, tan forearms and his gnarled hands could still close in a vice-like grip. He was a gentleman in every sense of the word and yet that word did not do him justice. He lived no pampered life of luxury, but rose before sunrise each morning to begin his workday. He often worked in the fields of his own plantation, where he grew tobacco for sale and crops for his own use. Dearborn was a man who enjoyed the beauty of nature and who took pride in the meticulous care of his flower garden. He had been born into an old and proud family, though one with little wealth. Through hard work and prudent investments, he had managed to earn a modest fortune. His needs were few. He liked a good meal now and then, and spent much time with his precious books. Often he was seen scribbling notes about things he saw, the weather, the different animals he encountered. He planned one day to write his own book about life in the Caribbean.

He lived well in Jacmel, but remained just outside political circles. He was known by those in power and was well-liked. But he remained aloof of partisan politics and, instead, entertained a wide variety of people. His dinner parties included well-cooked meals, the finest wines and stimulating conversation. Dearborn considered himself a student of human behavior. He would often go out onto the streets of Jacmel and spend the day wandering and watching people go about their business. He saw those merchants who laughed with their customers, yet sneered derisively behind their backs, the ones who sold fewer goods than the weight or count promised.

The strange career of the man now known as Carlomagno fascinated him. That Carlomagno was a native from North America was not unusual in itself. After all, many American Indians had been sold into slavery in the West Indies and the Caribbean. The practice began following the Pequot War of 1637 and continued through the end of King Philip's War in 1676. Over that 40-year span thousands of natives from New England or the mid-Atlantic colonies were sold into slavery. Most either died struggling against the system or intermarried within the boundaries that confined them and lived out their lives with all the quiet dignity they could muster. None had risen to the heights Carlomagno had achieved. He had escaped slavery and found his way to Tortuga, where he took to the sea. Piracy was a life that attracted the adventurous, the daring. But it also offered a means to wealth for one willing to take enormous risks. A successful privateer might gain modest wealth, vast land holdings and even some position within the community. Louis Dearborn could name a half dozen who had done just

354

that, starting with Sir Henry Morgan. But the others who had done so had one advantage that eluded Carlomagno.

They were European; the system in which they operated was in their blood, fed to them from birth. Carlomagno came from a different world, one that was vastly at odds with the life offered on the Spanish Main. That he had risen above these circumstances was a testament to Carlomagno's wit, bravery and uncanny ability to align himself with the right people.

One of those was Diego El Negro, the son of an African slave and a Spanish don. Dearborn considered Diego a friend, and it was for that reason he made his ride now. The heat of the day was growing increasingly unbearable as he aged and Dearborn would have liked to be sitting quietly in the shade with a good book open on his lap and a cool drink beside him. But there was time enough for that later. Today he had a ride to make. And there was no time to waste. Carlomagno had chosen well the location for this home, for access was limited. The Cordillera Mountains and the dense jungle loomed as natural barriers to keep travelers at bay. Dearborn rode southwest from Jacmel, where the road was narrow in many places. It was easy going for one or two riders, but moving an army would prove most difficult, Dearborn realized. He came to a place where the road became thinner and dipped down between two hills, and knew he was close to his destination. The best access to Carlomagno's plantation was from the sea and the road from Moagraine swung around to follow the coastline. Men and women were working in the fields as Dearborn entered the estate. He rode past, slowing only as he neared the main house. He swung down, using a shady hitching post for his horse, which immediately dropped its muzzle into a waiting trough.

The woman who met him on the porch smiled and ushered him into the sitting room. Dearborn settled into a chair, glad to relax after his hurried ride.

"Louis! This is a pleasant surprise." Diego offered his hand to his friend before taking a chair near him. "You look worried, my friend. I take it this is not a social call?"

Dearborn shook his head slowly. "Would that it were, Diego. But I have dire news. Most dire."

"Is it about Carlomagno?"

Dearborn had not seen Lady Pickford enter the room. He and Diego got to their feet. "My apologies, Lady Annabeth, I did not mean to cause you any concern."

"Sit, gentlemen," she insisted. "I've asked Beatriz to bring in a plate of fruit and something cold to drink. Now, *Monsieur* Dearborn, you spoke of news. Does it
concern my husband?"

"In a way, yes. I have it on good authority that the Spanish governor of Santo Domingo has ordered an expedition to be sent here to capture or kill him."

Annabeth had taken a seat; she carefully smoothed out her dress before replying. "As you know, *monsieur*, others have sought to capture or kill my husband. None have succeeded."

"But this time it is different! General Concepcion is leading a thousand men," Dearborn explained. "These are not riff-raff; the general will have battle-hardened soldiers. He marches across the land to strike you from the Jacmel road."

"This is serious, *monsieur*. We appreciate your warning."

"You don't understand, Lady Annabeth. The Spaniards are already on the march. You must flee from here."

Annabeth stood. "It is you who do not understand, *Monsieur* Dearborn. My husband is away; if I left he might return and walk into a trap. Then a thousand soldiers might just be enough to overpower the man I love."

"General Concepcion will be here within the week. He will destroy this place, burn everything down about your ears," Dearborn said. "I have sent for a ship, one of mine from Moagraine. It will be here any-time. I offer it for your safe passage."

"I will consider what you say, *monsieur*," said Annabeth. "Oh, where have my manners gone? You will stay the night? It will be good to have your company at dinner."

While Beatriz offered Dearborn refreshments, Annabeth and Diego stepped onto the veranda. There was a blazing determination in her eyes.

"We knew this day would come, Diego. Now we must put our plans into action."

"I will gather all the deeds and contracts, and the certificates and coin Carlomagno will need for the freedmen and their families. I wish he were here," Diego said.

"As do I," Annabeth agreed. "When you have the documents, begin to gather whatever valuables can be carried. Pass the word that every-one should prepare for the worst. When *Monsieur* Dearborn's ship arrives we will put as many as we can onto it. Perhaps they can safely reach Barbados."

"And you, Annabeth? And the children? You will have to be on that ship."

"You know my husband would not escape until he knew all of those who depended on him were safe. Did you think his wife would do any less?"

"But, milady..."

She held up her hand. "You cannot oppose me in this. In my hus-band's absence, I will take his place. I must be certain the others are safe before I leave. And remember, the *Pickford* is also due back any day now."

Diego had forgotten about the *Pickford*; it had been rebuilt after the Santo Domingo attack and was again seaworthy. It was on a trade mission to the Yucatan Peninsula and should have returned by now.

"Yes, she is due, milady. I had better start gathering the documents."

"You will go to Barbados, Diego. You will have to look after things there," Annabeth said. "On your way out, please ask Beatriz to join me."

Annabeth turned and stared out the window. No wonder her husband loved this view, with the calming emerald waves washing up on the white shore! This place was a paradise and it would be a shame to leave it. But they had always known this day would come. They had been expecting it ever since word of the allied attack on Tortuga had reached them. The European powers had finally stopped fighting each other and had turned their attention to the privateers and pirates that roamed the Spanish Main. The fall of Tortuga had only hastened the day that now faced them.

"Anna, is it..?"

"Yes, Beatriz. It is time. We will be leaving, probably forever. Get the household staff moving right away. Rochambeau should go after my husband. And ask Shabaka to come to me, please; I must speak with him."

{ 30 }

The Shadow of Hate

World events had moved faster than the pirates of the Spanish Main realized. Boldly, the freebooters, privateers and buccaneers sailed their three-masted schooners and swift barques across the Main, preying on any vessel that moved too slowly, or seemed to sit too deeply in the water. But while men with a hunger for action and a lust for wealth terrorized the honest shipping merchants, the great nations of Europe gradually came to terms with one other. War, they now understood, was not good for business. The Caribbean offered riches enough for all, if they could only stop fighting amongst themselves. That left the pirates out in the cold. Yet few of the pirates sensed the change that came with the new century, most did not understand that the noose of justice was slowly pulling tight around their necks. Gone were the days when a king might cry outrage against piracy, while secretly rewarding a man like Sir Henry Morgan. The smart captains, like Carlomagno, attempted to move into legitimate trading and to diversify their holdings.

As Carlomagno's confidante and business manager, Diego had invested wisely and the pirate found himself owning various plantations, farms and businesses from ship works to candle making spread across the Indies, in Barbados, St. Kitts and Nevis. Agreeing with Diego that land was of high value, he also had undeveloped estates in North America, Peru and on the Yucatan Peninsula. Anna's brother, Connor, had been sent back to London to partner with one of his father's business associates. He had taught Connor what he needed to know to manage the English holdings.

"The day is coming when a pirate will find no port open to him," Diego had warned. "By the time that day arrives, we must be businessmen and traders. Let them whisper we got our start as pirates, but let no man accuse us openly!"

But, piracy did not die out altogether, despite the truce between the rival countries. A new breed of buccaneer arose, one who plundered not out of national pride, but strictly for profit. They preyed upon any ship, from any country. The sun had set on the glory days of old, and a new era of piracy was dawning. Men like Henry Morgan, Drake and Carlomagno were replaced by a younger, bolder set of rascals. The seas were no safer for the old guard's passing, for in their place new brigands would rise; with names like William Kidd, Edward Teach, Stede Bonnet and Ann Bonney.

But Carlomagno was not concerned with these developments; life, for him, had calmed down considerably at *Sequanakeeswush*. There, he worked the fields beside the others, for each shared in the profits from their labor. Any who wished to leave were given a stake and passage on a ship to take them where they wished to go.

"Can I try it, father?"

Carlomagno bent over a fallen tree trunk, meticulously scraping out the trunk to make a place for sitting. Now he straightened and smiled as his eyes fell upon his first-born son. Tamerlane, nicknamed Lane, was six and a boy of unbridled exuberance. Once the English had derisively forced the name of an ancient king on his father, and then on himself, but Carlomagno had defied them, giving his son the name of a strong Mongol leader.

"It is hard work, Lane," Carlomagno said softly. "Some men try for years and never have the gift for making a canoe."

"I've been watching you for days, father. I want to try it. I want to help make a canoe! Jennie Poke can't even do that."

"All right, son. But you must be very careful."

With eager anticipation Tamerlane Pokanoket grabbed the tongs that held the turtle shells and scooped some of the hot coals from the fire. He dropped them into the hollow his father had started. The hot coals burned away a little more of the wood and, using another sea-shell, Lane began to scrape at the log.

Carlomagno watched his son with pride. "Make slow, even strokes, Lane. Hurried workmanship is poor workmanship."

"Can we ride in it on the way home?" Lane asked hopefully. "I want Jennie Poke and Mama to see what we made!"

"Yes, son, we'll ride it home." Carlomagno had already begun work on two paddles. He started to finish them as his son worked on the ca-noe. After 11 years of marriage, Carlomagno still couldn't bear to be apart from his Anasarani. It was a glorious morning on Hispaniola, with a bright, yellow sun and a cooling breeze to temper it. The golden rays of sunlight danced on the greenish-blue waves rolling evenly against the shore. As he worked on the paddles, Carlomagno's thoughts were thousands of miles away as he recalled the day he helped his father, Metacomet, make a birch bark canoe. He had been as excit-ed as his own son was now—and as eager to show it off to his mother.

Sadness touched his heart as he thought of Wootonockuse, his mother. He had been sold into slavery beside her, only to have events tear them apart. It was only by the will of the Great Spirit that he had found her again, crippled by age and malnutrition and blinded by a vengeful slave master. He had brought Wootonockuse back to his home and made her final days as pleasant as possible. She had died quietly in her own bed, at peace, a free woman.

Her final words were for her husband: "Prepare a seat beside the fire for me, Metacomet, I come to join you."

Carlomagno had buried her in the tradition of his people and worn the soot on his face as a show of mourning. That was in the past, and Carlomagno thought now of the future. He wanted the best life possible for his children. Jennie Poke was a girl of ten, with auburn hair that fell in curls past her shoulders. Her face held a perpetual smile, yet there was a deep thoughtfulness in her eyes and she seemed to be bursting with energy. In many ways she seemed older than her years. Carlomagno smiled to himself. Jennie Poke had appointed herself little Lane's guardian. She doted on her younger brother.

Carlomagno caught a faint rustle of leaves; someone was coming toward them—and coming swiftly. He grabbed up his musket and motioned for Lane to stay out of sight. He moved behind the nearly-finished canoe; it might provide him with a little cover if needed. He had his bow and arrows near him; the ancient weapon of his childhood was faster than a musket and in Carlo's hands nearly as deadly. He slowly raised his musket as the bushes moved and Rochambeau stepped out in the open.

"I was trying to see if I could come up on you," the Frenchman grumbled as he stared at the musket. "I guess there's just no sneaking up on an Indian."

"You move well in the woods, my friend. None but an Indian would detect you."

"The lady sent me, Carlomagno. There's trouble home, and plenty of it."

"The Spanish?"

"Spanish, all right. And the English!" Rochambeau warned. "They're all moving against us. It may be too late even now. Louis Dearborn brought us warning from Jacmel. He had heard talk of a large Spanish force under General Concepcion. Dearborn reached us with word and had already sent for one of his ships."

"And the English?"

"Dearborn's ship came all right, and with whispered news of an English fleet heading our way. Lord Halifax is leading it himself, with orders from the crown to bring you in—dead or alive."

"I don't care much for either option," Carlomagno said glumly. "Help me get this canoe in the water, Rochambeau. We'd better not waste any time getting back. Come on, Lane! We must return home at once!"

Little Lane came out of the woods at a run and Carlomagno noted with approval that his own small bow and arrow had been ready.

As they paddled along the shoreline, Lane insisted on hearing again the familiar story of how his great-grandfather, Massasoit, had welcomed the Pilgrims to the colonies, and of the terrible war that bore his grandfather's name.

"Great-Grandfather Massasoit was so nice to those Pilgrims; why did they do bad things to our people, father?"

"I don't know the answer, son."

"It comes from trying to change folks," Rochambeau offered over his shoulder as he paddled in the bow of the canoe. "My people trapped up north of the colonies. They got along right smart with the Indians—Abenaki, mostly. Some even married into the tribes. But they respected the Indian ways and their religions. That's how people get along, Lane. Trouble always starts when one group of people looks down on another and decides to 'save' or 'civilize' them. Usually turns out bad for the saved, who never knew they needed saving in the first place."

"And then there's the land," Carlomagno interjected. "The Pilgrims came first, and then more Englishmen and they all wanted their own farms. They built them by taking away our hunting grounds."

"Father, do you hate the Pilgrims?"

"God knows, you got cause," Rochambeau added.

363

"Do not give in to hate, son. Hatred is like scooping up a handful of cool water on a hot day. It might feel good for the moment, but soon it runs through your fingers and you are left holding nothing but memories of something that is gone—and cannot be returned to the way it once was.

"The man who starts down the path of hatred never reaches the end, for the road always curves and there is always something else to hate. I could have remained a slave and spent my life hating those who put me in chains—as well as those who would keep me shackled. But I chose, instead, to fight for freedom, to insist upon the right to live my life as I choose. I fought when I had to, my son, and killed when the need was forced upon me. But I never hated.

"Hate clouds a man's thoughts, Lane, and leaves a shadow over everything he would do, or say. I refused to hate, for I would not leave my children that legacy. I fought because that was the way of the world in which I found myself. But always I fought with the idea of building a better life for my wife, my children and myself. I fought all the harder, son, so that you might not find your road in life as difficult as mine."

Sequanakeeswush was abuzz when Carlomagno returned. Despite some objections, Anna had put many of the families aboard Dearborn's ship, which had arrived in the harbor, and saw them off to the lands Carlomagno owned on Barbados. Diego El Negro was among them and would see to Carlomagno's affairs from there.

"He did not want to leave, but I insisted. 'You must protect my husband's finances,' I told him," Anna explained. "Poor Beatriz, I heard her crying in her room all night. She was so torn. She didn't want to abandon you in your time of trouble. I told her that her children needed her now and, reluctantly, she agreed."

"How did you get Diego to go?"

"I said the deeds and important papers he carried were like children and needed to be nurtured and cared for so they could grow."

"He was always loyal, Anna."

"He has the deeds and paperwork. I kept some of the deeds for our holdings in the colonies."

"The colonies?"

"We need a place to start over, a place out of reach of the English and Spanish," Anna explained. "I think we can lose ourselves in the American colonies. I have sent a letter to Connor to alert him of our situation."

And so it was decided. But there was still the matter of whether or not the *Pickford* would return to *Sequanakeeswush* in time. A man was placed in the watchtower on the hill overlooking the harbor. He had a spyglass and was to raise the alarm as soon as any ship was spotted. They had known the day might come when they had to flee Hispaniola, and had taken steps to prepare themselves. Lady Annabeth had wasted no time upon hearing the warning from Louis Dearborn. She had sent scouts out to locate the advancing Spanish army. Word soon came that General Concepcion was but three or four days away.

"If we took horses, we could beat him to the Pass," Carlomagno said. "He will have to come through Mangas Pass or march his men an extra thirty miles to find another route to *Sequanakeeswush*."

Carlomagno was hoping to buy some time for the women and children still on the plantation. Every minute, every hour he brought them might give the *Pickford* time to arrive and rescue them.

Anna began to belt on a pistol.

"What do you think you're doing?" Carlomagno asked in wonderment.

"I am going with you. You are my husband, for better or worse," she replied. "Though I don't see how it could get any worse!"

"You can't go, my beloved."

"You are my husband, Carlomagno. You will not face death without me beside you. We shall fight together, husband. Or die together."

Damn, here was a woman! He swept her into his arms and kissed her hard on her soft, pliant lips. For a moment they forgot the world, and their own troubles.

"You are a woman to make any man proud, Anna," he whispered. "But you must stay behind to look after the old ones and the children—and our children, dear heart. I shall only make an attack on the Spanish and then withdraw. I shall return to your side in time to sail to the colonies together."

She looked deep into his eyes. "Are you telling me the truth? A quick raid and then you return to me?"

"That's it," he promised. He looked quickly away, for it was the only time he had ever lied to her. The only hope she had of rescue, he believed, was if he could delay the Spanish and buy enough time for the *Pickford* to arrive. The forces charging in upon him were vast, far too numerous to be halted by the few stalwarts that remained with him. Ever a realist, Carlomagno knew there was no hope of defeating such an army. And if they managed it? Within days they would be met by a larger British force from the sea!

This was a life or death struggle, and if the price of his family's freedom were his own life, he would gladly die. His enemies would finally win, they could gloat that they had slain the Barracuda of the Spanish Main. But Carlomagno would not cower; he would die in battle, a warrior; as Noank had done, and as his father had done.

{ 31 }

Sequanakeeswush

"It's a great risk to take, Carlomagno." Rochambeau had waited to speak until Lady Annabeth had left the room. "General Concepcion has a thousand men. We have less than 200 left here. We can't hope to defeat him."

"If we could surprise the Spanish, we might gain an edge," Carlomagno said. "Do you remember the story of Sir Henry Morgan and what he did at Panama City?"

Rochambeau nodded. "Panama's defender, Don Perez de Guzman, had far superior numbers to Morgan, didn't he?"

"Morgan was outnumbered three to one, but the pirates put on a bold show and Guzman's men were beaten even before the battle began. Morgan chased them back into Panama City and out the other side!"

"There's one problem, though, Carlomagno. Guzman was a gentle-man, a Spanish dandy who won his position through favors at court," Rochambeau said. "Concepcion is a fighting man, a soldier. He will not flee."

"Perhaps not, Rochambeau. But maybe his men will, without him?"

They rode horses and wagons to Mangas Pass, which was a notch in the ridge with steep walls on either side. Hastily, Carlomagno deployed his men. The scouts had sighted the Spanish force and it was marching swiftly toward them.

"He pushes his men hard," Rochambeau noted.

They would not have long to wait. The once smartly-polished Span-ish army was as dusty as the road, but marching with discipline. The officers signaled a stop as they spotted the two dozen men facing them at the mouth of the Pass. General Concepcion studied them with his field glass.

"I don't like it," one aide muttered.

The general shot him a fierce look and any further concerns were stifled. Even as Concepcion studied the ragged ruffians before him, they turned and began to flee.

"They see the size of our army and run like jackals!" Concepcion crowed. "What fools! Did they think could frighten us with a pitiful show of force? Signal them forward, lieutenant. Double time! We will catch those rascals and end this once and for all!"

Carlomagno's men fell back. The Indian himself, among the rear guard, pretended to stumble and then seemingly limped away. The Spanish swept forward like a great, uncontrolled tide; they spilled into the Pass, half-fatigued from their long march and being prodded for-ward by their officers. Suddenly, the fleeing men stopped and turned.

"Sell your lives dearly, men!" Carlomagno called out. His Toledo blade had been picked up by a crewman at Santo Domingo and returned to him. Drawing it, he urged his men on. "We fight for our wives and children!"

The Spanish came swiftly, storming toward the pirate's position. Suddenly a barrage from the left bank caught the Spaniards flat-footed and dozens of men fell. A lieutenant, knocked from his horse which ran off, stirrups flapping, rallied the soldiers, turning them to face the bank from which the firing had come.

With bayonets the Spanish prepared to charge. Rigger Bonham ordered his men to open fire, catching the Spanish from the rear. Mangas Pass turned into a mass of tangled, bloody bodies and the gunpowder blew thickly through the air. Carlomagno led his men as they charged back, as Rochambeau and Rigger surged down upon the soldiers. The situation deteriorated into a fierce hand-to-hand struggle.

Carlomagno was everywhere, slashing left and right with his blade. He sliced the arm from a man who had thrust at him with a bayonet. A second soldier charged, sword in hand, and Carlomagno met him with a fierce defense. The soldier, overmatched, began to fall back and Carlomagno advanced, awaiting an opening. It revealed itself as the man left his guard too low and Carlomagno went over it, ramming his blade through the man's belly.

Men screamed and muskets boomed above the carnage. The Spaniards suffered heavy losses, but still they came on. The defenders of *Sequanakeeswush* also faced mounting casualties.

"We can't hold out much longer!" It was Rochambeau. He raised a pistol and fired it point blank range even as he spoke. "We've got to fall back!"

"To the horses! We'll try to hold them. If we fail, we'll use the horses to get back to *Sequanakeeswush*," Carlomagno said.

Shouts went up for the men to retreat, though they continued fighting with each step. Carlomagno scrambled into the back of a Spanish wagon, where two soldiers were trying to load cannon. His blade pierced one soldier between the ribs. The second man swung his ramrod, knocking Carlomagno's sword from his hand.

"I have you now!" the soldier yelled triumphantly as he reached for his own sword.

Carlomagno yanked the hatchet from his belt and leapt forward, burying it in the man's head. He jumped from the wagon. Catching Rigger's eye, he gestured toward the gun.

"Get some men to turn it; we'll use it against them!" Carlomagno suddenly stumbled, as if an unanticipated blow had driven him to his knees.

"Carlomagno!" Rigger tried to lift him. "We've got to get you out of here!"

{ 32 }

Barracuda

Carlomagno waved Rigger off. "The cannon!" he rasped. "Fire the cannon!"

Forcing himself to his feet, Carlomagno swayed drunkenly as a finger of blood made a serpentine path down his face. He gripped his sword, prepared to sell his last breath at the dearest price. What remained of Carlomagno's small army surged forward, screaming like devils as they hit the Spanish with ferocious strength. A sudden confusion in the Spanish ranks indicated that a new element had entered the fray. Whatever it was, it had gotten the Spaniards' attention. With the inbred instinct of a warrior, Carlomagno knew this was the chance he had hoped for. A strike now would end the battle.

With a fearsome war cry that momentarily startled his foes, Carlomagno exhorted his men forward, leading a desperate assault with blood rolling readily from his wound. His Toledo blade slashed to and fro, biting deep wherever it struck. He gave himself wholly to the bat-

371

tle, shrieking and striking at any Spaniard within reach. Finally, exhausted and weak from loss of blood, Carlomagno fell forward into the dust.

"It's Carlomagno!" cried a soldier, who rushed forward with his naked blade in hand. He wanted to boast of being the man who killed the infamous pirate! Instead, his days—boasting or otherwise—came to an abrupt end as he ran into the point of a spear held by a tall, muscular black man. The Spaniards broke and ran, hundreds of dead and mortally wounded left behind, including the lifeless body of General Concepcion.

Carlomagno tried to force himself up, but nausea overcame him. Large hands touched him gently. Opening his eyes, Carlomagno looked into the smiling face of Koyamin Otigbu.

"It has been too long, my brother-friend," Koyamin grinned.

"How did you know?"

"The *Anasarani* sent word to me," explained the Cimaroon king. "I came as fast as I could."

"You came just in time," Carlomagno said, and promptly fainted.

He awoke in a fog, at first unable to comprehend where he was. Slowly, he realized he was in his own bed, and his own Anna was mopping the sweat from his brow.

"What happened?"

"You routed the Spaniards, sent them back toward Santo Domingo," she said. "General Concepcion was killed."

"It was Koyamin, he came at just the right time," Carlomagno recalled. "He saved the day, Anna. Where is he?"

"Gone, Carlomagno. He took his men to hunt down the Spanish, to make sure they don't regroup and come back here," Annabeth said. "Then he took those who wished to return with him to his mountain hideaway. They will be safe from the Spanish there."

"What of the ships?"

"We've had word that Dearborn's schooner passed safely through the straits toward Barbados."

Carlomagno forced a smile. "You did well, my wife. Is there any word of the *Pickford?*"

She turned her back so he wouldn't see the concern etched on her face. "Not yet. But, I'm sure she will be here any day now."

Without the *Pickford*, those that remained on *Sequanakeeswush* were trapped. Carlomagno gave in to a heavy, healing sleep; he awoke in the cool of the dawn. Annabeth, exhausted from days of stress, lay sleeping beside him. He looked over at her, wondering, as he often did, how he had been so fortunate to have a woman like her in his life.

Knowing the sun would soon rise and the day would become unbearable, he managed to rise from the bed. His side was bandaged and stiff, otherwise he felt good. He had no choice; he would have to leave Hispaniola forever. The thought filled him with sadness. Out of a childhood of uncertainty, he had created a safe haven in the midst of those who had oppressed him. But he knew that even the mightiest bear grows old and one day falls to a younger challenger.

Was this to be his day?

He glanced at himself in the mirror. He was still strong, though there was a touch of gray around his temples. His arms were thick and powerful and he did not feel old. No, he thought to himself, not today.

At mid-morning the bell at the watchtower began ringing; a ship appeared on the horizon. By noon their fears were put to rest: the incoming vessel was the *Pickford!* Wasting no time, they began moving supplies aboard as soon as she docked

"We had a tough time of it, but managed to slip past an English blockade," Gerard Labrosse explained. "We had a running fight near Cape Tiburon, but we outran them."

It would take several hours for the ship to be loaded and made ready to sail. But Carlomagno and Annabeth hesitated at the last moment.

"It seems so wrong for us to leave here, where we've been so happy," Annabeth said as they walked along the beach, hand in hand. "Yet I suppose we have no choice."

"It has gone too far now, my darling. The Spanish will be back, with more men next time. We have won our last battle here," Carlomagno said. "We always knew we'd have to leave *Sequanakeeswush* one day."

She stood on her tiptoes and kissed him full on the lips. "Have you any regrets, Carlomagno Pokanoket?"

Regrets? No, he could think of none. For had he not sailed boldly across the Spanish Main, scattering enemies before him? He walked as a man among men and was looked upon with envy, fear and respect. Carlomagno had been snatched from his boyhood homeland and stripped of his dignity, and yet he had created a new home from a barren wilderness and made a new life for himself. He had brushed shoulders with giants like Morgan and Modyford, measured his blade against devils like the Chevalier de Fortenay. There was no room for regret. He had walked with brazen abandon into Portobello and stolen the king's treasure, had looted the shining cities of Maracaibo and Santo Domingo. He had lived adventure enough for a dozen men! And along the way, he had fought for and won the grandest woman in the world, and sired two wonderful children.

"Can a man with such a wife have regrets? All that I have gone through helped shape me and make me the man you see before you. To regret any of it is to regret what I have become. I would like to make those sniveling cowards remember why they were once wise to fear the Barracuda of the Spanish Main. It galls me to leave now, to sneak away from my home like a common thief."

"We are not defeated," Anna told him, "we go on with our lives, to a land where we will watch our children grow tall and strong."

They heard voices in the distance as workers continued to load the ship and prepare to depart. Torches had been placed at intervals between the house and the shore so work could continue through the night.

They strolled along the beach, listening to the waves lapping playfully at the shore. In the shadows, away from prying eyes, they turned and gazed longingly into each other's eyes, the pirate and the gentlewoman.

"Regrets, my dear?" Carlomagno drew her close. "I regret that this is the last time I shall love you on this beach!"

{ 33 }

The Final Gamble

As they made their way back to the ship, a cry rang out from the crow's nest. A British warship was bearing down upon the little harbor of *Sequanakeeswush*.

"Get everyone aboard the Pickford," Carlomagno called. "Our only chance is to make a run for it."

The *Pickford* had been built for trading and carried now only four small cannon, used only for defensive purposes. The ship could neither outfight nor outrun the English warship. Carlomagno stood by the rail, a pair of pistols in his belt and a naked blade in his right hand. His left side was still sore; the ball had passed through him in the battle in Mangas Pass, but his ribs were unbroken and the wound showed no sign of infection.

"What do you think?" asked Labrosse, lowering his spyglass. "Her guns will be in range long before ours, Carlomagno. She will scuttle us before we can even get a shot off."

"Maybe we can go to the west, toward Cow Island. Our ship lies higher in the water, we can make it by the shoals without ripping out our bottom," Carlomagno suggested.

Labrosse whistled to himself. "That bad, is it? It's a last ditch gambit, Carlomagno. Is there no other way? We'd almost certainly damage ourselves on the shoals or get stranded on a sandbar near Cow Island."

"I know only one other way, Gerard. We could sail straight for her, maybe get close enough to fire off a volley. Then, we'd have to hope to grapple and board her."

"If we have to go down, Carlomagno, I'd rather do it in an attack than running away," Rochambeau said. "The old Vikings believed if you died in battle you went to Valhalla where you lived happily, forever fighting, feasting and wenching!"

"Sounds like a good life," Rigger agreed.

"It is much the same with my people," Carlomagno said. "Running at the British ship might confuse them enough to give us an edge. We have the advantage of a smaller, lighter ship, but the wind, it's with them..."

A call came from the crow's nest; the topsail of a second ship was spotted coming fast around one of the small outer islands.

"If that's another British ship, we're done for," Labrosse sighed. "We'd better get set to run up a white flag. We'll all hang, but at least the women and children will be spared."

Carlomagno opened the spyglass and trained it on the newest ship, but could not make out its colors, nor could the lookout. It wasn't British, or Spanish.

"English, Spanish, Dutch or French, it matters not to us," Labrosse said solemnly. "Either way, it's the end."

"Well, who is it, by gads?" Rochambeau spat.

"Maybe it's the ghost of Sir Henry Morgan, comin' back to help us," Rigger Bonham quipped.

Carlomagno was once again looking through the spyglass, but this time he was smiling. "It's not Sir Henry, Rigger! It's not Sir Henry—and it's not a ghost by a long shot!"

"Well, who the hell is it?" Labrosse persisted. "*Père Noel?*"

"Even better," Carlomagno lowered his spyglass. "It's Kerbourchard!"

As Persifal Kerbourchard, the French corsair, came full speed into the harbor, fate played its final hand in the struggle for life and death on the Spanish Main. The coy wind, which had flirted with the British, suddenly abandoned the mighty warship and offered its favors to the knowing sails of Kerbourchard's ship.

The wind shift knocked the warship's speed down to two knots, while Kerbourchard's schooner ran with the wind. The warship tried to turn, to meet the stronger enemy. Carlomagno's ship had been drifting slowly toward it, and now was their chance. With cannon ready they moved ever closer upon the English warship. It was still a long distance shot, but it was a chance they had to take.

"Lay into them, men!" Carlomagno cried, waving his sword overhead. Their two portside guns exploded. One fell short and the other seemed to be following. Turning too quickly in its attempt to reposition, the warship's bow swung about faster than her stern, and the *Pickford's* second ball slammed through the hawse pipe feeding the anchor line out of the hull. The great chain began to slide, and the heavy anchor plummeted into the sea. The warship's speed dropped and her return fire was poorly aimed, with two balls racing over the *Pickford's* bow. Against all odds, a third hit the mark, smashing a hole below the waterline: a fatal shot. The *Pickford* immediately began to take on water.

Kerbourchard's schooner came around fast, a perfectly synchronized broadside of six cannon ripping through the air and pummeling the British warship. Thrown off course by the heavy anchor, the warship fired its remaining guns, but the balls fell harmlessly into the sea. At full sail and dragging anchor, the warship's mainmast could easily snap under the strain. Hands rushed to desperately haul anchor, while others clambered into the rigging.

"I said it once before, and I say it again," Labrosse shouted, as he clapped Rochambeau on the back. "God bless Kerbourchard!"

The British ship, sorely damaged, limped eastward.

"Shall we give chase?" one of the sailors called.

Carlomagno shook his head. "Let them go about their business. We have done all the fighting we need to do."

The frigate grappled the floundering *Pickford*, and pulled it alongside. There was barely time to transfer the people and basic supplies before the *Pickford* began to list. There was no doubt the ship was going down, but she wouldn't be taking Kerbourchard's ship down with her. Kerbourchard was there, older and perhaps a little heavier, but still the same old rogue with the playful grin and devilish manner.

"I was in Trinidad when I heard about the plans to capture you, Carlomagno. I sailed at once, praying I would be in time."

"Your timing is impeccable, *mon ami*."

"Last we heard you was dead, or in Triana," Rochambeau spoke.

"I liked not the accommodations and was able to reach an understanding with an old friend, a greedy old friend who sought the ultimate treasure. Remember Souza, Carlomagno? It was he running Triana. I did my best to reward him. Though," Kerbourchard winked, as he patted his blade, "it remains to be seen if he found the ultimate treasure, or the hell he had spent his life working towards!"

The dashing Frenchman gave a splendid bow as he took Lady Annabeth's hand and kissed it. "And I know you, milady. You have captured the heart of the Barracuda. Do you remember, *mon ami*? That first time we met, I told you that the love of a woman is the only thing worth dying for. And you have found such a woman."

"But you were wrong, Kerbourchard. I have not found a love worth dying for, but rather a woman worth living for."

And they would rebuild their life together, in a new place.

Carlomagno stood by the rail watching the Caribbean sunset. He had grown up here, founded and lost an empire. His mother had lived to die a free woman at *Sequanakeeswush*; she was buried there in an unmarked grave.

"You made a paradise on Hispaniola," Kerbourchard said, coming from the shadows to stand beside his friend as the final crimson fingers of sunlight drew away. "You've lost so much."

"I've lost nothing, Percy. I have my family and friends around me, I am healthy and strong and young enough to start all over again. Perhaps, there is a paradise awaiting us in these American colonies? If not we shall push on. I have learned of a vast world my people knew only in legend."

Fate now steered them toward that world, to land he owned in Carolina. As a child, he had thought little of the world outside his village at Sowams; now he knew there was so much more to see, to do, to experience.

"What do you think it will be like, Carlomagno?"

He turned from the rail and leaned back against it. "I wonder if it will be any different. I have spoken with Diego many times about the situation in the colonies. Where we go will be much like the Main, only taking place on land instead of at sea," Carlomagno told Kerbourchard. "The American colonies are split between those loyal to the Crown and those wanting their own independence. To the north we will have the English colonies, the Spanish in Florida to the south, and the French cannot be far behind—"

"To be sure, *mon ami*," Kerbourchard agreed. "My countrymen have their eye on the great southern sea beyond Florida. There is a perfect harbor at the mouth of a great river. I have been there! The delta lands are rich and fertile, with access upriver to sell your goods, too! Yet it is also a wild place, protected by deadly swamps. The Spanish gave it up, and I doubt the English will do much better. Yet, I can envision a great city there before long. A great French city..."

They stood side by side for a while, neither needing to speak. They were two men from different worlds, with different values, yet they had forged a bond of friendship and respect.

"Come with me, Kerbourchard. We can build a new life on the land. Diego has told me of vast country to the west. He said Spanish explorers have written of cities of gold!"

"When you find a city of gold, summon me and I shall come post haste," the corsair smiled. "But otherwise, I do not see myself as a landlubber. The sea is in my blood, the salty air feeds my soul. I could no more live on land than a sailor could give up his grog!"

"The old days, the life we led, are gone now," Carlomagno told him. "Times change; every nation has turned against the pirates."

"Things change on The Main, only to give way to some new form of madness. *Non*, some old acquaintances are hatching a plan to turn New Providence into the new Tortuga," Kerbourchard said. "I shall go there and see what is afoot. Besides, my friend," he leaned in, a hand on Carlomagno's shoulder, "when it is my time to go, I intend to have a blade in my hand, not a plow!"

"Ha! If I know you, Kerbourchard, you will have a blade in one hand and a wench in the other!"

Kerbourchard retreated, chuckling, leaving Carlomagno alone. Alone, as he had been that night long ago when he fled through the jungle, pursued by the Arawak. He looked northward, wondering how it was in Sowams. Did the Wampanoags yet exist? Had the English destroyed them as they had the Pequots years earlier?

Did Wampanoag children still laugh, and run along the shores as their mothers waded in the water to find shellfish? Did the men still stalk the wild game? Did they sing the songs of their fathers? Did they remember the old ways?

And I, he thought, *do I remember them? Am I more Carlomagno than Pokanoket? Would the ancestors find me worthy? Have I helped more than hurt, Ezra?*

The sails snapped, sounding almost like laughter, and the old hermit's amused reply echoed in Carlomagno Pokanoket's ears: "Wait and see, my young friend, wait and see!"

ABOUT THE AUTHOR

Award-wining journalist John Christian Hopkins is a member of the Narragansett Indian Tribe, a descendant of King Ninigret, patriarch of the tribe's last hereditary royal family in Rhode Island.

Hopkins is a career journalist who has worked at newspapers across New England, in New York, Florida, most recently in Arizona. He was a former nationally syndicated newspaper columnist for Gannett News Service.

As a child Hopkins slept clutching books to his chest and dreamed of becoming an author. "I've never wanted to do anything else but write," Hopkins said.

Though proud of his native heritage—among his ancestors was Quadrequina, brother to Massasoit and the one that introduced popped corn to the Pilgrims at the First Thanksgiving—Hopkins is determined not to be pigeon-holed as a Native author, but as an author who happens to be Native American.

He and his wife Sararesa live on her Navajo reservation in Arizona.

Blog: http://authorjohnchopkins.blogspot.com
Email: johnchristianhopkins@gmail.com

www.bluehandbooks.org

OTHER BOOKS BY THIS AUTHOR

RHYME OR REASON: NARRAGANSETT POETRY

NACOGDOCHES

COMING SOON

LOKI: GOD OF MISCHIEF [REMASTERED TWILIGHT OF THE GODS]
FALL 2013

SONG OF SOLOMON
FALL 2013

ALL BOOKS AT WWW.AMAZON.COM

FAN PAGE:
HTTPS://WWW.FACEBOOK.COM/PAGES/JOHN-CHRISTIAN-HOPKINS-FAN-PAGE/144686789962